Vanilla
Without
You

Vanilla Without *You*

DEVIN EM

Book Summary

Vanilla Without You
By Devin Em

Thandi Elowen, the self-made billionaire behind a groundbreaking scent-based memory tech company, is on the cusp of taking her company public. Known for helping others heal through memory restoration, Thandi quietly battles the weight of one memory she cannot access—a pivotal moment from her childhood that changed everything.

When a threat from her past reemerges, the trauma she's long tried to forget rises with terrifying force. As public scrutiny mounts and the pressure to protect her company intensifies, Thandi must confront a danger that feels all too familiar.

Enter Ronan Thorne—a disaffected playboy-turned-strategist with an uncanny gift for reinvention. Brought in to help Thandi position her company for success, Ronan is the last man Thandi expects to depend on. But as the stakes climb and danger draws closer, Thandi realizes he may be hiding secrets of his own.

As sparks ignite between them, their connection deepens in ways neither anticipated. But the closer they get, the more dangerous the path becomes. To stop what's coming, Thandi will need more than memory. She'll need to risk her company, her heart—and maybe even her future.

Tropes:
- Enemies to lovers
- Female billionaire
- He falls first
- Found family
- HEA

Trigger Warnings
- Angst
- Childhood trauma
- Emotional abuse
- Parent sickness and death
- Erotic asphyxiation
- Explicit sex

Acknowledgements

This book would not exist in its current form without the generosity, insight, and care of a few extraordinary people.

My deepest thanks to my beta and sensitivity readers—**Kaycee, Jennell, Whitney, and Amanda**—for lending your eyes, your expertise, and your honesty to this story. Your feedback sharpened the work, strengthened the characters, and helped me see what the book was truly trying to become.

A special and heartfelt thank you to **Kaycee**, whose thoughtful, incisive, and deeply constructive feedback has strengthened my craft by leaps and bounds. Working with you has been a gift, and I am profoundly grateful for your care, clarity, and rigor. If you're an author looking for exceptional beta reading support, I cannot recommend Kaycee highly enough: https://retrospect-publishing.com/betareading

Finally, an unexpected but essential note of gratitude to **Rosemarie**, the nurse at my local urgent care who quite literally helped make the end of this book possible. Two weeks, three steroid shots, and a great deal of kindness later, the manuscript is finished. Thank you for your skill, your patience, and your compassion when I needed all three.

Heads Up

Before you dive in, there's one thing you should know: ***Vanilla Without You* is Book One of a two-part story**.

Which means—deep breath—yes, there is a cliffhanger.

Don't panic.

Wait—come back. I promise it's worth it.

Along the way, you'll find twists and turns, romance and intrigue, action and suspense, and a love story that's very much in motion. And while this chapter of the journey doesn't close every door, rest assured: this is a **guaranteed happily-ever-after romance**—you just have to take the full ride.

Details about the sequel, *Vanilla After You*, can be found after the final chapter.

Table of Contents

Off Note

• BY DEVIN EM

Anchor Park

Thandi

Twenty years ago.

It's hot. Too hot. Our dresses are sticking to our backs. Tess' is yellow, and mine is white with a pink sash. My scalp hurts a little from Mama's fresh cornrows, but I like the style, with the beads on the ends of each braid, so I don't complain.

Like always, Tess and I match. My plaits are longer, though. That's the only thing I can beat her in. She doesn't have pink beads in her hair like me. Hers are all different kinds of purple, like grape, violet, and the new color I learned in English class—periwinkle. The plastic beads make a fun clicking sound whenever Tess turns her head.

She looks pretty, so I know I look pretty too.

I watch as Tess picks up the crown of fake flowers Daddy made and puts it on her head. It's made of roses, daisies, and big sunflowers. I left mine at home because it's hot, and I don't want to mess up my edges.

There are lots of other kids playing in the park today. Tess and I are sitting in the grass, not far from the swing set, where there's a long line of kids waiting for their turn. I can see Andrea Sutton, who stole Maisha's lunch last week, Bobby Mace, and Tanisha James, who can draw the best in our grade. The way Tess keeps looking over, I know she'll line up too. I already had a turn on the swing, so I'll stay here and play with my LEGO blocks.

"What's that?" Tess points to my LEGO building.

"It's a lab." I show her the LEGO woman in a white coat. "She's a scientist."

Tess rolls her eyes. "Thandi, that's so boring. Let's play Barbies instead. Dee-Dee just broke up with Tom."

"Again?" I'm rolling my eyes now. Tess likes games with a lot of drama. "They were broken up last time we played. I think Tom is a bad boyfriend."

Tess is about to say something, but her eyes light up when she sees that the line to the swing set is almost empty. "I'm gonna swing. I'll be back!"

"Okay." I'm happy the swing is free, so I don't have to play break up with Tess' barbies.

I glance up and see Tess hopping onto the swing, the crown of flowers still on her head like she's some kind of princess. She calls over Maisha, who comes running, even though she never helps *me* when I ask.

"Push me!" Tess says, loud and excited. "Higher! Higher!"

Maisha laughs and does it, her arms pumping hard. Tess kicks her feet like she's flying, like she's not even a little bit scared. Her braids clap against her shoulders, the purple beads flashing in the sun.

"Higher!" she yells again, and Maisha listens, and soon the swing is going so high that Tess could probably see the whole park if she looked down.

When she finally jumps off—flying again—she lands with a little stumble, then throws her arms up like a gymnast. All the kids in line start clapping and laughing, and Tess bows like she's on stage.

In a second, she's in the middle of a circle, talking fast with her hands, her flower crown slipping sideways. Everyone's looking at her. Everyone's *listening*.

Tess always makes friends easy. She knows what to say, how to make people like her. I'm not like that. I'm the quiet one. The one with the LEGO lab and the scientist lady with no one to talk to.

The music is soft at first—tiny and far away—but as soon as it reaches the park, all the kids freeze like someone pressed pause on a movie. Then they explode.

"The ice cream truck!"

Everyone whoops and runs. Even the kids on the swings jump off in mid-air and start running. Maisha shouts that she's getting a Firecracker Pop. Bobby says he wants a Choco Taco, and a few of the littler kids just yell "ICE CREAM" over and over again.

The music gets louder as the truck pulls up to the curb, playing that same song it always does: "London Bridge is Falling Down," high-pitched and happy like it's being played on a music box. I don't know why, but it makes my neck feel funny. Like something's crawling on it.

Tess is still surrounded by her fan club, but now they're skipping toward me. Tess is in the front with her crown tilted and a sparkle in her eye.

"You stay and watch our stuff. I'll go get us ice cream," she says.

"Why do I have to stay?"

"Because you're the baby." She sticks her tongue out.

"I'm *not* a baby. You're only three minutes older."

We're identical twins, which Mama says means we were in her belly at the same time and that everything else about us is the same, but Tessa always acts like she is way older. She's bossy like that. And with the kids around, she's being extra bossy to make it seem like she is in charge, even though I know she spent all her allowance money last week, and she'll have to use mine to get our cones.

Bobby giggles when she calls me a baby, and it makes me want to say no, that I should go to the truck, but Tess grins at me and says, "I'll go get it, and then after we will play action hero."

I get excited by that. We both like climbing trees. "Promise?" I ask.

"Promise." She agrees and hugs me, so then I'm not mad at her anymore.

I nod and play with my LEGOs while she goes to the truck. The scientist lady needs a bigger lab, so I start working on that. Tess is lined up in front of the truck with the kids, and they're all bunched together, everybody yelling their orders at once. The old man, Mr. Dixon, tells everyone to calm down, go one at a time, but he's smiling. He's a nice man. He lives about three blocks from the grocery store on Oakton.

When it's Tess' turn, she passes Mr. Dixon my allowance money. Just before I go back to my blocks, a little boy with dark blond hair starts talking to Tess. I've never seen him before. I don't think he goes to our school.

I don't pay much attention, though, because the scientist lady is in trouble. She needs a place to keep her potions, and the crocodile tank is too close to the laser trap, so I move the clear bricks around to make a wall. Then I add some blue ones for her potion freezer.

I'm almost done when a group of kids runs past me, shouting and licking their treats. Maisha has one of those red-white-and-blue rockets. Bobby's whole mouth is purple from a grape slushie. Tanisha is already sticky with fudge from her Nutty Buddy, and she keeps laughing and saying, "Ew, ew, ew!"

My stomach grumbles. I try not to think about it, but I keep glancing at the ice cream truck. Mr. Dixon is still there, handing out change, but I don't see Tess anymore.

I stand up a little on my knees to look around.

It's taking her a really long time.

It's weird. Tess doesn't take a long time to do anything. That's why Daddy is always telling her to slow down.

Even before the truck leaves, I know something is wrong. Mama says it's our "twin sense." Like that time Tess got stung by a bee in the botanical gardens, and I knew she was in trouble before anyone found her. The crawly feeling on my neck is back again, and I don't like it.

I spot Maisha and Bobby sitting under the slide, finishing their cones.

"Hey," I say, hurrying over. "Did you see Tess?"

Maisha licks the side of her hand and nods. "Yeah. She was just at the truck. She got two vanilla cones. Said one was for you."

"She was talking to some boy," I say.

Maisha shrugs. "I dunno. I went to get napkins."

I turn to Bobby, who's still chewing. "Did you see where she went?"

He shrugs too, eyes squinty from the sun. "I was busy," he says, holding up the soggy bottom of his cone like that explains everything. "Maybe she went to the bench?"

That makes sense. The bench is the shadiest spot in the park, right in front of the big carved totem pole with all the strange animals stacked on top of each other. One looks like a dragon, but with wings made of feathers. Another has a lion's face and a fishtail. All the kids say it's magic, and sometimes we leave shiny rocks or dandelions at the bottom, just in case.

But when I run over, the bench is empty. No Tess. Just a melted patch of someone else's popsicle on the seat and a fly buzzing around it.

Confused, I walk back to where the truck was.

"Tess?" I call. "Tess, where'd you go?"

The first thing I see makes me mad—our ice cream cones, dropped and melting on the pavement. They still look fresh. The waffle cones smell sweet like hot cakes, and the scoops of vanilla are just starting to puddle in the heat.

Was Billy Maher here? Sometimes he bugs me and Tess. Tess says he's a bully, but I think maybe he just likes her. That makes me wonder—maybe they're off playing hide and seek, and nobody told me.

Tess did that once. It took me a whole hour to find her. I yelled when I finally did, because we missed dinner and got grounded, but she just laughed.

"Tess? This isn't funny," I say, my voice starting to wobble. "I don't wanna play hide and seek anymore."

I keep walking. Keep looking. When I reach the big tree where she hid last time, I hear a voice that sounds like Tess'. But she doesn't sound happy. She sounds… scared.

Then I see her.

A big man in a white shirt and khaki pants is holding her arm. I can't see his face, only his back, but he's pulling her toward the edge of the forest. The part we're never allowed to go to. It's too dark in there. Too quiet. Daddy says there are snakes, poison ivy, strangers.… Bad people.

My stomach twists. A good person wouldn't take a kid into a scary place.

"Thandi!" Tess screams.

I run.

I run harder than I ever have—harder than when we're playing action hero. I wish my legs were longer. I wish that I was taller. Faster. I can still see the yellow of her dress through the trees, her white socks flashing between the bushes.

My lungs burn. My tummy hurts worse than when I drank too much strawberry lemonade and played catch right after.

Tess is brave. She kicks the bad man. She *bites* him. He yells and lets go, and she starts running toward me. My heart jumps. She's getting away. Maybe she's going to be okay.

"Thandi!" she cries.

"I'm coming, Tess!" I scream back.

I don't care about anything else. Not Barbies, not being called a baby, not even if she says she's *five* minutes older. I just want her back so we can play action hero. I'll even let her wear my sparkly cape.

Now she's running, as fast as she can. He's chasing her, and I scream for help—for someone, anyone—to come stop him. But no one does.

Tess is crying. Her nose is runny. Her eyes are all puffy. I'm crying too, but the scary part is that *she* is. Tess *never* cries. She's braver than anyone in our whole class. The boys, too.

Her big brown eyes are wide with fear. I feel it. In my chest. In our twin sense. I just want to hold her. Tell her she's okay. We can go home. We can play action hero, and I'll let her win.

We're so close now. She stretches out her hand. I see the red nail polish we painted yesterday, already chipped on her pointer finger.

I reach out, too.

Almost—

Then he's there. Behind her. He yanks her back. She screams. He grabs her braids, and some of her purple beads scatter like marbles. The flower crown Daddy made hits the dirt.

"Tess!" I yell. "No! Stop! Let her go!"

I lunge—

And then everything goes black.

Base Notes

• BY DEVIN EM

Détente
Thandi

Have you ever tried winning an argument with a mouse?

Don't.

I watch as ISO E, my tiniest research assistant stares defiantly at the single dried banana pellet I've given him for successfully reaching the end of a maze and identifying Immerscent's new scent marker.

"Not this again," I grumble. "ISO, remember what the vet said about *someone* needing to lose weight?"

He rises on his back legs, nose twitching, his little red cape draping over his tail. If he could cross his arms, he would.

These salary negotiations have been going on for a week. We're currently in détente.

I lean on the lab bench, arms crossed. "You're not getting another pellet, ISO. You already negotiated a second breakfast yesterday and a mid-afternoon bonus snack. You're turning into a puffball with whiskers."

He squeaks once, indignant, and marches in a tiny circle of protest.

"Oh, don't you start with the theatrics." I flick a switch on the monitor to bring up his maze footage. "You did the task. You got the pellet. That's the contract. And unless you're planning to personally explain to Dr. Batista why you're too round for the blood pressure cuff next week, we're done here."

He freezes and makes eye contact. Then, he climbs back to the starting point of the maze and sits. Not moving.

"Really?" I huff. "Passive-aggressive, much?"

I sigh and scrub a hand over my face. Each scent marker is smaller than a postage stamp—just a thin absorbent square tucked behind a mesh port on the maze wall. Today's compound is Immerscent-β7, dosed at half strength. It's supposed to stimulate memory recovery without overwhelming the limbic system. It's elegant. Gentle. For survivors of trauma, I hope it will unlock key memories without sending the brain into defensive retreat.

But none of that matters if ISO E refuses to cooperate.

He gives a little sneeze. Dramatic. Pointed.

I pull out my data sheet and jot down: *Trial 14 — successful identification, refusal to proceed. Possible motivation: dissatisfaction with pellet distribution.*

Then I crack, because I always do.

"One more," I mutter, opening the canister. "But this is it. And you're doing the memory gate trial after."

ISO darts forward. Pellet secured, he zips down the first leg of the next maze module, cape fluttering like the world's tiniest hero— or super villain.

Shaking my head, I retrieve the used pads with tweezers and drop them into a baggie to prevent cross-contamination. My foot's already on the pedal of the waste bin when I pause.

I toss the bag, then reach for Immerscent's proprietary dispenser. Sleek and ergonomic, it looks like a cross between a vape pen and a nasal spray. I pipette a full dose of β7 into the cartridge and slot it into place.

I know I shouldn't. But I do it anyway.

I breathe deeply.

My eyes close.

My lungs expand on one inhale and then another.

The memory comes to me in pieces: The sweltering heat, the smell of grass, the creaking of the swing, Tess's bright, sweet laughter—

And then, the saccharine whiff of waffle cones burns my nostrils. I'm gagging on the creaminess of vanilla.

My vision darkens.

I'm running. Running through deep, sinister green, branches scratching at my arms. I hear Tess's scream … see the flash of her socks, the arm gripping her painfully…

Her purple beads scatter like drops of rain.

Then—

It's gone.

The memory collapses.

Just like last time, and the time before, and the time before that.

Every iteration of Immerscent's scent-tech has been better, more effective, more revolutionary.

For everyone.

Except me.

"Thandi?"

I watch as Sammie, Immerscent's head of patient assessment, approaches with a furrow in her brow.

Having completed his tasks and extorted double his treat allotment, ISO dozes lightly in his cage.

The bugger.

"What's up?" I ask, spinning my chair around to face her.

"I wanted to make you aware of an unusual intake assessment."

My eyebrows rise. "Anything I should be concerned about?"

"I don't think so," Sammie says slowly, "but I wanted to flag, just in case." She hands over a slim file. "White male, mid-thirties, no referral. Booked through our website, claiming an interest in addressing childhood trauma."

I nod. Our clients come to us in many ways. Most are medically referred, given the delicate nature of memory recovery and our rigorous eligibility protocols. But we allow self-referrals for clients without mental health access—or insurance.

"That's not so unusual," I point out.

Sammie inclines her head. "Here's the thing. He skipped scent fasting, showed up visibly disoriented, and was amped on Astor products. Couldn't sit still for the full olfactory mapping."

My lips flatten at the mention of Astor. Three years ago, Immerscent was a trailblazer. Now, Astor Pharmaceuticals is nipping at our heels with WhiffRush—their unregulated, unsupervised scent-based mood enhancer. Marketed as 'scent-powered confidence,' it's popular on college campuses. I think it's dangerous as hell.

"Did we get a neuro read?" I ask.

"Partial. The olfactory tech flagged erratic galvanic response. Neuropsych saw gaps in short-term retention. Emotional resilience screening is still pending, but the trauma therapist noted possible dissociative symptoms."

"That's not great," I murmur, flipping through the file. "Did ethics weigh in?"

"Yes. She's worried he's trying to reinforce a false memory through scent exposure. AI flagged similar patterns in two prior cases."

"So the full team's been looped in?"

"Yes." Sammie crosses her arms, expression tight. "He's exhibiting other behaviors that concern me."

"Like what?"

"This probably shouldn't bother me as much as it does, but it wasn't just that he was noncompliant; he was actively using WhiffRush in the waiting room. When I told him to stop, he looked around like he didn't know where he was. Kept repeating something about 'the incident' but couldn't describe it."

I frown. "Delusional?"

"Maybe. Not full-blown psychosis, but close. His scent responses are all over the place—peppermint triggered calm, then panic. We haven't mapped his trauma yet, but if this escalates, we may need the safeguarding officer or you to issue a decision."

I glance at the photo of the client on the top right of the intake form. Mousy hair, somewhere between brown and blonde. Green eyes behind thin glasses. Acne scars dot his cheeks. Unremarkable by every measure. And yet…

I lean back and tap my pen against the desk. Sammie's right—something feels wrong.

I believe in the research, but I trust my gut, too. And everything in this file is exactly why my team and I are so insistent on our approach.

"We could monitor him in the sandbox," I say. Then I shake my head. "But honestly? This feels like a no."

My voice sharpens. "Let's call it. We decline, and release him with an optional psychiatric referral."

"Got it." Sammie tucks the file back under her arm. "Thanks, Thandi."

The soft rustle of movement draws my attention. ISO blinks awake, ears twitching. He gives an exaggerated yawn, then stretches one tiny paw like a ballet dancer mid-rehearsal.

"Oh, so now you're awake," I murmur, unhooking the latch on his cage.

ISO scrambles up my hand and nestles into the crook of my forearm, paws tucked under his chest. He sniffs, then lets out a pleased chitter, as if signing off on the patient decision himself.

I rub a finger behind one of his ears as I watch Sammie retreat.

"Yeah," I say. "I knew you'd agree."

Thirst

Ronan

I'm sick of easy pussy.

The problem isn't the sex.

It's me.

Groaning, I roll over in the bed. I crack one eye open. The floor is littered with evidence of a night of passion—my clothes in a hasty pile, a lipstick tube, and a discarded condom near the dresser.

I should feel elated, thrilled to have charmed a beautiful woman with ease. Yet, I only feel empty.

Speaking of which—

Frowning, I pat the space next to me.

Where is she?

Nausea roils my stomach as I force myself upright against the pillows. My temples are pounding from the mix of wine and whiskey I drank too much of. I wince as light from the window pierces my brain. I'd give anything for some Ibuprofen and another three hours of sleep right now.

I watch as Brooke, the leggy brunette who came home with me last night, gathers her clothes and shimmies into the tube dress she arrived in.

"You're leaving?" I ask Brooke, feigning regret.

She shrugs. "This was fine, but you're not—" She pauses in the act of slipping on a pointy red-bottomed pump, as if searching for the right word.

"What?" I try to guess how I've disappointed her.

"Fun."

Ouch.

She rakes her fingers through her hair. It is dark chocolate, with hints of russet and caramel. My hands should itch to run through it.

They don't.

Brooke drops to the floor to hunt for something, disappearing out of my line of sight for a moment, before reappearing with a sparkly clutch.

"You're hot, but you're different from what I thought. Serious. Like you're ready to settle down." Her lips twist up. "I'm too young for that."

Me? Settle down? I almost guffaw at that. But she is not completely wrong. The thrill I felt in my twenties for the chase is over. At thirty-one, I'm starting to yearn for something different.

I'm surrounded by beautiful women. Tall, model types with impossible proportions who share a look I've started calling "The Template"—heaving breasts, waspish waists, subtle hips. No matter what flavor they're dipped in, they all have the same proportions and the Brooke—straight, hair, coaxed into touchable waves.

Most aren't all natural.

Not that I care. That's not the problem.

I'm missing something.

Something … *brave.*

Every time I think I'm close, it slips away.

Take Brooke. I picked her last night because when no one was looking, her eyes assessed the room with an almost brutal sharpness. That's when I walked over and suggested heading to the club's planetarium.

I could tell she hated the idea. The possibility of that small resistance thrilled me. I wanted her to say it was dumb, to insist that she preferred dancing. I didn't want another fucking person to agree with me for once.

Instead, I watched as Brooke deliberately snuffed out the discerning spark in her gaze and slid a mask in its place—warm, bubbly, accommodating.

Vapid. Uninspired.

Easy.

And now here we are, with neither of us getting what we want.

"I'll have one of my staff drive you home," I offer.

Brooke waves a dismissive hand, shooting me a final disappointed look over her shoulder. "My Uber is here. Take care, Ronan."

With a swish of her hips, she is gone.

I groan, feeling like a jerk, yet I also can't motivate myself to chase her.

My phone is lighting up next to the bed. I grab it and see a stream of texts from a blonde I named "Amber-Vixen" in my contacts. The array of sensual poses in her messages leaves little to the imagination.

They do absolutely nothing for me.

I sigh and toss the phone back onto the nightstand. I'm ready to trade all this full-frontal action for a frontal lobe and some executive functioning.

So, as I said: Done with easy pussy.

I'm cranky, and as if magnifying my irritation, the headache assaulting my temples only gets worse. I groan and, rolling over, yank a pillow over my head. I'm just about to numb myself into sleep when a whirlwind bursts into the room.

My best friend, Sofia Beltrán Zamora, breezes in, Hermes sweatshirt and leggings skimming her athletic form. Her dark hair is slicked back into a bun. When she tears the blinds open, I moan like a vampire immolating at dawn.

"Jesus Christ, Fia. Show a little mercy. I have the worst fucking headache."

"Too bad." Fia wheels over to my closet and begins grabbing clothes. "It's not my fault you spent the night drinking. We're not breaking our promise to those kids."

Was I complaining about boredom earlier? I remind myself that I can always count on Fia *not* to agree with anything I say.

Weeks ago, I promised I'd join her for Sports Day at Chesden's youth center, where she volunteers. I don't know what I was thinking. I hate team sports.

"Ronan," Fia growls warningly.

"Fine, fine, I'm moving."

I swing my legs off the bed and immediately regret it. "You know I'm not qualified to coach kids, right?"

"You're not coaching," Fia says, tossing a soft cotton tee at my head. "You're showing up. There's a difference."

"I liked you better when you were my sweet, gentle friend," I mutter.

Fia wheels over to the dresser, her hands moving confidently over the rims. Her posture is perfect, like always—shoulders back, chin up, every motion elegant. She opens one drawer, closes another with her elbow, eyes scanning like she's casing the place for intel.

"I've never been sweet," she retorts, rolling to the closet and yanking out a pair of joggers. "Up. Shower. Now."

I get up, still grumbling. As I shuffle toward the bathroom, I knock something off the dresser, and it clatters to the floor with a thud. I turn, and my heart is in my throat as I race over to pick up the picture frame.

Fuck! Please don't let it be broken.

I pick it up and breathe a sigh of relief. The frame is still intact, its glass unshattered.

It's one of the few pictures of Mom and me together before it all went to hell.

I remember that day so clearly.

Mom was weaker but still vibrant. We'd thought the cancer was in remission, so I took her to Roatán to celebrate. We did nothing all week but lounge by the pool and sip umbrella drinks. I'd never seen her that happy.

I'd never been that happy.

My fingers trace the edge of the black frame. Mom's eyes meet mine from the photo, bright and kind. I flip the frame face down onto the dresser as I feel the familiar sting behind my eyelids.

God, I miss her.

I close my eyes, breathing through the pain. I knew this week would get to me—the anniversary creeping closer, stirring grief I'm learning will never fully heal.

But I don't have time to dwell on that. I've got Fia and a bunch of kids I've never met waiting on me.

I get into the shower and turn on the water. Cold. Full blast.

By the time I make it to the kitchen, Fia's already packed a water bottle, painkillers, and a banana into my gym bag. She hands me a steaming to-go mug of coffee—just how I like it.

"Wow," I say, impressed. "You're very nurturing when you're bossing people around."

"You're welcome." She tosses the bag at me. "You can thank me by not being late. Even though the kids have been looking forward to this game all year, some of their parents won't be bothered enough to show up to see them shine. They need to know not everyone bails."

That sobers me. I think about every tennis match, every rowing competition I won as a kid. I try to remember one where my father was in the audience. I come up empty-handed.

I don't say anything. I just nod at Fia and follow her out the door.

I'm at the youth center water fountain, warming up.

Okay, more like chasing my hangover.

I bend over the nozzle, guzzling mouthful after mouthful until the cold seeps into my chest. I gasp, lifting my head.

Christ, I feel like shit. I'm getting too old for this.

Groaning, I stick my bottle under the stream and start filling it.

"You going to leave any of that for the rest of us?" a soft voice says behind me.

I spin around and am arrested by big brown eyes.

The owner of the voice stares up at me. She's holding a water bottle of her own.

She's... cute.

She's barely over five feet, but her presence is unmistakable. Her hair's natural—buzzed at the sides, a riot of hot pink spirals erupting from the crown. Her skin is warm brown and luminous, the kind of glow that suggests secret rituals of body oils and butters.

She smells good, too.

Shit. I suck in a breath. What the hell is wrong with me?

That's when I realize she's still talking.

"Huh?" I blink.

"You're not thirsty," she says.

I stare.

"Water is the easy part," she says. "But thirst is not what's making you miserable."

Is this the alcohol talking, or is she speaking in tongues? Because none of this makes sense. And with this headache, I don't have the bandwidth for riddles, no matter how adorable the riddler is.

"Sorry, what?"

"What your bender costs you is electrolytes—all the good stuff that keeps you in balance. That's why you feel like hell."

She nods at my bottle. "Without them, water doesn't help much." Her lips quirk. "And I'm afraid you just washed away the last of them."

She turns to leave.

I can't let that happen.

"Wait!" I lurch forward. "Are you—" I stop. "Are you a doctor?"

I stick my hand out. "Also—I'm Ronan."

Great. Real smooth, Thorne.

"Not a doctor," she says. "I just know that when something's really off, you have to fix the part that's actually hurting first."

Something about that hits me in the chest, but I ignore it, pushing it aside.

She takes my hand in hers. "Thandi."

Her palm is small and impossibly soft in mine. I want to say something clever, lean in with my usual charm. Instead, all I manage is,

"Good to meet you."

"Good to meet you, too, Ronan." She releases my hand. "There's coconut water in the rec room. That'll have more of what you need." She winks. "Potassium, magnesium—less drama."

She turns, fills her bottle, and walks away.

Heartbeat
Ronan

The youth center is nothing like I expected. I feel vaguely embarrassed that I'd pictured some *Dangerous Minds* movie stereotype.

This place looks like a tech startup and an athletic club had a very hip, very productive baby.

After hydrating, I headed to the full-sized basketball court. It rivals any professional arena—glass backboards, gleaming hardwood, the works. Just through the open doors, I glimpse a dance studio with floor-to-ceiling mirrors and a barre running along the wall. A child in a yellow tutu spins in the center of the room while an instructor claps along, marking time.

I glance at Fia, who is already waving to half a dozen kids like she's family. Of course, she is. She's alternating between rapid-fire Spanish and ribbing the teens in English.

As soon as we got to the youth center, she shifted to her athletic chair. This isn't the one she competed with in the Paralympics, but it's just as impressive. A marvel of engineering, its wheels are large and tilt inward. Honoring her Mexican heritage, the frame gleams red and green, and the spokes alternate the flag colors like a pinwheel caught in a breeze. Across the backrest, a bold, looping script reads: *Pura Furia.*

She's wearing a white Steph Curry jersey—number 30, of course—that gleams against her brown skin. It hangs loose over black leggings. Her whole vibe is chill, confident, and lethal.

The kids swarm her like she's a rock star. A few of them are already hyping her up.

"Yo, Coach Fia's chair is fire today," one says, eyes wide. "That paint job's *insane*."

"Is that glitter in the wheels?" a girl asks, crouching to look closer.

"Bro, she's so cool," another whispers with awe, nudging his friend.

Fia just laughs, spinning in a lazy circle. "Better watch your mouths," she calls out. "Y'all keep gassing me up, and I might go easy on you."

"Nah," one of the older boys says. "You never go easy. That's why we love you."

"*Bueno*. Let's get going then."

They're grinning. She's grinning. And for a second, I forget I didn't hate all the sports I excelled in before my father forced me into them.

"Where do you need me?" I ask, feeling out of my depth.

Everyone here seems so connected, so tethered to each other. Meanwhile, I'm an isolated balloon. For a minute, I wonder what having that sense of community must feel like. No wonder the kids love it here.

"Let's head to the court," Fia says, pulling me out of my thoughts and leading the way to the sleek arena, where a giant banner reading *Hoops for Hope* is stretched over the entryway. *All I Do Is Win* is blasting from the speakers, hyping up the crowd.

Families and kids are already clustered in the bleachers, the air electric with anticipation. I learn from a young mom juggling a hot dog tray and a toddler that the youth center runs intramural leagues during the year. Today's game, though, is a community scrimmage— kids, staff, and any adult Fia can guilt into lacing up. It's also one of the center's biggest fundraisers.

There are QR codes on posters, and volunteers hand out water bottles with tiny donation envelopes tucked underneath. I scan the code and donate ten grand without blinking. If Fia wants to yell about it later, as my portfolio manager, that's her problem.

The woman in question is now at the center of the court, briefing the players. While she speaks, two other women rush in. A tall, flinty-eyed blonde waves as they approach.

"Sorry I'm late," she says, just the slightest bit breathless. "Traffic was a nightmare."

She's stunning, with a commanding air—but it's the other woman beside her who grabs my attention.

It's Thandi from the water fountain.

If Fia is the rock star, Thandi is the group's beating heart. The moment she steps onto the court, kids and staff orbit toward her. She moves among them, offering hugs and smiles in equal measure.

"Ms. T, I got an A on that homework you helped me with!"

"Ms. T, look at my jersey! Cool, right?"

"Thandi, that last donation made a huge difference. Thank you."

She shakes her head. "No need to thank me."

The words are barely past her lips when a little girl with long pigtails and a bright red dress races across the room and launches herself into her arms.

"Ms. T!"

"Oof!" Thandi makes a show of stumbling under the girl's weight, but she's grinning. "Daysha, honey, I thought you were supposed to be at summer camp."

"Nuh uh." Daysha cocks her head back with a saucy look. "Wanna guess why?"

Before Thandi can answer, a soft voice chimes in from behind her.

"Someone got into Horizon."

A woman steps into view—tallish, tired around the eyes, but radiant with pride. She's still wearing her nursing scrubs, badge clipped to her breast pocket, and a to-go coffee mug in her hand.

Thandi spins, gasping. "She *did*?"

Daysha's mother nods. "We got the letter last night. Full placement, fall enrollment. They even want her in the science prep session over the summer."

"I told you she crushed it," Thandi says. "We did three rounds of baking soda volcanoes before she decided they weren't 'sophisticated' enough."

"It was a titration experiment," Daysha says, matter-of-fact. "We measured the pH of lemon juice and red cabbage water with—what was it?"

"Homemade indicators," Thandi finishes, beaming.

Watching from the edge of the court, I feel an unexpected pang at the center of my chest. There's laughter, a low-key reverence, and so much *care* in the space around Thandi that I can't look away.

I just know that when something's really off, you have to fix the part that's actually hurting first.

Maybe that's what it is.

I think of Brooke, Amber, my interactions with other women—all focused on status, on wealth, on what we can get from each other. On how much we can pretend to fill the empty places inside us.

I suspect there's no room for that with Thandi. She's too calm, too quietly self-assured. Like she's found a higher purpose. Like she's too focused on healing things at the root.

Not rolling around in the muck like me.

I'm struck. It's like watching the sun gently sweep away the clouds. For a moment, I wonder what it would be like—living with that kind of direction.

To be better, more honest. To stop chasing ghosts.

I wonder what it would be like to stand beside a woman like her.

The idea fills me with a feeling I can't name. It's a bittersweet ache, a vaguely protective instinct.

Which is ridiculous. She's not mine. I've never wanted a woman to be mine. And Thandi certainly doesn't need guarding.

I frown, shaking my head. I make a note to stay off the cheap stuff at the next party. I blame the cocktail, a pretty redhead sent my way last night. That must have tipped me over the edge, because what the fuck am I thinking?

A basketball lands at my feet with a loud *slap*.

"Ronan!" Fia calls. "I didn't bring you here to sit on the sidelines."

She rolls over and crooks a finger at me.

"We're down a player. Come on. You're in."

Pick-Up
Ronan

My head is still pounding, but I manage not to embarrass myself as Fia introduces me to the newcomers. The hard-ass blonde is Dani, and we're on the same team, along with a gangly teen named Marlon, an intense young woman with ash blonde braids named Mya, and Romero, who was bantering with Fia in Spanish earlier.

Fia and Thandi form the opposition, along with three others. I consider going over to talk to them, but then second-guess it, still feeling that strange sense of dislocation from earlier.

There isn't much time for chatter anyway. The whistle blows, and the game begins.

I sneak another glance at Thandi, but she's already in motion—sprinting down the court beside Fia, sneakers squeaking.

I see the gleam in my teammates' eyes and already know I'm the weak link—the only schmuck dumb enough to show up hungover and completely unprepared. I instantly regret every time I blew off Fia's offers to practice.

Because the only thing I hate more than team sports is losing.

And being the reason we get our asses handed to us? Yeah. Not exactly the impression I want to make on Thandi.

That thought revs me up a bit as I refocus on the ball.

Dani speeds down the court, our de facto team captain. She's a machine. Agile, fiercely competitive, and not afraid to play a little rough. She and Fia feed off each other, and I curse as she forces Fia to pull up short, almost rocking in her chair. Her grin is positively gleeful when Fia clips her heels.

These women are insane.

I pass to Romero, who sinks a clean shot from the corner. The ball hits the net with a satisfying *swish*.

We cheer as we pull ahead by two.

"Yeah!" Mya screams, springing for a high-five.

Dani throws her hands in the air. "That's what I'm talking about!" she shouts. "Scoreboard, Beltrán. Try to keep up."

Fia snorts and wheels into position. "Don't write checks your mouth can't cash, Whitlock."

Dani laughs, strutting backward. "From where I'm standing, your team is the one giving *broke*."

"Ooh," the crowd gasps from the sidelines.

Fia narrows her eyes. She and Thandi share a look—and I realize we've awakened a fucking beast.

There are no weak links here. Their team's play is synchronous, organic. Fia is the strategic brain, while the kids form an unforgiving offensive line.

As for Thandi, I'd wondered how she'd fare given her stature, but I've underestimated her. She's fast, skilled, and impossible to pin down. I curse as she ducks under my arm with the ball and races to the opposite end of the court, where Fia is waiting, ready to take a three-point shot.

"Ronan! Cover Thandi!" Dani's exasperated voice is yelling at me.

Can't she see I'm trying? I'd like to see her hold onto that slippery rocket. My legs pump, my lungs burn as I close in.

I catch up to her just past the center line, managing to cut off her path.

Her eyebrows lift. "Feeling better, I see?" she says, dribbling the ball between her legs.

I grin. "The coconut water helped."

Her eyes flash. "It won't help you here, though."

She pivots, fast, and I move with her—too close. My chest brushes her back, my hand nearly grazing her hip. She smells incredible—something fresh and sweet with a faint, citrusy sharpness, and underneath it, the clean salt of sweat.

My brain short-circuits.

My timing falters. I stumble—a hint too slow—and in that instant, she's gone. She slips past me like a shadow.

"Shit," I hiss, turning just in time to see her pass the ball to Fia, who's already at the three-point line.

Fia shoots.

The ball slices through the air before dropping into the net.

"Ronan!" Dani barks. "Are you playing defense or trying to get her number?"

I smirk and flip Dani the bird for the comment that hits a little too close to the mark.

I mean, I'm playing my ass off, but fuck it, if Thandi offered her number I'd take it. I'm already that curious, and she's barely spoken a word to me.

The next twenty minutes are a blur.

Mya sinks a layup that puts us ahead, and Romero follows it with a clean jumper from the key. For a moment, it feels like we've got momentum on our side.

But we can't hold it.

Fia's team is ruthless. They move like they've rehearsed this in their sleep—fast passes, perfect spacing, no wasted motion. Fia barks instructions like a general, and the team executes with deadly precision.

We're still in it, barely, when Dani steals the ball and drives down the court. She passes to Romero, who gets boxed in by two defenders. He lobs it back to me, and I lunge for it, but not fast enough to prevent Thandi from snatching it midair.

"Nice try," she taunts, but it's hard to process the jab when my head is spinning from just the timbre of her voice. *God, I'm hopeless.*

She's off again.

Thandi crosses half-court, weaving past Mya and Marlon so fast it's like she's possessed.

Then she pulls up at the top of the arc.

My heart thuds. No way. She's too far.

She jumps—and lets it fly.

The ball curves like a prayer, and I swear the whole gym holds its breath.

Nothing but net.

The crowd explodes.

"Damn," Dani breathes.

I stare, stunned, as Thandi jogs back to her teammates, grinning and glowing with sweat. Fia gives her a theatrical high-five as the buzzer sounds.

Game over.

I brace my hands on my thighs, fighting for breath.

Fuck it, we lost, but it's the most fun I've had in years.

The come-down from the pick-up game is better than any high I've ever experienced. Dani jogs up to me with a grin and offers her hand.

"Good game. I hope you'll come back and play with us again."

"Yeah, bro," Marlon echoes. "That was some nice footwork out there."

You know what? They're all right.

"Thanks," I murmur, feeling prouder than I should about a scrimmage.

Fia pulls up, victorious and radiant. "Thanks for coming, *Roncito*. You did well out there." She winks at me. "Imagine what you can accomplish when you're not hungover."

"You're a menace, you know that?" I growl, pulling her into a playful headlock. But my eyes are on Thandi behind her, chatting with Mya and Romero. She's wiping her face on her shirt, and the glimpse of her stomach has me in knots. Have belly buttons always been this sexy?

There's only one more thing to do. I straighten my shoulders, unleash the Thorne swagger—

And I am immediately intercepted by Dani, rushing to Thandi and barking into her phone.

"Thandi," her voice is urgent. "We have to go. KLTB5 just called in a media request."

Thandi straightens with a nod, all playfulness evaporated. She turns to the kids, offers a few quick hugs, and a wave.

And then she's moving with Dani toward the exit.

Our eyes meet for a millisecond, and my breath catches in my throat.

In that flash, all the sound in the room seems to go muffled. The buzz of the crowd, the children's laughter, all fade to a distant hum. Thandi's expression is still soft, still exuberant from her win, and when she looks up, the faintest smile touches her lips.

That's all it takes, and warmth like the sweetest honey floods my veins. I feel my own lips curving. I take a step, open my mouth—

Too late.

She's already slipped through the doors.

I look up, and Fia's eyeing me with an amused expression. She glances at the exit, then back at me. "You okay?"

"Of course," I scoff, rolling my shoulders. "Can we get out of here? Too much do-gooding and I start melting like the Wicked Witch of the West."

Fia rolls her eyes. "Fine. Let me grab my things and check the schedule for the rest of the week. I'll meet you out front."

I nod, but I don't move right away.

Fia disappears into the staff room, and I linger by the court, dragging a hand through my hair. The place is quieter now as the staff pack up their gear and take down posters. Someone laughs in the hallway. There's a lingering echo of joy in the air—but it's already fading, and I feel the absence like a shadow falling across the sun.

I sigh and shuffle out of the room, joining the slow current of bodies heading toward the lobby. I lean against a wall near the front windows, watching the sun bleed gold across the concrete outside.

Behind me, a chorus of kids' voices rises, full of leftover adrenaline.

"Yo, we won!"

"Let's hit the gas station and get some Sniffz!"

"I'm getting the cherry one—and the one that smells like fire!"

"I'm getting, like, five vials. I'm *this* close to finishing my PlayPack."

I smile, despite myself. Something about their chaos, their joy— the dumb names for whatever the hell those things are—sticks with me, reminding me of the guileless pleasure of the basketball game.

I glance over my shoulder, just once.

Still thinking of her.

Steady
Thandi

"And with regulatory due diligence cleared," I finish, "we are on schedule for the IPO launch in eight weeks."

I catch the eye of Dani, my head of communications, and she's nodding approvingly. From the pleased expressions of the board members around the room, she's right.

We've nailed it.

"This is impressive, Thandi, as expected from you and your team."

I watch as Trent Calhoun, Immerscent's Board Chair, stands. Balancing his daughter, Junie, on his hip, he passes her a bottle, then, with his free hand, deftly grabs the pointer, clicking through the presentation on the screen to return to this quarter's earnings.

Brilliant and intensely private, the Texan native has been Immerscent's angel investor since our launch.

"We're exceeding forecast metrics—" His gaze pierces mine. "But for how long?"

I frown. "What do you mean?"

"You're steady. Strong. Yet, what we need now is *extraordinary*. Something to convince investors this isn't the end of the curve—it's the next crest."

His words trigger a ripple of murmurs from the board members around the table. I can feel the shift in the mood.

"Calhoun's right," Clara Yuen, head of a Hong Kong–based AI governance think tank, says crisply. "There is also the question of the competition. Astor's *WhiffRush* may be crude, but they're scaling with alarming speed."

"There's also *Sniffz* and *PlayMist*." Heads turn as Dr. Niko Barasa, CEO of Barasa Biotherapeutics, leans forward. Charismatic and unapologetically blunt, Niko has a reputation for saying what others won't.

He continues, voice dry. "Scent-based behavior modulators—marketed to preteens. *Preteens*, folks. They're positioning PlayMist as both recreational and 'focus support for digital learners.'"

That earns a few sharp inhales.

"Let's be clear. Astor isn't just racing ahead. They're shaping a new market in ways that will influence long-term consumer preference." Niko folds his arms. "We all support safety. But is Immerscent being too cautious?"

A heaviness replaces the room's earlier buoyant mood.

My throat tightens. The question isn't just sharp; it's fair. And yet, I didn't start Immerscent to put profit over people, or to chase trends.

"These are key considerations, and you're right to push," I concede, walking to the end of the conference table. "Immerscent must do more on innovation. My team and I will take this feedback, and I'll present draft concepts for our next breakthrough when we reconvene next month."

I pause, looking each board member in the eye. "But let's be clear: our brand was never built on mass appeal. Rigorous science, evidence, and client care—these are the pillars Immerscent stands on. Astor may have the edge today, but the use of scent technology on developing minds is untested. It could cause long-term harm. Is that a risk we're willing to take?"

A silence settles in the room until Marisol Jennings, head of RiseWell, a community-based youth organization, speaks.

"Thandi raises a good point," she says quietly. "We're not just talking about a market. We're talking about our most vulnerable populations." She looks around the table. "This isn't something we should rush. It deserves real deliberation."

Inside, I breathe a sigh of relief for her reasonable voice, but I know it won't be long before we'll have to address these issues again.

As the meeting ends and the board members file out of the room, Trent lingers, and I can tell he wants to connect privately.

I nod at Dani. "Catch up with you in thirty?" I ask as she gathers her things.

"Of course."

"Good job in there, Thandi." Trent murmurs as we step into the hall. Junie coos and grabs a fistful of her father's hair as he speaks, her chubby brown fingers flexing around the soft blond strands.

Trent is entirely unaffected, and I can't help but smile, the tension from the board meeting easing from my shoulders.

"Should we grab some coffee?" I ask. I lift my arms, and Junie squirms, reaching for me.

Trent huffs at her. "What am I? Chopped liver?"

I laugh as I pull Junie into my arms, spinning her around with a grin. I bounce her on my hip, causing her to giggle, and it's all I can do to stop myself from melting.

"Come on, Dad, you've had her all day. Share the love."

"Fine." Trent pretends to grumble as we make our way to the cafeteria.

I grab a chai latte while Trent orders an Americano and a sippy cup for Junie. We sit near one of the windows, and we're so high up we can see clear across the city.

Chesden isn't New York, but the Northern Virginia hub is sleek in its way—with wide streets lined with old-growth trees, and sculpted green spaces tucked between glass mid-rises. A city designed for walking, connecting, and moving forward.

That's part of why I chose it. Sure, DC has legacy, and Maryland has its research corridors—but Chesden offers generous R&D tax credits and zero BPOL tax for start-ups like mine. It made scaling

Immerscent possible, and let me put more money not just into the product, but into our people.

Trent seems to be having similar thoughts as he glances at the cityscape beneath us. I'm quiet as I guide Junie's apple juice to her lips. She gurgles and pats the table.

"I know I was tough on you in there," Trent murmurs after a moment. "It's because I believe in you, Thandi."

His pale green eyes meet mine. "Not just your product—*you*. Your leadership. That's even rarer than all the new tech combined. I want this IPO to make everything you've ever dreamed of possible."

I never doubted his motives, but it feels good to hear him say it. I think of Tess, and I blink, swallowing past the sudden lump in my throat. I nuzzle Junie's silky mop of curls to hide my emotions.

"Thanks," I croak.

"What do you know about Thorne Consulting?"

I frown. "The name doesn't ring a bell."

Trent leans back, cradling his cup. "That's not surprising. The company keeps a low profile by design."

I tilt my head, intrigued despite myself.

"Thorne doesn't even have a website," Trent goes on. "But his fingerprints are all over half the biggest tech turnarounds in the last five years. Sometimes he builds. Sometimes he guts. But when he gets involved, things shift."

I narrow my eyes. "So, he's a fixer."

Trent shrugs. "More like a strategist. What he does is see patterns before they fully emerge—and helps founders make the hard calls while there's still time to steer the ship."

The description hits uncomfortably close to home. I glance down at Junie, who is smearing juice across the tray in wild arcs.

"And you think Immerscent needs someone like that?" I ask quietly.

"I think we're at that moment," Trent admits. "The pressure you're feeling? That's the price of being first. Immerscent didn't follow a trend—you *created* it. Now everyone's scrambling to catch up, and they're willing to cut corners to do it."

He pauses, his gaze sweeping the skyline. "People keep acting like Astor is the trailblazer. They're not. They're the reaction. *You* set the terms. It's time to remind them that they still don't measure up."

I run my thumb over the edge of Junie's half-empty sippy cup. Trent must sense my uncertainty because he smiles.

"You don't have to commit," he reasons. "Just talk to him. I'll pay for the consultation. Think of it as another investment in Immerscent."

"Trent," I say, more sharply than I intend. "Immerscent is hardly strapped for cash."

He chuckles and reaches for Junie, who's started rubbing her eyes and fussing. It's clearly nap time.

"This isn't about what you can afford," he says, lifting her into his lap. "It's about showing up for the people I believe in."

He cocks a brow. "So? Will you meet him?"

I sigh. This man is far too persuasive for his own good.

"Alright," I agree. "I'll meet him."

Junie
Ronan

"Sorry to drag you all the way out here." Trent shifts his daughter in his lap. "But this was halfway between Junie's daycare and my next meeting."

His daughter, an adorable eighteen-month-old with big brown eyes and a riot of dark curls, coos. She clutches a stuffed bunny in one hand. With her other hand, she bangs a yellow teething ring on the table. A black diaper bag is draped over the back of Trent's chair.

Trent's call was a pleasant surprise after losing touch over the years. When the investor and my old grad school buddy invited me to lunch to chat about a potential client, I wasn't expecting him to have a guest of his own—albeit a very cute one. From the way Trent calmly switches between checking his phone, straightening Junie's headband, and scanning the menu, I can tell she's a regular business partner.

"Not a problem," I say, glancing around the bustling Bethesda café. "This is a great spot. And it's nice to have a change of scenery."

Trent smiles. "It is, isn't it? This is Junie, by the way."

"Hey, Junie." I wave across the table.

"Say hi to Ronan, Junie," Trent says, and miraculously Junie seems to understand—sort of. She makes a happy gurgling sound and bounces in her seat.

I laugh. I think that's the best I'm going to get.

The waitress comes by to take our orders. Trent and I both order burgers, and he orders oatmeal for Junie.

I watch as Trent feeds himself with one hand and gently spoons the oatmeal into Junie's mouth—with not a single drop spilled on his crisp navy suit.

It's… absurdly smooth.

Trent has never been a flake, but at MIT, he was the imp of the group, always up for anything, never one to turn down a dare—the cheerful troublemaker who never actually got in trouble because he could charm his way out of anything.

The charm isn't gone. The gleam of mischief still dances in his green eyes, but the man I'm facing is grounded, centered in a way I hadn't expected. Like he's channeled all that rogue energy into something much more meaningful.

Purposeful.

Unbidden, my mind flits back to Thandi and the pickup game. I shift uncomfortably in my chair.

"So … fatherhood, huh?" I say, tracing the filigree on my napkin.

"Yeah." Trent's expression softens. "We've come a long way from our MIT days, huh?"

"I'd seen the rumors in the tabloids, but I didn't really believe it," I confess.

He shrugs. "Life has a way of throwing curveballs. But you know what? I wouldn't have it any other way."

"Really?" I ask, unable to conceal my surprise. It's none of my business, but Junie's mom doesn't seem to be in the picture.

Trent doesn't look exhausted, though.

"You know my Dad died when I was a kid." Trent leans back in his seat, his eyes growing distant. "Not having him around—I wasn't sure I was cut out for this, but the truth is, I love it."

Junie spits out her oatmeal and begins to fuss. Squeezing her forefinger and thumb together like pincers, she picks up a blueberry and flings it across the table. It bounces off the tablecloth and rolls onto the carpet.

Trent makes a clucking sound and kisses her forehead. Without a raised hand or a harsh word, he extricates her fingers from the bowl and brings the spoon of oatmeal back to her mouth.

Something inside me twists at his easy tenderness. I think of my own upbringing and can't recall a single moment like this with my father.

Maybe I was just too young to remember, I tell myself.

I don't believe it.

"Hey, I heard your mom passed," Trent murmurs. His eyes are full of sympathy. "I'm so sorry. I know how close you were."

"Thanks," I say hoarsely. I clear my throat. "It'll be a year this week."

Junie twists suddenly, knocking her spoon against the bowl. Oatmeal splatters the table.

She freezes, lip trembling.

Trent glances down. "Hey," he murmurs, bouncing her once. "You're okay."

She isn't. Her face crumples, and she lets out a low, unhappy whine. Then she wails.

Brow furrowing, Trey lifts her to his shoulder.

"She's teething," he explains. "So she hasn't been sleeping well."

"Not a problem. I'm in no rush."

When Junie remains inconsolable, Trent shakes his head. "I should take her back." He stands abruptly. "Can you hold her while I make a quick call? I need to reschedule my 2 PM."

Before I can answer, he plops a crying Junie in my lap and strides to the nearby alcove, phone already to his ear.

Junie's cries hit a higher pitch as she squirms in my arms. I freeze, instinct short-circuiting for half a second. Then I shift her, tucking her into the crook of my arm the way I saw Trent do. She's warm and lighter than I expect, her small body rigid with indignation.

"Okay," I murmur, pulling a ridiculous face. "I see you."

She pauses. Just for a second. Big brown eyes lock onto mine. Her lip wobbles as if she's deciding whether I'm worth the effort.

Then she lets out a surprised, gummy laugh.

Something warm rushes through my chest, catching me off guard. I adjust without thinking, lifting her gently and giving a careful little toss before settling her back against me. She squeals, all tears forgotten, gurgling with delight as I repeat it once more.

"Well," I mutter. "That wasn't so hard. And for the record, it wasn't the blueberries."

Junie kicks happily.

"You just needed a better face to look at."

"Seriously, Thorne?" Trent raises a brow as he slips his phone away, eyes crinkling with amusement.

"Hey," I say. "Take it up with your daughter, not me."

Trent shakes his head as he takes Junie from me. "Sorry for the abrupt exit, but quickly, before we run, I wanted to talk to you about the client I mentioned."

He slings the diaper bag over his shoulder. "I know your process, so I won't interfere with your blind assessment, but I will say she's brilliant—the real deal."

I raise a brow. "So why does she need me?"

"Her company is young, and she's preparing for a public offering. The board is pushing her to prove to investors that her tech has the staying power to edge out the competition."

I frown. "Well, you know how I work. Let's see what the foundation looks like before we talk about the competition or anything else."

Trent raises a hand. "I know, I know. You'll do your thing with your algorithm, but I wanted to meet because this isn't a random request. This one is personal. I want the premium package, top of the line. Money is no object. That's how much I believe in her."

That was a high endorsement—especially coming from Trent.

"All right," I say slowly, "I'll meet with her—" My gaze sharpens. "But no promises."

"Of course." Trent turns to leave. "Good to see you, Ronan. And great job with Junie. Let me know if you want another shot. I'm always looking for great babysitters."

He grins and disappears into the cafe rush.

I lean back in my chair, intrigued despite myself about this new client.

"Everything okay over here?" The waitress asks.

"Perfect," I say. "I'll take the check."

Mind Fuck
Ronan

I can't concentrate.

The truth is, my focus has been shot since the game at the youth center. I've been trying to figure out why something so trivial has hit me so hard.

Somehow, seeing Trent yesterday only makes things worse.

I'm a loner. It's essential to the Thorne Consulting image: *The best leaders are those the people hardly know exist, and all that jazz.*

The less anyone knows about Ronan Thorne, the more they want access to me—and the more they value what I offer.

Scarcity is a currency, and I've built a career on it.

Yet, for the first time, I wonder if I've pushed too far into mystique.

I think of Thandi and Fia surrounded by a cluster of loving kids, and the sense of belonging I witnessed at the youth center. I remember Trent with Junie in his arms, open, centered—not living a life of compartments—and everything that I thought mattered seems hollower now.

My mind drifts to Thandi, to the moment I looked up and saw her at the water fountain. I remember the pickup match, and how embarrassingly off my game I was around her—how I could barely catch my breath when our bodies touched.

She's a little slip of a thing, and yet, after just one meeting, she's managed to eclipse every waking moment. I'm still as off balance as when I flubbed the pass from Romero.

My phone flashes with an incoming call.

Just seeing the name makes my chest seize.

It's my mother's lawyer, Frederick Ellison.

"Fred," I answer, trying to keep my voice neutral. "How can I help you?"

I already know. I've known this moment was coming. Still, now that it's here, I'm not ready.

"Ronan, I'm calling to confirm the will reading," Fred says. "It will be held three days from today, at Whitlow Estate. Your mother was clear: She wanted all parties present, in person."

My mouth goes dry. "Three days," I echo, because my brain is slow to process the rest. Three days from now means—

"It aligns with the first anniversary of her passing," Fred says gently, as if I haven't already done the math. "She felt it… appropriate."

I go silent. For a minute, I can't breathe.

"Ronan?"

"Yes," I gasp. "Yeah. I'm here."

"I'll send you the formal notice. In the meantime, you know where to find me if you need anything," Fred finishes, a note of regret in his voice.

"Thanks, Fred," I murmur and hang up the call.

I stare at the wall, my hand still clutching the phone. My stomach is in knots.

Three days from now, I'll be back at Whitlow.

Back in the home I grew up in.

Back in the house where she died.

Back in the same room as my father.

And suddenly, nothing I've built feels like enough armor. I'm flooded with panic, with pain so searing it feels like I'm being flayed from the inside.

I'm sweating. My hands are shaking. Mom was my rock—my everything—and I'm not sure I can survive this. Without her, I'm adrift.

Anchorless. Useless.

I squeeze my eyes shut. No. Not now. Not here. I've got to pull it together.

Besides, there's no time for wallowing with a new client arriving in under an hour.

Work.

That's the solution. That's the anesthetic.

I drag my attention back to the matrix glowing across the screen. Time to drown in it.

In the circles that matter, the Thorne process has become legendary.

And with good reason.

My method is a proprietary three-step process. First, my team anonymizes the data, stripping key identifiers that could introduce bias—name, age, race, gender, and education level. Then I run the initial analysis, arranging the output into a cognitive map that lets the sharpest details stand out, like seaglass sifted from sand. The final step is applying Thorne Consulting's unique algorithm to measure probabilities of success.

What people pay me for isn't hyper-specific knowledge of their field but my distance. I don't follow markets. I don't track blogs or tech chatter. My isolation is image, yes, but it's also intentional.

Like I told Trent, my goal is to push past the noise to unearth what's real underneath.

What I see about his client intrigues me: A company approaching a public offering, valued at $5.5 billion in just three years. A brand built on ethical leadership in an industry where an egotistical, high-handed style is the norm. It's rare, especially in scent tech.

I feel a twinge at that—then bury it. I stepped out of that world five years ago, and I'm not going back. It's just one more thing my father took from me.

Still, a small buzz of anticipation hums through me. Now I see why Trent was all in. It feels good to have a real challenge.

As if on cue, my assistant raps on the door. "Mr. Thorne, your client is here."

"Excellent, send them in."

I stand, going to the window. Outside, the garden glows in the late summer sun. Neat rows of ashwagandha, skullcap, and holy basil line the beds—plants selected not for beauty but for what they do under the microscope. Past them, the glass atrium gleams in the sun. Through the haze, I can just make out the spiraling growth of kanna and the fine-leafed sprawl of gotu kola.

Someone approaches the desk. The soft click of heels lets me know it's a woman. But it is her scent that hits me first—fresh and sweet with the faint sharpness of citrus.

I'm immobilized.

My breath falters.

My pulse spikes.

Without a doubt, I know it is *her*.

I turn, trying to project calm, even though my world has tilted on its axis. My center of gravity is gone.

Thandi stands across from me, separated by my massive desk, but still close enough to touch.

She's here in a polished navy jacket and slim pencil skirt as though my week of longing has conjured her. I don't know why this woman has seized my imagination, why my mind cannot cease its endless wandering to her.

And now, as if by fate, Trent has brought her to me.

"Mr. Thorne," she begins, "It's a pleasure to meet you." She stops. Those wide, bewitching eyes stare up at me.

"Oh," she breathes. "It's you. From the water fountain and the pickup game."

I rub a hand behind my neck. "Yeah, though those were hardly my most memorable moments."

"We all have our off days." She laughs. "Ronan, right?"

"Yes. It's good to see you again, Thandi."

And it is.

She is even more beautiful than I remember. It's a punch so forceful it knocks the wind out of my lungs. That same grace, that same purpose radiates from her. She's nothing like the dispassionate opportunists who usually seek me out.

Not with that warmth, those gentle eyes. Not with that smile. Not with what I saw of her at the youth center.

The funny protective instinct I felt last week washes over me again.

That's when I know there's no way I can take her on as a client.

She's a true believer, and I don't do bleeding hearts. I stopped believing in goodness or kindness prevailing after Mom died. And I can't bear to see her story repeated.

"Thank you for seeing me," she's saying, "I'm grateful for—"

"No." I cut her off.

"Pardon?" Her eyes widen.

"No," I repeat, my voice flat, my jaw tight. "Unfortunately, you'll have to leave," I say. "Because I will not be taking you on as a client."

Lazy
Thandi

There's remote work, and then there is this.

Thorne Consulting's headquarters are an hour outside the Beltway, deep in the affluent Kenleigh neighborhood in Northern Virginia.

Ever since Trent suggested the meeting, I'd scoured the Internet for any crumbs I could find on Thorne Consulting's mysterious proprietor. But Trent was right. The man may as well be a ghost.

The little I could uncover suggests Thorne is the Rick Rubin of the biotech space, while also shunning the industry. It's very confusing, and I wonder yet again what Trent is thinking.

Thorne's ethos seems to contradict everything Immerscent stands for—transparency, accessibility, and collaboration. At first, I was uncomfortable with Trent covering the consultation. Now I'm glad he is. Based on Thorne's business model, I couldn't justify the expense.

I glance at the GPS and turn onto the tree-lined avenue that leads to my destination. As I drive past modern mansions and stately historical homes, I realize that Thorne's headquarters aren't just located in a residential area; they *are* his home.

I expect a showy entrance, but the home I pull up to is modern but restrained. The house looms in three levels of glass, stone, and wood, tucked so naturally against a rocky slope that it seems to grow out of it. A stone driveway curves upward, bordered by native grasses and evergreens.

Compared to the ornate colonial next door, Thorne's home speaks a different language. Not louder. *Smarter.* As I approach the entrance, I can see what looks like a greenhouse further back on the property.

I ring the bell, and a young woman in a crisp pantsuit opens the door.

"Ms. Elowen, welcome. I'm Belinda. Please, follow me."

Inside, the home is light and bright, with sleek furniture and breathtaking views. Belinda leads me to a room with heavy double doors.

She raps softly. "Mr. Thorne, your noon appointment is here."

"Come in," a deep voice commands.

When we enter, Thorne's back is to us. He is standing in front of a dramatic floor-to-ceiling window overlooking the garden. He is dressed all in black, but instead of diminishing his presence, the muted color magnifies it. Even facing away from me, something about Thorne's posture, the line of his shoulders, feels familiar, but I can't place it.

As soon as Belinda excuses herself, he turns.

His eyes widen, as if shocked to find me here.

I'm used to that. There aren't many Black twenty-seven-year-old female billionaires in this town—or anywhere, really. Not that money has ever been my motivation. It's always been about Tess.

This time, though, I also do a double-take.

Now I know why he looked familiar.

I almost laugh. Trent's consultant is the guy from the water fountain?

Thankfully, he seems mercifully more stable here.

When I introduce myself, his easy smile and self-deprecating comment about his performance at the pickup game release some of my tension.

I have whiplash as my emotions struggle to catch up. This isn't what I expected. Maybe I've misjudged Thorne Consulting.

"Ronan, right?" I say, approaching the desk. For a moment, I feel inexplicably breathless.

He looks … different here.

At the youth center, amidst the kids and the game, I didn't register much beyond his obvious hangover. Maybe it's the all-black outfit or the imposing desk. But this man feels nothing like the one I met a week ago.

Thorne is easily six and a half feet of solid muscle. So much taller than me that I have to take a step back so that I don't crane my neck looking at him.

His auburn hair is pulled into a heavy knot at the base of his neck. The color is surprisingly rich, deeply autumnal. The heavy shadow of stubble across his jaw does nothing to blunt the striking lines of his face—a sculpted brow, angular cheekbones, and a strong, uncompromising chin. There's not much softness there.

Except for his eyes.

They're amber. Not hazel or gold, but the rich, clear hue of sunlit honey. Unusually bright, disarmingly beautiful, there's intelligence there—but also something quiet and wounded. That part is familiar. I noticed it at the water fountain too.

It makes me wonder if that flicker of melancholy always lives there.

"Should we get started with the consultation?" I ask, but Ronan doesn't seem to hear me.

He's gone quiet. He stares—longer than is polite, longer than is comfortable.

"Thank you for seeing me," I begin, now uncertain. "I'm grateful for—"

Something shifts, and Ronan's expression shutters. Those honey-sweet eyes narrow into golden slits. All his earlier warmth vanishes.

"Unfortunately, you'll have to leave," he cuts across my words with unexpected violence. "Because I will not be taking you on as a client."

At first, I am stunned.

Then, fury sweeps through me with a force so powerful I shock even myself.

All my life, I've been the calm one—the voice of reason. I'm used to biting my tongue and sanding down my edges. Shouldering every condescending remark and burying the resentment from every slammed door.

But today, I am so tired of these indignities. The arrogance and entitlement would be more tolerable if they weren't so damn predictable.

I've worked too hard and come too far to let a spoiled man-child make a mockery of me—or Tess' memory.

"No." The word explodes from me before I can stop it.

Ronan jolts as if I've struck him. Like every bully, he doesn't expect resistance.

"What?" he growls.

"I said no." I meet his gaze head-on. "I left my team during our busiest season because you're supposed to be the best. I even had to endure an hour-long drive in traffic since *you* refuse virtual meetings."

"I don't—" Ronan starts, but I fold my arms, refusing to let him regain control of the conversation.

"I'm here for a consultation, and I am not leaving until I get it. I don't care if you work with Immerscent afterward. I'm a paying client, and this is the minimum I deserve."

My voice tightens. "If I were a white man, we wouldn't even be having this conversation. My time is valuable, and I will not be *dismissed*."

Ronan stares.

The silence in the room is deafening.

He parts his lips. His eyebrows lift, then lower. Whatever script he's rehearsed doesn't apply here, and for a moment, he looks like he's trying to recalibrate. It's obvious he's not used to being challenged like this. Certainly not by someone like me.

"The contract states I have an absolute right of refusal."

"It does," I say evenly, "but I'm asking for a reason. What is the basis of your rejection?"

"My method is proprietary. I don't have to—"

"Let me guess. I'm just not a 'fit,' right?" I make quotation marks in the air with my fingers.

What a joke. It's always the same tired story. Bias cloaked as brilliance; discrimination concealed as discernment. I'm unimpressed and disappointed. Trent has never been wrong before. I guess even he isn't perfect.

Ronan glowers. "Are you calling me a bigot, Ms. Elowen?"

"No," I answer. "Worse. I think you're lazy. Unimaginative. Boring, even."

I'm almost breathless in my anger. Not because he's hurt me. I've overcome far worse than Ronan Thorne. No, I'm upset because too much rides on the IPO for me to be distracted by false starts or hollow promises.

I *know* I'm getting closer to perfecting Immerscent's formula. Going public means more investment to unlock the next iteration, so I can get justice for Tess.

That's all that matters.

I don't have *time* for this.

I'm already twenty years too late. I can't squander another minute.

"Boring?" Ronan repeats, circling his desk. His voice is incredulous, but also a little wounded.

It's almost funny. After all his dismissiveness, *this* is what gets to him?

I swing my handbag over my shoulder. "You know what I love most about science, Ronan?"

He glares. "No, but I'm sure you're going to tell me."

"You have to show your work." I hold his gaze as I say it. "You don't get to just wave your hands and say, trust me—I'm smarter, taller, or richer. If it doesn't withstand scrutiny, it's not valid. Period."

I take a deep breath to center myself and the truth. He doesn't know me. Doesn't know what it feels like to go to sleep every night to Tess' screams. Doesn't know my team or the thousands of hours we've poured into a dream we refuse to give up on.

He doesn't matter, and I'm sorry I let myself think for a moment that he did.

"Trent said you were a genius, but I've met a million small-minded men like you. There's nothing here for Immerscent."

I pivot on my heel and stride towards the door, crossing the expensive hardwood as fast as my feet can carry me. I'm almost half-way there when Ronan catches my arm.

"Wait," he says quietly.

"For what?" I snap, wresting my arm free.

Our eyes lock, and for the briefest second, I see a crack in the mask. Something buried in those honeyed depths sparks. Anger? Guilt? Regret? It's gone too quickly to name.

With the light no longer directly on his face, Ronan's eyes are warm and deep, like the color of whiskey. His lashes are thick, ridiculously long for a man, and for a moment, I'm arrested by this unexpected glimpse of vulnerability.

The spell quickly fades when I remind myself that his beauty is only skin deep.

Thorne keeps studying me. His Adam's apple bobs as he swallows. I brace myself for whatever insult he'll come up with next, but he doesn't speak. Instead, he steps back, his body half-turned away from me.

"I was wrong," he says quietly. "Have a seat, Thandi." He gestures to the desk.

"Please."

Livid

Ronan

She's livid, and I don't blame her.

That was a dick move, and I regret it. She's called me out, and I face the uncomfortable truth that she's right. She deserves better than this.

I look across the desk at Thandi. Even in her fury, she's still magnificent. I hate what she said, but I have to admit, I respect the way she defended herself.

The only other people who've ever checked me this thoroughly are Fia—and my mother.

Mom, who was a scientist, just like Thandi.

Thandi's accusations ring in my ears: Biased. Unimaginative. Lazy. Cruel too. She doesn't say that part aloud, but her eyes transmit it.

I'm not that person ... *am I?*

I know I don't want to be.

Something's happening to me. It's been happening to me since Mom passed away last year.

It's like I'm grasping at the foundations of who I am, but keep coming up empty-handed.

Maybe that's why I feel so haunted by Thandi, by the youth center and Trent. Now, three days away from Mom's will reading, I'm teetering again, questioning whether any of the things I've told myself make sense.

Seeing Thandi's face and the wounded expression I've put on it doesn't feel like a coincidence.

If cosmic pushes exist, I'm getting a giant kick in the ass.

I know I have to fix not just this, but everything. It's time to stop wandering around in the wilderness and be the kind of man my mother would be proud of. The kind of man she always pushed me to be.

"I'm sorry," I say to Thandi. "You didn't deserve that. We can move forward with the consultation."

Thandi's eyes widen. Everything in her body language says she's still ready to bolt.

"So you *want* to have the consultation now?"

"Yes. Unless you're so disgusted with me that you no longer want anything to do with Thorne Consulting."

I sigh. "I *am* good at what I do, Thandi, and I *can* help you. Allow me to redeem myself—and my work."

Thandi is quiet. Her eyes reflect her uncertainty, but I can see my apology has earned me the tiniest sliver of respect.

"Alright," she says at last.

The air rushes out of my lungs. Thank God.

I gesture at the chair. "Shall we begin?"

Thandi nods, and I explain the first stage of my method—the fundamentals. Before the IPO, before the competition, before the next best product, I need to understand a CEO's vision. What drives them? What legacy do they want to leave behind?

"Thandi." I lean forward. "Why did you found Immerscent?"

Thandi's throat works. Her gaze leaves mine for a moment, fixing on an invisible point somewhere out the window.

Her eyes are full of pain when they meet mine again. "I had a … difficult experience as a child that caused me to lose my memory."

She shakes her head. "Having a piece of your life missing is torture I wouldn't wish on anyone. I founded Immerscent so no one would have to go through what I did."

She describes Immerscent's rigorous referral and evaluation processes, the committed team she's built in three short years, and the governance structure she's established to ensure profits align with purpose.

She's amazing, fucking brilliant. No wonder Trent insisted on the highest investment package.

But the more Thandi speaks, the more panicked I become. My pulse is racing, and my neck is clammy with sweat.

It's just as I thought.

It's just like Mom all over again—a beautiful dream and a brilliant executive thinking an IPO will make all the difference.

Is she really ready for everything that comes with going public?

And can I prevent the jackals from circling this time, when I failed before?

I meet her gaze. "Are you sure you're ready to go public?" I ask. "It's not so easy to maintain a bright line in the sand when shareholders are calling the shots."

"I'm sure." Thandi's jaw is set. "We've weathered storms before. As long as we stay true to our purpose, we'll navigate this as well."

She believes it.

I wish I could believe it, too.

Thandi Elowen is the most brilliant client to come to my office in years—maybe ever. But what impresses me the most is that somehow, despite the pain she carries, she hasn't lost her idealism or her humanity.

And that's precisely what terrifies me.

"I need twenty-four hours to review the data before I can make a decision," I say slowly. "I'm attending a mixer tomorrow evening at Sky Lounge. Could we meet there to discuss next steps?"

"Of course," Thandi replies, rising.

"Perfect. I'll email you the details."

We shake hands, and she leaves, her perfume lingering faintly in the air.

I stare at the door long after she's left.

What the hell have I gotten myself into?

Mixer

Thandi

Mixer?

Yeah, right.

I step through the doors and enter the exclusive space that is Sky Lounge.

This is a full-blown party.

When Ronan asked me to meet him here, I imagined a sterile networking event. Not this.

Three-hundred-and-sixty-degree floor-to-ceiling windows define the rooftop bar, revealing a skyline so vast it feels surreal. Chesden glitters below like a tray of spilled diamonds.

Music pulses through hidden speakers. The room is packed. Even though the evening has just begun, the atmosphere is already charged. Raucous guests float past in designer outfits, while waitstaff offer artistic hors d'oeuvres balanced on matte-black trays.

In one corner, a bottle of Cristal arrives with a lit sparkler jammed into the top. The flame hisses while a booth full of model types shrieks in delight. Across the room, a darker corner thrums with low laughter—bodies hunched over a table, fingers darting over a flash of white powder. I don't let myself think about what they're sniffing. I just look away.

I realize belatedly that I'm one of the few people here in anything resembling business attire. Everyone else is dressed for an evening that doesn't end with a handshake.

My dress is crimson, with clean lines, cap sleeves, and a fit that hugs without demanding attention. No one ever expects it, but somehow with my fuchsia hair, it works. Paired with my patent black pumps and the fresh fade I got yesterday, I know I look sharp. But in this sea of sequins, bare backs, and slinky silhouettes, I feel out of step.

Best to find Ronan, complete the consultation, and get out of here.

I hate feeling out of place.

I scan the room, searching for a towering figure with honey eyes and a knot of auburn hair, but with so many people milling about, it's hard to see beyond the gaggle in front of me.

I slip past couples grooving on the dance floor to find a better vantage point near the bar.

Still no sign of Ronan.

The bartender, a young Black man about my age, nods at me, his golden forearms flashing as he wipes down the bar. "What are you having, miss?"

I hesitate. I hadn't planned on indulging, but it's been a hell of a week. I've earned one drink at least. I lean over so he can hear me over the din.

"I'll have an Old Fashioned with a cognac base—Pierre Ferrand, if you've got it. And lavender honey instead of simple syrup, please."

"I got you," the bartender nods and gets to work.

"Thanks."

I'm about to scan the room again when a living heat radiates behind me. I spin and find myself staring into a warm amber gaze.

"A honey-lavender Old Fashioned? You're full of surprises, Ms. Elowen."

Ronan's voice is so deep it seems to vibrate in the space between us. He's wearing a tailored black suit with a crisp white shirt and no tie. With his build, I can only imagine that the ensemble is bespoke. Diamond-studded platinum cuff links flash at his wrists. He's too close, and between his voice, his height, and the faint irritation I still feel from our first meeting, I can't help thinking that everything about this man is *too much*.

"*Mr. Thorne*," I say wryly, "You finally decided to grace us with your presence."

Ronan smiles like I've just complimented instead of chided him. He doesn't answer but focuses on the bartender, who's adding the curlicue of orange peel to my drink.

"The lady's drink is on me. My tab is already open. Last name, Thorne."

"Yes, sir."

"That's really not necessary, Ronan, I—"

"I insist," he says, handing me my drink. I watch as he orders a pour of Macallan Rare Cask, neat.

Thanks to my Dad, I know enough about whiskey to be a little dangerous, and I find myself surprised by the choice. I know nothing about this man, but based on our volatile first meeting, I'm expecting something a little less … *acceptable* in Ronan's drink preferences. It's what every other sensible rich executive would order. But what do I know?

Besides, it's not like I care what someone as insufferable as Ronan Thorne drinks.

He's watching me again with that intense, inscrutable look, and I raise an eyebrow. What on earth is he staring at?

"Cheers." Ronan clinks his glass against mine. "Sorry for pulling you into this circus. My client just posted his highest earnings in four years, and he wanted to celebrate. Not an ideal location for business, but after our rocky start, I didn't want to keep you waiting any longer than necessary for my initial assessment."

"Ah," I say softly.

Something inside me softens at that. The problem was never the party. No, part of me just wondered if Ronan had chosen this place on purpose, to keep me off balance.

To remind me, like last time, that I don't belong.

But I see genuine sheepishness on his face now, and a hint of uncertainty. I take a breath. I'm relieved this space isn't ideal for him, either. It means he's not as petty as I was bracing for. The tension in my shoulders relaxes a fraction.

"I've booked a private conference room if you'd like to discuss the analysis in detail, but my assessment is pretty straightforward," he informs me.

"Oh?" The tension is back with a vengeance. It shoots down my spine as every cell in my body prepares for battle. I sip my Old Fashioned to hide my resentment at this Thorne-induced emotional siege. Sharp, sweet, and herbaceous, the drink's flavors are perfectly balanced. The universe has spared me one disappointment at least.

"Yes," Ronan murmurs. "I'll share a hard copy of my assessment, but it should also be in your inbox by now. Immerscent's fundamentals are magnificent. I'd be honored to have you as a client, Thandi."

I came here to give Ronan the benefit of the doubt and to salvage whatever I could of Trent's investment. But mostly, it was to show Ronan that I refuse to be intimidated. Needless to say, my expectations were in hell.

This is the last thing I thought he'd say.

And now, I'm speechless.

Ronan laughs. "Not what you were expecting?"

"Honestly, no," I say with a shrug. "Not after the way you treated me yesterday."

Ronan's expression tightens. "I'm not proud of that. I won't make excuses, because I know they're meaningless, but for what it's worth, I really am sorry."

Those honey-sweet eyes bear into mine, and I almost want to believe him.

I hesitate. It's barely a breath, but Ronan doesn't miss it.

"Say it," he prods.

"I'm glad you think Immerscent is on solid footing, but with all due respect, I would not be going public if we weren't. This isn't going to work if I'm jumping through hoops to prove myself worthy of the basics."

I square my shoulders. "I'm not interested in this collaboration if we can't approach it as equals, and if there is no mutual respect. I won't stand for a repeat of our first meeting—no matter how brilliant Trent says you are."

Now it's his turn to go silent.

I'm surprised to see what looks like real contrition flash across Ronan's face. I'm puzzled as he pulls out his phone and types for a few minutes before returning to me.

"You're absolutely right. And that's why I've just texted Trent to amend our contract. Twenty percent up front instead of the full amount I usually require. You'll only pay the balance if my behavior exceeds your standards."

Is this man insane?

"You don't even know what my standards are," I stammer. "I could demand anything."

Ronan shrugs. "Trust goes both ways. If I'm asking you to trust that I'll be my best self, I'll have to trust that you'll be yours too."

Ronan extends his hand. "What do you say, Thandi? Do we have a deal?"

I stare at that wide palm, those long fingers, for far too long. I'm not sure what to make of this. Which Ronan Thorne is the real deal—the reasonable man in front of me, or the one who spat venom at me just twenty-four hours ago?

"I…" I begin, but I can't finish. I'm assailed by doubt. My hurt and anger from yesterday are still too fresh.

"I understand," Ronan says softly. He can't hide his disappointment. Damn it.

Something in that dejected look tugs at me despite my misgivings.

I don't know why, but I make a split-second decision that's nothing like me. It's the kind of leap of faith Tess would take if she were still here.

Ronan's palm falters, already lowering, but I grasp it before it can drop to his side. His hand is warm, faintly callused, and it completely engulfs my own.

I hope it's not a symbol of how Immerscent's future will be smothered under the Thorne signature touch.

Too late now to go back, though.

My heart is beating way too fast when I meet Ronan's gaze again.

"Deal," I agree.

In Sync
Ronan

Thandi's palm is soft. So soft.

And small.

My hand looks like a fucking bear claw next to hers.

I thought I'd completely blown it, but here she is, agreeing to work with me.

And touching me of her own volition.

A current of electricity crackles from the pulse in my wrist all the way to my heart.

She could order me to follow her to the ends of the earth right now, and I'd ask if she wanted me to shuttle off to the next galaxy, too.

There is such kindness, such gentleness in this woman. And now I've also seen the core of steel under it. I've already glimpsed Thandi's fire and her unwavering determination. I've done nothing to deserve the grace she's showing me, yet she's extending it anyway.

That funny protective feeling consumes me again. Paradoxically, the more I learn of her strength, the more I want to make sure it's never compromised. I failed miserably at honoring that yesterday, but things are going to be different moving forward. Not just because I made a vow to Thandi, but because I'm making one to myself.

We're frozen, as if the moment our bodies touched, we both short-circuited. She's staring up at me, eyes wide, hand still clasped in mine.

I have the insane urge to pull her close. I don't.

I do manage to find my voice.

"Let me buy you another drink," I offer.

That seems to break the spell, and she releases my hand.

"Thank you, but I shouldn't. I need to head back."

I glance at my watch. "It's 8:30 on a Friday night. You can't be going back to the office?"

She ducks her head guiltily. "I'm in the final stages of developing β7, our newest compound. With a few more tweaks, it could be ready for the IPO." She waves her hand. "I'll sleep then."

"Nope," I say, already lifting my finger to signal to the bartender.

"What?"

"That's the only condition I wrote into the new contract with Trent. No working on a Friday night." I wink at her. "Besides, we haven't even toasted to our new partnership yet."

Thandi makes a surprised sound, then laughs. "I'm going to have to take a close look at this new contract. Otherwise, I suspect we're going to be discovering new clauses every day."

I feign a hurt look. "You're expressing doubt about our Friday night clause? You wound me. That demands a second drink, for sure."

Thandi mutters something under her breath while the bartender chuckles. I take her empty glass and hand her the fresh drink.

"Stay," I plead with her.

And she does.

"Hey, hot stuff, I missed you."

Amber slides into the booth next to me in a cloud of bubble-gum-sweet perfume. She looks stunning with her golden hair falling in waves over her shoulders, and a plunging black mini dress that leaves little to the imagination.

I should be entranced by her charms. Instead, I'm tracking a tiny inventor across the room.

"Hey, beautiful," I murmur, kissing her distractedly on the cheek.

Amber follows my gaze over to where Thandi is chatting with Adrien Vaillancourt, one of my European investors. Of course, Thandi would find the only other serious person in the room tonight.

Young and ambitious, the Frenchman comes from a long line of famous perfumers. Brilliant, Adrien keeps pushing his hidebound aristocratic family to be on the leading edge. Right now, he's focused on emotion-responsive scent wearables and smart diffusion systems for home environments—tech that makes venture capital lean in.

It's exactly the type of connection Immerscent should be exploring, and Thandi once again demonstrates her razor-sharp business acumen. Yet, I only feel irritated at how easily they seem to be getting along. Thandi is laughing, and her eyes sparkle as Adrien leans in to murmur something in her ear.

I've always been aware of my size—six-six, and built like a goddamn linebacker, thanks to my father and too many years of competitive rowing. There's no casual way for me to stand next to someone like Thandi, not when she barely clears five-two. Adrien is tall too, maybe six feet, but lean and fine-boned, with a build that makes a well-cut suit look effortless. Tonight he's wearing a navy blazer with slim lapels and tapered trousers. No tie, but just enough structure to look polished without trying.

He's easy on the eyes. Next to him, Thandi looks like she belongs. The proportions make sense. She's not swallowed by his presence. There's a rhythm between them—her quick smile, the way she leans in when he speaks. It's nothing. And it's everything.

It shouldn't matter.

But it does.

"Her?" Amber laughs beside me. "Oh, honey, that little thing will never satisfy you."

I turn to her with a frown. "I didn't know you'd be here tonight." My tone says the rest: push this, and you'll wear out your welcome.

"I thought I'd surprise you." She rests a hand on my thigh and starts to trail it upward. "I have other surprises you'll like too."

I try to listen, but the piped-in music shifts, and the DJ, a wild-haired woman with a tattoo sleeve, slips on her headset and spins a new track.

The low hum of the lounge turns into a rhythmic pulse.

In that pulse, I catch movement.

Adrien has abandoned his drink. In one smooth motion, he asks Thandi to dance. He takes her hand, and just like that, he pulls her from the bar and into the fray of bodies on the floor.

Son of a—

Adrien's hand is at the small of Thandi's back, his mouth near her ear. Thandi's fingers are splayed against his chest. I try to catalog the sequence: the tilt of her head, her other hand on his shoulder, the way his eyes move over her face. Every detail needles me, in a way I can't articulate. I want to look away, and I can't.

I stand without even thinking. Amber's hand falls away.

"Sorry, Amber, I've got to run. I'll catch you around, okay?"

"What?" She sputters. "You can't just—"

I don't catch the rest. I'm already moving, pulled by magnetic force toward the dance floor.

Flow
Thandi

Adrien is sweet, and I'm glad I've met him.

He's not like most people I spoke with this evening. Of course, our business interests align, but he's easy to talk to. He's not looking for the edge in every conversation or infatuated with being seen. He just wants to chat and treat the night as its own reward.

He's a good dancer, too. I laugh as he swings me into a spin. Adrien catches me with a hand at my waist. His smile is genuine, and I realize with a pang that I haven't smiled like that in weeks.

He takes me for another turn, and I fall into rhythm. It feels good to let loose after the pressure of perfecting β7, the board meeting, and the looming IPO. With the music pulsing and my feet matching his, the stress starts to lift.

We pivot, and the motion gives me a glimpse across the room. Of their own volition, my eyes find Ronan. Since he left me at the bar, I keep catching flashes of his shock of auburn hair and that tall, imposing body. I can't stop seeing him, even when I'm not looking for him.

It's not like I *want* to find him. Ronan Thorne simply doesn't *blend*.

He's sitting next to a blonde determined to hold his attention. She's leaning toward him, one hand on his thigh. But Ronan looks... detached. Not annoyed. Just somewhere else.

I wonder what has him so distracted, but when I look again, I find him staring.

Right at me.

Our gazes collide.

I expect him to look away, but he doesn't. He just watches me with a focus that steals the breath from my lungs. Even across the chaos of the dance floor, those whiskey-colored eyes pin me in place. There's something dark in his gaze.

Dangerous.

Not the hostility from yesterday, but something much more disconcerting.

Something intense.

I grip Adrien's shoulder and tear my eyes away.

"Everything alright?" he asks, leaning close to my ear.

"Yes, of course," I murmur, though I can't account for the flutter in my stomach.

When the music shifts to 90s R&B, I shake off Ronan's brooding intensity, smiling as *"Why I Love You So Much"* by Monica comes on.

"Okay!" I say, giving my hips a little shake. "Now they're taking us back. I love this song. Man, our generation doesn't have anything like this. We missed out on the good old days."

Adrien laughs, trying to match my enthusiasm. "I'm not sure this is my genre—" he starts.

He doesn't get to finish.

I feel the shift in the air, the almost electric presence behind me, even as Adrien's eyes widen.

I know who it is without looking.

Ronan.

"Sorry to interrupt, Adrien, but I'm afraid I'll have to steal the lady from you for a minute." The words themselves are polite, even bland, but Ronan's voice carries something else. A warning. Maybe a challenge.

Adrien hesitates. Whatever he sees in Ronan's face makes up his mind.

"It was a pleasure, Thandi. I hope we can continue our business conversation soon," he says.

"I'd love that," I say, smiling at him.

Adrien nods, and with a small dip of his waist, steps away.

My lips part as Ronan looms in front of me. For the second time this evening, he extends his hand to me.

"May I have this dance?"

My thoughts scatter. Why is he here? Of all the things I've pictured Ronan doing—and honestly, that list is short—dancing was not on it. After all of our earlier friction, he can't really want to dance with me.

Can he?

I make a questioning sound, but he doesn't lower his hand. Of course, he'd be stubborn as hell.

I sigh. I might as well do it and get this over with.

Rolling my eyes, I slip my hand into his. Monica's raspy voice croons from the speakers as Ronan pulls me close. A spark tingles through me, catching me off guard.

I frown. Maybe I'm just aware of the contrast between his power and his restraint—that gentle hand versus the muscles lying dormant beneath the clean lines of his suit. He could overpower me easily, but somehow I know he won't.

I'll be honest. I assumed Ronan would have two left feet. I've never met anyone his size who's graceful. Plus, he's a rich white guy. What does he know about rhythm and blues?

Well, I can't speak for the blues, but it turns out Ronan Thorne has a hell of a lot of rhythm.

He draws me in, and suddenly I'm pressed tight against him. We move together like we've done this a million times before. His movements are loose and natural, his center of gravity low in his pelvis. If Adrien's touch was the warmth of sunshine, Ronan's hand on my lower back is the core of a furnace. His grip is confident, his finger-tips pressing just shy of a caress. Hot. Possessive. The opposite of Adrien's polite grip.

Even my body reacts differently. There's a spike in my pulse. My cheeks flush. I try to step back, but Ronan follows me, thinking I'm just changing up the pace. We sway, locked together from chest to knee.

I'm hyper-aware of every part of him—the breadth of his shoulders, the pull of muscle across his back. My cheek grazes his chest. With every breath, I catch the clean edge of his aftershave and something underneath it. Something I can't name that makes me want to lean closer.

I resist. Barely. My skin hums with sensation, and I still can't catch my breath. When my chest brushes his again, my nipples prick to rigid points. I stifle a gasp.

"Ronan," I say sharply, pulling away.

This makes no sense. Yesterday, I wanted nothing to do with Ronan Thorne. Now, after a couple of drinks and a slow dance, I'm lighting up like a Christmas tree. If this is my body's way of telling me I've been pushing too hard and need rest, I'm receiving the message loud and clear.

Time to go.

"What's wrong?" Ronan's words are barely more than a rumble against my temple, but even the soft exhalation of his breath leaves me reeling.

"I… I need some water," I croak.

He pulls back, face softening with concern. "I'm sorry, Thandi. Let me grab you something."

"That's not—" I start, but he's already making his way to the bar.

I don't need him to wait on me. But I'm grateful for the break from his presence. I smooth a hand over my dress and try to breathe. I don't know what the hell is happening, but I need to get my head back in the game.

Ronan orders at the bar. Then, he turns and ambles back to me, holding a glass aloft.

"Here you go."

"Thanks," I murmur. The condensation on the glass slicks my fingers, cooling the heat he left behind. I expect him to walk away. Instead, he gently guides me off the dance floor toward a booth that looks like it was reserved for him.

The thudding bass softens here. It's quieter, tucked away—a small alcove of almost-peace.

Ronan gestures for me to sit, but I shake my head.

"Ronan, this is really thoughtful, but I should probably head back."

"Head back to what, exactly?" Ronan leans forward, arms folded on the table. He fixes me with an expression that's equal parts question and challenge. His eyes are bright, the honey of his irises deepening to almost caramel in the dim light.

I scramble for an answer. "There are worse things than a shower, a little paperwork, and maybe some Netflix before bed," I say, trying for levity.

"I'm sorry." Ronan rises and makes a show of peering at my head.

"What on earth are you doing?"

He grins. "Checking for gray hairs. For a moment, I thought I was talking to a sixty-year-old, not a young, vibrant billionaire in her twenties."

"Are you calling me boring, Thorne?"

"Apparently, I would know," he says wryly, reminding me of the dressing down I gave him yesterday. There's no reproach in his tone, though, and his eyes are dancing.

"Fine," I say, "but even if I don't go home, I need to get out of here."

"You don't want to stay?"

"No, I've stayed much longer than I intended." I shrug. "Besides, this isn't my scene anyway."

Ronan's gaze turns thoughtful. "What is your scene, Thandi Elowen?" he asks, and the question lands with more weight than I expect.

I frown, fingers tightening around the sweating glass, unsure how to answer without sounding ungracious. "Casual. Less performative," I say finally. "More genuine—no offense."

"None taken." Ronan smiles. "I'm only here because I promised my friend I'd come to support. I'd much rather be somewhere we can talk."

There's something quieter in his voice now, something that catches me off guard. I study his face, and what I see there seems ... real.

My stomach picks that moment to growl. Loudly.

The thread snaps. Ronan blinks, then bursts out laughing.

"Wow, my company's that bad, huh?"

"What?" I ask, flushing. "Don't tell me those tiny hors d'oeuvres filled you up. If I'm still hungry, you must be starving."

"I'll have you know I have a rather dainty stomach, Ms. Elowen," Ronan teases, but his expression settles. "You're right. I could use a real meal."

I can't believe I'm doing this, but I say, "Then let's get out of here. I know the perfect spot."

Tino's
Ronan

Tino's is as far from Sky Lounge as I can imagine.

There's nothing glitzy about the hole-in-the-wall pizza joint. Tucked between a dry cleaner and a shuttered yoga studio, the storefront is easy to miss. But inside it's warm and alive—all wood and brick, the air thick with the smell of fresh bread, charred wood, and slow-simmered tomato. There are no pretentious flourishes or curated playlists. Just voices rising over clinking glasses and the crackle of the oven.

It's rustic. Homey. Welcoming.

I can see why Thandi loves it.

As we step through the door, I glance around. The space is small, maybe eight tables total, with a long marble counter stretching along the far wall. Every seat is filled. At nearly eleven PM, people are still waiting: some with drinks in hand, others clustered near the door, trading stories or glancing toward the kitchen.

I start to wonder if this was a mistake, but Thandi doesn't bat an eyelash.

"This crowd is insane," I say under my breath. "You think they'll seat us?"

Before she can answer, a voice booms across the room.

"*Architetta!*"

A stocky man in a flour-dusted apron barrels toward us, arms already outstretched. His salt-and-pepper curls are plastered to his forehead, and his smile could outshine a marquee.

I glance around, half assuming he's talking to someone else. But no, Thandi is already moving forward, laughing.

"Tino," she says as he pulls her into a hug that almost lifts her off her feet. "You're working late. Think you can squeeze us in?"

"For you? Always." He releases her with a pat on the cheek. "Got your regular spot ready." Then his gaze shifts, and for the first time, he notices me.

He pauses, eyes twinkling. "*Il tipo tuo?*"

I don't speak Italian, but I don't need to. The way Thandi flushes tells me everything.

"No!" she says quickly, pressing her hands to her cheeks in a way that's—honestly?—kind of adorable. "A friend, Tino. Just a friend."

I'm flushing too now, but for a different reason. Hearing Thandi call me a friend feels good, even if I know she's only saying it to get Tino off her back.

"Welcome, *amico,*" Tino says with a wink, then claps me on the shoulder. "You're in good hands with this one."

He leads us past the counter to a small alcove tucked off the side of the main dining room. It's not quite hidden, but half-partitioned by a low wall and flanked by shelves full of cookbooks and framed photos. It feels quieter here, more intimate.

Tino pulls out two chairs. "You want the usual?"

Thandi nods. "I was thinking the margherita. And maybe the speck with hot honey and burrata, as an app? That okay with you, Ronan?"

"Sounds perfect." I lean back in my chair. I don't really care what she orders. I'm just grateful for the glimpse into her life. Like at the youth center, I'm realizing Thandi leaves a little bit of sunshine wherever she goes.

Tino grins, already retreating. "Coming right up."

As he disappears into the kitchen, I let my gaze wander. The walls of the restaurant are cluttered with framed photographs, some yellowing at the edges, others crisp and recent. There's a black-and-white shot of a former president mid-bite, sleeves rolled up. A jazz saxophonist I recognize from an old vinyl cover twirls a forkful of pasta not far from him. There's a famous chef. A late-night host. Even a blurry picture that looks suspiciously like two Supreme Court justices sharing a pie.

And there—tucked between a photo of a young Aretha Franklin and a local sportscaster—is Thandi.

She's younger in the picture, maybe fresh out of college. She's wearing a hoodie and holding a half-eaten slice, eyes squinting in mid-laugh. She's seated at the counter, the oven glowing behind her, and even though the photo is candid, it's obvious she belongs here.

I gesture at it with my thumb. "That you?"

She groans. "I wish Tino would take that down."

"He's not wrong for thinking you're famous."

She rolls her eyes. "He thinks *anyone* with a feature in the *Post* is famous. I've known him since I was a kid. This was our Sunday night spot growing up, every week, like clockwork. He still calls my mom *Professore*."

"And *Architetta*?" I ask, remembering the nickname he used at the door.

Thandi smiles. Before she can answer, Tino calls back from behind the counter.

"Because she was always building!" He waves a floury hand. "LEGO castles, towers, whole cities—right in the booth while I made their pizza. I kept telling her she could've won a national competition."

He winks, already halfway to the oven. "Still got the little model she made of this place in my office."

Thandi shakes her head. "He exaggerates," she huffs.

But I catch the look on his face, and I don't think he is.

Tino reappears with two water glasses and a basket of bread-sticks wrapped in paper napkins. He sets a menu on the table, even though all the choices are on the chalkboard behind him.

He glances between us. "So," he says, "is she letting you share her pizza, or do you want something of your own?"

Thandi shrugs. "Up to him."

Tino turns to me. "Well?"

"I'll share," I say. "But I'd also take the shrimp and pesto—if I can add pickled banana peppers to it."

Thandi lifts her head, staring at me. "*That's* your order?"

I shrug. "What can I say? I'm complex."

She narrows her eyes. "You're insane."

"Hey, I'm eating the speck and burrata too," I say. "I'm not unreasonable."

Tino barks a laugh. "I like this guy. Shrimp and pesto with banana peppers. Coming right up."

He heads back toward the kitchen, but Thandi calls after him.

"Tino—one more thing? Can you get him a gin and tonic? Extra lime?"

I blink at her. "How did you…?"

Thandi just smiles, reaching for a breadstick. "You just seem like a G&T guy."

I stare at her. And for a second, I forget whatever I was about to say. Just when I think I've got a handle on her—her brilliance, her humility—she goes and surprises me again.

She leans in, elbows resting lightly on the edge of the table. "Did I guess wrong?"

"No," I say, still watching her. "You didn't. But I need to know—what gave it away?"

She looks pleased with herself and a little amused. I expect her to say something smug, but instead she tilts her head. "I saw you nursing that whiskey all night," she says. "You didn't look like you were enjoying it. You never even finished it."

I start to respond, but she keeps going.

"A man who wears *Sel Marin* is *not* a whiskey guy. Don't get me wrong, it's my vice of choice, but citrus notes and clean botanicals seem more consistent with your scent profile.

That catches me off guard. She's right.

I don't know when I started ordering the Macallan at public events. It seemed to project the image I wanted for Thorne Consulting—cultured, mature, discriminating. Eventually, it stopped being a preference and became a prop. A tool.

I never expected anyone to notice.

Then again, Thandi isn't just anyone.

"You could've ordered something lighter. A G&T with extra lime would've hit the right note." Her voice softens. "So I guess I'm wondering why you didn't."

She doesn't press. The question lands lightly, like mist off the Potomac—soft, but weighted with more than it seems.

The most remarkable part is that she's not trying to prove anything. She's just paying attention. It's impressive and … unsettling, the way she sees past the walls I've built. I know she's brilliant, but her precision, her impeccable nose, remind me again why she's the best at what she does.

I feel the gentle heat radiating from the wood oven. I glance at the worn brick, the old photo of her laughing in a hoodie.

Tino's is a place where you don't have to posture to be welcome.

And Thandi is a person who doesn't need the excess to think someone matters.

For the first time in a long time, I wonder what it would be like to stop performing. To put aside all the props and tools and show up. Just as myself.

We demolished the speck and burrata, and only half of Thandi's pizza is left.

She laughs at something, and in the amber light, she's radiant. She's so genuine, so present, so thoroughly herself. There's a looseness in her shoulders I haven't seen before.

And I don't want to look away.

Tino returns with a dark bottle tucked under one arm and two long-stemmed glasses balanced in the other.

"I brought you something special," he says, setting the glasses down on the table. "Picked it up on my last trip home."

The label is Italian, hand-lettered and elegant—a bottle reserved for special occasions.

Thandi squints at it. "Tino, this is too much."

He waves her off with a snort. "It's the least I can do. After everything you did for the renovation, a bottle of wine is nothing."

Her smile falters. "We agreed you wouldn't make a thing out of that."

"And I'm not." He deftly pops the cork and gives her a wink. "Just being a good host."

I watch the exchange in silence. Now that he's said it, I notice the new tile on the oven and the upgraded stonework around the alcove. Tino decants a generous pour into each glass and slides one toward me.

"She insisted we keep it rustic, but made sure the bones were solid," he murmurs. "The oven alone—don't even get me started."

"Tino," Thandi warns, but there's more exasperation than heat in her voice.

"Fine, fine." He raises both hands. "Enjoy, you two. Just don't forget to save room for dessert. That chocolate budino isn't going to eat itself."

He disappears with a smile, and Thandi sags back in her chair. She looks acutely uncomfortable, like she's been caught sneaking out of a good deed, instead of getting credit for one.

I twirl my wine glass, observing her. "So, just how many people has superhero Thandi saved?"

She glances at me, flustered. "It wasn't about being a savior. Tino put in all the work. It just needed to be done."

"Mm hmm." I don't press, but I'm not convinced.

"This is nice," Thandi says after a moment. Her expression says she didn't expect it, and I once again feel like a cad for my behavior yesterday.

"Thandi," I murmur. "I really am sorry."

She looks up, eyes wide. "About what?"

"About yesterday."

"Oh." She nods. "Thanks for saying that. I honestly didn't know what to think."

"You were right to be confused. A lot's been going on in my life lately … and I haven't handled it well. I shouldn't have taken it out on you."

She hesitates. "Is that why you were so unwelcoming yesterday? So angry at me?"

The sadness in her eyes kills me. Damn it, I really fucked up.

"No." I stammer. "I was an idiot, plain and simple." The words come before I can stop them. "I could never be mad at you, Thandi."

My heart's racing. God, I probably sound like a lunatic.

She's quiet for a long time. When she meets my gaze, the look in her eyes completely unravels me. "How about we start again?" she says. "Properly this time."

She extends a hand. "Truce?"

I grin and take her hand in mine.

"Truce."

Willpower
Ronan

"Are you sure you want to do this?" I ask Fia as we wait outside Whitlow Estate's massive entrance.

Everything about my childhood home is as I remember it, from the heavy oak door we're waiting in front of, to the sprawling gardens. Equally familiar is the volatile mix of anger, resentment, and dread I feel being here.

Fia shoots me a look and squares her shoulders. Today her hair is in a soft halo of spirals, and she's wearing a crisp slate pantsuit with magenta pumps that add a sophisticated pop of color to her ensemble.

"Your father doesn't intimidate me. Besides, I'm your financial advisor and your best friend. I *should* be here for the reading of your mother's will."

Of course, she should be here. And my father doesn't intimidate me, either.

He lost any leverage he had over me when I took my mother's name and forfeited my inheritance.

But I know the man I grew up with well. Not only is he petty, but he thrives on control and humiliation. He's also the type of bastard who's never approved of my having a Black best friend. He approves even less of a woman owning the types of spaces Fia has dominated.

Fia might not be worried, but I know before even entering the house that my father has prepared something to isolate or insult her.

He'll do it to undermine her and because he knows it'll enrage me and throw me off my game. Which is why I offered Fia the option of joining virtually, since my lawyer will be physically present. In fact, Aamir already texted when he arrived ten minutes ago.

I've tried to anticipate the worst, but I know whatever is waiting on the other side of that door is nothing Fia deserves. I've tried to prepare her, to give her an out in the hope that she might be deterred.

Of course, I should know better. This is a woman who has never backed down from a challenge. And she isn't about to start now.

That has my thoughts drifting to another woman who faces the world head-on: Thandi.

The dinner at Tino's still feels like an unexpected gift. I don't have much time to dwell on it, though, as the door swings open, and Whitlow's House Manager, Mr. Hensley, appears as impeccably turned out as ever.

In a tailored charcoal vest and polished shoes, he looks like he's stepped out of another century. His silver hair is neatly combed, and his eyes, a warm hazel, crinkle with something close to fondness when he sees me.

"Mr. Thorne. It's good to have you home."

He reaches for my hand and briefly clasps it in both of his. Knowing what we're here for, the small gesture grounds me more than I'd like to admit.

Mr. Hensley turns to Fia. "Ms. Beltrán Zamora," he says, his smile widening. "We're honored to have you at Whitlow. You are most welcome."

His manners are perfect. But more than that—he means it. Most people would call Mr. Hensley staff, but I never have. As a boy, I thought of him as an uncle who just happened to work with us. He certainly was more present than my father. He'd slip me extra candy when my mother wasn't looking and cover for me when I needed to disappear to play with the other kids.

His presence is probably the most pleasant interaction we'll have today.

I mentally brace myself as he ushers us inside.

Despite its age, the house is beautiful with an understated elegance. The foyer opens into a broad hall with wide-plank pine floors. The walls are decorated with pale cream wainscoting, and the morning light pours in through the tall windows.

The home is my mother's; a wedding gift from my grandfather that has been in the Thorne family for centuries. As soon as my parents were married, my father—obsessed with the Thorne name, the bloodline traceable to the Pilgrims and the Quaker virtue it carries—commandeered it as the ultimate status symbol.

And a foil for his depravity, in the same way that he ultimately used my mother.

Through one of the arched windows off the main corridor, I catch a glimpse of the vineyard—it's neatly trellised rows cutting across the eastern slope. My chest tightens.

The land had been forgotten and overgrown for decades, until my mother insisted it could be transformed. Whitlow Vineyards was her last project—part science, part stubborn poetry. She designed everything, from the irrigation to the fermentation profiles.

Her signature wine, Thorne Run, a full-bodied red with a surprising mineral finish, won her accolades. But it was Rosalind's Trace, a delicate rosé with notes of wild strawberry and sage, that became a quiet cult favorite, especially among women like my mother, who preferred precision to pretense.

The success thrilled her.

Now, it's my father who benefits from the vineyard instead. He takes meetings in the tasting room she built and assumes credit for her inspiration, without ever having lifted a hand in the work. It's a bitter irony, but no surprise.

As we move towards the grand hall, the air smells of lemon polish and peonies. My mother's favorite flower is still arranged in fresh bouquets throughout the foyer and halls. It's a subtle but unmistakable reminder: the staff hasn't forgotten who this home truly belongs to.

The grand hall opens before us, the polished floors reflecting the light of the massive chandeliers above. The staircase curves upward in a graceful sweep, its banister worn smooth by generations. Oil portraits line the walls. The room is hushed, formal, but alive with memory.

At the center of it all stands the House Stewardess, Mrs. Jackson.

Her posture is ramrod straight, her salt-and-pepper hair twisted into an elegant knot at the nape of her neck. She's wearing navy today, with a string of pearls that sits neatly against her mahogany skin. Her features are severe—cheekbones sharp, lips unsmiling— but the moment her eyes meet mine, they soften.

"Ronan," she says quietly. "Welcome home."

No one else could make that word—*home*—sting and soothe in the same breath. I know she'll scold me for it, but I do it anyway.

I step forward and envelop her in a hug.

In my mother's final days, Mrs. Jackson was her fiercest defender, sparing no expense to ensure her comfort. That alone makes her a heroine in my eyes, never mind her razor-sharp management skills.

None of that warmth is reserved for the man behind her, however, with whom I share so much. I may have my mother's hair and eyes, but even I can't deny the resemblance.

He's tall—only an inch shorter than me—but he carries himself as if the world belongs to him. His shoulders are broad, his waist still trim despite his age, though his thick blond hair has gone almost silver. He exudes the same poised strength I used to admire before I knew better. I glance at his face. We share the same angular cheekbones, but where my gaze is muted amber, his eyes are a dark, polished brown. They reflect no emotion.

They never have.

Dressed in slate wool and a silk tie so perfect it might as well be armor, he stands with one hand braced on the banister.

There, at the foot of the stairs, is James Astor, CEO of Astor Pharmaceuticals.

And my father.

Bloodlines

Ronan

"Ronan." My father descends the staircase and closes the distance between us. He doesn't offer a handshake, nor do I extend one.

"James," I respond without emotion. He ceased earning the title of father long ago.

James looks so far down his nose at Fia that he practically sneers. "Ms. Beltrán."

Fia, of course, is unfazed. "Mr. Astor. You look well."

"Thank you." James half-turns, glancing over his shoulder. "Shall we head upstairs to my study? Our counsels are already here, and of course, Frederick is waiting."

"Your study?" I frown as I realize his disgusting ploy. Whitlow was built in the 1600s—not exactly the height of accessibility. With successive renovations, that has been mitigated, especially under Mrs. Jackson's leadership. But those changes are mostly restricted to the main level. There is no elevator to James' study on the second floor.

"Why aren't we in the library?" I demand. "It's larger, and it's where we usually conduct business. Isn't it more appropriate for a gathering of this size?"

James makes a show of looking contrite. "I'm afraid a recent leak has forced some renovations. The space is not suitable." The lie rolls off his tongue with ease. "Shall we get on with our business?"

I'm so livid, I could throttle him.

It's reprehensible. His scheming leaves Fia with an impossible choice: be excluded from the proceedings—or be forced to abandon her chair and be carried upstairs.

Fia notches her chin, refusing to show my father any sign of weakness, but I know her too well. I see the tremor in her fingers that she tries to conceal by smoothing her hands over the rims of her chair. She hates feeling helpless, and my father's move is intended to make her vulnerable—to publicly undermine her power and bodily autonomy.

I see the determined look in her eyes, and I know she will endure it for me, but I refuse to let her make this degrading sacrifice.

I can sense the tension rolling off of Mr. Hensley, who has been standing off to the side since ushering us in. No doubt he is appalled. This goes against everything he stands for, every protocol that demands that each guest at Whitlow be afforded the highest level of dignity and comfort.

Plus, he's always loved Fia.

I exchange a look with Mrs. Jackson, who tips her head in acknowledgment.

Thank goodness we have a contingency plan.

"I will not proceed without my financial advisor in the room," I announce emphatically, and irritation flashes across James' features.

I don't care. He may think he has the upper hand, but I know Fred won't start without me. My bastard of a father can wait.

"Mrs. Jackson, is there a private room that Ms. Beltrán Zamora and I can use to discuss how we'd like to handle this?"

"Of course. Arthur, why don't you settle our guests with some tea in the south drawing room?" Mrs. Jackson says to Mr. Hensley.

"Certainly. This way, please."

Hensley leads us towards one of the smaller drawing rooms. Once we are past the grand hall and out of earshot, he pauses. "Come, Mr. Ronan, everything is ready as you requested."

We pivot to the staff quarters, a space most visitors will never see. Of course, James does not deem it worthy of his presence.

Except for Hensley and Mrs. Jackson, he never interacts with the estate team.

It's appalling, but his arrogance will be our blessing.

The staff quarters are behind the main kitchen, just off a wide corridor that once served as the estate's delivery passage. This is the beating heart of Whitlow—where supplies are received, linens are sorted, and meals are staged before being carried out to more formal wings. Even now, I glimpse a sous-chef plating something delicate on a rolling cart. Someone from housekeeping disappears through a side door with an armful of pressed napkins.

It's not a grand space, but it's alive with purpose. The service stair anchors the corner, wide and straight—nothing like the dramatic curve of the main hall's balustrade. Designed to move staff and goods swiftly between floors, it now serves another purpose.

At its side, tucked into the paneling, is the chair lift I installed with Mrs. Jackson's help. Without it, my mother would have been exiled upstairs in the final months of her life. When her illness left her too weak to walk, my father did nothing. For weeks, Mom couldn't feel the sun on her skin. Couldn't reach the gardens or the vineyard—all the places that brought her joy.

But Mrs. Jackson and I made sure she had a way down.

I still remember the tears in Mom's eyes the first time she used it.

If James saw her outside of her rooms, he never cared to ask how. To this day, he still doesn't know the lift is here. Mrs. Jackson kept it, even after Mom passed. For practicality, yes, but more than that, for the dignity it ensures guests like Fia.

Fia wheels toward the lift now, and I catch the change in her posture—the way her shoulders relax. I'm still angry that James created any anxiety in her.

"Roncito," she murmurs. "Thanks."

"Hey, I'll always have your back," I say, squeezing her into a hug. "Besides, you're more family to me than James has ever been. I'd walk out of here first before I'd allow him to disrespect you. Mom's already in the ground. The will isn't going anywhere."

Mr. Hensley steps forward without a word, fingers brushing the control. Fia eases onto the platform and gives him a nod.

The lift hums to life.

I watch her rise to the second floor, and I take the stairs beside her.

Mrs. Jackson is already waiting, a folder tucked beneath one arm. She must have paused en route to whatever fire she's putting out this time. When the chair clicks into place at the upper landing, she offers Fia an approving nod. "You made good time."

Fia flashes a smile. "Just needed the right equipment."

Mrs. Jackson's lips curve before she sweeps past us. "The study's just ahead," she says over her shoulder. "And Mr. Sen is waiting."

Fia and I step forward. The determined set of her shoulders reflects the tension rising in my own.

James may have tried to diminish us.

But we're ready to meet him—on our terms.

Canyon
Ronan

James' study, concealed behind a paneled door on the second floor, is cold in its order. The room faces a row of windows that frame an expansive view of the estate. The study's walls are painted a deep oxblood, and the scent of aged leather lingers in the air. A single oversized painting commands the space behind the massive oak desk—*Napoleon Crossing the Alps*. It's the only artwork in the room. There are no family photos. Not even a picture of James himself. Just a wall of shelves lined with hardbound classics, both ancient and modern—Cicero, Marcus Aurelius, Sun Tzu, Machiavelli, Greene, and Chernow.

In front of the desk are two matching leather chairs. For the occasion of the will reading, two smaller club chairs have also been added to accommodate the additional guests. Behind the desk, James's seat is high-backed. Built to support his frame, it's more like a throne than an office chair.

As a child, something about the majesty of the study always struck me with awe and dread. Awe at the man whose love I was desperate to earn, and dread because I knew, even then, that I'd never be good enough for him.

First, it was because I was a sickly infant. Then, when I surpassed even James' muscularity, it was because I was too unpredictable, too intellectual—not interested in leading Astor Pharmaceuticals and following in his footsteps.

Too wedded to my own ideas.

Of course, my worst sin was my loyalty to my mother.

And that leads us here.

As soon as Fia and I enter, my lawyer, Aamir Sen, rises to greet us. We shake hands, and he and Fia do the whole European cheek-kiss routine.

I can't help feeling smug at James' shocked look when he sees Fia breeze into the room. I meet his stare head-on, and he glowers. This has always been our dance: him, brutish in his attempts at control, and me, bucking his pathetic authority.

I take the seat nearest Aamir and make sure Fia is comfortably positioned at my side. Fred has ignored his appointed seat and is standing. James' lawyer, a dour, balding man named Griffin, is to Aamir's right.

There's not much time for pleasantries as Fred calls us to order.

"Should we begin?" he asks with a glance around the room. He's grimmer than I've ever seen him, with deep lines bracketing his mouth. He looks as exhausted as I feel.

"Let's proceed," James barks.

Fred nods. "Then let the record reflect that we are gathered for the formal reading of the last will and testament of Dr. Rosalind Thorne Astor."

Hearing her full name lands harder than I expect. She rarely used it in life. It sounds too formal now, too final.

James' posture is relaxed, but his anticipation is palpable. Despite his callousness towards my mother, he expects to benefit most from this reading. I'd like to think he's wrong, but Mom was always too kind for her own good.

This is all just a formality, anyway. Thanks to her foresight, I received a $250 million trust in my mid-twenties—enough to let me walk away from my father and the Astor name entirely. No other gift matters more than that. Thorne Consulting has grown that initial investment many times over ever since.

Anything revealed today is just a bonus.

I *am* sentimental about a few things, though. Like the vineyard, because it was so precious to Mom.

Unfortunately, I doubt I'll have much say over it. Thorne Run is part of the estate, and Whitlow has always been a symbol of the kind of legitimacy James—with his oil wealth, his ruthlessness, his new money—could never buy outright.

There's no chance he'll let it go.

Fred begins reading, his feet tracing a weary path across the carpet.

"As outlined in the Thorne Family Trust, my son Ronan received his first disbursement upon turning twenty-five. These funds were intended to grant him the financial independence I feared he might otherwise be denied."

James' expression tightens at the phrase, and I smirk. Let him stew. Mom understood him perfectly.

"The remaining assets of my estate—" Frederick continues, *"including all private accounts, stock holdings, intellectual property, Whitlow Estate, Thorne Run Vineyard, and its associated revenues—shall pass in full to my son, Ronan Ansel Thorne, through a trust designed to ensure immediate and uncontested transfer upon my death."*

What?

This isn't—

I lean forward, gripping the armrests of my chair. My pulse hammers in my ears.

"Fred—" I manage, barely.

"She loved you so much, *Roncito*," Fia whispers, reaching over and squeezing my hand.

My chest aches. The wound that has been pulsing inside me since Mom died tears open—a canyon swallowing me whole. I don't even realize my fists are clenched, or that I'm hunched over, until I feel Aamir's hand on my shoulder.

"Breathe, Ronan," he whispers. "This isn't a mistake. She wanted you to have this."

I try to speak, but if I open my mouth, I'll shatter.

She left me everything.

Everything.

Whitlow, her life's work, and the vineyards she loved so much.

I am stunned.

I didn't think I wanted it. Didn't think I needed it.

But now that I know, I am grateful.

It's not about the money. It's never been about that. I'm just thankful for the chance to honor her one last time.

"What!" James slams his hand on the desk. His nostrils flare. "This is ridiculous. Rosalind was always a sentimental fool. This is my home. I'm not going anywhere."

"James," Frederick bulldozes over him. "We are not finished."

James jerks his head up, startled by the sharpness. For a second, I expect him to erupt again—hurl some insult. But he stills, every line of his body coiled with fury.

Fred resumes.

"Given the unambiguous designation of Thorne Run as my personal asset, and in light of my declining capacity during my final year, I hereby direct that any profits, revenues, or benefits derived from the vineyard's operation during the twelve months preceding my death be fully audited and, if found improperly allocated, returned in full to my son, Ronan Thorne."

I frown, caught off guard. It's an oddly specific clause; one I'm not sure I understand. The words make sense. I just don't know why Mom would draw such a fine point on it.

But Fred is continuing, plowing through the rest of her wishes:

"To my beloved son, Ronan Thorne, I bequeath all intellectual property rights associated with Thorne Therapeutics, including patents and proprietary formulations developed under the company's name. Additionally, I leave to him the rights to the specific cultivars and formulations of Thorne Run Vineyard.

It is my deepest hope that these legacies, born from our shared love of discovery and creation, may rekindle in him the joy and fulfillment that comes from scientific pursuit and innovation."

My throat works. Of everything she could have left me, this—her formulas, the intellectual heart of her life's work—is the most intimate, the most sacred.

I know what she's asking. And the weight of it nearly crushes me.

I haven't been in the lab since James wrestled Thorne Therapeutics away from her. Since I watched him gut everything she built and repackage it under the Astor name.

I stopped believing in any of my creative gifts long ago. What's the point when the woman who was my mentor isn't here to share them?

But Mom did believe.

And now, she's asking me to return to that place, to find something redemptive in the ruins. Not for her. For me.

A moment ago, I thought I was ready to carry her legacy. Now, faced with the truth of what she's entrusted to me, I'm not sure I'm brave enough. I'm shaken. My mind spins, a swarm of doubt unraveling my sense of purpose.

It's Fia's name that pulls me out of my spiral.

"To Ms. Fia Beltrán Zamora—" Fred intones, his voice gentler now as he meets her gaze. Beside me, I see Fia's lips part. Her spine straightens.

"In gratitude for the steady light you have been in my son's life, I leave a founding gift of twenty-five million dollars to be held in trust for an initiative of your choosing. It is my wish—but not my instruction—that you consider using these funds to advance research, equity, or access in the field of spina bifida or another cause close to your heart. I trust your judgment entirely, as I did in life."

Fia gasps, and tears spring to her eyes. My own vision blurs. I wrap an arm around her, drawing her in.

She deserves this after everything she's done for Mom and me. And after the way James tried to diminish her earlier, this feels like a vindication.

But Mom isn't done with us yet:

"To Frederick Ellison—" Fred begins, and here, his voice catches. He pauses, clears his throat, and lifts his chin.

"For your decades of unwavering service, loyal counsel, and quiet companionship, I leave the stone cottage and adjoining acreage in Istria, near Grožnjan. The cellar and library are yours as well. I trust you'll know how best to preserve what we built there."

I blink. The words settle, their meaning unfolding slowly.

Fred's grief, so controlled until now, trembles at the edges of his expression. His devotion has been so absolute that I'd always wondered whether he and my mother had ever been more than colleagues.

Now I know.

It soothes the ache a little, knowing she found joy before the end. If anyone deserved to be loved—really loved—it was her.

James scowls, his face sour and petulant. A thick vein pulses at his temple. His jaw ticks so violently that the tendons in his neck stand out in sharp relief. With each word Fred utters, his complexion darkens—first pale, then blotched with splotches of crimson. By the time Frederick finishes, he's beet-red, fists clenched.

"That's it?" he explodes, pushing back from the desk.

Where he once seemed imposing, now he just looks bloated and impotent—a king without a kingdom.

"You!" he snarls, jabbing a finger at me, then thrusting it at Fred. "The two of you colluded! Rosalind would never leave me hanging."

Normally, this is the moment I would shoot to my feet, ready to lock horns with him. But today, I barely register it.

I'm too proud of Mom. Too moved by the fact that she found the strength to stand her ground.

It matters, even if she did it at the end.

Especially at the end.

"Don't think we won't contest this," James growls.

"James, you were aware of the prenuptial agreement Rosalind entered your marriage with." Fred shuts him down with a terse look. "It clearly separated her pre-existing assets, such as Whitlow Estate and any intellectual property related to Thorne Therapeutics. The wealth accumulated under the Astor name during your marriage—such as the joint ownership of the Astor Plaza building, the Aspen Ski Resort property, and the investment portfolio in Ventura Holdings—is yours to control. Rosalind made no claim on that in her will."

He's right. I know enough about their finances to recognize that what Fred just listed far exceeds what Mom left to me. Not to mention the empire James built through Astor Pharmaceuticals.

But facts don't matter when ego is in play. James doesn't just hate losing. He hates being outwitted. And today, he's made a rare miscalculation.

"You won't get away with this!" he bellows, spittle flying.

"Mr. Astor," Griffin ventures quietly, "perhaps we should pause to discuss—"

"Be quiet! The only thing you should be focused on is undoing this farce."

Griffin recoils. "Yes, sir," he mumbles.

I frown. I'm used to my father's abuse. What's new is the whiff of desperation beneath it. Being outmaneuvered by my mother is humiliating, sure—but this feels excessive even for him.

I study him more closely. Is it possible he's hiding something? Illness? His volatility is worse than usual.

He still looks strong—broad-shouldered and imposing in that slate-gray suit—but a lot can be concealed behind custom tailoring and bluster. I don't know enough about his medical history to guess at dementia or something else, but he seems far from invincible.

If he were another man—if I were a different son—I might ask. I might even care.

But James has never prioritized anything above control. Whatever's going on, I don't give a damn.

In fact, I smile as I glance around the study and through the windows framing the estate grounds.

Because now that Whitlow is mine?

I won't waste a second before kicking his sorry ass out of here.

Lemonade
Thandi

"Blouse and skirt, a weh de sign deh man? A which one a unnu move dis? Caa me know seh me put it yassuh inuh!"

Uh oh. Dad only switches to patois when he's truly vexed.

A muttered stream of curses is the only warning I get before a trowel sails past me.

I duck and peer carefully around the garage door.

Inside is chaos—shelves emptied and crates overturned. Buckets of lime plaster sit open near Dad's workbench, and strips of copper sheeting are curled like snakes across the floor. Tools are everywhere: rasps, clamps, soldering irons, wire cutters, and an angle grinder.

At the center of it all is my father, encircled by a ring of sculptures—some finished and gleaming, others still skeletal, welded armatures poking through layers of carved wood or unfinished plaster like creatures half-emerged from the chrysalis.

He doesn't notice me because he's too busy glaring at an old garbage can filled with discarded plywood and metal piping. He's wearing thick utility gloves, and there are flecks of plaster in his salt-and-pepper locs.

"Dad?" I call out, suppressing a laugh. The man is insane.

"Peanut!" Dad's whole face lights up. He fights his way through a wall of boxes just to squeeze me into a hug. "I'm so glad you're here. I can't find the posts for the damn yard signs. You always know where I stash that stuff."

I smile up at him. "No problem, Dad. I'll find them. I'm sure they're in here somewhere."

I peer over his shoulder at the disaster zone behind him. "It's worse than Hurricane Allen in there," I say with a grin, deliberately invoking the storm that has reached near-mythic status in our family lore thanks to the story Dad loves to tell—how it ripped through his home in Jamaica when he was a teen.

He sputters, then laughs. "You've got jokes, huh?"

"Just a little," I wink at him. "I can see why you're overwhelmed. Maybe take a break?"

"I agree," says Mom. She steps into the garage carrying a tray of her signature lemonade, frosted glasses clinking as she walks. A scientist to her core, she swears she's precisely calibrated it to be the perfect balance of sweetness and tang. I rush over to take the tray from her, and she kisses my cheek.

"Hey, baby," she murmurs. "Thanks for coming by."

"Don't be silly. You know I'm happy to help."

I set the tray on the workbench and gesture at the war zone that is the garage.

"Is this for the yard sale or the youth center auction?" I ask, trying to make sense of it all. I scan the overflowing bins, the leaning sculptures, the piles of things-that-might-be-useful-one-day. Then I tap a finger to my lips. "You know what, Dad? I'm pretty sure we put the signs in the attic last time. I don't think they're in here."

"Of course!" Dad breathes a sigh of relief as he reaches for a glass of lemonade. "I forgot that we put them there after I lost them *last time*."

I can only laugh at that.

"And to answer your question—both," he says. "We need this place cleared out to get ready for Ricky, and I've got to finalize which sculptures to include in the exhibit. I'll need your opinion, Peanut."

"I don't know who this '*we*' is Winston keeps referring to," Mom mutters, brushing past a stack of boxes. "He's been at this since morning, and I still can't get to my filing cabinet. I need to mail a copy of the permit to Ricky's caseworker today."

"Go easy on me, Iris," Dad says, stealing a quick kiss. "You gotta have more trust."

"This *is* trust," she replies dryly. "I could have called that junk removal service instead of our daughter."

Dad gasps in mock betrayal. "Do you even love me?"

I laugh. "Okay, okay. Focus. What does a permit have to do with Ricky?"

Ever since Tess disappeared, we've been a tight little triangle—three corners holding each other up through grief and memory. Her kidnapping tethered us together in ways that wouldn't have happened if she were still here.

In a strange, painful way, I guess that was Tess' gift to us.

I remember how hard it was on my folks when I left home. To their credit, they never tried to pressure me to stay close. They wanted me to spread my wings as wide as I needed to.

And I did.

But choosing Chesden for Immerscent's headquarters was a lot easier, knowing they were nearby.

Now, our lives are intertwined again.

When I started volunteering at the youth center, my parents joined me as mentors and quickly fell in love with Ricky Harris, a sharp, funny little boy in the foster system. Last month, they were conditionally approved as a Resource Family. Which means that if Ricky's current placement falls through, they're near the top of the early match list.

I'm excited for them. Ricky's a sweet kid, and my parents still have so much love to give.

"The home study went fine," Mom says, brushing plaster dust off the folder in her hand. "But they want documentation proving the addition we built in the back was permitted."

"The one Grandma Moses stayed in when she had her hip replacement?" I ask.

She nods. "That's the one. We're updating it for Ricky now. I already have the certification letter, but if I can find the original permit, we can include it with the revised packet. One less reason for anyone to drag their feet."

There's a moment of silence as the weight of how much this means to them lingers in the air.

"Okay," I say, taking a breath. "Put me to work. Where should I start?"

"How about the finished sculptures?" Dad replies. "Now that you're here, the three of us can move them safely. Then maybe you can help your mom find those documents."

He props his hands on his hips. "Everything else is just excess for the yard sale. If you see my old welder, let me know. Mark wants to borrow it for his balcony project."

"Got it."

We get to work. With a little grunting and several admonitions from me to Dad to avoid straining his back, we get the sculptures out onto the front porch. There, the shipping company will wrap them up and ship them to the youth center. I'm so touched that he's doing this. It's going to be a great event.

"Thanks again for doing this, Dad," I murmur.

"No thanks needed, Peanut. This is all part of the karmic circle. We've got to always keep paying it forward."

My dad is the sweetest and humblest guy I know, but he's a big deal in the modern sculpture world. He just finished an exhibit at the Hirshhorn, and in a few months, he'll have a new show at *Kunstverein München*—a contemporary art space in Munich known for elevating spiritually and politically resonant work.

Anything with the Asa Winston Elowen name draws collectors, and for the youth center auction, he's releasing early pieces no one has seen before. The show will pull in heavy hitters—and even more funding for the youth center, where he still leads a weekly art program.

Once we've hauled all the sculptures to the front of the house, we take a break, sitting on the porch steps, and drinking the last of the lemonade. I close my eyes as the tangy-sweet flavor bursts over my tongue. It really is perfect.

"We've been talking your ear off so much, we haven't even asked how you're doing." Mom shakes her head. "This was a big week, with your board meeting, wasn't it?"

"Yeah," I sigh. "The last few days have been intense. It's not just the IPO. The board is worried that Astor is stealing our market share. But I can't bring myself to compete on the front that matters most to them." I glance across the street, where the Tranh girls are chasing each other barefoot through the grass. "I won't target kids. It just doesn't feel right."

"Because it isn't," Dad says softly. "And we're proud of you for holding the line."

I hang my head. "I just want to do right by Tess."

"We know, Peanut," Dad murmurs. He pulls me into his side and kisses the top of my head. "Give yourself grace. Trust the timing of the universe. We may not understand it; it may even hurt, but it's never wrong or too late."

I nod, though I don't share Dad's faith in cosmic order. I believe in what I can observe, measure, and replicate. I believe in effort. And accountability. I don't think I'll ever accept that there was some higher purpose in Tess' suffering—or in the brutality of how we lost her.

How I lost her.

Mom reaches over, patting my hand. "We know you're doing your best, honey."

"Thanks," I murmur. "I am. I'm trying but…."

"But what, Peanut?"

"As if I didn't have enough to deal with, Trent's asked me to work with a consultant to help conceptualize a signature product for the IPO launch."

"That doesn't sound unreasonable," Mom says.

"In theory, no. But Ronan Thorne *is* unreasonable. Selfish. Spoiled. Confusing—" I throw my hands up, still reeling from his ridiculous behavior during our first meeting. Just thinking about it sends my blood pressure rising again.

"Confusing?" Dad echoes, raising an eyebrow.

"Yes." I launch into the saga—Ronan's initial rejection, the abrupt 180 at the mixer. "I guess he's not *the* worst," I admit grudgingly, "because we did have a nice time at Tino's. But I have so much on the line right now. I need to be laser-focused on perfecting β7, not wasting time on some prima donna with esoteric methods and a condescending attitude. I really don't know what Trent is thinking."

My parents say nothing.

They just stare at me.

"What?" I ask, glancing around to make sure I'm not missing something.

"You took a *man* to Tino's?" Mom asks gently.

"Not a *man*—Ronan. That hardly counts."

Dad scratches his beard. "Wait, now I'm confused, Peanut. Ronan isn't a man? It's not like you to ignore someone's pronouns."

I groan and slap a hand to my forehead. "Dad. I'm not misgendering Ronan. I'm saying it's not a big deal that I took him to Tino's."

Dad looks instantly relieved. "Ah. Got it. I just thought Tino's was your special spot—your sanctuary to decompress. You know Micah's always wanted to go there with you."

What is happening right now?

How have we gone from Thorne to my ex in under sixty seconds?

"There wasn't enough food at the mixer, Tino's was nearby, and we were hungry. We just popped in for a quick bite. That's it."

I lift my hands in surrender. "Also, Tino's is a public restaurant. Micah can go whenever he wants. Heck, why doesn't he go with *you*? He's your apprentice."

"That's actually a good idea," Dad muses. Then he frowns. "Although I think Micah might be gluten-free now."

I splutter. "What does that have to do with *anything*?"

"You said his last name was Thorne?" Mom interrupts, as always, the voice of reason.

"Yeah. Do you know him?"

Mom shakes her head. "No, not the young man you're referring to. But the name sounds familiar. I know I've come across it before. I'm sure it will come back to me."

"Well, let me know if you remember," I say, intrigued. If Mom had ever crossed paths with Ronan or his family, I definitely want to know. Still, he hasn't said anything about a neuroscience connection to his method, and I doubt he would've forgotten meeting *my* mother.

"I will," she says, and when I look up, she's smiling.

So is Dad. Actually, he's full-on grinning, with an extra sparkle in his eye.

"What now?" I fold my arms. "You guys are seriously being weird."

"We just want you to be happy, honey," Mom says gently. "And I hope you remember it's not always about giving back to the world. It's okay to receive good things from it, too." She leans in to kiss my cheek, then rises. "Shall we head back in?"

Dad stands too. *"Being and non-being create each other. Difficult and easy support each other. Long and short define each other. High and low rest upon each other,"* he quotes, nodding like a mystic.

I roll my eyes. "Whatever you say, Dad."

Mom laughs. "Will you stay for dinner, honey?"

Now I'm the one smiling.

"Yes."

De-risking
Thandi

It's Monday evening, my first day of the week at the youth center. I'll be back again on Thursday and possibly the weekend if there's a tournament or special event that needs support.

I step through the double doors and wave to Miguel at the front desk, already ticking through the rhythm of my night: chess and homework with Ricky, then dinner with Fia to plan Dad's fundraiser. Basketball practice started at six, so Fia has a head start. She's probably already giving them hell on the court.

I'm halfway down the hall when I stop short. The rotating kids' art exhibit is gone. In its place, the pop-up booth, draped in purple fabric and stamped with the Astor Pharmaceuticals logo, feels much less innocent.

Vinyl banners shimmer under the lights, each one emblazoned with the slogan: "Focus Better. Feel Better. Be Your Best with PlayMist EDU™." A ring light glows over a digital tablet with an animation. Cartoon kids inhale mist and suddenly solve math problems with heroic ease. Behind it, more screens cycle through footage of classrooms and libraries, accompanied by soft, insistent music.

I frown, my anger already beginning to rise.

What the hell is this? And what are they doing here?

Two Astor reps, a man and a woman in matching blazers, beam with Disney-cast-member energy from behind a desk. In front of them, informational pamphlets are fanned out like casino cards alongside trays of inhalers.

These are not the jewel-toned WhiffRush inhalers or the disposable Sniffz dispensers I'm used to. They have been redesigned in sleek white and navy, featuring a minimalist gray "EDU" stamped along the side. The effect is serious and streamlined, made to look clinical but still approachable.

The man beckons to a tired-looking mom with two restless middle schoolers.

"Ma'am, are you interested in making dinner time easier? How about those hectic school mornings? Astor can offer focused cognitive and behavioral support. All natural, scent-based, and totally safe."

"Designed specifically for kids," the woman chimes in with a megawatt grin. "Ideal for transition points—before school, after recess, and end-of-day regulation."

Designed for kids? I suppress my audible scoff. But that's not what's most alarming.

I've never been comfortable with Astor's tactics, but at least WhiffRush and Sniffz are confined to the recreational space—overhyped mood boosters, nothing more. This is the first Astor product that attempts to step into the same clinical domain as Immerscent.

But it's all junk science.

The mother is shaking her head, already pulling her boys toward the exit. But when one of them bumps the other hard and bickering erupts, she hesitates.

I watch with dread as she slows down, then stops in front of the desk.

"Sure," she says after a moment.

"Excellent," The man extends a pamphlet. "I'm Dale, and we're offering a special promotion this evening. Thirty percent off all Play-Mist EDU inhalers, plus an extra fifteen percent if you opt into the subscription plan for cartridge replacements. Lock in the price tonight, and Astor guarantees your rate won't go up for two full years."

The mother turns the pamphlet over. "Can you explain what this does again?"

"Of course," Dale replies, "Why don't I start the video? Sheila and I can walk through the finer points afterward."

By now, a cluster of parents has gathered, and he waves them over.

"Come on in, folks, we're just about to watch the demo."

My blood is already pounding, and before I know it, I'm stalking towards the desk. I don't even know what I'm doing or what I plan to say, but one thing is certain: Astor won't sink its evil claws into any of my kids if I can help it.

"We'll be right with you, ma'am," Sheila calls to me, flashing a smile.

I don't answer. My eyes are locked onto the large monitor behind the booth, where the looped branding melts into ambient music. The video opens with a breathtaking vista of soft blue skies, then pans into a classroom filled with chaos.

A frustrated teacher rubs her temples near a chalkboard as middle schoolers giggle, throw paper, crayons, and chewed-up gum. Two boys brave the crossfire to chase each other, while at the other extreme, two sullen, disaffected girls stare at their phones.

The music swells, dramatic and urgent, before dissolving into tranquility.

The classroom is transformed. The teacher is smiling, scribbling on the board. Now every student sits upright, nodding in time, repeating after her in unison. We flash to recess, and the boy who was in hot pursuit earlier draws on an inhaler, visibly relaxing. Music pulses beneath a voiceover:

"PlayMist EDU introduces children to emotional regulation through scent association. Built for classrooms. Backed by science. Trusted by parents."

The product flashes on screen: the squared-off navy and white inhaler. Beneath it, color-coded cartridges—Focus, Confidence, Calm, and Joy—are fanned out like crayons.

The voiceover continues with more marketing-speak:

"In the face of rising behavioral challenges, overstimulated learning environments, and growing emotional needs, PlayMist EDU™ offers a screen-free, teacher-friendly tool to help students self-regulate, reset, and refocus in under 60 seconds."

The next vignette opens on a sunny, softly lit kitchen. A blonde woman moves between the stove and fridge, packing breakfast for her son. The scene transitions to a close-up of the pair on the couch, the woman's arm curled around the boy's shoulders.

Her brow furrows and her voice trembles as she begins: "I'm a single mom and military wife. We lost Hayden's dad in active combat three years ago."

She swallows hard. "Early on, Hayden was diagnosed with ADHD. But after Jack passed, we were down to one income. I didn't know how I could keep up with Hayden's meds—"

Her voice breaks. Blue eyes shimmer with tears before she smiles, straightening.

"PlayMist saved us. It's more affordable than what Hayden was on before, and it's organic, which is great. Hayden has food allergies. Not only does he feel better, but he's so much more independent now that he can manage his doses through the app."

A brief animation follows, touting the Build Your Boost™ app: *"Track your scent usage, collect emotional wellness badges, and build your character profile, all inside our COPPA-compliant platform."*

The segment ends with a smiling teacher giving a thumbs-up as a classroom of students lifts their PlayMist devices in unison.

The voiceover lowers to a murmur:

"Can't afford PlayMist? Astor may be able to help."

The crowd has swelled. Parents murmur around me, excitement building, and hope flickering in their eyes. Two families immediately rush forward to place an order.

I am so enraged, I can't remain silent.

"Hi. Yes, hello." I project my voice above the noise.

Sheila beams. "Yes? You have a question?"

I cross my arms.

"Thanks for the video. How is Astor justifying the use of this product for children, especially neurodivergent minors, when current data suggests scent-based cognitive therapy isn't well-adapted to developing brains? That it could actually harm the frontal lobe, undermining the very executive functioning you claim to support?"

The chatter dies.

A sneaker squeaks on the court down the hall. A microwave beeps in the distance. I can feel the shift in the room. Parents are turning to look. Listening.

Dale's eyes narrow. He lets out a short laugh.

"You know what they say about damn lies and statistics. I can assure you, Miss, that all Astor's products are safe and rigorously tested. As we said before, PlayMist EDU is non-invasive, organic—"

"Organic? Then what about Mathers, Johnson, and Odeyemi?" I interrupt.

I scan the crowd, meeting the eyes of parents.

"All peer-reviewed research endorsed by the American Academy of Pediatrics and the American Psychiatric Association. Their data shows that repeated exposure to scent-based adaptogenic therapy in children may lead to adrenal dysregulation."

Sheila stiffens. "Thank you," she says tightly. "We ask that you direct any specific formulation questions to the corporate hotline at 155-ASK-ASTOR."

She's still smiling, but her eyes are cold now, her voice edged with irritation. Dale is furiously texting someone on his phone.

The spell is broken.

Parents glance at one another.

One mother pulls her hand away from the sign-up sheet. Another tugs gently on her child's sleeve.

They start to walk away.

I'm just about to puncture the last of Astor's hot-air-filled claims when Janice, the center director, steps out of one of the conference rooms. I spin on my heel and jog after her instead.

"Janice?" I call. "Can we chat?"

Back in her office, Janice sighs and leans back in her chair, fingers resting on her keyboard. "I think I can guess what you want to talk about. The Astor booth?"

I nod.

"Hard to miss, huh?"

I raise an eyebrow. "Purple isn't exactly subtle."

"Yeah, well. Astor just made a significant contribution. It's multi-year, too, and you know how hard that is to come by." Janice's tone is even, but I see the weariness behind her eyes.

Still, my outrage hasn't cooled. If money is the issue, I'm happy to think about a new investment—anything to get Astor's dirty money out of here. I open my mouth, but Janice cuts me off gently.

"We love you, Thandi. You know that. But you can't support this operation single-handedly." Janice frowns. "And I wouldn't be doing my job if I weren't thinking about diversification and the center's long-term sustainability. Donor priorities shift all the time. What if—"

"Mine won't," I insist, leaning forward. "How much did they offer? I'll match it. This isn't about pride, Jan. These products are dangerous."

"I don't like it any more than you do," Janice says, "but this isn't just my decision. I'm getting pressure from the board to de-risk our portfolio." She gives a dry laugh. "Even as they're asking me to sniff out your capacity for another gift. I'll tell them you're open. But I can't turn down the Astor contribution."

I get it. I know she's right, but it still stings.

I nod, my fingers curling around the laminated flier I took from the booth. "Did they ask to integrate PlayMist EDU into the center's programming?"

Janice's expression is wry. "They tried, that's for sure. But I told them that any new intervention has to go through the independent Therapeutic Review Committee. No exceptions."

She swivels her monitor toward me, tapping a neatly labeled folder. "They submitted their paperwork, but it didn't pass muster. Too many gaps, not enough peer-reviewed data, and a little too much marketing gloss for something they want tied to kids' behavioral health."

I breathe, feeling the tension in my body ease. I feel foolish for barging in here so hot under the collar. Janice has always been stellar. I should have known she'd be a step ahead.

"So the booth's a compromise?"

She gives a one-shouldered shrug. "Two days and outreach only. They're allowed to talk to parents. That's it."

"Thanks, Jan." I sigh. "Sorry for bending your ear like this, and thank you for always fighting for the kids."

Janice smiles. Her voice is tired but warm. "I do what I can here, but it's the schools I'm worried about."

She swivels back to her screen, tapping at the edge of her keyboard. "They don't have donors like you to fall back on. That means no leverage. I talked to the superintendent down on Fifth. He's uncomfortable, but it's either take the money or keep using the same textbooks from thirteen years ago."

I nod, even as a pit of anxiety resettles itself in my stomach. I think about the parents who signed up before I interrupted the demonstration, and I know I have to do more.

Janice's voice lowers. "Sounds like it's been smooth sailing for Astor across most of the middle schools in the district. In a month, half the kids in this area are going to be hopped up on PlayMist."

And there's the problem.

What good is protecting the youth center if kids all over the city are still at risk?

I stand and thank Janice, but my thoughts are already churning.

I have to find a way to stop Astor for good.

Off Days
Thandi

The clack of plastic chess pieces echoes in the corner of the rec room. Ricky sits cross-legged across from me, brow furrowed, lips pressed into a thin line. He's been staring at the board for a solid minute.

Usually, by now, he'd be narrating possible moves in rapid succession, complete with trash talk and a victory dance. Today, he just sighs.

He picks up the rook, then stalls. The piece hovers in midair. His knee starts bouncing in an agitated rhythm.

"I used to be good at this," Ricky mutters, slamming the rook back into place without committing to anything. "Now I just suck."

I glance up, but he's already hugging his arms to his chest like he regrets saying anything.

Worry and empathy for this sweet young boy fill me. "You're still good at this, Ricky. Everyone has off days."

He shakes his head, and he won't meet my eyes. "It's not just chess. I can't focus in class either. And my math grade dropped. Mr. Sanders said I've been zoning out."

My heart twists. I watch him fidget, hands picking at the sleeves of his hoodie. His eyes dart around the room. I want to tell him he's wrong, but something *isn't* right. Before, Ricky's energy was kinetic, coiled, and brilliant. Now it just seems like something has snuffed out his spark.

"Come here," I say, patting the spot beside me.

He bites his lip, then shuffles over. I tug him to me and squeeze him tight. "What's going on?" I ask, rubbing his back.

He wraps his arms around me and buries his face in my neck.

"Dunno," his voice is muffled. He sniffles, then I feel wetness against my neck. My own eyes fill with tears.

"Oh, Ricky, I don't care whether you're good at math or you beat me at chess. You'll always be my rock star."

More sniffling. My shirt is crumpled in his fist.

"If I'm not good at stuff, the Glens will stop liking me," he mumbles. "They don't like me so much now, but I heard Mrs. Glen tell Mrs. Houghton she's proud I topped my math class."

He pulls back to stare at me with wide brown eyes. Tears are still clinging to his lashes.

"I got a C in social studies last week. Then they put me in a time-out in the laundry room. Mr. Glen said I was acting out, but I wasn't. It's just sometimes I get things mixed up. I kept saying revolution when I meant *constitution*. You have to believe me, Ms. Thandi," he pleads in a watery voice.

"Of course I believe you, honey," I murmur, trying to reassure him the best I can, even though I am getting more alarmed by the minute. Time out in a laundry room? For his first C? I'm no parent, but it seems unduly harsh. Especially for a kid with ADHD.

"If I fail math, they'll send me back to the group home," Ricky whispers, tightening his grip on me. His voice cracks, and the tears come again. "I *know* they will."

I'm so hurt, so angry for him, that he's been made to feel unworthy. That he's been made to feel that he deserves anything other than unconditional love. I stare down at his soft curls, his quaking shoulders, and I can feel the tumult radiating from every line in his body.

He's not just dejected and confused; he's terrified.

I hold him tighter. Sweet, brilliant Ricky, who never skips his meds, who tries so hard even when his thoughts spin sideways, and his mouth can't catch up. He's done everything asked of him. But that doesn't matter if the family doesn't understand his flare-ups. And most don't. Not really.

His caseworker told my parents that he's bounced from home to home. His current placement with the Glen family has lasted almost five months, which is practically forever in Ricky's world.

I frown as his words about the Glens not liking him echo in my mind. I hope that's not true. Not when my parents would move heaven and earth to be his next placement—or his adoptive family.

"Look at me, sweetie," I say fiercely. "You are smart and kind, and I'm sure the Glens love you."

"Okay." Ricky nods, but he looks both sad and skeptical.

I draw him into another hug. As he shifts against me, I notice something sticking out of the pocket of his hoodie. A navy and white PlayMist EDU inhaler reads: *Still Lavender – For Calm Moments!*

A sinking feeling grips me. Suddenly, it all makes sense.

"You using that?" I ask, nodding toward the device.

Ricky shrugs. "Yeah. The school says it helps." He sniffs. "They said it's better than the pills."

I swallow past the rage bubbling in my throat. "Do *you* feel better?" I manage to say, keeping my voice steady, so I don't upset him further.

Ricky shakes his head. "No. I feel worse … I … it's scary, Ms. Thandi. I used to be popular, since I'm good at science and fixing stuff. But yesterday I overheard some kids saying I'm weird now, and they won't eat lunch with me anymore." His eyes fill with tears again.

My hands are shaking as I hold him. "Did you tell the Glens?"

"Yeah, but they said I need to try harder. My homeroom teacher told Mrs. Glen that the inhalers are supposed to work, but they take time."

That's it. I refuse to stand by and let this continue.

I give Ricky another hug, and we return to our chess game, even though inside my emotions are boiling.

No wonder he's lost his spark. No wonder he can't hold a thought in his head. He's being tortured with this stupid Astor PlayMist, and whoever is responsible for this will have hell to pay.

I'm sick of adults harming kids when they should be protecting them.

Ricky's only ten; he should be having fun, not carrying this awful weight.

We throw ourselves into our game, and now that the pressure is off to be perfect, now that his panic has eased a little, Ricky ekes out a win. The spark of hope in his eyes and his tiny smile are enough to break my heart.

Next, we tackle his homework assignments together, and I feel his tension building again as he questions his abilities. When I see his bottom lip quiver over a long division problem, I lean over and tickle him.

He shrieks and nearly kicks over his books and the chessboard.

"Traitor!" he gasps, squirming away. But then, with lightning-fast vengeance, he lunges for my side and tickles back.

"Hey!" I yelp, twisting away, but he's relentless. We dissolve into a full-blown tickle war, all flailing limbs and squeals, knocking over cushions and scattering homework pages like confetti.

This time, I'm victorious. Waggling my eyebrows, I loom over him, fingers curled like claws, ready to strike at a moment's notice.

"Do you give up, Captain Harris?" I growl in my best cartoon villain voice.

"I give up!" he cries, breathless with giggles, even as he launches one final poke. "But I'll get you next time, Villain Lady!"

We collapse in a heap, wheezing, tears of laughter in our eyes.

It's the most fun I've had all week.

By the time we finish—after he's made me double and triple-check every answer—I realize it's already 8 PM. Fia and I are connecting at 8:15, so I'm safe, but Ricky's session was only supposed to last an hour. I frown. Is he always here this late?

I won't leave Ricky to wait alone, so I'm thinking about whether I need to cancel with Fia when I remember that Ms. Ortega is usually here in the evenings, prepping for the nutrition program.

"Quick break, Rickster?" I say, standing. "I need to find Ms. Ortega."

"Okay, Ms. Thandi," he murmurs without looking up from his favorite Juicy Crush game on his phone.

I find Ms. Ortega in the center's cozy kitchen, just off the rec room, surrounded by plastic containers. She's got a classic bolero playing low, and the air is warm with the scent of cumin, tomato, and slow-simmered beans. Three open lunchboxes sit on the counter in front of her, each carefully packed with arroz con pollo, slices of ripe mango, and little bundles of foil-wrapped tamales.

She's wearing her usual navy apron over a patterned blouse, sleeves rolled to the elbow, her silver hair swept into a tidy bun. A clipboard rests nearby—today's check-in sheet for evening activities.

Ms. Ortega used to be a school principal, but now she volunteers at the center, helping with evening registration and running the Healthy Start nutrition program. She always says kids can't learn or play on an empty stomach.

She's frowning in concentration as she nestles thinly sliced carrots, cut into smiley faces, into the vegetable compartment of one bento.

I can't help but grin. "What's all this?"

Ms. Ortega glances up and returns my smile, but it's faint. Her hands keep moving as she answers.

"It's for Ricky." She hesitates.

"Ms. Ortega," I say gently, "Is something wrong?"

She keeps her eyes on the last lunchbox, tucking a folded napkin next to the tamales. When she finally speaks, her voice is hard.

"You see how late he's here. It's been like this for the past two months. At first, it was nothing noticeable. Ron or Carla Glen arriving ten, maybe fifteen minutes late after his mentor session. Now he eats dinner with us every evening," she finishes with a huff. "It's no problem for me. I'm here cooking anyway, and I love Ricky. But I found out today he has no lunch money. I don't know if he ever did."

Ms. Ortega arranges the lid on the final bento, her hands smoothing over the plastic before looking at me. "Greenwood used to be my district, so I try to keep up with things. With the budget cuts, school lunches were the first to go."

She swallows, then presses down hard on the lid. "I don't know what that poor baby has been eating."

I'm gutted. Everything I learn about Ricky's situation is worse than I imagined.

"You think he's going hungry?" I gasp.

"Well, you know what they say about assumptions...." Ms. Ortega leans against the countertop. "But I've been doing this a long time, Thandi. And the signs... *no se ven bien.*"

"What do you mean?" I ask, pulling out a stool and sitting across from her.

"Ricky's smart, so he doesn't make a fuss," she says slowly. "But he eats like he's on a timer, and he never leaves a crumb behind. The other day, I caught him wrapping half a sandwich in a napkin and slipping it in his backpack."

Ms. Ortega smooths her apron. "He always shows up early, too, no matter what time his sessions are. Right before snack trays come out. I don't press, but it happens a lot."

She pats the stack of finished bentos. "Anyway. This should tide him over until his next visit."

The words are matter-of-fact, but they land like a punch. My chest aches. I wait until she finishes packing the boxes into a cotton shopping tote, then ask quietly, "Do you know anything about Ricky being taken off his meds?"

Ms. Ortega mutters something in Spanish under her breath. "They're all idiots," she snaps. "Fools who don't know what they're doing."

Her eyes flash. "I make sure he takes his guanfacine and fluoxetine every evening—been consistent with that for months. We had a system, and it works."

"But?" I prompt.

She looks up at me, mouth tight with frustration. "But for the last three weeks, it's just been these." She nods toward two PlayMist EDU inhalers beside Ricky's backpack. "He's been miserable. Withdrawn. Snapping at the other kids." She shakes her head. "I'm no doctor, but I am worried."

"I noticed the same thing tonight," I say. "He's struggling. And I know for a fact those inhalers are useless at best—damaging at worst."

Ms. Ortega folds her arms. "I believe it. I've tried to speak with his foster father, but he's always in a rush—out the door before I can get a word in. I don't want to stir up trouble, but Ricky can't keep going like this."

If I had any doubts before, everything she's just described confirms what I already feared.

"It's time for an intervention," I say.

I don't often throw my weight around, but I'll break that rule in a heartbeat for Ricky. I plan to reach out to Janice and Lena Aduba at the Family and Youth Services Division. The mentorship program is a formal partnership. She'll take my call.

Ms. Ortega nods. "Maybe you could say something? People listen to you. Besides, you're an expert in this scent stuff. When I try to push back, I just look like a paranoid *abuela*."

"You're not paranoid," I say firmly. "You're right to think Ricky's in trouble. Thank you for looking out for him."

"It's why we're all here, no?" she says with a smile.

She slips the bundled lunchboxes into Ricky's faded backpack, layering in handwritten notes—little neon squares with cheerful doodles and messages like, *"You've got this!"* and *"Ask good questions today."* Then, with a sigh so soft it eviscerates me, she slips the two PlayMist

EDU cartridges in beside them. The contrast is heart-wrenching—care and harm, nourishment and negligence coiled together.

The front door chimes.

Ron Glen strides in, Bluetooth clipped to one ear, keys jangling in one hand. I slip off the stool and move to intercept him. Ms. Ortega follows, Ricky's backpack slung over one shoulder.

Ron doesn't slow down. "Yeah... okay. Send the paperwork to my personal email," he says into his earpiece.

"Mr. Glen," I step forward and extend my hand. "I'm Thandi Elowen, Ricky's mentor. I'd love a quick word."

"Uh huh... well, somebody screwed up, because they shouldn't have been eligible for the bid in the first place. Yeah—Sandford?" Glen lifts one finger without making eye contact and shoves a business card into my palm.

"Ricky, let's go," he calls, not unkindly, just... brusque. Abrupt.

Ms. Ortega catches my eye over his shoulder and shrugs, as if to say, *I told you so.*

I'm disappointed and a little stunned at being so summarily dismissed. Meanwhile, Ricky is scurrying to grab his bag. He's a little slower today, and his shoelace is half untied.

As soon as Ron notices, he frowns, his mouth thinning into a disapproving moue.

Ricky's eyes widen. He nearly topples under the weight of his backpack, scrambling to lace his sneakers in record time. He's at Ron's side so fast, I barely have time to pull him in for a goodbye hug.

He leaves without a glance back, his tiny shoulders vibrating with tension. He and Ron walk side by side toward the exit, but there's no hug, no hand on his shoulder. Ricky's backpack jostles against his spine, the bentos and PlayMist vials inside rattling like marbles.

Just before they reach the door, Ricky tilts his head up.

"Mr. Glen? I won today. At chess. I beat Ms. Thandi." There's a flicker of pride in his voice, fragile and eager.

But Ron's phone buzzes again. He answers mid-step.

"Yeah—no, just grabbing the kid now."

Ricky's shoulders drop. He doesn't say another word.

And as the door swings shut behind them, the silence left behind feels heavy enough to drown in.

"Whoever the hot guy is you've been texting all evening, better be worth it," Fia says, eyeing me over her glass of wine.

I sigh and put my phone face down on the table. "I'm sorry, Fia. And I wish it were a guy. I had to reach out to Janice and Youth Services about one of my students. You remember Ricky, right?"

Fia brightens instantly. "Of course, I do. He's our resident physicist. That kid's gonna change the world one day." She leans in. "What's wrong?"

"Not if Astor has anything to do with it," I mutter. Then I tell her about Ricky's missing meds, his fear, and the Glens' neglect. By the time I'm finished, Fia's eyes are blazing.

"How can I help?" she demands, slamming her napkin down. "What pisses me off most is they always pull this shit with *our* kids. I guarantee Astor isn't roaming the halls of Thomas Jefferson."

Fia snorts. "And the Glens? There's a special place in hell for people who hurt kids. How could anyone meet Ricky and not fall in love with him?"

"I don't know, Fia." My voice wavers. I keep seeing his shoulders as he walked away. "Honestly? It's breaking my heart."

"Oh, Thandi, I'm so sorry." Fia reaches out and squeezes my hand.

"Thanks." I swallow past the lump in my throat. "The crazy part is my parents fell in love with Ricky from day one. They'd give anything to be his foster parents, but by the time they met him, he'd already been placed with the Glens. The best they could do was get certified as a Resource Family and ask to be added to the priority waitlist."

"Well, something tells me the Glens aren't going to be in Ricky's life much longer. Give me the name of your contact at Youth Services. It'll help to have someone who isn't as close to this reach out, too."

Fia slides her phone across the table. She's already tapped into a new contact, so I can enter Lena's number. "Besides, it's good you told me. I'll keep an extra eye out for Ricky and any other kids who might be caught up in Astor's mess."

I smile, the sadness that's been dogging me finally starting to ease. I enter Lena's info into her phone and hand it back.

Fia and I haven't known each other long—just in the last year since she started volunteering at the youth center—but I like her a lot. And she's already made a huge impression on the kids and me. She's also brilliant. After a couple of conversations, I knew I had to switch from Schwab to her boutique firm.

Let's just say my portfolio's performance speaks for itself.

Fia's one of those old souls—the kind of person who makes you feel like you've known each other for a lifetime, even if it's only been thirty minutes. And she cares. *Really cares* in a way most people don't.

I love that about her.

And now, she's helping me plan Dad's fundraiser. She knows a lot of impact investors who want to support the arts. I have a few donors in mind, too, so we decided to strategize over dinner. Fia also recommended an event planner to the youth center's art director.

I tap through the list of names on my tablet. "What about Marianne Joseph?" I ask, just as our server arrives with our mains.

"Of the ethical apparel company?" Fia's fork is poised over her leg of lamb as she considers. She always gets the lamb when we have Afghan food. I don't blame her. Zarafshan's is the best in the DMV.

"Yeah. There was a piece about her in the *Post* a couple of months ago. She supported the *Wings of the Diaspora* exhibit at the African American Museum of Art."

Fia nods. "Okay, that's a definite yes. I've got Johnson Fowler on my list."

"The banker?"

"The very same." She winks. "We need to get some old money in that room."

I laugh. "Sure, then. Why not?"

We continue like this, sharing names, cross-referencing notes until we've built a guest list of damn-near superstars. I sigh around a mouthful of aloo baloo pulao. This is going to be an amazing event.

"You know," Fia murmurs, "I was thinking we should host something."

"Host something like what?" I ask.

"A little soirée ahead of the main event. To whet the buyers' appetites. Maybe your dad could stop by, say a few words, give a sneak peek of the collection."

"Oh, I love that," I say, brightening. "A cultivation moment."

"Exactly!"

"Should we book a venue? I've heard Brick & Echo has an amazing event space. You know which one I'm talking about? The converted warehouse in NoMa."

"We could." Fia grins. "But how about we make it personal—host it at my house?"

"Isn't that a lot of work?" I ask, uncertain.

"Chica, please. I love entertaining, and it'll make the whole thing feel even more exclusive. And you'll be my fabulous co-hostess."

"I mean, if you're up for it, I'm game," I say, already catching her excitement. It would be fun to co-host something with Fia, and Dad would love the unpretentious vibe.

"It's settled then." Fia raises her glass, and I clink mine against it.

"I should invite Trent," I murmur, mentally running through a few more names. "Maybe Clara Yuen, too. She'll be in town in two weeks."

"And I'll invite Ronan," Fia declares as she signals for another glass of grenache.

My stomach somersaults.

Of course. How could I forget they were friends? The memory of Ronan reminding me that Fia invited him to the pickup game flashes across my mind. It still surprises me. Fia's so steady and Ronan is so... *Ronan*.

I frown, picking at the edge of the tablecloth. "Hey, there's something I've been meaning to ask you...."

"Sure. What's up?"

I don't get to finish because a deep voice says behind me:

"Fia?"

And as if conjured by my thoughts, Ronan Thorne strolls up to our table.

Reality TV
Thandi

Ronan emerges fully into view. He's wearing a charcoal jacket over a crisp white shirt, the collar open. Fitted dark jeans complete his casual but tailored look.

He's not alone. A beautiful blonde woman is clinging to his side, and for some reason, I feel a surge of irritation.

Our eyes meet, and Ronan looks vaguely … embarrassed? Regretful?

I don't know why. It's not like I care who's in his bed.

"Roncito!" Fia exclaims. "What are you doing here?"

"Just having dinner with a friend, he murmurs, still looking my way. The blonde on his arm frowns. She looks familiar.

Then I realize she's the woman who was practically sitting in Ronan's lap at the mixer.

"Hi, I'm Amber," she announces in my and Fia's direction. Apparently, Ronan is so magnetic, she can't even offer us a proper handshake.

Amber is wearing a navy sheath that hugs her supermodel proportions, and in sky-high heels, she's almost as tall as Ronan. She looks so much like she stepped off the pages of *Vogue* that I'm convinced she works in fashion. But when she introduces herself, she says she's in real estate.

Still clinging to Ronan's arm, she leans forward, voice breathy. "We're celebrating."

I suppress the urge to roll my eyes. "Oh? What's the occasion?"

"Amber just got confirmation that her pilot for *Billion Dollar DMV* on HGTV has been greenlit," Ronan says evenly.

Fia and I exchange a look across the table.

It's the universal *Girl, can you believe this shit?*

And damn it—now I'm suppressing a giggle.

"That's... wonderful," I say, nearly choking on my water.

"Ronan, honey, is that you?"

I stare in disbelief as another woman approaches the table. A redhead this time. She beelines straight for Ronan and cuts in front of Amber like the blonde is nothing more than a graffiti scrawl in need of scrubbing.

Damn. These women are cutthroat.

"Ronan," she coos, dragging a pointed red nail down the centerline of his chest.

"Kelly," Ronan says, clearly shocked. He shifts, trying to bring Amber back into the conversation. "This is Amber. We were just—" he begins.

He needn't have bothered.

The two women turn on each other, like Zeus facing Typhon.

"Well, *this* is awkward," Kelly snipes, folding her arms.

"Only for you," Amber shoots back. "I heard you didn't get a callback for your show."

Kelly's eyes shoot such a cutting look at Amber that I check myself for splinters. "Honey, I just signed with *Bravo*, not that knockoff network you're piloting with. I mean, who still watches *HGTV*?"

Kelly laughs, all dazzling, veneered teeth. "Good luck entertaining sixty-year-olds."

"You little—" Amber's eyes narrow.

Their voices rise in tandem, bickering with such viciousness that it makes me think: No wonder Amber's getting her own reality show.

Ronan mutters something that sounds like, "This is not the time or place," but it's hard to tell over the women's shrill voices. People are starting to stare, and Ronan edges between Amber and Kelly, hands lifted like he's trying to disarm a bomb.

But it's too late. They're fully locked into the showdown.

"Shut up with that fake-ass Birkin. You're not fooling anyone, darling."

"What?"

And that's when Kelly's elbow bumps Fia's half-empty wine glass.

I watch, horrified, as the red liquid tips—slowly and inexorably tumbling toward Fia's fine camel silk blouse.

It doesn't happen.

"Whoa, hold on there," a deep voice murmurs, thick with a Texas drawl.

I glimpse a flash of honey-blonde hair. Then Trent swoops in with lightning-fast reflexes, catching the glass just before it spills.

His cowboy hat slips off and flutters to the carpet.

For a moment, everything goes quiet. Even Amber and Kelly are frozen mid-sneer, fingers still thrust in each other's faces.

And there's Trent—crouched in front of Fia, glass in hand.

Their faces are inches apart.

Fia's eyes are wide.

"Th-thanks," she stammers.

Trent's mouth curves into a slow, sultry smile I've never seen before. "Anytime, *darlin'.*"

Somewhere between Kelly and Amber's bickering and Trent's dramatic entrance, our server reappears—with the manager in tow. One look at his glowering face and the two women instantly spring apart, no doubt calculating what bad press might do to their burgeoning reality TV careers.

Kelly leaves entirely. Amber, not to be outdone in the drama department, announces she's heading to the ladies' room.

"Ronan, babe," she coos, lashes fluttering. "Maybe we can finish our conversation at my place after I powder my nose?" Her lips part in a pout I'm sure has charmed many men.

Ronan rubs the back of his neck. "Sorry, Amber. Like I said, I've got a client call on the West Coast after this. But I'm happy to give you a lift home if you didn't drive."

The pout morphs from coquettish to genuinely annoyed. "Fine," she huffs, giving a sharp nod. "I'll be back in a minute."

She pivots, but not without firing a death glare in my direction.

I raise my eyebrows and think in my Nene Leakes voice: *Now why am I in it?*

This dinner has officially spun off the rails. Between Amber and Kelly's shenanigans and the emotional minefield of Ricky's situation, I'm exhausted and ready to go home.

I glance at Fia, hoping to catch her eye so we can wrap this up. But she and Trent seem deeply embroiled in … banter? An argument? It's hard to tell. Fia's glaring, but Trent looks completely unbothered. If anything, his smile is even brighter.

They're no longer inches apart, but he's still standing pretty damn close.

And Fia, whom I've seen elegantly eviscerate many a fool who dared to overstep, might be frowning, but she's *not* chasing him away.

I stare.

I've never seen either of them behave like this.

I need to get going.

I signal for the check and quietly pay for dinner. Ronan is still standing at the edge of the table, looking a bit lost when I rise.

"Sorry, guys," I call, raising my voice just enough to get Fia's and Trent's attention. "I'd better head out."

Fia's eyebrows shoot to her forehead. "What? No saffron ice cream for dessert?"

I laugh softly. "Let's do a rain check on that, okay?"

Fia smiles. "Okay, girl, but don't think I didn't see you paying for dinner. Promise me, I'll get you next time?"

"I promise. Scout's honor." I grin and cross my heart before turning to Trent.

"Trent, I'm going to send you an invitation for a charity event that Fia and I are planning. Oh, and can we chat tomorrow? It's about the IPO and some new—and very concerning—developments with our competition."

That seems to refocus Trent. He rises from his crouch next to Fia. "Of course, Thandi. 9:30 alright? I'll have Jessa block an hour."

"Perfect." I grab my purse and push back from my chair. "Nice to see you again, Ronan."

I'm almost two tables away when I hear footsteps behind me.

Ronan gently catches my arm.

"Thandi, wait."

I pause, and my irritation sparks again. Of all the things I think I will say, the last thing I expect to hear myself ask is, "Shouldn't you be looking for Amber?"

Surprise flits across Ronan's face—followed maddeningly by pleasure. Now he's the one with the Cheshire Cat grin.

"Are you *jealous*?"

I fold my arms. "Why would I be jealous? We have a business arrangement. Your harem of women has nothing to do with Immerscent or me."

"Harem? Hardly," Ronan laughs.

"Tell that to the real housewives of Montgomery County," I mutter.

He rocks back on his heels, more sober now. "Look, Thandi. I know we kind of started off on the wrong foot—and that's on me."

I take a breath. "Okay," I say slowly.

"That's why I wanted to talk to you. Make sure you didn't get the wrong impression back there."

Ronan's gaze holds mine. "My focus isn't on Amber or Kelly. It's on you, Thandi. And doing everything I can to make sure the IPO succeeds. Anything else is just noise."

I stare at him for a moment, wondering why the idea of Ronan focusing exclusively on me makes my stomach feel like I've swallowed a lightning bug. But I nod.

"Oh, and Thandi?" he calls as I turn to go.

"Yes?" I glance back, heart inexplicably lodged in my throat.

He smiles, and this time it's not smug or teasing. It's warm, gentle. Unmistakably genuine.

"Sorry for ruining your dinner. I hope one day you'll let me make it up to you."

Mr. T
Ronan

My relationship with RT Laboratories has been distant. Schizophrenic.

The building is a glass-and-steel structure nestled on a wooded research campus near Kenleigh. There is no signage beyond a discreet "T" etched into the entry doors. Even the landscaping is understated—a gravel and rock garden, almost zen-like in its aesthetic.

All of it reflects my ambiguity about the work I once thought would be my life's focus.

I've owned the biotech firm for almost a decade, and apart from installing a CEO, a capable team, and fulfilling my duties as board chair, I've been hands-off. I was too heartbroken over Mom's illness to continue, but too conflicted to let the company go.

But her will has me rethinking everything.

I press my hand against the biometric scanner, and the doors hiss open. Inside, the lobby is flooded with natural light from the atrium. The young receptionist does a double-take when she sees me. She jerks to attention so quickly, her headset slips sideways.

"Mr. Thorne? Oh! I didn't realize you were scheduled—"

"I'm not," I say, gently, offering a smile. "Just stopping by."

"Of course. Let me know if I can get anyone for you."

"I'll find my way," I say with a shake of my head.

I pass the familiar etched glass wall of the central lab, then turn down a side corridor where I nearly collide with Dr. Evelyn

Yanagawa, our head of R&D. She's in flats and a loose-knit sweater, clearly between bench work and a meeting. She stops short when she sees me.

"Ronan, it's been a while." I can see the question in her eyes, but even I don't have the answer for why I'm here.

Not yet.

I shove my hands into my pockets and rock back on my heels. "It has."

"It's good to see you."

"You too."

"Everything in your lab is as you left it," she says, glancing down the hall. "And if you've got time, I can give you an overview of where we are on the neuroplasticity trials. There's some new promising data from the Singapore lab."

"I'd like that," I say, meaning it. "But let's schedule something instead. I need a moment to catch up on things."

"Of course," Evelyn nods, eyes shrewd but warm. "Whenever you're ready."

"Thank you."

I head toward the private lab I designed when I still believed I'd be the next great olfactory disruptor. The specter of who I once was lingers here—loud, unfiltered, and embarrassingly intact. Thank God that identity is long-buried. A lot can disappear online for the right price.

The office is filled with state-of-the-art equipment: modular benches, adaptive airflow hoods, triple-insulated freezers humming in the corner. But surrounding it all are the disjointed accolades of a past life—one I'd rather forget. A YouTube Diamond Play Button gleams beside two Fragrance Foundation awards: *Perfume Extraordinaire of the Year* and *Instagrammer of the Year*. Both are from roughly a decade ago.

The screens on the far wall flicker with looping videos, and I wince.

A bass drop hits like a warning shot as the first video begins: **Scent Showdown: Can Shezmu the Scent God Identify 30 Essential Oils Blindfolded in Under 3 Minutes?**

The camera zooms in on my nineteen-year-old self—oiled up, bare-chested, kohl-rimmed eyes fixed on the camera with a smirk I'd like to punch. I'm wearing a makeshift shendyt, some gold chains, and sitting at a table lined with essential oil vials on top of a wrinkled white tablecloth. A papyrus-style scroll in the background declares NOSE OF THE GODS in faux calligraphy.

A thin haze of smoke clouds the makeshift studio—weed, I recognize in retrospect, and not incense.

To my left is my cohost Evan Copeland: lanky, pimpled, and unmistakably high. He was never really a friend, but we were co-conspirators—two ultra-wealthy sons bored enough to chase infamy together. Most of our plans revolved around one goal: becoming more attractive to women. Now he runs a hedge fund.

The thumping intro trap beat fades under a dazed voice:

"You've heard of photographic memory," Evan slurs, swaying in front of the camera, pupils dilated. "But have you ever met someone with *perfect scent recall*? Folks… witness *eidetic olfaction*." He throws out his arms like a magician before a reveal.

The camera pans to me, blindfolded and smirking, while Evan wafts a vial under my nose.

I fold my arms. "Lemon, verbena. Cold-pressed. Moroccan origin."

Another vial.

"Indian vetiver, sun-dried, not steam-distilled—solar extraction," I declare with an imperious sniff.

Evan swears and produces another.

"Ylang ylang. Mid-grade. Sulawesi, not Madagascar."

Each response is rapid-fire and confident. The camera jumps back to Evan, who is now doubled over with laughter.

"Okay, okay, okay. Get this. He doesn't just *recognize* smells. He can *recreate* them." He stumbles to his feet and dramatically pulls off a dingy sock. "Scent challenge number one: *my sweaty gym sock.*"

The camera cuts to me, smirking again. I pull down beakers from the shelf with theatrical precision. I swirl, mix, dilute, and shake. The screen flashes, *SHEZMU FORMULATION #001*. After a few minutes, I hold it out to Evan with aplomb.

He sniffs, then recoils in horror. "Bro. That's *exactly* it. That's my *foot.*"

The video smash-cuts to a series of quick street interviews. Plastic vials are handed around, capturing a montage of shocked reactions:

"Oh god, that is *definitely* a sock."

"Gym locker realness."

"How did he even *make* that?"

"Gross. But like… impressive."

Back in the studio, Evan grins directly into the lens. "All hail Shezmu, the Scent God."

The video ends on that image—me, shirtless, blissfully lacking in self-awareness—vials lined up like trophies on the table.

The second video is marginally less damning.

It's cleaner and glossier than the first. Gone is the smoke, the faux-Egyptian getup—the most egregious cultural appropriation—though the Shezmu brand remains. I'm 21 in this one, sitting at a table beneath a spotlight, wearing a black button-down and the stupid leather cuff I thought made me look mysterious. Evan's gone after a bitter fight over his cut of the sponsorship revenue.

I peel back a velvet cloth to reveal the YouTube Diamond Play Button. Just months after the award was introduced, it was in my hands. I remember the adrenaline rush, the way the pride swelled in my chest.

"It's official," I declare in the clip, pausing for dramatic effect. "Shezmu has hit ten million."

A collage of my most dramatic scent "wins," then plays: me calling out perfume notes mid-breath, fans screaming in Tokyo, a woman sobbing as I recreate her grandmother's scent from memory.

The screen behind me changes to bold serif text over a marble background. It reads, SHEZMU x Maison Orphée. It was my first fragrance collaboration with a Parisian niche house known for smoky, animalic base notes and a proud refusal to sell through major retailers.

"You asked for it," I announce, "Coming this Fall."

Then the video fades to black.

I reach for the remote, shutting off each of the screens in turn. The silence that follows is stark. I lean against the desk, letting out a breath I didn't realize I was holding.

I remember the giddiness of those years—the sponsorships, the viral highs, the niche fame. At the time, it felt like nothing could compare. But now, the footage, the awards, the absurd moniker—they all feel like artifacts. A shrine to entitlement and recklessness.

What strikes me most isn't the spectacle.

It's how much of an *Astor* I was in those videos. Cocky, callused, and combative. Not once considering anything beyond the rush of attention or the next check.

I scan the room and finally land on the one thing here I'm not embarrassed by: A photo on the bookshelf of Mom and me, both grinning in our lab coats, holding up a copy of *Modern Neuroscience*. Framed next to the photo is the reason for our joy—the first peer-reviewed piece we published together: *Targeted Olfactory Cues and Emotional Regulation: Mapping Compound-Specific Mood Modulation in Neurotypical Adults*.

I was twenty-two, and it was just before we found out about Mom's cancer diagnosis.

She'd done the heavy lifting, of course, but I'd contributed. For the first time, I'd stopped performing and started asking whether my gift could be more than just a gimmick or a way to get richer faster.

It was the first time I began to think that I could contribute to something bigger than myself.

After that article, RT Laboratories became an official partner of Thorne Therapeutics, so I could support Mom more directly. She'd spent her life studying how scent could modulate mood: calm the nervous system, ease depression, even support palliative care by addressing pain or nausea.

Not memory.

Not exactly what Thandi's chasing. But close enough to explain why her work calls to me so much. It isn't just because Thandi's brilliant, or because she's beautiful. It's because she's reaching for something bigger.

I want to remember what that feels like.

And thanks to Mom, maybe now I can.

I cross the room and unhook the Diamond Play Button from the wall. It's heavier than I remember. The framed fragrance awards come down next. Then the gilded "Shezmu" placard. I tuck them into a banker's box, sealing the lid with a final press.

I shrug on a fresh lab coat. The fabric is stiff, starchy from disuse.

For a long moment, I stand there, poised on the precipice between the past and the present.

Then I begin to move; slowly at first, reacquainting myself with the equipment, opening drawers, inspecting vials. My hands remember more than I thought they would.

I don't know what I'm building yet.

But for the first time in years, I want to try.

A sweet, heart-shaped face, gorgeous brown skin, and determined eyes bloom in my mind.

I want to see what it feels like to use my gift for the right reasons again.

And this time, I know exactly who I want to share it with.

Mortal Combat
Thandi

I stare down the bowl of vanilla ice cream like it's a mortal enemy. To be fair, I've never won a battle with it yet.

My only armor is the mask covering my nose and mouth. The industrial-grade respirator clings to my skin, twin filters extending from either side. It's bulky, a little ridiculous—but it's the only thing standing between me and complete sensory derailment.

For now, I can't smell a thing.

Unlike the controlled dose of $\beta7$, a confrontation with these creamy scoops, and the fresh waffle cone smashed on top of the dessert could produce violent, unpredictable results.

But I'm getting desperate.

It's been too long. I've made too little progress. And I can feel the IPO, the board's push for a new product, and this entire process with Thorne Consulting pulling me further and further away from my original purpose.

Finding my way back to Tess.

No. Finally bringing her home.

I don't mean a body. I gave up hope of that long ago. But this is where Dad and I align. Tess's bright, buoyant spirit deserves peace. She deserves justice. She deserves to be free.

Sometimes I wonder if Maryland had a statute of limitations on kidnapping, would I have found peace? Closure? Would I have stopped? Would I have founded Immerscent at all?

But I already know the answer.

I can't stop. Would never stop. Not in this state, not in this country, not in this universe. As long as Tess isn't with me, she'll always be my life's work.

My hands go to my mask, and ISO E looks up from munching on the organic oat-and-raspberry pellets my dad packed when I left my parents this weekend. My tiny research partner is clearly skeptical of this course of action.

"I'd like a little less judgment from you, mister," I say, stroking his soft white fur.

He nuzzles into my fingers, then twitches his nose as if to admonish, *'Don't say I didn't warn you.'*

Fair enough, but I'm more stubborn than he is when I set my mind on something. And this is the most important thing of all.

There's no going back now.

I close my eyes.

I remove the mask.

Bending close to the sundae, I take a deep breath.

The reaction is immediate—swifter than even I expect.

My lungs seize up. Sweat beads on my skin. All the fear and helplessness of that day in the park rush forward as I'm assaulted by image after image: Tess jumping off the swing, my LEGO blocks scattered in the grass, the tinny, repetitive music of the ice cream truck.

And then terror.

Tess screaming.

A man's hand clamped around her wrist.

He's turning … turning … so close now I can almost—

Please.

Just a little more.

I try to focus, but bile surges in my throat. My breath comes in shallow gasps—too fast, too sharp. Dark spots bloom across my vision, swimming and clustering at the edges.

I'm going to faint.

I clutch at the edge of the table, but my grip is weak. My limbs feel boneless. At the blurry edges of my narrowing vision, I see ISO E darting frantically back and forth on my desk, his small body a blur of white. I hear his high-pitched, panic-stricken squeak.

But it's too late.

Everything tilts.

My knees crumple, and the floor rushes up to meet me.

I'm falling.

And somewhere, in the slow, suspended seconds before impact, I know something is wrong. The way I'm collapsing. My angle is off. I can see it in the sharp edge of the desk rising in my vision, directly aligned with my temple.

I'm too far gone to twist away.

It's too late to save myself.

Guess ISO E was right.

Fuck.

Ronan

I feel a little guilty telling Thandi's receptionist that Trent asked me to stop by.

Technically, I could've called, but I can't stop thinking about Thandi, and I need to propose the focus of our next session. Why not do it in person?

As for the vial in my pocket—well, I'll decide later if it's worthy of her attention.

When the receptionist turns away to call up to Thandi's office, I slip into the elevator behind a very serious-looking woman in a lab coat whose badge reads *Sammie*. I have no idea where I'm going, but I'm betting wherever Sammie's headed, Thandi's close by.

The good thing about being born an Astor is that we're genetically predisposed to walking around like we own the place, even when we don't belong. So when the elevator dings and Sammie and I stride into the hallway, no one questions my presence.

I lean into the Astor DNA and clear my throat. "I'm here to see Thandi Elowen," I say, just as Sammie starts to peel away. From the speed of her stride, she's clearly got somewhere important to be.

"Ronan Thorne," I add quickly. "Forgive me, but I've forgotten the room number the receptionist gave me."

Sammie pauses, eyebrows lifting. "Mr. Thorne. Of course. Thandi mentioned your project. She's in Lab 33. Just down the hall and to the left."

"Thanks." I nod and head in the direction she indicated.

I know enough about Thandi now to recognize she accepts nothing short of excellence from herself or her team. But I'm still struck by what I see as I move through Immerscent's halls.

Of course, she explained it during our consultation—the rigorous protocols, the attention to detail, the uncompromising commitment to client care.

But it's different, seeing it in person.

Different, seeing the warm, bright evaluation rooms where patients sit side by side with their counselors instead of being separated by a desk. Different, seeing the state-of-the-art equipment in use and the diverse staff hard at work.

The craziest part? Everyone looks … *happy*.

Scientists, interns, and administrative staff chat in the corridor, laughing as they walk. Through glass walls, I glimpse teams working in beautiful synchrony; heads bent over monitors, pipettes passing from hand to hand, gestures smooth and easy.

There's intensity here. And focus. Even anticipation, like they all sense they're on the edge of something significant.

What's missing is the tension I've come to expect in institutions like this—the brittle anxiety, the performative overwork. The misalignment between values and daily reality.

In other words, the usual.

But not at Immerscent.

The truth here is undeniable.

Thandi has built something different.

I find Lab 33 at last and knock softly. There's no response, but I'm not surprised. I know what it's like to be deep in the zone. My presence might be unannounced, but I'm not here to be disruptive.

I try the handle and slide open the bamboo door.

No wonder Thandi didn't hear me. She's across the room, half-turned away, completely absorbed. There's a bowl of ice cream on the desk, topped with a crumbling waffle cone. Is this what lunch looks like for her?

I almost chuckle, but the sound dies in my throat.

Something's wrong.

She's gasping. Swaying. Her hand scrabbles for the table, but she can't find her balance.

I watch in horror as her knees soften. Her legs give out.

Her body lurches forward, her head pitching unerringly toward the sharp point of the desk.

Panic floods me, hot and sharp. My heart is pumping, my legs are moving before I can even think.

I lunge forward and slide across the floor like a baseman diving for home. My arm wraps around Thandi's waist in a single, desperate motion, yanking her back from the brink.

She collapses into me. Unconscious. Limp.

Shit.

I press my hand to her cheek, then her clammy forehead. Her usual lovely brown complexion looks gray and ashen.

What the hell happened?

I lean in, listening. Her breath is faint, but steady. My fingers find the pulse in her neck, and the fist squeezing my heart eases just a fraction.

It's strong.

Sure.

There's a high-pitched squeaking in the room, and at first, I wonder if my ears are ringing. Then I spot the frantic white mouse on Thandi's desk, chittering and gesturing like his tail is on fire.

At least someone else in here shares my distress.

That's when I notice the tiny red cape.

I blink and shake my head. I'll figure that out later. Right now, I need to focus on Thandi and making sure she's okay.

I gather her close. She's impossibly light in my arms, and that only sharpens the storm of fear and protectiveness battering me.

I rise to my feet and sprint for the door.

"Help!" I shout, voice ragged as I barrel down the hallway.

"Someone, please—help!"

Recovery
Thandi

"Thank goodness," a voice murmurs. "She's coming to."

A light flickers across my vision. "Thandi, can you hear me?" the voice repeats, and this time I recognize it as Aisha, our director of clinical programs.

I stir. Everything is soft and slow. I register sound, weight, and warmth. I'm woozy, but my head isn't cracked open like I expected. I touch my temple. No blood. No pain.

Strange.

Even stranger, I feel comfortable.

Grounded.

The hands stroking my back are gentle, anchoring. A calm settles over my body, quieting the panic still close to the surface. For a moment, the shadows that have hunted me for twenty years retreat.

I'm being held, and whoever it is smells *amazing*—fresh and resinous like bergamot, birch, and crushed vetiver. A sigh escapes me, and I burrow deeper into my comforting nest.

There's strength behind me: solid muscle, bulging biceps, and a wide chest. I marvel at the fact that, rather than sporting a concussion, I've landed in a fortress, one that is both solid and tender, protecting me from the world—and nefarious, sharp-edged tables.

I curl closer, and I decide that's not a bad thing. Not when their presence is so warm and soothing.

"Will she be okay?" a man's voice says, close to my ear. The sound vibrates through me, rough and familiar.

I inhale, filling my lungs with masculine freshness. Slowly, the notes begin to coalesce. It smells like a rooftop in the dark, a pulsating beat, and a hard body moving with heat and grace I didn't expect to enjoy.

My senses sharpen. Clarity burns through my fog, piercing it with dread.

Wait.

No.

No, it can't be. There's no way he'd be here.

No reason he'd be at Immerscent.

I crack one eyelid and shift just enough to glimpse sun-warmed skin and corded forearms dusted with auburn hair. The hand cupping my hip is large, with long, blunt fingers and a platinum ring etched with a single, unmistakable letter: T

My heart stutters.

No.

Oh, God. Please don't let this be—

I open my eyes and stare into an amber gaze. Of course, it belongs to the man I least want to see:

Ronan Thorne.

I jerk upright and instantly regret it as the room tilts sideways. A wave of nausea pulses behind my eyes. I press a hand to my temple, wincing.

"Hey, hey, easy," Ronan murmurs, steadying me with a hand at my back. "Slowly. You've had quite a tumble."

My fuzzy cocoon of comfort evaporates. The world reassembles around me. I smell coffee, hear the beep of a microwave. I see the scuffed game table and the bright upholstered chairs, and realize I'm in the staff lounge.

I squint against the overhead lights. A cluster of worried faces surrounds me: Sammie, Rashid from clinical trials, Javier, and Colleen from intake. Their expressions are wide-eyed and uncertain. They're all here for me, and guilt churns in my gut. My reckless experiment hasn't yielded a breakthrough. Only chaos and worry.

Dani is on the phone, pacing near the door, but when I move, her face softens with relief. "What do you think, Aisha? Should I hold off on calling the Elowens?"

I shake my head sharply at Dani. The last thing I need is to send my parents into a spiral.

"No," I gasp. "Please don't bother my parents. I'm fine."

"I'll be the judge of that," Aisha says, her tone warm but firm.

She kneels in front of the couch, clipboard balanced on the coffee table, a compact emergency kit open at her knee. I glimpse the tools she must have used before I woke up—an oximeter, a blood pressure cuff, and a digital thermometer.

She reaches up and tilts my chin. "You with us now?"

I nod, though my thoughts still feel disjointed.

That's when I realize exactly where I am, and how I'm being held.

Ronan is seated behind me on the couch, legs braced wide, one arm curled around my waist. His other arm is at my shoulder. My entire body is cradled across his lap, like I'm something fragile.

Or precious.

My lab coat is gone. My collar has been loosened, my silk blouse unbuttoned down to the third clasp. I'm decent, but the thin silk feels like a shoddy barrier against Ronan's vital heat. It's enough to make my head spin again—this time for entirely different reasons.

I try to sit up, desperate to put some distance between us, but Ronan's grip tightens, holding me in place.

"Stop. Let her finish her evaluation," he admonishes.

"What are you even doing here?" I hiss.

"I came by to talk about our next consultation," Ronan says. "You were collapsing just as I got to the lab. What happened?"

"I…"

Aisha's eyes are on me now, kind and curious.

"I'm fine," I mumble. "Just waited too long to have lunch," I lie, and I hate myself for it.

Aisha checks my pulse again. "Has this happened before?"

How am I supposed to answer that?

What can I say? That vanilla ice cream is my only remaining link to the day I failed my sister? That it's my tether to a memory so painful I've spent my whole adult life trying to reconstruct it? That its scent is the proof of the guilt I can never erase?

My lips part. "Yes... no. I—" I stop, defeated.

Aisha doesn't push. She just nods. "Humor me, Thandi. Let's step into the med suite for a quick check, okay?"

"Aisha, I'm fine. Really." I swing my legs off the sofa, and the world spins just enough for me to list sideways.

Ronan is there instantly. He stands, gathering me up in his arms like I weigh nothing. Like it's the most natural thing in the world. His arms are firm, his voice brooks no protest as he says calmly, "Where's the medical suite?"

I see Dani's raised eyebrow, and my face burns.

God, I've created a mess.

"Mr. Thorne, I'll have to ask you to leave, for privacy reasons," Aisha says, drawing the blinds to the medical suite.

"No, he can stay." I'm already halfway off the examination table, eager to get back to work. Eager to put this all behind me. "This'll be quick."

Nothing's wrong with me.

At least, nothing modern medicine can fix.

Aisha sighs. "If you won't stay for a more thorough exam, then at least promise you'll follow up with your physician. I'd also like to get your vitals one last time."

I nod reluctantly, and she gets to work. She clips the pulse oximeter onto my finger, straps on the blood pressure cuff, then presses the stethoscope to my back and chest.

"Vitals look fine," she says. "But since you mentioned skipping lunch, can I do a quick blood glucose check?"

It's phrased like a request, but the way she settles her hands on her hips and lifts one eyebrow, I know it's not a question.

"Fine," I mutter.

Aisha pulls out a glucose monitor, inserts a thin strip into the device, and reaches for a lancet. "Just a little pinprick," she says, pressing it to my index finger.

I wince as the needle pierces my skin. A single drop of blood wells up. She absorbs it with the strip, and we wait.

"Eighty-five," she says a moment later. "Low, but not hypoglycemic. With some food in you, you should be fine."

"I'll take her to lunch," Ronan says, as if it's already decided. "We'll get her something with actual nutritional value."

"What?" I twist to face him. "That's not necessary. I'm perfectly capable of feeding myself."

"Not from where I sit."

I glare up at him. "Good thing you're not sitting, then."

His lips twitch. "I'm not the one who fainted, remember? Can you even stand on your own?"

And here I was, starting to think he might not be totally insufferable. What makes him think he can waltz in here—*unannounced*—and boss me around? The man is delusional.

I hop off the exam table, ready to storm out and prove it. But I'm not exactly tall, and with my feet already dangling, it's a longer drop than I account for. Naturally, my traitorous heel chooses that exact moment to snag on the hem of my slacks.

I stumble. Teeter.

And fall right back into Thorne's arms.

He raises a brow. "You were saying?"

Heat rushes to my cheeks as I find myself once again pressed against his chest. His arm is firm beneath my thighs, as unyielding as steel.

"Put me down," I grit. "I'm not an invalid."

"Not a chance. Not after that display." He smirks. "Besides, where are you rushing off to now? To grab some chocolate ice cream instead?"

I make an indignant sound. The nerve of this man.

"For your information, what you saw in the lab wasn't a meal. And even if it were, is there nothing you eat just for enjoyment?"

Ronan's gaze darkens, lids lowering. The amber of his eyes deepens to something molten as they drift over me.

"I can think of a few things, yes."

"I—" The word snags in my throat.

I'm suddenly breathless.

My gaze drifts to his lips, and I notice for the first time his pronounced cupid's peak, and how full and firm his bottom lip is— surprisingly sensual against the rough stubble on his cheeks and the hard angles of his jaw.

He catches me staring.

His lids droop, becoming even more weighted as his gaze drags across my face and lands on my own lips. When his eyes meet mine again, I almost gasp. His pupils are dark, dilated, irises narrowed to hot whiskey-colored rims.

My entire body prickles with heat. This is—

I try to shift to escape Ronan's burning gaze and the dark, swirling emotion I see behind it, but his hold is immutable.

I'm too aware of his scent, the breadth, and depth of his chest. It's like the mixer all over again. There is just so much of him. *Too much of him.* All of it unutterably male, and my body doesn't seem to understand that Ronan Thorne is off limits, that he is not even a friend.

"Ronan," I whisper.

He misreads it as distress. His expression softens, and one callused hand glides up to my neck, pressing at the frantic pulse fluttering beneath my skin.

"You sure you're alright?"

Well, I *am* distressed. Just not in the way he thinks.

That single touch ignites a million electric impulses over my skin. My nipples tighten, and I curse myself for pulling on a softer bra this morning in my rush to get to the office. I don't dare look down to see if I've embarrassed myself. To see if my sudden arousal is telegraphing itself through thin silk.

"I'm fine. *Please.*" I'm not above begging. Not when the alternative is drowning in this slow, confusing undertow.

Ronan sighs. "Talk some sense into her, doc."

"Thandi," Aisha says gently. "Go. Eat. We need you too much for you not to be well."

That gets me. The staff lounge flashes through my mind—the worried eyes, the pall of concern—and I'm instantly chastened.

She's right.

This isn't just about me.

And I've already caused enough chaos for one day.

"Alright, let's go," I tell Ronan.

He shifts me in his arms and starts toward the door.

Oh, God. I'm positive everyone is staring as we pass. I can feel the curious looks, the awkward energy in the hallway. My cheeks flame. This is worse than fainting. Worse than the failed experiment.

I hate being an inconvenience, hate being the center of attention, hate being the focus of anyone's scrutiny unless it's business.

Unless it's for Tess.

I groan and press my face to Ronan's chest, humiliated. Angry at myself. But I can't seem to help it.

I brace for his mockery. Some smug quip, or a sarcastic jab. But none comes. Instead, his hand comes up to cradle the back of my neck.

Shielding me.

Holding me steady.

I don't understand what's happening.

Right now, I don't even understand myself.

And whatever it is Ronan Thorne and I are barreling toward—

I understand that least of all.

Haze
Thandi

I'm grateful when we're in the parking garage. It's quieter here, and there are no more prying eyes reflecting questions I have no answers to.

Ronan is silent as we take the elevator. He's still cradling me. I should protest, but after that walk of shame, I'm too emotionally wrung out to do anything other than close my eyes and let him lead us away from here.

Outside, the air is warm, the afternoon sun diffused by a fine haze. Once we get to Ronan's car, I expect him to set me on my feet, but instead, he opens the door of a midnight gray Mercedes May-bach and lowers me into the passenger seat. The leather is the color of butterscotch and as soft as kid gloves. I sink into it with a sigh.

Ronan moves around to the driver's side, and before I can reach for the seatbelt, he leans over me, one arm braced on the headrest, the other tugging the belt across my chest. The strap tightens, pressing between my breasts. My breath stutters as his fingers brush the curve of my shoulder, then dip to click the buckle into place at my hip.

"How are you feeling?" Ronan glances over as he backs out of the parking lot. His large hands caress the wheel and move over the gear shift with easy, confident motions.

"I really am okay," I insist.

"Hm," is all he says, and he doesn't sound convinced. "How's the temperature for you? Too cold?"

"It is a little chilly, I admit," fiddling with the vent in front of me so that it's no longer pumping an icy blast in my direction. Before I can finish, Ronan's long fingers are sliding over the console, coaxing the temperature into something more comfortable. I remember the way they brushed over my skin, both rough and tender, and I shiver.

"Still not warm enough?" he murmurs, not taking his eyes off the road.

I'm startled at how observant he is, at how much he's absorbing even when I think he's not paying attention. It scatters my thoughts in all the wrong directions.

"No," I whisper. "It's perfect."

"Good. Whatever you need, let me know."

He leans forward. His arm stretches across my body, brushing the edge of my thigh. His delicious scent surrounds me as he opens the glove compartment and pulls out a small bottle of water. I watch in helpless fascination as his hand engulfs the bottle and twists it open before placing it in the cupholder nearest me.

"Just in case you're thirsty," he says.

I nod, unable to speak.

I need to stop thinking about Ronan's scent, his hands, his massive frame, or the unexpected kindness in his eyes. After the tumult of the morning, I need the security of the expected. And the expected is supposed to be that Ronan Thorne is distant and arrogant—not the thoughtful, gentle man beside me.

I take a tremulous breath.

Outside, the world speeds past. Inside, the silence between us thickens. Not awkward, but humming with something I'm afraid to put a name to.

"You scared me back there," Ronan says quietly.

"I did?" I turn to him, caught off guard. Why should he care what happens to me?

"I saw you falling and I panicked." Ronan's breath escapes in a huff. "Also, that mouse was losing his shit. Not that I blame him."

"ISO E?"

"Super," he blurts, then laughs, the sound full-throated and warm. "I was trying to figure out what the fuck was happening with that cape."

"Yes." I smile, despite myself. Few people get the molecular pun behind ISO's name and outfit. "Poor little guy. I must have terrified him."

"Yeah, well, he's not alone." Ronan glances at me, his amber gaze filled with hidden fire. "You're special to a lot of people, Thandi. We don't want to see you hurt."

We?

Ronan thinks *I'm* special?

I have no idea what to do with that. No idea why the thought makes my heart trip over itself.

So, I ignore it instead.

"Where are we having lunch?" I ask.

"Verdance. Have you been? It's one of my favorite spots. Not vegan, but plant-forward. Everything's organic. I figured you could use something healthy after your fall."

"It sounds perfect, thank you. And no, I've never been." I shoot him a sideways grin. "Is ice cream on the menu?"

Ronan chokes.

He stares at me.

Then he tips his head back, and he's laughing all over again.

Verdance looks like a converted greenhouse with a glass ceiling. Light filters in from every direction. The walls are a grid of tall windows framed in blackened steel, and a living installation of mosses, orchids, and trailing vines runs the length of the space like a suspended jungle. Natural wood tables, linen-colored banquettes, and slate tile floors give the place an earthy elegance.

A hostess appears, tablet in hand and a welcoming smile on her face. "Mr. Thorne, your table is ready."

We follow her into the main dining room, and Ronan's hand settles at the small of my back. His touch is light, but impossible to ignore. Not inappropriate, just…warm. Unexpectedly intimate.

He's standing too close. And my body won't stop noticing.

The hostess keeps glancing over her shoulder at us, her lips twitching like she's trying not to smile.

"Is everything okay?" I ask.

She stops walking, cheeks blooming pink. "Sorry. I didn't mean to be weird." Her voice dips into a whisper. "Are you Thandi Elowen? The founder of Immerscent?"

I nod. "Yes. That's me."

Her eyes widen. "I thought so! I'm a student at George Mason. I read your *Forbes 30 Under 30* profile last year. You really inspired me. I never thought I'd see you in person." She hesitates, biting her lip. "Would you mind if I asked for a selfie?"

I smile. "Of course not."

Honestly, I love talking to young people. And her request gives me the perfect excuse to slip away from Ronan's touch. We shift, and I lean in as she lifts her phone and snaps a picture, her grin impossibly bright.

When we're done, she bounces on her toes. "Thank you so much, Ms. Elowen. My friends are never going to believe this."

"No problem at all. What's your name?"

"Kara. Kara Matthews."

"It's a pleasure to meet you, Kara. What's your focus at GMU?"

"I'm doing an MBA with a concentration in health care management. I want to start something one day. Something focused on menstrual health." Her eyes sparkle. "You made me believe it's possible."

I'm so touched and energized by her passion.

This. This is why I wake up in the morning.

I hand her my card. "I'm so glad we met. Let's stay in touch. Immerscent has a few roles opening soon. Not menstrual health, unfortunately, but a good way to start wrapping your head around the sector."

Her face lights up. "Are you serious? I'd love that." She takes the card like it's made of gold. "Everything online says you're nice, but now I *know* it's true."

Now that the ice is broken, she dives into full girl-gab mode. "I *love* your hair and your outfit, by the way. That *Forbes* photo was so badass, I thought you were taller. You're so tiny in person!"

It's my turn to flush. "I'm not *that* short. I'm just wearing lower heels today."

Ronan snorts beside me.

I turn and shoot him a glare. "Not a word from you, Thorne."

Kara giggles. "You guys are *so* cute. Please—your table's right this way."

I arch a brow. *Cute?* As in *a couple?*

I glance over, and Ronan looks entirely unbothered by the implication. His hand has also somehow migrated to the small of my back again.

This man seems determined to invade my space no matter what.

When we reach the table, Ronan pulls out my chair. His hand brushes my shoulder as I sit, and I realize he's still watching me, quietly attentive to the way I move, still scanning for any signs of unsteadiness or nausea. It's thoughtful. Disarming, even, and I find myself reassessing everything I know about Ronan Thorne, yet again.

"Still doing okay?" he asks as he takes his seat.

Kara ducks out with another breathless thank you, leaving us with a couple of menus and a promise that our server will be with us soon.

"You don't have to keep asking," I huff. "I thought Dani was the worrier, but you've got her beat."

Ronan doesn't reply. He just watches me, that unreadable gaze resting on mine. Finally, he says, "What do you feel like eating?"

"Hmm, let's see," I murmur, grateful for the change in subject. I flip through the menu. "The eggplant looks good, but the seared Pacific halibut with preserved lemon, sorrel emulsion, and roasted fennel sounds amazing."

"That *does* look good. I was leaning toward the tempeh myself."

"Oh. Are you vegan?"

"Hardly." Ronan laughs. "But it's protein-rich. Good for my workout regimen."

"Workout regimen? Is that why you're so…so…" The words slip out before I can stop them. I pause, pressing my lips together.

"Why I'm so…?" Ronan raises an amused brow.

Chiseled? Gigantic? Muscular? Built like a tree, I'm increasingly interested in climbing?

I clear my throat. "*Big.*"

"Are you calling me fat, Thandi?"

"No, of course not. That's not what I meant," I groan. "Not that it would matter if you were. Health is more important. Size doesn't matter."

"Oh yeah?" Ronan leans back in his chair, legs spread. His voice is low, edged with heat. "That's never been my experience."

The air abandons my lungs.

I don't—

Is he… flirting with me?

"Hi there! How are we doing today?" our server appears, pulling out a tablet. "I'm Jessica, and I'll be taking care of you. Have we decided, or do you need another minute?"

I shake my head, trying to refocus—definitely ignoring the smoldering look Ronan is still casting across the table.

"I think we're ready."

"Great," Jessica says, tapping her screen. "What are we having?"

Ronan gestures toward me. "The lady will order for us."

I blink, surprised. It's not that I thought he was a chauvinist—okay, maybe I did, a little—but Ronan moves through the world with such authority, I never expected him to defer to me.

"Ah," I say, recovering, "I'll have the halibut, and he'll have the tempeh with beluga lentils and charred vegetables."

"Excellent choices," Jessica intones. "And for drinks?"

"Sparkling water with lemon, please."

Ronan nods. "I'll have the same."

"Perfect. I'll put that right in." Jessica collects our menus and disappears into the rush of the dining room.

There's a brief silence, then Ronan says, "No lavender-honey old-fashioned today?

"Ronan, it's one in the afternoon."

He smirks. "Aren't you the boss? Who's going to stop you?"

"Not because I can means I *should*."

Ronan regards me for a moment, his gaze thoughtful. "Is that specific to work, or a general life philosophy?"

"You disagree?"

He pauses. "A few months ago, I might've said yes. But lately I've been thinking a lot about choices and what they cost us. Where the line is between desire and duty."

I don't fully understand what he's referring to, but I can feel the weight behind it. There's something in his eyes—quiet and bruised—that looks a lot like sorrow. There's a lot I don't understand about Ronan Thorne. But that is a language I speak fluently.

"You said you wanted to talk about our next consultation?" I ask.

Ronan nods just as our food arrives. "I've looked at your fundamentals, which are, of course, phenomenal. I've also thought about the IPO. And there's one question I keep coming back to."

"What's that?" I ask, spearing a piece of halibut.

He sips his water. "Is Immerscent only about nostalgia?"

I turn that over. "But memory isn't the same as nostalgia, is it?" My mind skitters back to the bowl of ice cream melting on my desk.

"Not everything we need to remember is pleasant. For our clients, accessing the good is important—but confronting the nightmare is what heals."

I don't say, for some of us, that's the only thing that matters.

Ronan nods, drumming his fingers on the table. "Right. Yes. But…"

"But?" I prompt.

"Right now, Immerscent is an album," he says. "A way to revisit the past. But what if it could be a vision board too?"

I frown. "I still don't follow."

"Come with me on Saturday," he says abruptly. "I have a theory. But you have to trust me."

"Why Saturday? Where are we going?"

Ronan's eyes glint. "If I say more, I'll ruin the surprise. Just wear something casual. And comfortable."

I set down my fork. "Why is this sounding a lot more like a date than a consultation?"

Ronan's smile is slow, sultry. He leans forward until our fingers nearly touch.

"Thandi," he murmurs. "This is a consultation. Because when I decide to sweep you off your feet—"

His voice drops to a velvet murmur.

"You'll know it."

Maestro
Thandi

We're back at Immerscent, and of course, Ronan insists on walking me up like I'm some Regency-era damsel liable to faint at any moment. He seems convinced that if he's not there to guard me, I'll wither into dust.

Despite my trepidation, lunch turned out better than expected. Verdance was beautiful, and I'm still pleasantly full. Two hours with Ronan also passed more quickly than I care to admit.

I thought Tino's was a fluke, a rare moment of camaraderie. But this is the second meal I've shared with Ronan Thorne, and both times I've … *enjoyed* myself. I knew he was smart. I didn't expect him to be funny. Or kind. Or good at listening

I can't believe I'm thinking this, but I may even like him.

Strictly personality-wise, of course.

I still haven't processed the tenderest aspects of care he showed me earlier. There's no place in my reassembled worldview for that yet.

I can hear ISO E's indignant squeaks even outside Lab 33's door, and I rush over to atone for my sins.

Sammie must have come by. ISO's bowl is rinsed and stowed, and he's back in his cage. I unlatch the door, and he bolts out like a tiny, caped fury, launching himself onto the desk with a barrage of squeaks aimed at my soul.

"I know, I know," I murmur. "I didn't mean to abandon you."

I reach to scratch his favorite spot behind his neck, but he turns his back on me, cape fluttering as he tosses a haughty look over his shoulder.

"Damn. That bad, huh?" I whisper.

Behind me, Ronan laughs. "Apology not accepted, apparently."

"He'll forgive me when I bring more of Dad's treats. I might have to upgrade to the mango flavor now that I'm in the doghouse."

Ronan crosses his arms and leans against the desk, still smiling. "Sounds like bribery."

"Call it restorative justice. He's a critical research partner."

"Right," Ronan says, his voice dry with amusement.

I glance up at him. "I guess I should formally introduce you two. I'm afraid he's as much your business partner as I am now."

I wink. "You'll be negotiating royalties by the end of the week."

"I'd be honored to officially meet Mr. Super, especially if he's the genius behind Immerscent's success," Ronan says with mock solemnity.

"Then, ISO E Super, meet Ronan Thorne. Ronan, meet ISO E Super." I bow, sweeping my hand toward the desk like a game show host.

"Hey, little man," Ronan murmurs, bending closer. ISO sniffs the air, then rises onto his hind legs, curious.

"Careful," I warn. "It usually takes him a while to warm up to new people. He's been known to nip a few fingers—Wow. Really? ISO, *seriously?*"

Before I can finish, ISO darts forward without a hint of caution, scaling Ronan's arm and nestling into the crook of his shoulder like he's found his new soulmate.

Ronan is cackling now, nearly doubled over. "Look at that. You let him down, so he's decided to place his bets elsewhere."

I plant my hands on my hips, glaring at the little furry traitor. "After all those treats, all those ear scratches? That's all it took for you to abandon me?"

ISO squeaks as if to say, "*Whatever.*"

I shake my head in disbelief, even as the moment settles into quiet. But it's a good quiet—leftover easiness from lunch and the breathlessness of genuine laughter.

Ronan's eyes are sparkling, and he looks relaxed and approachable—nothing like the brooding playboy I first met.

Even I feel uncommonly mellow, which is impressive given how my day started. I may not understand what's happening between Ronan and me, but I have to give credit where it's due.

He saved me today.

In more ways than one.

"I guess I owe you an apology," I murmur, my gaze dropping to the edge of the desk.

"For what?" A long finger brushes my chin. Ronan tips my face back up until I'm looking into those honeyed eyes.

"For all of this," I whisper. "The chaos. The drama. I'm sure you didn't plan on spending your entire afternoon here cleaning up after me."

"Thandi," Ronan brushes his thumb over my cheek. "There is nothing more important to me than spending time with you." Both of his large hands come up to cup my face. "And as for this morning, I'm relieved I was here to help."

"Oh," I breathe, the sound so small I barely recognize it. I shiver and let my eyes fall shut. It's easier this way—easier not to see the fire in his gaze, easier not to fall into it. My fingers tighten at my sides. I can feel myself leaning in.

I force myself to pull away.

"Well," I say, stepping back, severing the connection before I do something I'll regret. "Thank you anyway. I'd be in a hospital bed if not for you."

"Sure." Ronan tucks his hands into his pockets. On anyone else, the gesture would be ordinary. On him, it manages to embody masculine ease and power.

"Thanks again for lunch," I offer. Now the silence between us has shifted, stretched taut, awkward in its fullness.

"Thandi…" he begins,

"Yes?" I swallow.

"Are you sure you'll be alright? I'd like to check in on you. Just in case something like this happens again."

"Ronan," I say gently. "That's really nice, but I don't need you wasting more time on me. Today was an aberration. I promise I have friends and family who look out for me. This morning, I just couldn't bear calling them. I felt so…" I pause.

"So what?" he asks, not letting it go.

"Foolish. The experiment was a catastrophe. Putting myself in harm's way is bad enough. Panicking everyone else is even worse."

Ronan frowns. "The ice cream was an experiment?"

I wince. We may have evolved past mutual loathing, but there are places I'm not ready to go. Not with anyone, and certainly not with him.

"It doesn't matter," I say, shaking my head. "The point is, I messed up."

Ronan's frown deepens. "Okay, but take my number at least. I'm not a friend or family," he says with a bitter twist to his lips. "So you don't have to worry about inconveniencing me."

"Ronan…."

"Thandi, whatever you were up to imperiled your safety and the IPO. Which means it also imperiled our contract. I can't help you if you're out of commission. Take the damn number."

When he brings it back to business, I think of Trent and how disappointed he'd be in me. Actually, he wouldn't, and that's the worst part. He'd be kind, but I'd never get over letting him and the board down.

"Fine," I mutter. I swipe to a new contact and thrust my phone into his hands. "You can enter it in here."

As Ronan taps out his number, ISO E—who's been oddly quiet on his shoulder—suddenly springs to life. Without warning, he scampers down Ronan's arm and dives into his left pocket.

"Jesus," Ronan mutters, freezing mid-text. He cranes his neck. "What the hell is he doing?"

"If you've got gum or candy in there, it's over," I warn. "You'll never get him off your case."

Ronan stiffens as ISO wiggles deeper, rustling around like a furry excavator.

"You know," I add, "he once stole half a protein bar from Dani and wedged it in a centrifuge. It took three of us to get it out."

Ronan reaches into his pocket, clearly trying to salvage what remains of his dignity. "Alright, alright. Out you come," he growls, pulling ISO out by the scruff.

My research partner emerges, but not empty-handed. Clutched between his front paws is a 3ml vial with a handwritten label. ISO squeaks triumphantly, holding it aloft like he's just retrieved the lost grail.

"What's that?" I ask.

I expect Ronan to say it's a gift, maybe a sample from a client, but I watch in amazement as his eyes widen. Then, incredibly, he blushes.

Ronan Thorne—blushing!

"Ah." He raises a hand to the back of his neck. "I forgot about that. Just a little experiment of my own. For you."

"For me?"

Did I miss something? I know Ronan is a marketing and algorithmic genius, but this is the first I'm hearing about expertise in chemistry.

I tuck my phone away and take a still-wriggling ISO E from him. The little guy is holding onto the vial like his life depends on it, and I wrench it from his paws.

"Yeah, it's just a small token. Not a big deal." Ronan's voice is gruff now, the warmth from moments ago gone. "Anyway, I should head out. Saturday?"

"Of course," I murmur, utterly bewildered as he strides toward the door.

Yet another 180 from Ronan, Whiplash Thorne. A minute ago, he was looking at me like—

No.

I banish the thought.

We are not going there.

Still, it's jarring. Seconds ago, he'd lingered like there was nowhere else he'd rather be. Now he's retreating like the building's on fire. I barely have time to process the shift, let alone say goodbye, before the door swings shut behind him.

Frowning, I return ISO E to his cage and turn the vial over in my hand. The neat, handwritten label reads simply: *Tino's*.

My curiosity flares.

I hold the vial to the light, then uncap it. I take a cautious sniff.

The effect is immediate.

The scent slices through the air like the first piercing note of a maestro's symphony. My breath catches. I stumble back into my chair.

I'm no longer in the lab.

I'm outside Tino's on a summer night, pressed in among the crowd waiting for a table. The scent of magnolias drifts in on a sultry breeze. There's woodsmoke, and beneath it, the yeasty, grape-dark richness of wine.

My heart thuds. My hands are trembling. I have to set the vial down and grip the edge of the desk to steady myself.

Somehow, Ronan has taken the first evening we shared, refined it, compressed it, and capped it in a bottle.

What it evokes isn't just memory. It's something closer to teleportation. It's that vivid, that precise. The image doesn't fade. It lingers—shimmering like a fragment of stained glass, catching the light from a hundred angles.

No. Not glass.

A diamond, blazing in the sun.

I thought Ronan was only analytical, doggedly left-brained. But this is science transfigured into art. The calibration is so precise I'm rattled. My emotions are in chaos. My thoughts spiral.

Scent has been my life's work, but this simple vial hits faster and harder than anything Immerscent has ever produced. Sharper than my best efforts.

Sharper than β7.

I bring the vial to my nose again.

The volatile top notes have lifted, revealing a softer heart: the salt-slick heat of pepperoni, the comforting lactonic haze of melted cheese. If I hadn't just eaten, I'd be drooling.

But even here, there's progression. The scent shifts again.

The final, resounding base notes leave me the most shaken: mimosa petals, gardenia, and citrus. And beneath that, a whisper of warmth—the nutty richness of shea butter.

I set the vial down with a gasp.

I'd know the scent anywhere.

It's me.

Heart Notes

Sunset Peony
Ronan

It's Friday evening, and I'm a wreck. My stomach's more knotted than a clown balloon. I haven't heard from Thandi since ISO E outed me and forced me to hand over *Tino's*.

That bastard. I thought we were becoming friends. I hope Thandi's dad is out of mango treats.

After lunch at Verdance, I'd decided to wait until Saturday to gift the vial, but that little bugger jumped the gun. Now she has it, and I have no idea what she thinks of it.

No idea what she thinks of *me*.

I've replayed that precious Wednesday more times than I'll admit. First, the terror of seeing Thandi hurt. I've never felt more helpless. She was so soft, so small in my arms, and all I could think of was Mom—how life can change in a breath, and how it doesn't care how brilliant or prepared you think you are. Mom's illness taught me that we're all on borrowed time, and we can't afford to waste a minute.

I told myself that if Thandi was okay, I would stop hesitating and just show her how I feel.

Verdance was a start. And when Thandi didn't run, my heart sang. I noticed how she stared at me in the car, felt the way her body leaned into mine when we were back at Immerscent. There's something between us, and it's not one-sided.

I'm sure of it.

Still, I wasn't *quite* ready to lay it all on the line. Not yet. Because even beneath Thandi's attraction, I could sense her hesitation. Even as she looks at me with those big brown eyes, I hear the unspoken question behind them about whether she can trust me. Whether I'm *safe*.

Meanwhile, Tino's is an emotional milestone oceans ahead—a statement, a breathless confession of everything I've felt since the day we met. And those sweet closing notes are the most damning.

I only hope I haven't scared her away.

I pull out my phone again, hoping she's texted, but of course, the screen is dark. I don't know why she would, or what I expect her to say. I only know I'm a starving man desperate for whatever morsel she'll offer.

I could reach out. I've thought about it a dozen times. But I keep second-guessing myself, and my gut says wait. Give her space. Let her process everything that's happened this week.

Tomorrow will come soon enough.

I sigh and turn my attention to the message that *did* come through—the one from Fia, asking me to come over tonight to talk next steps on managing Mom's estate.

The sky is dark, the air heavy with the promise of a storm. It starts as a sullen drizzle as I pull out of my garage, but by the time I'm halfway to Fia's, it's a full-blown deluge. My hands tighten on the steering wheel, and I feel a bit of exasperation at my best friend. Even knowing the storm was coming, she insisted on our meeting.

Fia would never admit it, but nights like this are hard on her. I looked it up once—the connection between storms and nerve pain. Something about barometric changes causing tissues to expand, increasing the pressure on nerves. Add in the damp and the cold, and it's a recipe for discomfort.

She'll still greet me like nothing's wrong, breezing through like it's just a minor annoyance.

I've given up trying to understand why she insists on being superhuman.

Then again, Thandi did the same thing—pulling away the second I offered help, like it's a badge of shame instead of just the reality of being human.

I sigh again, this time deeper. Why am I surrounded by women determined to prove they're invincible?

Good thing I checked the forecast before leaving the gym. I'm bringing reinforcements.

Fia's on the other side of the river in Montgomery County, not far from Chevy Chase, and the drive takes me twenty minutes longer than usual thanks to the downpour. I'm not saying Maryland drivers are the problem, but I also don't see any other state tags slipping and sliding out here. Between that and the abysmal drainage, I wouldn't be surprised if we're under a flash flood warning soon.

Fatouma, Fia's home care assistant, is locking the side gate as I pull up to the entrance, umbrella raised high over her head. I roll down the window and smile.

"Hey, Fatouma. You're sure you'll be okay out there?"

"If I leave now, I will be," she says with a grin, nodding toward her red Camry. Then she gives me the same look we've exchanged regularly over the past five years.

"She's a little tense today," she says in her soft, French-tinged accent. "Storm's sitting in her hips. Don't let her overdo it—and tell her to do the stretches. She'll listen to you more than she listens to me."

I snort. "Doubtful. But I promise to try."

"Good luck!" She calls, skipping over puddles with surprising speed before getting into her car and heading off.

I'm sure I'll need it.

I park in the driveway and don't bother with an umbrella as I sprint to the trunk, grabbing a plastic bag and two thickly folded bundles.

I'm stamping my feet on the mat when the front door flies open and Carmen, Fia's younger sister, bolts past—takeout in one hand, book bag in the other, her burgundy braids flying behind her.

Carmen's a student at GW, and technically lives on campus, but you'd never guess based on how much time she spends here. She pauses when she sees me, smirking.

"What's up, Ronan? You staying over?"

"Yeah, might as well. We've got a lot of paperwork to get through tonight."

"Sounds like a plan. Oh, and don't let her bully you into the celery juice. There's birria in the fridge."

"Sure thing," I chuckle, waving as her Uber pulls up and she slides in.

The door is barely closed when Fia's voice bellows down the hall. "For the love of— Whoever's letting the draft in, shut that front door. And if you're tracking mud on my hardwoods, I swear—*que la Santísima Virgen te proteja!*"

Now I'm really laughing.

Yup, that's Fia.

"So where's this famous birria I heard about?"

I set my stuff down and head toward the kitchen.

Fia narrows her eyes as she follows, circling the low, custom island in her lightweight manual chair. She's wearing an ivory cashmere lounge set, and her curls are pulled into a messy bun. True to Fia, the outfit strikes the perfect balance between high fashion and weekend casual.

"That Carmen," she mutters. "I'm trying to get us all to eat healthier. Mama's blood work just came back, and would you believe her LDL is 150?" She throws her hands up. "And don't even get me started on her A1C. Six point three!"

I open the fridge and stick my head in, hunting for the stew. When I spot the Pyrex container, I pull it out and raise it to the light.

"Right. So you're telling me Carmen single-handedly demolished two-thirds of this in one afternoon?"

I glance over my shoulder just in time to catch the blush spreading across Fia's face.

"Aha."

"Okay, so maybe I had a little," she huffs.

"A little?" I hold up the nearly empty container. "There's barely enough in here for me."

Fia begins to stammer, and grinning, I saunter to the microwave. "I propose LDL vigilance starting Monday instead."

"Fine," she grumbles, though the color's still high in her cheeks.

I shoot her a sidelong glance as I rummage through the cupboards and pull down two mugs. The microwave hums in the background.

"You want some tea? Got a new recommendation from Jack, my trainer."

"Oh? What kind is it?"

"Turmeric, ginger, and a root I'm forgetting. Apparently, it tastes like ass but works miracles for soreness and inflammation. I pulled a trap bar deadlift personal record this morning and then got crushed on the rower."

"You're really selling this." Fia's voice is wry. Our eyes meet, and there's a flicker of softness in hers, a hint of acknowledgment, before she nods. "Sure, I guess I'll have some too."

"I mean," I add, leaning against the counter, "I can't say I'm opposed to eating a little—"

"*Ronan!*" Fia interrupts with a glare, and I laugh, holding up my hands.

"Fine, fine," I call over my shoulder as I grab the boxes of tea, which I conveniently plan to "forget" here. Of course, my thoughts flicker to Thandi despite myself. She can cure my inflammation any time.

By the time I return to the kitchen, the birria's ready. I plate it, steep two strong mugs of tea, and press one into Fia's hands. Its pungent aroma curls upward, promising heat and healing. It doesn't taste that bad, actually.

Fia's fingers curl around the ceramic, and for just a moment, I glimpse the tired slope in her shoulders, the ghost of exhaustion from fighting pain all day.

"You wanna stay in here," I ask softly, "or get comfortable in the living room? I could use being horizontal for a bit."

"Living room," Fia says, already balancing a tray on her lap as she wheels away.

I follow with birria and tea in hand, waiting while she settles onto her stylish couch. It's pristine ivory, all architectural lines and soft angles that take nothing away from its comfort. I've crashed more than a few nights on Moby Dick (yes, that's my nickname for it), and I've slept better there than in my own bed.

Fia has yet to meet a neutral she doesn't love. Not that there aren't any vibrant tones in her life, but according to her, the rest of the color spectrum is strictly rationed.

"So," I say, already fighting a grin, "I brought something."

"What is it?" she murmurs, adjusting a tray table with her tea and MacBook across her lap.

I don't look at her as I start peeling back the packaging. I unfold the combo Snuggie-weighted-heat-blanket in a shade of pink so blinding it would offend even Barbie.

"They called this one 'sunset peony.' Figured it suited your vibe."

Fia gasps in horror. "Ronan, what the hell is that?"

I cackle like a cartoon villain. "Impulse late-night QVC purchase. You gotta admit, it's genius."

"Absolutely not."

"Oh, come on." I advance with the fuzzy monstrosity fanned out like a threat. "Give it a try."

"Over my dead body. Why would you buy me something like this?"

"Don't flatter yourself," I say as I help her ease her arms through the sleeves and make sure her legs are tucked beneath the fleece. I switch on the heat. "I just didn't want you to feel left out."

"Also, I'll take the sunset peony if you prefer this color." I shake out the second blanket—phosphorescent Nickelodeon slime green. "Monster Mash. I think it brings out my eyes."

"You're an idiot," Fia mutters, but I note with satisfaction how she sinks deeper into the couch as the warmth kicks in.

"And what's with your obsession with this stuff?" she adds, eyes narrowed. "Should I be putting QVC in your portfolio now?"

"Look, I'm allowed one vice," I say, slipping on Monster Mash and curling up beside her. "And I looked it up, by the way. Qurate. Ticker QRTEA. I'm only boosting their margins, not their long-term viability."

"One vice? Yeah, right."

I narrow my eyes. "You've got some birria on your chin."

"I do not!" Fia protests, swiping at her face.

"Ha! Knew it."

"Shut up." She glares. "You are such a child."

"And you love me for it," I coo, nudging her with my shoulder.

Fia huffs, but after a moment, she relaxes, letting her head rest against me.

"We've got a lot of ground to cover tonight," she murmurs. "Want me to share some quick analysis, or do you already have a sense of where you want to start?"

"Well," I mumble into my tea, "I… got back into the lab this week."

Fia jerks upright, eyes wide. "*Roncito*," she breathes. "That's amazing."

I shrug. "It just felt like the right thing to do. I'm thinking about reviving RT Laboratories."

"I'm so proud of you." She clicks through something on her laptop and starts typing. "When you say *revive*, are we talking expansion, rebranding, or something else?"

I meet her gaze.

"I mean an entirely new wing. Dedicated to Mom's research."

Fia's quiet. She doesn't have to say it. We both know how big this is for me.

"Okay," Fia says simply. "What next? The lab's been coasting under existing grants and private funding. Are you planning to inject capital from your estate or spin up a new revenue stream?"

"Definitely a capital injection," I say. "I ran some preliminary numbers. To get the new division off the ground—equipment, staffing, space redesign, maybe some IP counsel and early trials—I'm thinking ten to twelve million in the first year."

Her brows rise, but she doesn't interrupt.

"That gets us a dedicated facility, a small but sharp team, and six months of operational runway before we need to think about partnerships or licensing. I'd rather not take outside funding until we're clear on scope and control."

Fia taps a few keys, already refining. "I'd probably adjust up by twenty percent to account for regulatory and compliance costs, especially if we're dealing with scent-based therapeutics. But you're not far off."

She does a few more calculations, scanning the spreadsheet. "You mentioned outside investors. Is RT Laboratories finally going public?"

"No," I say—too quickly. "I'm never exposing Mom's work to that kind of vulnerability again. But I've been thinking about a couple of strategic partnerships."

Fia nods, fingers flying across the keyboard. "Names?"

I pause, trying to sound offhand. "How about Immerscent?"

Fia swivels to face me. "Immerscent? As in Thandi? *My* Thandi from the youth center?"

"She's not *yours*," I growl.

Fia blinks, then grins. "Whoa. Down, boy."

She eyes me over her mug. "So… you gonna say more about this? Not that I have any objections to Immerscent, by the way—great sector alignment, and their numbers are stellar."

I grimace, annoyed at myself for the outburst and at her obvious delight. "Forget it."

Fia's grin only widens. "Oh hell no. You like her, don't you?"

"I told you Trent asked me to work with her on their IPO, right?" I mutter, knowing damn well I haven't mentioned it. I'd trust Fia with my life—that's not the issue. I've just been too embarrassed by how far and fast I'm falling for Thandi.

Fia only raises a perfectly arched brow.

"It's only been a few days. A week-ish on Saturday." (Not that I'm counting every minute of contact with Thandi.) "But I'm already impressed with Immerscent's potential," I add, trying for neutral. "Seemed like a great fit."

If I think that'll stop Fia, I'm an idiot. She sets her MacBook aside, inheritance forgotten. There's a dangerous glint in her eye, and I groan.

"Okay, I *may* have a crush. But can you blame me? I've never met another woman like her."

"It doesn't hurt that she's beautiful and kind," Fia says sweetly, twisting the knife. "When did this start?"

I sigh. "At the pick-up game."

"*Dios mío.* You've got it bad."

I glare. "Aren't you supposed to be comforting me or something? Offering sage advice?"

"*Do* you want my advice?" Fia asks seriously.

I nod, not even bothering to hide my desperation.

"No shade to your past dating habits, but that approach is not going to work with Thandi."

Don't I know it. I want to latch onto the "dating habits" comment for spite, but I behave myself. "What do you mean?"

"Thandi is a pure soul, but she has trauma, and it's serious. You know I love you, Roncito, but I couldn't share it without her permission, even with you." Fia sighs. "If you want her heart, you have to be gentle with her. She's been through too much to give it easily."

Fia smiles, easing the weight of her confession. "I'm not gonna lie, though. You guys would make a cute couple. Two of my favorite people together—*and* I could get you to spend more time at the youth center? Win-win for me."

"Thanks, Fia. I owe you one," I murmur, pulling her into a hug. But my thoughts are already churning.

I'm worried—more than that, I'm mad as hell that anyone would hurt Thandi.

Still, what Fia said rings true. I'd seen it myself. There's a caution in Thandi, a wariness that only comes from pain.

Now I'm glad I didn't bother her with some inane text. Tomorrow looms larger than it did this morning—heavier, more urgent.

I sigh, but I'm filled with new resolve. *I have to get this right.* Thandi's too special for me not to.

I square my shoulders and turn to Fia. "So… are we watching it?"

She frowns. "Watching what?"

"You know what. Don't play dumb. I saw you fumble the remote when I walked in earlier. You paused mid-recoupling."

She stares, then sputters. "That could've been a *documentary*."

"Sure. A deeply educational piece on emotionally stunted influencers in matching swimwear."

Fia groans, yanking the pink blanket up to her chin.

"Fine. But if you say one smug word during *Casa Amor*, I'm turning off your blanket."

Perspective
Ronan

10 Years Ago

"I'm just saying," I mutter, slumped on the couch, legs stretched out on the coffee table. "Cancun isn't *wasting* spring break. It's… culturally enriching. Sun, ocean, cheap beer—all important life experiences."

From the kitchen, I hear the clink of china. Tea for Mom's afternoon ritual. She steps into the living room, a linen wrap dress knotted loosely at her waist, her auburn curls piled high in that regal way that makes her look more like an artist than a chemist.

She gives me a look. "Ronan. You're twenty-one. You've had your fill of cheap beer."

"Not quite. I'm still calibrating the data set."

Mom doesn't laugh. Instead, she sets her mug down on the coffee table and folds her arms. "What if you used the week for something different?"

"Like what? A monastery?"

"Like perspective." She takes a breath. "You know the communities we've talked about. The ones your father's facilities border. The ones no one from corporate ever sets foot in."

I groan. "Mom…"

"I'm not asking you to fix anything," she says gently. "Just to go see it for yourself."

I'm quiet. I don't get it, but I'll do anything for her, and she knows it.

"Fine. You win. No *senoritas* and *cervezas* this year."

Mom smiles, and it's not smug, just full of an emotion I can't name. She turns to walk back to the kitchen, but after two steps, she stumbles.

My feet are under me before I even realize I'm moving. "Mom?"

She catches herself on the back of the armchair, one hand flat on the cushion. Her face is pale. Too pale.

"I'm okay, son," she says, mustering a wan smile. "Just a little tired."

But I'm already at her side, one hand on her shoulder, the other catching her elbow. And suddenly, Cancun feels like a million miles away.

I might have agreed with Mom to cancel Cancun, but that doesn't mean I can't add a little Ronan Astor flair to her vision. One quick search of where my father's factories are located turned up a bunch of podunk towns I'd never heard of. A couple are border towns. Quaint. Dusty. Irrelevant.

Evan and I doubled over laughing, picturing ourselves lost in backwater farm country. That's when I came up with the new Shezmu series: *Top Five Smelliest Cities in America.*

I pitched it as a joke: "Come on, Evan. One long weekend, an epic road trip, and a camera. What could go wrong?"

That sold him.

Now we're about twenty minutes outside this Great Value Marfa, and I'm already tired. The AC in the U-Haul Evan rented died two hours into our drive from Cambridge, and I'm melting. The straw hat and overalls I've put on aren't doing a damn thing to cool me down.

Evan's sweating like a mofo in the passenger seat, but he's hopped up on weed as usual, so he's chill, camera pointed out the window.

Those shots better not be shaky, or I'm gonna beat his ass.

Ahead, black smoke puffs from red and white factory spires above the town. They stick out like cigarettes against the bright blue sky.

Or giant spliffs.

I snort. "Yo, Evan, they must've heard you were coming." I point at the towers and laugh. "Rolling out the welcome kush."

Things stop being funny, though, the closer we get to Main Street.

We park the van and get out, but right away, I know something's wrong.

The air is thick with a sickly-sweet odor that clings to the back of my throat and coats my nostrils. Beneath the burnt sweetness is something harsher and synthetic. Like bitter almond extract soaked in battery acid.

"Well, you were right," Evan drawls, hoisting the camera on his shoulder and filming a sweeping panoramic shot. "Smells like shit out here."

I don't need a lab to know what we're breathing in. I've smelled low-grade organophosphates before. Years ago, on a field visit with Dad, we drove past a field just after it had been sprayed. One of the workers had mishandled the gear, and the air was so thick with chemical residue that our handlers rushed us back into the car.

My stomach churns as I watch kids skipping on the sidewalk, tiny hands clutched in their parents' palms. A pregnant mom is slipping into an ice cream shop just as we arrive, and elderly couples are rocking lazily on front porches.

They're all breathing in the same air.

This air.

Do they not know what's in it?

Because I do.

For the first time, my *Shezmu* gift feels like a curse.

Each of the compounds rattles through my head—chlorpyrifos, malathion, diazinon. Pesticides that can damage lungs, scramble neural pathways, and even warp DNA.

I rip off the straw hat and toss it into a trash can. I wish I could take off these dumb overalls, too.

Behind me, Evan is alternating between getting scenic shots and zooming in on pretty girls as they walk by. I slap him upside the head.

"Cut that shit out. And turn the fucking camera off," I snap. "We need to find some masks."

"Ow! What was that for, you dick?" Evan rubs his head, but the complaint dies when he sees my face. "Wait. You're serious?"

"Yeah."

A sinking feeling is building in my chest, and it feels a lot like regret. And deep, blistering shame.

I don't know if what I see next makes it better or worse.

I realize that once again I'm an idiot. Because, of course, they know. No one needs Ronan Astor sniffing the air like a bloodhound and spouting revelations.

They've been breathing this in for years.

They've always known.

Mom's face flashes in my mind.

I'm the only dumbass who chose to be in the dark.

We keep walking down Main Street, looking for a pharmacy or supermarket, and the fact that it's even hard to find one is a sign in itself.

Just past a chain-link fence, a dozen kids are stringing wire between raised garden beds. Behind them, a mural catches my eye: Black and brown hands cupping sunflowers. Down the street, a camera crew is filming elders in front of a low-slung building that reads *Community Resource Center*.

The sidewalk is buzzing with motion: A teenager with a fresh fade is handing out brochures in front of a pop-up tent marked *Know Your Rights*.

I take a brochure. The font is bright, urgent. One side is printed in English, the other in Spanish. Both warn about the dangers of pesticide exposure, including spina bifida, cleft palate, low birth weight, respiratory complications, and childhood leukemia.

My gut is churning, and I want to sit down, but there's nowhere to rest.

I guess that's fitting.

Because why should I get to when they don't?

That's when I see her.

Seated in a wheelchair, arguing—calmly but firmly—with a middle-aged man about the problem with *Citizens United*. Her voice carries, clear, measured, and full of conviction.

She can't be older than nineteen. She's wearing a Princeton sweatshirt, the sleeves pushed up to her elbows, and a floral scrunchie that holds her curls off her neck.

Her name tag reads *Fia*.

Her presence is like a live wire. Powerful, magnetic—and ten times more focused and mature than I've ever been.

Suddenly, everything I've been doing until this moment seems useless. Frivolous.

The red-hot rain of shame drenches me again.

This was a mistake. We need to go. I open my mouth to tell Evan just that, but she's already rolling toward us, brows drawn.

"You lost?"

Soft Hands
Ronan

10 Years Ago

"You lost?"

"No." The word catches in my throat. "I was just… looking."

Fia gestures at the factory spires behind me. "You can't smell that and still need to look."

My face burns. "Yeah. It's no joke."

"Nope." Her voice is even. "Neither is organ failure, neural tube defects, or miscarriages."

I flinch, but she just stares at me. Waiting.

I gesture toward the garden beds. "This is… incredible."

Her expression softens. "Yeah, well. We're not gonna wait around for a settlement that may never come. We build what we can with what we have."

"What are you studying?" I blurt, jerking my thumb at her sweatshirt.

"I started with environmental law," she says. "Then I realized the law doesn't mean much without power. Power comes from capital. So now, it's finance."

"Oh."

Back home, I'm considered the big man on campus. And thanks to Shezmu, I just got my YouTube diamond play button. I've never been at a loss for words. In fact, my friends joke that their biggest problem is getting me to shut up. But in front of this fierce young woman, I'm tongue-tied.

Apart from a few glitzy fundraisers that I attend with my parents twice a year, and one flashy trip to donate food to poor kids in Uganda, I haven't thought much about other communities or vulnerability.

Heck, I feel more vulnerable now under Fia's gaze than I have since I outgrew my father's sharp words and his even heavier fists.

But Fia is not asking for arbitrary pain and submission.

She wants accountability.

Before today, I would have scoffed. What do I owe a town hundreds of miles away? But that's a hard line to maintain when my family's crimes are staring me in the face.

Next to me, Evan has a zoned-out look on his face that has nothing to do with weed and everything to do with disengagement. I'm still not sure any of this is landing for him.

"What about you?" Fia asks suddenly. "What are you studying?"

"Who me? Oh. Biochemistry."

Her mouth tightens. "Figures."

"Huh?" I frown. "What's that supposed to mean?"

Fia just shakes her head. "Never mind."

"You're from here?"

That gets me a brief smile. "Yup. Back home for spring break. And to welcome my new little cousin."

Fia tips her head toward a woman setting up folding chairs. She's young and heavily pregnant, with the same glossy curls and golden skin as Fia. She's wearing a t-shirt that says *Born Free* stretched over her baby bump.

"That's Amaya," Fia says. "She's due any day now."

"She lives here?" I ask, dread seeping through my veins. Because I know what that could mean for her and the baby.

"Just like everyone else," Fia sighs. "All we can do is hope for the best. Things worked out for me, but not every kid with spina bifida in this town gets a scholarship to Princeton. In the meantime, we're building our case against Astor."

"You're building a legal case against the company?" I echo, the weight of guilt sinking deeper in my gut. And what's stranger, what should feel disloyal but doesn't, is that I *want* her to win.

"Yeah," Fia says, watching my face now. "They've got another plant outside town. Nothing flashy—just chemicals for adhesive bonds, scent carriers, that sort of thing. But we've collected residue samples and health records. The proof is there. We just don't have enough traction. Not yet."

"Okay," I say slowly.

Fia lifts her chin. "We'll get there. The ACLU's already interested. Now we just need more data."

I hear the conviction in her voice, and somehow I believe her.

"And in the meantime?" I ask.

She flashes a tired smile. "In the meantime, we keep raising the alarm to anyone who'll listen. And we take care of each other."

"Is there… anything I can do to help?" The words tumble out before I can stop them.

"Well—" Fia stares up at me. She points at the cluster of raised beds behind her. "We always need help in the gardens. But that might be tough on those soft hands of yours."

I wince, because she's right. I've done as much gardening as I have housework. Which is zilch. Zero. A housekeeper comes by every day to keep my condo near campus spotless.

Fia's gaze shifts toward a cluster of people beneath a pop-up canopy, where a camera crew is adjusting lights and sound.

"There's a news crew over there," she says. Her eyes meet mine. "You know what would help our campaign more than anything?"

"What?" I breathe.

"If James Astor's son made a statement about the harm his father is causing this community."

My breath catches. "You… you knew who I was this whole time?"

"Of course I did." Fia crosses her arms. "This is a small town. Word travels fast. Faster still when we're being reduced to one of the smelliest towns in America by the son of the very man polluting our air."

"I…" I make a choked sound. "It wasn't … we thought.…"

"Hey, man," Evan mutters, already backing away. "I think I'll wait in the car, cool?"

He's gone before I can say a word. But Fia doesn't flinch, and there's no mistaking the steel in her voice when she speaks again:

"Look, if you're just here for shock value, leave. But if you meant what you said about helping, this is it. Time to put your money where your mouth is."

I look at the mural. At the garden plots and the kids weaving between them with plastic watering cans.

Then I look up at the air, hazy with invisible poison.

And for the first time in a long time, I feel something sharp and urgent in my chest that isn't shame, guilt, or insecurity.

It's conviction.

And the exhilarating freedom of finally pulling away from my father's shadow.

"So what's it going to be?" Fia demands. "Are you going to keep feeling sorry for yourself, or are you going to do something that matters?"

I square my shoulders and meet her gaze head-on.

"I'll do it."

Funnel Cake
Thandi

I don't know why I'm obsessing over what I should wear today. It's not like this is a date.

Still, I check my reflection one more time in the mirror. The navy sleeveless sundress I've chosen is simple and versatile. Casual, like Ronan requested, but sleek enough that I can shrug a blazer over it if I need to.

I make a mental note to toss my favorite jacket in the backseat. Men like Ronan don't always read the room the way they think they do, and as a Black woman, I won't get grace if I show up underdressed.

I'm moving on autopilot, applying sunscreen, lip gloss, and a spritz of my usual perfume when my gaze drops to the vial of *Tino's* on my dresser.

I freeze, suddenly hyper aware of Ronan's keen nose and even sharper sense of observation. Should I switch things up? Throw him off the scent, so to speak?

But then, I shake myself. I've never hidden who I am, and I won't start now.

Putting the address Ronan shared into my phone, I get in the car and back out of my driveway. The location, deep in PG County, past Upper Marlboro, is not familiar.

At least it should be pretty out there. It's a beautiful day. The sky is startlingly blue after yesterday's storms, as if all the world's troubles have washed away. The usual August humidity is gone, replaced by gentle sun and a playful breeze.

I roll the windows down and let the wind caress my skin. It helps soothe the hum of anxiety lurking just beneath my emotions. I remind myself that this is the very unpredictable Ronan Thorne and to keep my expectations neutral.

That way, I can't be disappointed.

Still, I'm shocked by the theme park looming ahead.

This is where we're meeting?

Chrome turnstiles gleam in the sun. Candy-colored flags ripple overhead, fluttering above striped awnings. Somewhere in the distance, a rollercoaster lets out a whoosh, followed by the faint shriek of riders. The candy-apple red main gate, crafted from curlicued wrought iron, forms a pair of arches, each crowned with a neon sign that declares "Sugar Hill Park." Beneath it is a ticketing pavilion shaped like a giant popcorn box.

Even from the parking lot, the air is thick with the aromas of sno-cone syrup, fried batter, and caramel popcorn. A speaker hidden somewhere in the landscaping plays a looping barbershop quartet version of Beyoncé's *Texas Hold 'Em*.

Of course, it's Saturday and the place is packed, teeming with giggling groups of teenagers and flustered families with young kids. Costumed mascots are enthusiastically working the crowd. The tallest and most ridiculous is Captain Funnel Cake, the park's signature lead. He's a golden spiral of fried dough with powdered sugar eyebrows, a captain's hat, and foam boots shaped like whipped cream swirls. A cluster of kids squeals and chases after him while he pretends to salute.

To his right is Rocket Pop Rina, a swaggering popsicle with blue lipstick, wraparound shades, and a red leather jacket that reads *Chill Happens* on the back. She's posing for selfies and giving out fist bumps. Two girls race past, breathlessly commenting that Rina has over 12 million TikTok followers.

I don't know if to laugh or cry. What is Ronan thinking?

What kind of business meeting requires concession stands and roller coasters?

I haven't left the car. I sit with one hand on the door, the other on the steering wheel, as I contemplate turning around and texting Ronan with an excuse about a meeting or a personal emergency. Anything to get out of this.

But I don't.

This is the least I owe him after his kindness this week

Besides, I know the real reason I'm hesitating.

Theme parks like Sugar Hill haven't been the same since losing Tess.

There are too many ghosts. Too many memories of my daredevil sister. Too many painful reminders of what might have been.

I may be the athletic one, but that's because I've always succeeded at anything that requires focus, discipline, and structured effort. Tess, on the other hand, was the true free spirit. Her well of spontaneity was endless. Sugar Hill Park is exactly the kind of place where she'd be in her element, racing towards rides and using her charm to get free funnel cakes and to cut in line.

And just like that, I feel her.

Everywhere and nowhere.

Still sprinting ahead, turning to see if I'll follow.

I close my eyes and draw a slow breath, then step out of the car. With every step forward, I'm less sure I should be here.

It's too late now, though, because Ronan has spotted me.

He's standing to the right of the main gate, hands in his pockets. He's wearing jeans, a navy t-shirt, and a pair of weathered Chuck Taylors. The shirt isn't technically a muscle tee, but it might as well be. It clings in all the right places, hugging his chest and the impressive span of his shoulders.

Despite myself, my gaze lingers.

Funnily enough, he's wearing blue like me, magnifying the feeling that I am now part of some weird couples' activity.

"Ronan," I gesture at the surrounding chaos. "What exactly are we doing here?"

He grins. "What? You don't like theme parks?"

"Not for business."

"Don't worry," he nudges me lightly with his elbow, "I promise this is all above board. Should we grab some tickets?"

"Fine," I sigh, not entirely pleased with his lack of explanation, but I follow him to the ticket booth anyway.

The girl at the booth, barely sixteen and chewing her gum with studied indifference, looks up from her screen. "You two together?"

I blink. "Oh—uh—"

"There's a couple's bundle," she says before I can answer. "It's a special for the park's tenth anniversary. You save, like, thirty percent and get a free photo with Captain Funnel Cake."

Ronan raises an eyebrow as I glance at the pricing and do some fast math. It's a no-brainer to do the couple's bundle, even if we're anything but.

"We'll take it," I say briskly. "We don't need the photo, though."

The attendant shrugs, and before I can interject, Ronan taps his card to pay.

"Hey!" I glare. "You've got to stop doing that."

"Doing what?" Ronan asks innocently, passing me my ticket and tucking his wallet back into his pocket.

"I can pay my own way."

"Thandi, it's twenty bucks. I think I'll manage."

"It's the *principle*," I grumble. "You paid for lunch at Verdance, too."

Ronan's eyes gleam. "If you're so concerned about equity, you can owe me a favor."

"A favor."

"Mm-hmm. My pick."

His tone is offhand, but he's practically glowing with satisfaction.

I narrow my eyes. "Why does this feel like you're benefiting from a situation you orchestrated?"

Ronan shrugs. "Hey, I don't make the rules."

"Isn't that *exactly* what you're doing?"

"No, now I'm being a gentleman." He places a hand over his heart. "Honoring your desire to restore balance between us. Righting a great economic injustice."

His smile is sudden, disarming. The corners of his eyes crinkle, and a dimple appears in his left cheek—a perfect little divot of masculine charm. Somehow, it makes him look impish and boyish. A far cry from the inscrutable man who arranged this meeting, whose purpose I still don't understand. My thoughts scatter, and my heart gives a little flip.

"Yeah, right," I manage, smoothing a trembling hand over my skirt. "Also—"

"LOVERS OF SUGAR AND SUNSHINE!"

We both startle as Captain Funnel Cake lumbers toward us, arms flung wide like he's coming in for a bear hug. The glittery faux sugar flakes on his costume glint as he barrels forward with alarming agility.

"No," I say, holding up a hand. "Absolutely not."

"Yes!" he cries, herding us toward a corny backdrop plastered with cartoon hearts, roller coasters, and doves in sunglasses. "For love! For legacy! For the Captain's Bundle!"

Ronan bursts out laughing.

Not just a chuckle, but a deep belly laugh. I stare at him as the mascot cheerfully corrals him into place. Is he serious?

"*What are you doing?*" I hiss, resisting the urge to drag him out of the frame.

"Come on, you have to admit it's fun. We should get a quick shot." He grins, leaning close. "Imagine the kick the kids at the Youth Center will get out of this."

Damn him for mentioning the kids.

That's the *only* reason I'd consider this. He's right. I can just see Daysha and Ricky laughing their heads off. They'd never let me live it down—in the best way.

"Okay," I sigh. "Just this once."

Ronan immediately drapes his arm around me, and his woodsy scent, clean and warm, surrounds me.

"That's the spirit!"

"Say funnel cake!" Captain Funnel Cake shouts, flinging confetti into the air as the camera flashes. He does a dramatic little jig while the Polaroid develops, twirling and shaking it with flair.

"Oh, you two are cuter than me and Rocket Pop Rina!" he booms.

I slap a hand to my forehead, torn between amusement and existential concern. How would that even work? Then again, Rina's a popsicle who doesn't melt in the sun. Funnel cake romance is probably the least of her worries.

Beside me, Ronan chuckles again. "Come on, Captain," he calls. "Let's see it."

Funnel Cake tap dances in place, then makes a grand show of selecting the "perfect" photo. He slides it into a frame and hands it over with a wink.

It's a glossy 5×7-inch shot mounted in a plastic sleeve. The border is outrageously saccharine: funnel cakes stacked into hearts, whipped cream rosettes, sparkly gumdrops, and a bold red banner across the top that reads, "Sweetest Pair in the Park!"

I brace myself, preparing to cringe.

But the Captain is right. It's a great picture.

Ronan and I are both squinting, mid-laugh.

I'm staring into the lens.

And Ronan?

My breath catches as my fingers brush over the photo.

He's not looking at the camera at all.

He's looking at me.

Joy Ride
Thandi

Once the photo foolishness is over, Ronan ushers me off to the side, away from the crush of bodies streaming through the entrance. I can't look at him. Not fully.

Between *Tino's* and the photo, I can no longer deny that he feels something for me. I'm not some wide-eyed ingénue. I know what desire looks like. Sex, attraction, and chemistry are all familiar terrain.

But there's a part of me I've always held separate.

Because of Tess.

Not deliberately. However, I learned at an early age that joy can vanish in a flash, and that love doesn't always get to stay, even when you hold onto it with both hands. Somewhere along the way, I started believing that if Tess isn't here to have all this life, all this sweetness, then maybe I'm not meant to either.

Now, Ronan is throwing all of that into chaos.

I'm still trying to decide if I like him, except that something as banal and mild as likability wouldn't be a problem. Instead, the magnetic spark he inspires feels volatile. Dangerous. Like nothing I've ever experienced.

Ronan Thorne isn't a gentle spin in a teacup. He's an extreme rollercoaster with death drops, sharp turns, and no seatbelt. If I'm not careful, I'll be flung off the track and never find my way home again.

And yet, I'm already hurtling toward devastation.

I don't know how, but he's already under my skin.

Like right now. He's not even doing anything, and I still feel the pull of him. I'm aware of his every move and how the light magnifies the amber of his eyes like he's an extension of the sun.

I'm also drawn to his scent. To the fresh, bottled notes that tease my senses and the invisible isotopes that are uniquely his. I'm no whimsical savant like Ronan, but the vial of Tino's rattled me because it proved how much we were *both* anchored to aroma that night.

I noticed his cologne the moment I saw him at the mixer. Something about it set off a chain reaction I haven't recovered from since. It's why we ended up at Tino's in the first place. Why I insisted on ordering him that gin and tonic.

It's not that I'm afraid of Ronan's arrogance. Or even his unpredictability. When he looks at me, I feel something I've never allowed myself to feel:

Selfishness.

Like there's something I want to hoard. *Just for me.*

I'm terrified that Tess is the scent I'll never remember.

And Ronan Thorne will be the one I can't forget.

It's the scariest and most exhilarating sensation at once. Like I can't tell if I'm going to fly or if I'm going to fall. And my treacherous mind is reminding me of Wednesday and murmuring that Ronan's arms are strong enough to catch me even if I tumble.

My fingers tighten around my copy of the cheesy photograph, and once again, I wish I hadn't agreed to this.

"So," Ronan drawls, pulling me back from the edge. "I know you're wondering why we're here."

"To put it mildly," I say, trying to tamp down my frazzled emotions.

Ronan spins in a circle. "Can you feel it? The air here—it's pure anticipation. Right now, there's no place on earth more obsessed with the future. No other place where fear of the unknown is not just anticipated, but relished."

A family rushes past—a couple mid-argument, dragging a toddler in a chocolate-smeared play suit—and Ronan laughs.

"Even they're looking ahead. Aching to get home, I'm sure, to put that little guy to sleep."

I purse my lips. "Okay. I think I'm following."

Ronan grins. "Isn't it funny? Once we leave, our memories will betray us. We'll edit the chaos—the crowds, the gut-churning food, the gleeful terror. We'll take it all and put it in a safe little box. Sugar Hill Park will be nothing more than a shrine to childhood and perfect nostalgia. But the truth of it? The reality of today?"

Ronan pauses, eyes sparking. "It's nothing but adrenaline—movement. Hurtling so fast and so hard, you're flung off the edge of who you are into whoever you're about to become."

He stops, breathless.

I realize I haven't blinked since he started speaking.

My lungs are full of fire, and my mind is electrified like a thousand Christmas lights. I'm teetering on the edge of the very precipice he's describing.

"That's why I brought you here today, Thandi." Ronan murmurs. "*This* is what I want for you and Immerscent. To use what you've built to shatter the line between the past and future. To help others not just remember who they were, but to realize who they can *become.*"

He extends his hand to me. "Want to try it together?"

I stare at his palm with its long fingers, and the heart line etched in a deep, generous arc. I've been so caught up in finding justice for Tess that I never considered Immerscent could be aspirational. But now, I'm already reconstituting β7 in my mind.

No, not that.

Something else.

A new compound that will stimulate different neural pathways and ignite the limbic system. Not to build closure but confidence. To divine the pressure point where the aquifer of memory erupts into imagination.

No, this isn't β7 at all.

It's possibility. ∞: *Ápeiron.*

No limits.

And when I slip my hand into Ronan's, I wonder, not who I've been.

But what I'm about to become.

We've dropped the photo bundle off in a rented mini locker, and now we're standing in line for the Dragon of Doom, a massive rollercoaster with five death-defying loops. The sun is pleasant enough, but we've been behind the turnstiles for twenty minutes, and I'm starting to schvitz. Tilting my head back, I squint up at the gleaming metal track. Every few minutes, a centipede of cars shoots past us with riders screaming at the top of their lungs.

This had better live up to the hype.

"Thirsty? Want me to grab you something from that guy with the cart?" Ronan asks.

Before I can answer, he snags a flyer from a clown in neon pink overalls and starts fanning me with it. It's useless, barely a whisper of air, but the gesture sends a flush across my skin that has nothing to do with the weather.

"No, I'll be okay. We're almost to the front of the line," I murmur.

Ronan nods, but his gaze lingers, studying me as if I might suddenly drop from heatstroke. I almost laugh. He's the one in danger of sunburn, not me.

I don't know what to do with his attentiveness. I'm usually the caregiver in my family, the one anticipating needs and looking out for everyone else. Being the center of all this focus is… disconcerting. I want to tell him to cut it out, but it's not like he's doing anything wrong. Still, from the corner of my eye, I catch a few sidelong looks—women glaring like I'm not grateful enough for his presence.

The ride screeches to a stop, and the current group of riders stumbles out, dazed and breathless. One or two look green around the gills.

"Alright, up next," calls the attendant, a lanky guy with a shock of red hair and diamond-studded ears. "How you guys doing?"

I mutter something vaguely in the realm of "excited," and he grins like I've passed a test.

"Sounds good. Hey, man." He nods at Ronan. "Since you're bigger, I'll have you here. Your girl goes on the inside."

"Got it," Ronan says easily.

I huff as he helps me into the high-backed seat, sculpted like a dragon's spine, then settles in beside me.

Does everyone think we're together?

I don't have much time to dwell on it. The attendant double-checks our harnesses and gives a thumbs up to an invisible operator somewhere overhead.

"Ready?" Ronan glances over, grinning.

"As I'll ever be." I smile back, and my heart's pounding—in the best way. Just like he described earlier.

But right now, there's nothing deep or philosophical about what I'm feeling. Just the joy of the wind rushing past, the sun on my skin, and my legs dangling 150 feet above the ground.

This is the most fun I've had since I started Immerscent. And it's crazy that it's Ronan making me feel this weightless.

Then we're moving, picking up speed, hurtling toward the first loop at an insane pace. I brace myself, adrenaline humming in my veins. The chain clanks us to the peak, and for a breathless second, the park falls away below us, leaving just steel and endless blue sky.

Then gravity kicks in.

We plummet, whip into the first loop, and I let out a scream that rips from somewhere in my gut. Beside me, Ronan's harness jerks tight, and the sound that escapes him is…

Not a roar.

Not a grunt.

But a high-pitched, startled shriek. A castrato's discordant G6.

My own cry cuts off mid-loop. I twist toward him, stunned, and then I'm howling with ugly, gleeful, shoulder-shaking laughter.

He glances over, wide-eyed and wind-mussed, muttering something I can't hear over the roar of the track.

But his ears are definitely pink.

By the time we get off the ride, we're both in shambles. Whatever ribbing I was about to give Ronan dies when I nearly throw up on the last corkscrew loop.

We're giggling like teenagers. The release is exhilarating—almost innocent in its purity. I'm still snorting as Ronan gallantly offers me his arm while we make our way down the ramp. I think back to how nervous I was before, and I'm glad I didn't bail.

I glance up at him from beneath my lashes. I have the ridiculous urge to slip my hand into his again. But that way lies peril. *His girl* territory, not the safe boundaries of a client.

My fingers twitch, curling reflexively at my side.

Ronan beats me to it.

A jolt—no, an electric current—sparks through me as he threads our fingers together. I startle, caught in his snare. He's looking down at me with the softest expression, the gentlest smile.

"That was fun, wasn't it?" he rumbles.

Heat is pooling, spiralling, settling low in my belly.

"Ronan," I whisper. "What's happening between us?"

Ronan's fingers tighten. He pulls me fully into him, until his body is flush with mine. "Thandi, I—"

"Vanilla cones, two for five! Cream straight from Lancaster cows!"

A combination bicycle and ice cream cart lurches to a stop beside us, its driver ringing the bell like an overeager acolyte. The vendor is already flipping open the lid on a tub of creamy ice cream.

"Two for five!" he crows. "Your choice of Captain Funnel Cake or Rina Pop Rocket sprinkles!"

I don't hear the rest.

My breath stutters. I'm suddenly fighting for air, strangled by the oppressive sweetness of vanilla, sugar, and warm waffle cone.

The world begins to blur.

No.

Not now.

Not here.

But, my body is already reacting: skin prickling, vision narrowing to a hazy shimmer; stomach churning with the nausea I've come to dread.

Panic blooms, and just before the dizziness overtakes me, one thought breaks through my fog.

It's happening again.

Come Clean
Thandi

Well, at least I didn't faint this time.

It was close, though.

Thanks to Ronan's quick thinking, we're sitting on a bench, in a shady green space removed from the worst of Sugar Hill's madness. Well, Ronan is sitting, and I'm slumped against him, leaning on his strength.

Again.

I remember the violence of his reaction—his barked, *"Get the fuck out of here,"* at the poor, confused ice cream vendor, then the ground shifting beneath me as he whisked me away.

Now, I'm pulled tight against his side. I'm too weak to look up at him, but just based on the tension radiating from his arm curled around me, I suspect his face is set, his jaw clenched.

My shallow breathing is evening out, but my brain still feels like it's stuffed with cotton. Irritation follows swiftly on its heels. Vanilla ice cream may trigger me, but I'm not some fragile flower wilting at the slightest gust, and I hate that Ronan is forming that impression of me. Once I knew we were spending the day in the park, I should have been more vigilant. But somewhere between that candy-apple red gate and here, I lost my head.

The moment I try to shift, Ronan's arm tightens. The world has stopped careening enough for me to meet his gaze at last. His brows are lowered, and his lips are pressed into a worried line.

"How do you feel? Should we go to the medical bay?"

"No, I'm okay. This will pass in a few minutes," I say, raising a hand to my throbbing temples.

"Thandi…"

I know what's coming, what he's going to ask.

"Yes?" I sigh.

"This is what happened on Wednesday, isn't it?" The question is quiet, but it lands like a hammer. "The reason you said the ice cream wasn't an experiment."

I nod, unable to speak. Besides, I'm shattered in so many ways that I've given up any illusion of pretense. Physically, I'm exhausted from the endless cycle of trigger and failure. Emotionally, my soul will never recover from losing the most precious person in my life.

The weight of Tess' kidnapping has been heavy for so long, but I manage, usually through discipline and careful planning. No revisiting Anchor Park, where Tess disappeared, and always doing a scan of new environments to orient myself. That often means arriving a bit earlier than everyone else, and building in contingency plans in case I need medical help.

Lately, though, it feels like I'm increasingly failing in my responsibility to Tess, and this silly incident is just one more proof point of how much further I need to go to be worthy of my sister's memory.

But of course, Ronan doesn't know that. He couldn't have known any of it when he planned our meeting. I was careless, and now this outing, this rare moment of joy, is ruined.

And I have no one to blame but myself.

By now, my throat is aching, and I'm blinking back tears. I turn away, hands shaking, shoulders heaving under the effort of control. I can count on one hand the number of people who know about my reaction to vanilla ice cream and its connection to Tess: my ex, Micah, Dani, Fia, and, of course, my parents.

I never intended Ronan to be one of them.

God, I'm such an idiot. I need to escape, to go home. I can't make a fool of myself by crying here. I struggle in Ronan's arms, but he holds me fast.

"Shh, what's going on? Where are you going?"

"Let me go. Please, I can't—" I start to insist, but to my horror, my face crumples and tears burst forth despite my efforts. "Oh, god," I sob.

Is there no end to my humiliation?

"Thandi!" Ronan's voice is urgent. His hands are on my shoulders, then he's cupping my face, his large thumbs wiping away my tears.

I hate this. Hate that I still haven't figured it out after two decades. I close my eyes and try to suppress the pain ripping through me.

"Come on, Pink," Ronan growls. "Talk to me."

But I can't. Not for what feels like an eternity. Maybe it's stress, or the pressure of the IPO, but a dam has collapsed, and I can't stop the rain of tears.

So Ronan simply holds me, offering comforting words until I'm quiet. When the worst of the storm has subsided, he reaches into his back pocket and presses a handkerchief into my palm. My composure is already hanging on by a thread, and for some reason, that little detail threatens to pitch me over the edge.

It's such a quaint gesture; a gallant act of care, that I'm left floundering. Who still carries a handkerchief in the 21st century? Ronan's is sharply pressed with a crisp blue border, and it smells just like his cologne. There are even tiny initials cross-stitched into one corner of the fine linen-cotton blend.

It feels like a crime to ruin something so pristine, but there's nothing I can do about it now. I dab my eyes, then blow my nose, crumpling the cloth in my fist.

"Thank you," I mumble.

"Better?" Ronan asks, rubbing my back.

I nod, even though a few more frustrated tears escape me before I can stop them.

"Pink?" I finally demand with a sniffle.

Ronan smiles. "Because of your hair."

"Oh."

I'm unsure how to feel about the fact that he has a nickname for me. Nickname or pet name? My traitorous heart dares to ask, even through the chaos of my emotions. I'm seriously such a fucking mess.

Next to me, Ronan is quiet, patient. He won't push, but I know it's too late to turn back. Not after he's saved me twice in one week.

I stare at the crowds beyond our green little boundary. At the mascots committed to projecting joy no matter what, the couples walking past with linked hands, and the tight-knit families buzzing with excitement.

A little unit with two dads and two girls under the age of seven walks past. Their voices carry over to us, revealing plans to ride the Churro Tower of Chaos and for dinner at Chuck E Cheese's. The two girls link arms and skip ahead, and I pray for their sakes that they always remain whole.

"I'm a twin. *Was* a twin," I say. I'm staring at my hands, because it's easier to tell it if I'm not looking at him.

"When I was eight years old, my sister was kidnapped in Anchor Park while getting us ice cream. The smell of vanilla waffle cones has triggered a psychosomatic reaction in me ever since."

There. *Psychosomatic* puts a neat bow on it. Inserts clinical distance between me and what is in reality an all-consuming emotional and physical siege.

"Oh, Thandi." Ronan gasps as if the wind has been knocked out of him. His voice is low and rough. "I'm so sorry. I never would have brought you here if I'd known."

Both of his arms come around me, and he pulls me fully into his chest. I don't fight it, pressing my cheek against the warmth of his shirt, letting the steady thump of his heart anchor me.

"It's my fault. I should have paid more attention," I whisper.

"How can you think that? God—" Ronan cradles the back of my head. "You don't have to say anything else. Just know that I'm here. I'll always be here."

How does he do this? How does he keep showing up in ways that make me feel more seen than I have in years? I'm crying again, but the tension in my shoulders eases a bit.

"I tried to stop him," I blurt. "I even ran after them into the woods... And then, I can't remember the rest." I lift my empty hands, as if the memory is slipping through them yet again.

"Oh, sweetheart. You lost your memory of that day?"

I nod, sobbing harder now. "I failed her, and now matter how hard I try, no matter how many formulas I develop, I can't fix it."

"Thandi, look at me," Ronan says fiercely. "You haven't failed anyone. You were a child, bravely facing an evil no one should ever have to confront. It could have broken you, made you lose all faith in humanity. Yet, you chose to become the brilliant, kind, and resilient woman that you are today instead. Your sister would be so proud of you."

I stare, rendered speechless by his vehemence. It's strange, but the way he says it, I almost believe him.

Ronan raises a brow as if daring me to contradict him.

"Thank you," I say softly. "For everything."

I'm so tired, wrung out from all the emotions, yet I *am* grateful for Ronan's presence. For his unfailing kindness.

"So what now?" I ask. I'm guessing our time at Sugar Hill is over.

"Now, we face this as a team," Ronan declares. It's the last thing I expect him to say.

"As a team?" I stutter.

"Yes ... I need to confess something." Ronan captures me in his gaze. There's a softness in his eyes, a yearning I've seen before but was afraid to acknowledge. "Thandi, this isn't just business to me."

My breath catches. "It isn't?"

"No. Of course, the IPO matters—and trust me, we're going to kill it. I was serious about what I said earlier," Ronan vows, taking my hand. "But it's more than that. I like you, Thandi. Really like you. And now that I know about your past, I want to help you recover your memories."

"I…" My heart is beating so hard, so fast, I can hear the blood pounding in my ears. This electric current between me and Ronan has been sparking from the moment we met, but somehow, hearing him confess his feelings changes everything.

All my life, Tess has been my paradox—my north star and my secret shame. I never thought to ask for help. Of course, every day, Immerscent is on the front lines, breaking down the barrier of memory, but my team doesn't know my torment. That has always been my unique burden to bear.

And in just a week, Ronan has shown me that it might not have to be that way. I've been guarding my heart, sitting off to the side—shoring up my defenses brick by careful brick. But Ronan's leaping off the swing, somersaulting straight into the terror of love, grabbing life by both hands.

Just like Tess.

And just like her, he's forcing me to change, forcing me to catch up to him. I'm stunned by how much relief there is in leaning on someone. How much tenderness lives in the simple act of naming my fears—and not being judged for them.

I can't deny this fire anymore.

"Yes," I whisper, my fingers tightening around his. "I want this too."

"Thandi," Ronan breathes. He leans closer until his face is inches from mine, his warm breath caressing my skin. His eyes are the most beautiful that I have ever seen—imperial topaz lit with all the warmth of sunlight. He leans in further, and my heart beats faster, every sense heightened with anticipation, with a scorching realization of the inevitable. We've been tumbling into this moment from the very beginning.

Ronan's lips brush mine, and just like that, I choose to let him in.

His kiss is so soft, so sweet, a masterclass in hunger and restraint. And beneath that, something hot and sinful. Shameless. Selfish in exactly the way I need it to be. Every trace of my earlier disorientation flees as I'm swept up in a different tide, a gentle, all-consuming fire.

My lips are tingling. I'm melting, my entire being dissolving into the warmth of his touch. Ronan licks along my bottom lip, coaxing me to open up, to let him in. I do, my mouth parting to allow him access. I should care that we're in public, that anyone can see us, but none of that matters when his tongue slides against mine.

Moaning, I clutch him tight as I deepen the kiss. Our tongues tangle together, and it's like the entire world has come to a standstill. He tastes like minty gum, funnel cake, and the lure of freedom. I'm lost in the sensation of his mouth on mine, and I only want more and more and more.

Ronan cradles my face, even as a rough, urgent sound escapes him. His fingers trace the contours of my cheekbones, and the hand at the back of my head slides to my neck—tender, but possessive. I shiver, instinctively tilting my head back, baring the column of my throat as I imagine all the ways he might steal my breath.

"Jesus, Thandi," Ronan wrenches away with a gasp. His hands are trembling as he pulls me against him, and this time, the pounding of his heart matches the frantic rhythm of mine. The world is more alive than it was a minute ago, like Ronan's kiss chased all sorrow's sepia tones away.

He's staring at me, and we're both panting, with heat, with hunger.

Ronan's lips are swollen, flushed, and I realize that my first taste was not enough. May never be enough. I want to bite his bottom lip. Trace the curve of his cupid's bow with my tongue. Just like in my dreams.

He's awakened the beast in me. Not the Thandi who carries the guilt of being the wrong survivor. But the one who storms into boardrooms.

The one who refused to be told no when investors couldn't see what Immerscent would become. The one who doesn't focus on what she's lost but on what she's *owed*.

The one who only plays to win.

She's alive now, and she's ravenous.

"Fuck it," I mutter, and drag Ronan back to me.

Barbie
Thandi

"What do you think?" I ask Dani. "The white or the pink?"

We're at my condo, and Dani is helping me choose what I'm going to wear to the donor event that Fia and I are hosting. I need to strike the right tone. Tonight isn't just about Dad's art. It's also about a room full of people who could be Immerscent investors. With the IPO looming, I can't afford to leave anything on the table.

"Hm," Dani looks up from her phone. "Let's see the pink one again."

I slip on the sleeveless tailored pant set, the delicate hue of cherry blossoms. The jacket's structured cut tucks in elegantly at the waist, complementing the sleek, fitted trousers. It's polished. It's versatile. And yet....

"Too much?" I ask. "With my hair, I don't want to look like Barbie."

"Fair." Dani grins. "Let's strike it from the list."

I laugh. With her subdued wardrobe palette and no-nonsense attitude, I'm not surprised she's ready to move on the second I voice doubt.

"Okay, white dress it is. Help me with the zipper?"

I pull on a flowy, halter-style dress that's giving "hostess" and a little Marilyn Monroe.

Dani tugs the zipper, then steps back. "That's it. You look incredible."

"Thanks," I murmur, meeting my own eyes in the mirror. She's right. The white is luminous against my skin, pulling my hair into sharp relief. Pointed pumps in the exact shade of my fade pull it all together—a nod to Barbie without becoming her. My legs look damn good, too.

Unbidden, my mind wanders to Ronan.

We haven't seen each other since our kiss at the park two weeks ago because we've both been traveling for work. I was off to San Diego for a research conference, and Ronan flew to Tokyo to strategize with a reclusive, high-maintenance client.

The distance, however, has done nothing to dim the memory of that afternoon. I can still feel his heat, his strength—the way his stubble rasped against my skin, even as his lips lit a fire in me that I still can't quench.

It doesn't help that Ronan has been checking in every day despite the thirteen-hour time difference—two calls and a volley of texts that range from mundane to teasing to disarmingly sweet.

Unable to help myself, I pull out my phone and scroll through them again:

Have you eaten?

Can't stop thinking about you.

Is red bean paste safe for mice?

Beneath that, timestamped a few hours later, is a photo of Ronan grinning like he's just conquered Mount Fuji. In one hand, he's holding a packet of kabocha seeds and freeze-dried fruit bits. In the other, a tiny indigo-and-white yukata for ISO.

Mission accomplished, the caption reads.

Idiot. I'm smiling before I can catch myself. I can almost hear the satisfaction in his voice. But his most recent message, sent just after he landed this morning, is the reason I can't stop thinking about him:

I missed you.

I stare at those three simple words, and my hands are shaking so much I have to put my phone down. My heart, meanwhile, is doing a traitorous little tap dance.

We haven't defined what this is, but one thing is clear: Once a door is open, nothing will stop Ronan from hurtling through it. He's open with his feelings in a way that's both a little arrogant and surprisingly guileless. It's there in his grinning selfies, in the unfiltered declarations, in the ease of a man who is very much aware of his charms. And beneath that—the rich little boy who's lived in the world's acceptance and protection.

I can't fault him for it. Not after the care he's shown me. Still, it's going to take me a little longer to jump off the deep end.

"Everything okay?" Dani asks, and I realize I've been quiet for too long.

I sigh. One kiss, and already I'm losing my head. "Yeah. Sorry, just checking messages. Looks like Ronan should still make it tonight."

I wince as soon as the words slip out. I didn't mean to reveal how much he's been on my mind.

Dani raises a brow. "Since when do we care about Ronan Thorne's schedule?"

"I mean, I don't," I stammer. "I was just thinking—"

"Are you blushing?"

"Of course not."

"Are you two fucking?"

"Dani!" I gasp.

Now I'm warm for reasons that have nothing to do with embarrassment, as my mind joins in my heart's betrayal and supplies me with a vision of me and Ronan in flagrante delicto.

Dani only seems amused.

"Thandi, that man was cradling you like a Fabergé egg when you fainted," she says, folding her arms. "And he wouldn't let anyone else take you away. You're telling me that's just business?"

"It was. We're not—" I press my hand to the bridge of my nose. "Okay, we kissed."

Dani smirks. "I knew it! When did *that* happen? Also, I thought you hated him."

"I've … revised my assessment," I say, searching for the right words. "I wondered how he and Fia could be friends, but now I see it. He's more thoughtful than he looks. Kinder, too," I finish softly.

"And the kiss?"

"That happened at the Sugar Hill Park consultation." I busy myself putting away the other outfits I haven't chosen. "I didn't mean for it to happen. But it just did."

"So you like him," she says, and it's a statement, not a question.

Sighing, I meet Dani's eyes again. "I do."

"Well, you're both consenting adults. Ronan is a bit of a wild card, but maybe that's good for you."

"What do you mean?" I demand, crossing my arms over my chest.

"Don't act like you don't know what I'm talking about. When was the last time you were on a date?"

"I've been busy," I mutter.

Dani's gaze is sharp. "That's exactly my point. I love you, Thandi, but everything in your life revolves around Immerscent or the youth center. That's very noble, but what in all of this is just for you?"

"The company and the youth center *are* for me."

"Thandi…" Dani's voice is kind. "I worry about you. You take on too much. If you're not careful, you'll burn out."

Nodding, I bite my lip. What can I say to that? She's not wrong, and yet stopping is not an option. Will never be an option until I do right by Tess.

"Anyway," Dani says brightly, picking up her handbag and ushering us out the door. "If it takes someone as bullheaded as Ronan Thorne to draw you out, then I'm all for it."

Of course, Fia's home is as elegant as she is. The decor's palette is soft, with muted tones of ivory, taupe, and ash accented by warm wood. All around the house, fresh flowers punctuate the space with vibrant bursts of color.

Fia wheels up to me in a sleek red sheath dress. Her curls have been pulled into an elegant chignon that emphasizes her luminous eyes and amazing cheekbones.

"You look amazing!" she says, and we hug. "I'm so glad we're doing this together."

"So do you." I grin. "That red dress needs to find its way into my closet after the party."

Fia winks. "It's yours if we double our money tonight."

I laugh, as energized by a challenge as she is. "Don't complain when I come to collect."

"Girl, if we pull that off, I'll put it on you myself."

I give her another squeeze. "Thanks for doing this with me. The space is incredible."

And it is. The room feels both expansive and intimate. Pale oak beams span the vaulted ceiling, their warmth mirrored in the built-in shelves flanking a limestone fireplace. Low, plush seating in sun-warmed neutrals invites lingering, while floor-to-ceiling glass doors dissolve the barrier between indoors and out.

Beyond them, the branches of an old oak sway lazily, sunlight spilling through its leaves in restless, dappled shapes across the floor. Even with the soft undercurrent of staff voices drifting around us, there's a stillness here, a curated calm that feels both intentional and natural.

A young man in a crisp navy jacket approaches, clipboard in hand. "Pardon the interruption, Ms. Beltrán Zamora, but the chef would like a word."

"Of course." Fia nods. "Sorry, Thandi. I'll only be a minute."

I wave her off. "Go ahead. I should probably run through my speech again and figure out where Dani disappeared to." I lost track of my head of communications right after her wife, Evelyn, arrived.

As Fia leaves, I watch the jazz quartet setting up. The technician murmurs, testing audio levels, and the lead singer, a voluptuous, almond-skinned woman with a glorious Afro, leans into the mic and lets a few honeyed notes unfurl into the air.

It's all so lovely, so thoughtful, that I pause to draw a breath. To center myself. To take in the stillness while it lasts. In a few minutes, the first guests will arrive, and I doubt I'll get another moment like this all night.

My phone buzzes.

I pick it up to see a text from Ronan:

On my way. Looking forward to seeing you this evening.

Of course, my heart is thumping again, and a chorus of butterflies flutters in my stomach.

Me too, I reply, and slip the phone back into my clutch.

So much for that zen feeling.

"Peanut, you look stunning."

I turn to see my parents crossing the room. Dad has set aside his usual Bohemian riot of color for a black silk shirt and tailored trousers. His salt-and-pepper locs have been freshly twisted into an intricate basket weave over his shoulder. He looks striking, distinguished, every bit the celebrated artist.

Beside him, Mom is luminous in a flowy robin's egg blue dress.

I hug them both. "Forget about me, you two look stunning. We've had a lot of interest from some high-profile collectors. I think it's going to be a great night."

Mom scans the room, her eyes warm with appreciation. "This is all so lovely. You guys have outdone yourselves."

"You always make us so proud, Peanut." Dad kisses my cheek. "Where's Fia? I need to thank her, too."

"She's with the chef. I just—"

"Pink."

I freeze. My thoughts scatter. I don't have to look behind me to know who's speaking. The deep voice, the magnetic heat, the masculine scent that's becoming increasingly familiar—I know them all in a heartbeat because already, Ronan is tattooed on my senses.

Pink.

It's a silly nickname, the least romantic thing ever. I don't know why he's using it in public, or in front of my parents. But the way it rolls off his tongue—low, certain, almost possessive—sends a shiver through me.

I should be irritated, but I'm not.

Instead, it feels like Ronan has just thrown me over his shoulder, Tarzan-style, and yelled, "mine" for all the world to hear.

And since when do I find *that* sexy?

"Ronan." I turn to face him, my heart thudding in my chest.

His hair is pulled back, and as usual, a faint shadow of stubble darkens his jaw. He's wearing a black suit without the tie, and his crisp white shirt is unbuttoned to reveal a wedge of muscled chest. The elegant lines of the jacket do nothing to soften the breadth of his shoulders or the quiet power in the way he moves.

Civilized on the surface. Something far less tame underneath.

Only his eyes give him away.

Golden. Molten. They sweep over my face, then linger over my dress.

"You are beautiful," he says, leaning in to brush his lips against my cheek. The kiss is light, chaste, but I feel it all the way to my toes.

Not, "you look nice," or "your dress is beautiful."

You are beautiful.

The words alone are a caress, a slow stroke of heat along my skin. Desire sparks and smolders. I stare up at Ronan, and I can't seem to catch my breath.

"I—"

My father clears his throat.

I spin to face him and Mom, my face hot with embarrassment. *God.* What am I doing?

"Ronan," I say hoarsely, "These are my parents, Iris and Asa Elowen. Dad goes by Winston, though. He's our guest of honor tonight."

Am I babbling? I'm definitely babbling. Ugh. I press a hand to my forehead.

"Ronan Thorne. A pleasure." Unlike me, Ronan is smooth as he steps forward to shake my parents' hands.

"Ronan and I are working together on the IPO launch," I add quickly. "Trent introduced us."

"Thorne…" Mom murmurs, staring at Ronan. She tilts her head. "Forgive me, by any chance, are you related to the late Dr. Rosalind Thorne?"

Ronan's eyes widen. He stiffens, and a shadow flits across his features. "Yes, she was my mother. Did you know her?"

"I thought so. The resemblance is striking. Your eyes, your hair—" Mom stops herself, shaking her head. "We worked together many years ago. That was very early in our careers at Smith Laboratories. It feels like yesterday and a lifetime ago."

"Mom's a neuroscientist," I tell Ronan.

He nods, and for a moment, something crumples at the edges of his expression. There's a softness there, and beneath it, something raw enough to make me want to step closer. The sadness I've sensed in him suddenly has a shape, a name.

Without thinking, I slip my hand into his and give it an encouraging squeeze.

He startles, then meets my gaze. Something quiet passes between us. Gratitude, recognition, and shared understanding of the weight of loss. His fingers tighten around mine.

"You and Mom worked together?" he asks my mother softly.

Mom nods. "We did some early work together on neural pathways and scent. Even published research on it."

She turns to me. "Remember when you came over to help us with the garage? I told you the name was familiar. I just couldn't place it. Now that I see Ronan, it all makes sense."

"Yeah," I murmur, still reeling from the fact that my mother and Ronan's were connected at all.

Beside me, Ronan's brows lift. Slowly, the shadow in his expression dissolves, replaced by a grin that builds with each passing second. He tugs on our conjoined hands, drawing me closer to his side.

"What?" I huff.

"You talked to your parents about me?"

I wince as I think about that conversation. Talked to them about him? More like ranted. "It wasn't like that…" I begin.

"You made an impression, that's for sure," Dad declares. Now he's grinning, too. Just like that weekend when I first mentioned Ronan.

Dad steps forward. "Son, why don't you join us for dinner this Sunday?"

What? What is he doing?

"Dad," I say quickly, "I'm sure Ronan doesn't have time—"

"I'd love to." Ronan interrupts. "When should I be there?"

"How about seven? Iris, does that work?"

"That sounds perfect," Mom replies.

She's smiling, Dad's beaming, and Ronan, the most incorrigible of them all, has a wickedly gleeful glint in his eye.

God, I'm in so much trouble.

Chicken Tikka Masala
Thandi

Now that the guests are arriving in a steady stream, I leave Ronan and my parents to join Fia in the greeting line.

We'd budgeted for a few last-minute cancellations, but so far, there's been no drop-off.

"This is an amazing turnout," I say after welcoming Clara Yuen and two venture capitalists. "Will we be okay with catering and space? This is definitely more than we expected."

"We'll be fine," Fia says, smiling like she knew this would happen. "Your dad's early works rarely hit the market, so it's not so surprising. Catering can handle twice our number, and we've got the overflow room ready."

"Of course, you thought of everything," I tease, but I am grateful. I really couldn't have done this without her.

"Anytime," Fia grins. "We make a good team."

"We do." I squeeze her shoulder. Studying her elegant profile, I marvel at how, with the right people at your side, everything feels lighter.

And speaking of the *wrong* people, I frown as Amber sashays up the walkway, clinging to an older man's arm.

"Incoming," I mutter. "How on earth did she get on the guest list?"

"She's not. Not directly, anyway," Fia counters. "Looks like she's Fowler's plus one."

"The old money banker?"

"The very same."

"At least she didn't drag a camera crew behind her," I say with a huff.

"Yeah, but damn," Fia whistles under her breath. "Gotta hand it to old girl. Already scouting new opportunities now that you've taken Ronan off the market."

"I haven't taken him off anything," I immediately protest.

Fia just gives me a look.

I can't mount my defense because Fia and I have just enough time to plaster smiles on our faces as Johnson Fowler and Amber step up.

"Mr. Fowler," I say, offering my hand. "I'm Thandi Elowen. Fia's told me such wonderful things." I nod at Amber. "Amber, good to see you again."

"Oh, Fia's always far too kind. And please, call me John." Fowler's grip is warm. He bends to kiss Fia on the cheek. With his ruddy cheeks and white beard, he could pass for Santa Claus—if Santa traded velvet for business casual.

Fia laughs. "That's not what you said after the Falworth merger, but I'll take it."

He chuckles, rubbing his chin. "Elowen," he repeats. "Not the same Elowen behind Immerscent, the scent technology firm?"

"That's right."

Beside him, Amber's eyes go so wide it's almost comical. "*You're* the billionaire behind Immerscent?" she spits the question out like an accusation.

"The very same," I say brightly. I'd bet every one of ISO's mango treats that she assumed I was Fia's assistant.

"But … that's not possible," she mutters, brows knitting together.

John shoots her a puzzled glance before turning back to me. "Well, my dear, it's truly an honor. I hope we can spend a few minutes this evening discussing your IPO. I'm *very* interested."

"Of course, John. Why don't we connect at the first break?"

"Excellent." Fowler heads inside, dragging a miffed Amber along.

I shake my head, watching their retreat. "Goodness, that woman is insufferable."

"*But that's not possible,*" Fia mimics Amber in a snooty voice. She reaches over and hooks her arm in mine. At this distance, our eyes are level—close enough that I can see the spark of mischief in hers. God, I love this woman.

She's petty and wicked in the very best way, and I can't help leaning into her with a snicker.

In the pause between the next wave of guests, we share a hearty laugh, heads leaning together, until it's time to be serious all over again.

"And thank you to all of you for supporting the arts," I finish my speech. "And, now, for the man of the hour. Dad, over to you."

A roar of applause and cheers swells as Dad takes the proverbial stage. We hug before I release him to slip in among the guests.

I'm so proud as he begins explaining the origin of each sculpture in the exhibit and its significance. It never gets old, watching him in action. He's an amazing public speaker, and there's something magical about seeing my quirky, absentminded dad transform into this charismatic powerhouse. You can hear a pin drop as the room leans on his every word.

He's wrapping up and raising a glass now. "At the end of the day, the reason I do this is simple. It's thanks to Thandi, my daughter and my greatest gift. She reminds me every day that the most important thing we can do is be kind to each other—and pay it forward for the next generation." Dad's eyes meet mine over the crowd. "I love you, Peanut."

Damn it, now, why'd he have to go and make me cry? Sniffling, I fish through my clutch for some tissue, and curse when I come up empty-handed.

"Here."

I look up to see a familiar blue and white handkerchief.

Ronan grins. "We've got to stop doing this."

"Thanks." I take the handkerchief and dab my nose. "Why do you have one of these anyway?" I mumble into the cloth.

Ronan's smile is a little sad. "My mother always said it was the hallmark of a true gentleman."

That bittersweet look stirs an ache deep within my chest. I reach out to touch his arm. "Well, you're doing her proud."

Ronan takes my hand and kisses my fingers. "Thank you, Pink."

Silence settles between us, warm with the tenderness of something still unfolding.

"Thanks for inviting me," he says after a moment. "I'm glad I could make it. For a minute, I wasn't sure. Koichi was playing hardball at the last minute."

"Oh?"

"He owns one of the most pioneering distilleries in Japan. He's about to launch a new blend, and we disagreed on the length of my contract."

"He wanted to shorten it?"

"Lengthen it. He's nervous about first-quarter earnings and wants room to pivot."

I smile. "Well, at least you're in demand?"

Ronan shakes his head. "It's been too long. This is where I need to be. Plus, you and Fia hosting something together? I wouldn't miss this for the world," he says, his eyes soft on mine.

His hand finds the back of my neck, thumb stroking lazily. My mind jumps to our kiss in the park and how his fingers rasped against my pulse then. The neck seems to be his thing. Unfortunately for me, it's also mine, and I shiver, my body flooding with warmth and hazy pleasure.

"Ronan," I say shakily. "You can't—"

"Can't what, baby?" His fingers tip my chin up until I'm looking straight into his eyes.

Baby? My heart stutters. Ronan, the consultant, is intense, but Ronan, the potential boyfriend, is a force of nature. Powerful, inexorable, and single-minded in his attention.

His fingers haven't stopped moving, and I'm not even sure he realizes he's caressing me. Touch seems to be his hallmark. A reflex that has sparks igniting all over my skin and gathering to a conflagration between my thighs.

I make a soft sound and begin pulling away.

"You okay? You're not feeling faint, are you?" Ronan's voice is pitched low, so no one discovers my secret.

I appreciate the concern, but he's missing the point entirely. Now his other hand has settled at my waist, anchoring me against his chest. It's too much. Too intimate. And far too public.

Besides, every time he touches me, I lose my head.

"Ronan, I—"

Something jolts me sideways, breaking Ronan's hold. My heel skids backwards as someone wedges between us with too much force to be an accident.

"Oh—sorry," Amber gasps, her voice syrupy with mock innocence. Her shoulder clips mine as she twists just enough to force me off balance.

I scramble backward, fighting to keep from going down on Fia's polished hardwood.

But Amber's not done with me yet.

She tips her hand, and the bright orange sauce from her chicken tikka masala skewer arcs through the air—

And lands squarely across the front of my white dress.

An audible gasp ripples through the crowd, just as Ronan leaps forward and grabs my arm, preventing me from adding injury to my humiliation.

"Amber, what the fuck do you think you're doing?" he growls. His fury is so palpable, even I'm shocked into silence.

Whatever Amber intended, this is not the reaction she was expecting.

"What? Ronan, honey, surely our connection is stronger than this." She punctuates "this" with a derisive nod in my direction.

"There is no connection between us—and there never will be." Ronan's voice is ice. "Your behavior is disgusting."

"But—" Amber's lip quivers, eyes glistening with crocodile tears.

There's a commotion as Fia and Dani push through the crowd. God, now we're making a scene.

"Thandi!" Fia's eyes widen as she takes in my dress. "What happened?"

"We all saw it," Clara Yuen calls from a few feet away. "She shoved Thandi." A few guests nod grimly, and I catch one woman rubbing her shoulder in unconscious sympathy.

"And that sauce spill was no accident," adds one of the venture capitalists I'd greeted earlier, his tone clipped.

Another ripple of murmurs surges through the guests. When I glance up, the event photographer—an intrepid journalist moonlighting for us tonight—already has her camera up, firing frame after frame.

John Fowler appears in the gap between two onlookers. His expression, when it lands on Amber, is more effective than any reprimand. Shaking his head, he simply turns and strides toward the far end of the bar, leaving her standing alone.

"Alright," Fia says, with an authority that brooks no argument. "Amber, I'm going to have to ask you to leave."

Amber's gaze darts between the shrinking space where John vanished, the cluster of people watching, and the relentless snap of the camera shutter. Then, cheeks blotched with crimson, she pivots on her heel and stalks toward the door.

My breath is tight, my skin hot under the scrutiny of too many curious eyes. I can feel the sauce drying against my dress, and I can just imagine what it looks like—an exclamation point of humiliation.

While attention is still trained on Amber's retreat, I slip away from Ronan, weaving through the crowd,

"Thandi!" Ronan calls after me.

But I keep moving, the sound of his voice chasing me as I disappear into the swell of strangers.

Right now, I just need space. Away from the mess, away from the stares, and the feelings I'm developing for the man who has rescued me yet again.

Marilyn Monroe
Ronan

I lose sight of her almost immediately.

Just like at the pickup game, Thandi moves fast—faster than I expected. And being half a foot shorter than most of the guests makes her damn near impossible to spot once she's in motion. The crowd swallows her whole, a blur of cocktail dresses and tailored suits converging in her wake.

I start with the kitchen, drawing startled glances from the catering staff as I push past stacks of canapé trays and rows of bubbling champagne flutes.

Nothing.

The library is next, quiet and shadowed, but that's a dead end.

Outside, the air is cooler, threaded with the mellow notes of the jazz quartet. A knot of guests has gathered under the patio string lights, swaying to the music. But Thandi isn't here either.

I grit my teeth and head back in.

"She'll be okay."

I turn to see Fia gliding up beside me, her hands resting lightly on her rims. Her expression is calm, but there is also a watchfulness in her gaze.

"I'm sure she just needs a minute to gather her thoughts."

I sigh, though it doesn't quite take the edge off. "Yeah, you're probably right," I say, scanning the crowd again, unwilling to let it go.

"I know you're worried," she adds, her tone softening, "but you already have her trust. Give her a little space. She'll come back to you."

Every protective instinct in me wants to ignore that. To keep searching until I see her with my own eyes. But this is Fia, and she's rarely wrong about people.

So I force myself to nod, bowing to her wisdom, even as worry and the lingering embers of rage at Amber burn in my chest.

I don't understand what she was thinking. We were never serious, and I've made it clear I'm not interested in anything other than friendship. The fact that she assumed attacking Thandi would somehow endear her to me drops her even further in my estimation.

As if she could ever hold a candle to Thandi.

I frown, scanning the crowd, desperate despite Fia's words, for a glimpse of a petite, pink-haired beauty in a pinup dress.

When I first saw her this evening, my heart stopped. There she was, with her warm eyes and gentle smile, mingling with guests, her white dress luminous against her skin.

My very own Marilyn Monroe.

Except more unique, more brilliant, and with none of the coquettish pretense. A true diamond in a sea of boring, predictable wealth.

No wonder Amber took one look at her and felt threatened.

"Roncito," Fia says warningly.

"What?" I grumble.

"You're doing it again. Relax; have a drink." She smirks. "Go charm her folks if you really want to lock things in."

My brows lift. Fia might be onto something. If I can't be at Thandi's side, I'll do the next best thing: make sure that when she comes back, the room is already buzzing in her favor. I know how much is riding on this for her.

If Thandi's taking her time, then when she walks back in, she'll do it to a crowd that's already half in love with her.

So I work the room, easing into conversations, buying a round at the bar for Johnson Fowler and two other heavy hitters Fia flagged earlier. I talk up Immerscent just enough to intrigue, dropping hints about a "major upcoming project" that I can't discuss. By the time we clink glasses, I've gotten three more IPO investors all but locked in—and a bladder reminding me how many drinks I've shared.

The downstairs powder room is occupied, with two guests already queued outside the heavy oak door. The two men are debating the merits of regional bourbons as if the fate of humanity hangs in the balance.

Chuckling, I head for the staircase.

The upstairs landing is blissfully clear of guests, the noise from downstairs fading into an indistinct hum.

Fia's primary bath has always been my fallback. I know the route by memory, each step soft on the plush runner leading to her suite.

My head is still half in work mode—replaying conversations, mentally drafting follow-ups, deciding who to loop in—when my hand closes around the cool brass knob.

I push the door open without thinking.

And freeze.

I stumble as the air is punched from my lungs.

The splash of running water hits my ears.

Thandi is at the face basin, furiously scrubbing the stain from her pretty dress.

But that's not the problem.

Thandi is in Fia's bathroom.

With her dress pooled around her waist.

Topless.

Her breasts are perfect—pert, and neither too lush nor too small for her slight frame. No, they're round and full, with sweet brown nipples that are just beginning to pucker from either the wet dress or the cool air from the vents above.

My immediate thought is how perfectly her breasts would fill my hands. Not enough to overflow them, but they're full enough that I could map them completely. I imagine myself running my thumbs over her nipples and the sound she would make.

A hot and possessive feeling rushes through me. I don't even remember what I came to the bathroom for. But I know I need to get out of here before I do something dumb.

"I'm sorry," I blurt, trying to kickstart my brain, struggling to get my body moving, now that the blood in my veins is flowing unerringly south.

Thandi looks up and gasps.

Shock and then deep mortification bloom over her features, like stages of the sunrise. Her hand hovers mid-scrub above her dress. Little bubbles of soap cling to her fingers.

I've never found the lime and verbena scent sexy before, but it's redefining itself as we speak. The fragrance fills the air in a cloud of freshness, which only seems to reinforce ideas about bathrooms, showering, and myriad delightful things I could do naked with Thandi.

Especially after that kiss in the park. Especially after the way she felt in my arms earlier.

I should go. Say something. *Do something.* But my body refuses to obey the commands that my brain is giving my limbs.

Thandi can't seem to move either.

Time freezes.

No, it doesn't stop.

It slows. Stretching and magnifying each passing second, as if they're infused with molasses.

My pulse is throbbing.

The running faucet is impossibly loud.

I feel drugged. Overwhelmed by Thandi's beauty.

It's not just her gorgeous breasts. It's her adorable heart-shaped face, those big brown eyes staring at me now in shock, the smooth skin of her shoulders, her taut stomach, the feminine dip of her waist.... Every part of her is a feast for the senses.

And every nerve in my body wants to reach for her, touch her, devour her.

Cherish her.

"Excuse me," I mutter, then lurch backwards, slamming the door behind me.

Jesus fucking Christ.

I'm so cooked.

Euphoria
Thandi

I just flashed Ronan.

The horror plays out in slow motion. Almost like I'm watching from a distance, I see Ronan freeze. His eyes widen. He inhales sharply as his gaze drops to my breasts.

I want the ground to swallow me whole.

That doesn't happen.

I can't seem to move.

I'm aware that the stain is still on my dress, that the fabric is getting soggier and soggier under the rushing tap water, and is probably ruined. I'd only intended to flush the one spot.

I look up, and Ronan isn't even being a jerk. He seems as stunned and confused as I am when something snaps him into awareness. He mumbles and bids a hasty retreat out of the bathroom.

The door slams behind him with a thud.

It shakes me out of my stupor. I yank my dress up and tie the straps around my neck, grimacing at the cold, wet fabric against my skin.

When I was thinking about making an impression on Ronan with my dress, this is *not* what I meant.

I can't go out there again. Not only is my dress ruined, but I'll need a minute before seeing Ronan again. I sink to my knees, hot with embarrassment. My heart is pounding. I'm so frustrated and humiliated that tears smart behind my eyelids.

This debacle is bad enough, but the worst part is the missed opportunity with the investors. I'm sure Dad is also wondering why I've disappeared. All because of Amber's petty nonsense.

I don't know how long I sit on Fia's bathroom floor, my arms wrapped around my knees, but just as I've scolded myself to get my act together, I hear a knock.

"Thandi?" Ronan's deep voice is muffled on the other side of the door.

I groan. *No, I don't want to face him yet.*

I shoot to my feet, panicked, even as I know I can't hide in here forever. I take a deep breath, notch my chin, and yank the door open. "Yes?"

Ronan makes a pained sound.

His eyes are glued to my chest, and I immediately see the problem.

My dress is on, but the white linen is now almost transparent. My dark, peaked nipples are visible, standing in sharp relief against the thin cloth. I've gone from flashing him to the equivalent of a wet t-shirt contest.

Squeezing my eyes shut, I cross my arms over myself.

"What do you need?" I say through gritted teeth.

"Here," he says gruffly. "Fia asked me to give you this. She would come up herself, but she didn't want to leave the guests."

"Of course," I mumble.

That's when I see the stunning cobalt dress he's holding. Fia's taller than me, but the sheath is made of a supple knit forgiving to any figure. As usual, she's thought of everything. The dress's plunging back means it has a built-in shelf bra. A relief, since I don't have one.

I sigh. Maybe the night isn't lost.

"Thank you," I croak, grasping the bundle with numb fingers. "Sorry for this mess. And now I've wasted so much time instead of supporting Dad and promoting the IPO."

"Thandi." Ronan's deep voice is exasperated. "Why are you apologizing for something that's not your fault? As for the investors, you're fine. I worked the room—hyped Immerscent up. Fowler is convinced, and Mathers and Adaku are almost there. I've got your back. Have some faith in me, please."

"Faith in you? Of course, I have faith in you, Ronan. That's not the issue." I point to my soiled outfit. "Tonight was important, and I just hate not being my best."

I'm so frustrated. I still don't understand how it turned out like this. I don't even know Amber. Not really. Besides, Ronan and I are so new that there's nothing to be jealous of yet. Closing my eyes, I take a deep breath, trying to find the calm I felt when I first walked in.

"Please thank Fia for the change of clothes. I'll be down in a minute," I say, once I've regained some composure. "If you could just help me with my zipper, I'll be out of your hair."

"Of course."

I turn, offering my back. It was easy to tug the closure halfway down to wash my bodice, but the narrowest part of the dress, just before the flare of the voluminous skirt, is the trickiest. It's what Dani helped me with earlier.

Ronan grips the zipper. He pulls for a moment before pausing.

"I don't have enough leverage. I'm afraid you'll have to untie the straps. May I?" He murmurs. His warm breath over my ear smells of mint and a hint of whiskey.

I nod, my throat too tight to answer. Holding up the bodice, I feel Ronan's fingers brush my shoulders as he loosens the halter. The straps slip free, whispering against my skin. I'm already out of sorts, but his nearness—the living heat of him at my back—only tangles my nerves further.

He reaches again for the zipper, his touch deft but careful.

Nothing happens.

The slider refuses to move. Ronan tries again, tugging more firmly, but the stubborn metal won't budge.

"It's stuck," he mutters, the words hot against the curve of my neck.

I groan. "Of course it is. Because tonight hasn't been humiliating enough already."

His low chuckle vibrates far too close to my skin. "Hold on. I think some fabric is caught in the teeth."

"It's probably the lining," I sigh, already resigned. "It always happens."

Ronan tests the slider, moving it down a fraction and up again. His knuckles skim my spine with each movement, leaving sparks in their wake. I suppress a whimper, praying for the zipper to cooperate.

"You're right," he says finally. "The lining's jammed."

"Well, can you—" My words cut off in a gasp as Ronan tugs harder, bracing one hand against my hip for leverage.

The zipper jerks an inch, then halts with a sharp pop of thread.

My eyes widen. That doesn't sound good. "Ronan, wait—"

But I'm too late. Ronan's already giving the zipper another pull.

"Just a little more…" he mutters with a forceful yank.

The awful sound of tearing fabric rips through the room.

I jerk, gasping as I lose my grip on the bodice.

"Shit, Thandi, I'm sorry, I—" Ronan's voice dies in his throat.

Our eyes meet in the mirror. His shocked gaze, my own wide and stricken—just as the ruined dress slips from my body and puddles in a heap at my feet.

I close my eyes, as I'm utterly exposed. Left in nothing but pink stilettos and my black underwear.

I'm stuck in some awful karmic loop.

That's it.

This must be my punishment for not doing enough for Tess. Or maybe some animal deity is exacting retribution because I refused to give ISO those new sweet potato treats he wanted. That can be the only reason my evening keeps spiraling into chaos.

"Please go," I whimper, my voice breaking as I jerk my arm up to cover my breasts. My eyes are still scrunched tight, humiliation burning through me.

For a heartbeat, the room is silent except for the thundering of my pulse. I assume Ronan is leaving.

But then he makes a ragged sound. And suddenly his arm is around my waist, dragging me back against him. My naked back is pressed to his chest, my hips nestled against the cradle of his body.

"Thandi…" he rasps.

The kiss he presses to my shoulder is feather-light, but it scorches me like a brand.

"Look at me, baby."

I hesitate, then let my eyes flutter open. My lips tremble at the sight before me.

Our shared reflection in Fia's vanity is decadent. Ronan is fully clothed, and I'm all but naked in my pink pumps. He's caressing my shoulders, and my breasts sway as he tucks me even more fiercely against him.

It's too much. I start to pull away, but he stops me with a tender hand on my shoulder. His other hand splays low on my stomach, as if he already knows about the heat blooming within me. Like he already knows that my womb is fluttering with the most intimate ache.

I make a distressed noise. "Ronan, *please.*"

"Stop." His fingers slip from my shoulder to trace the shadow of my spine. "You are far too beautiful to be ashamed of anything."

I don't know what to say. I stare at him in the mirror. The heat in his gaze is so scorching it takes my breath away, burning away the shame of exposure and transforming it into something else. My pulse pounds to a crescendo. It's so loud I'm shocked that I can still hear him.

When his mouth drops to my shoulder again, my nipples tighten.

"Thandi…" Ronan's hungry eyes miss nothing. A ravenous sound bubbles from his throat as his gaze settles on my breasts. "You're so gorgeous. Can I touch you, baby?"

This is—

I whimper, trembling. Heat floods my body, and I'm wet, so wet as Ronan watches me with his burning golden eyes, waiting for my answer.

"Yes," I exhale, and I don't care that it sounds desperate. Like I'm gasping, gagging on the promise of his touch.

Still, I jolt at the first brush of his fingers. He cups my breasts, bouncing them gently in his hands.

"You have no idea what you did to me when I saw you earlier. How long I've wanted to touch you like this."

He licks the whorls of my ear, and his teeth close on the round of my earlobe just as he starts kneading my breasts. He flicks his thumbs over my nipples, and I jerk, whimpering as an electric current sears through me. Ronan rolls my nipples between his fingers, then tugs them into aching points.

A ragged sound bursts from me as a live wire of sensation twangs between the sensitive buds. I writhe, my hands helplessly coming up to cover his.

"Ronan, I—"

"That's it, baby. I knew you'd be sensitive," he purrs as he keeps teasing and plucking, fingering the tender points of my nipples, shaping them upright.

My words disintegrate into a cry. I arch, heat flooding my body. My desire rushes forth, wetting my inner thighs.

Ronan growls. "God, you're so fucking beautiful. My sweet, sweet Pink. "

Each word is punctuated by a kiss. One ghosts across my back, another skims along my neck, and finally, Ronan tilts my head back and claims me. That's the only way to describe the savage plundering of my mouth that happens next.

Our tongues tangle, and his taste bursts across my senses. Fresh, sweet, and that boozy wildness that makes my head spin. The kiss is hot, dirty—the agile thrust of Ronan's tongue against mine mimicking what he can do elsewhere, where I already yearn so much.

He slides his hand down my body, and I gasp into his mouth. But he holds me fast, preventing me from breaking our kiss. My entire body shudders when he slips his hand into my panties.

"Fuck," Ronan groans, tearing his mouth away. "You're so wet, baby."

A long finger slips between my legs, gliding back and forth, luxuriating in my desire. "Is this all for me?"

I nod, my head lolling on his shoulder. I shout as Ronan's thumb brushes my clit. *"Ronan!"*

"That's it. Sing for me," he purrs, his arm tightening around my waist.

Ronan's free hand smooths over my belly, then dips to the side, following the curve of my hip. He hooks his fingers under the lacy band of my thong. A sharp twist, and the fabric gives way far too easily beneath his touch.

"Ronan," I choke as my panties flutter to the floor.

"Look how pretty you are," He murmurs, cupping me possessively. His hand envelops my pussy. I'm covered again, but in a very different way, now. I squirm, squeezing my thighs together as the ache between them grows to an all-consuming hunger.

"I'm … I…"

"I know. You feel so good. So soft, so wet. I can't wait to get inside," Ronan murmurs, and it sounds like both a promise and a threat.

Well, now I know Ronan is the type to talk you through it.

My cheeks heat at his sinful praise, even as I feel myself spilling all over his hand. I've never been aroused so quickly, and I haven't even touched him yet. My knees almost buckle when he pulls free long enough to lick my essence off his hand.

"You're delicious. I need more."

He circles me, dropping to his knees, making sure I can still see us in the mirror. He squeezes my left calf as he drapes it over his shoulder. The vanity reflects it to me—my hot pink pump dangling over his back, in a vision of utter debauchery.

I'm overwhelmed by the sight of us, by his touch between my legs. He holds me open with his thumbs, staring at me for a heated moment, before diving in and burying his nose against my clit.

"God, Ronan, that's—" I shudder.

"You smell so good, Thandi. And look at you, so damn pink and pretty everywhere. Just like your name."

"That's not my name." I blurt, shivering against him. My fingers tangle in his hair.

Ronan smiles wickedly against my thigh. "It is now."

His tongue is light as he first tastes me, but it quickly becomes more insistent. I moan as he suckles my labia and worries my clit with gentle suction, then with the careful nip of teeth. He's lapping over my entrance like a starving man, sipping all of my secrets. When he probes me with his tongue, I call out his name. He thrusts in deep, wet strokes, even as his thumb presses hard against my clit. The contrast between the soothing wetness of his tongue and the insistent pulse of his finger against my tender flesh rocks me to my core.

Ronan is insatiable, relentless. His hand keeps moving, finding me with uncanny precision. Pressure gathers and intensifies until the sensation rolls my eyes back in my head. My heart is beating between my legs, and I cling to his shoulders for support. My fingers fist in his hair, but the prickling pain only seems to egg him on.

I'm shocked at the violence of my need, at the intensity of his hands and mouth. Stunned at how quickly I'm tumbling towards the edge.

My entire body is trembling with pleasure. Wild, desperate sounds reach my ears, and I realize they're coming from me.

"That's it," Ronan breathes. "Let it happen. Come for me."

How could I do anything but obey? I shatter, my release dripping down my thighs as tremor after tremor seizes my body. My knee buckles, threatening collapse, but Ronan holds me up.

"*God, you're perfect.*"

Groaning, he licks a hot trail from my quivering core to my ass. When he slips a finger inside my still pulsing pussy. I make a keening sound—twisting, almost frantic, in his arms.

"Wait … Ronan, I can't. I'm too sensitive," I plead.

"Hmm?" he rumbles, almost petulant. "Fine."

Reluctantly, he pulls away. He rocks back on his heels, shooting me a sultry grin as he rises to his feet. He makes a show of licking each of his fingers before he captures my lips again.

His mouth slides down to the side of my neck. I feel the puff of his breath before his hot tongue licks across my skin, tracing the tendon that connects my shoulder to my ear. I'm trembling so much that I have to hold tight to his torso.

There's something I want.

Something I've been ashamed to ask any other lover. But somehow with Ronan, I know it's safe. Not only because he is kind, but because he's just a bit broken, like me. He'll understand; he won't judge me. I felt it in our kiss at Sugar Hill Park.

I grab his free hand and press it to my throat. "Please," I whisper.

Ronan freezes.

The world goes quiet.

So quiet I can hear my heart hammering.

Ronan's heavy breathing echoes between us.

He stares down at me, and I can see all the flecks in his eyes: honey, amber, and warm whiskey. His pupils are wide, dilated, almost as black as the darkness that chases me.

But I can't put this genie back in the bottle. Ronan closes the remaining space between us. He slides his large hand to my throat and tilts my head back.

I see it all in the mirror.

Then, without a word, he's bending to me, his lips brushing once, twice, like he's examining my flavor. He kisses my neck, applying a suction so hot, so sweet, that it forces me onto the tips of my toes. I'm gasping, straining against his living heat—arching into the mountain of his strength that's protecting me even now.

Cradling me in the crucible of a desire even I don't fully understand.

Ronan's fingers brush along my collarbone, tracing delicate patterns that make me shiver all over again. With every touch, he murmurs words of affirmation—whispers as tender as his embrace.

"You're so lovely," he breathes against my neck.

He's said it many times tonight, but the conviction, the sincerity in his voice, still sends a rush of pleasure through me. He makes me want to believe him. Makes me want to believe that I could be whole again.

Ronan circles my skin in slow arcs, as if he's writing syllables into my flesh—sigils of yearning just for me. His hand moves down, the heel of his palm resting along the hollow of my throat.

My breath speeds up. The ache inside me is deep, wet, and full of longing. I throw my head back.

Offering him everything.

He finds the vulnerable place just below my jaw, and he presses a kiss there. His lips are velvet, hiding the sharpness of his teeth as he nips my sensitive skin. His stubble grazes my skin in bristling warmth, and my head lolls, my hand clutching at the front of his shirt for balance, for an anchor in the storm. I'm suspended between anticipation and surrender, caught on the precipice of a dark, exhilarating freedom only he can give me.

When he finally grasps me, I marvel at how easily his large hand encircles my neck. His thumb rubs over my pulse and the throbbing artery there. On the other side of my neck, his middle finger mirrors the movement. Both squeeze and my lips part on a moan as the world telescopes to the pressure of Ronan's touch.

"*More*," I plead.

"Look at me, baby."

I stare at him from beneath heavy eyelids. "What?"

"Are you sure?" he grips my chin, forcing me to hold his gaze. "I'll give you anything, but I have to know you're certain."

"Yes," I hiss, leaning into him. "*Please*, Ronan."

"I'm not going to choke you. It's too dangerous."

"But you just said—"

"I know what I said," Ronan coos, kissing my temple. "I'm not going to strangle you."

"I'm not some fragile doll. I can handle it."

I clutch at Ronan's shirt.

"I need it," I whisper.

"Shh, it's all right, baby." Ronan slips his hand between my legs, and I moan as he rubs gently over my entrance.

"I tore your dress just pulling down your zipper," he says. "What you want is riskier than you think. But I can give you the next best thing."

"The next best thing?" I whimper as he slips one finger inside of me.

"Mm hmm." He presses his thumb against my clit.

Pleasure flares, hot and fierce, and I cry out. *I'm so close.*

"Give it to me, please," I beg.

"I will," Ronan soothes me. "It'll just be a little different—a tweak to a technique I learned long ago. I'll press both sides of your neck until you feel lightheaded. You'll get the same sensation with less danger. That work for you?"

"Okay," I agree, adrenaline spiking, voice shaking with frustration—and anticipation.

"Good, because it's the most I'll allow. You're far too precious for anything else," Ronan growls.

Precious? I want to scoff, but my words evaporate as he pinches my clit.

That's when his other hand returns to my throat. His thumb and middle finger are just beneath my jaw. And this time, when he squeezes, the pressure doesn't stop. The compression is steady, precise.

All the while, his fingers work inside of me, thick as a dick, filling me up. The wet slide and retreat take over my senses, stealing my ability to think. Pleasure crashes over me, pulling me under its riptide. I can only feel as Ronan curls his fingers, reaching for the spot deep inside that's already causing mini sparks to spiral upwards, summoning ecstasy.

His hand on my neck, the expert way he's stroking my pussy— the dual sensations are intoxicating. A low buzz fills my ears, and the edges of my vision blur to gray. My head swims under the weight of dizziness.

It's like every other time, every other trigger, except this is so much sweeter. More powerful than any whiff of vanilla. Sharper than the spice in any waffle cone.

Ecstasy instead of fear—pleasure instead of shame.

The world fades to velvet black euphoria. My orgasm is so powerful it leaves me shuddering, gasping for the very breath I'd asked Ronan to take.

For so long, I've been afraid of the darkness, but it welcomes me now, urging me higher. I call Ronan's name as I shatter into a million pieces. It's not quite freedom, but something close.

No guilt.

No pain.

Only the deep seduction of darkness.

And sweet blissful oblivion.

Kites
Ronan

I don't usually spend my Friday afternoons in parks. Not even as a kid. I've certainly never been to Anchor Park.

The oddity of being a rich, spoiled kid is missing milestones like this. Astors don't go to parks. Playmates come to them.

But today I'm on a mission. Still floating from what Thandi and I shared in Fia's bedroom.

Who am I kidding? She owns me now.

I can still taste her.

And I'll never recover from her scent.

Her quiet request is seared into me—the need in her eyes. Her trust.

It's why I'm here. Before the party, I knew what she'd been through, but now I understand how deep it goes.

I'm not trying to fix her—there's nothing to fix. Thandi is already perfect. But if I can use my gift to ease her pain, that's all that matters.

I'm in Shezmu mode, fully in the zone as I catalogue the park's cacophony of scents: the sharpness of soil still damp from last night's drizzle, grilled onions wafting from a cart nearby, sunscreen, hot dogs sizzling on a food truck's grill, and spun sugar from cotton candy.

Shielding my eyes from the glare, I jot a few notes into my tablet and dab the back of my neck with my handkerchief. The DC humidity is living up to its reputation, and the sun is bright as hell. I curse myself for forgetting my Ray-Bans and move on to the next notes: asphalt baking underfoot, sweet clematis, and the tang of sawdust drifting from the jungle gym. Then something less pleasant drifts through. Yeah. That's dog shit.

I'm jotting down the formulas when I hear kids shrieking. But these aren't the usual arguments about favorite toys or taking turns on the swing. This is about angles, lift, and drag; a debate sharp with scientific certainty.

I round the bend and nearly trip over the budding Nobel Laureates. Two kids are crouched in the grass. One is a girl with tape stuck to her sleeve, her brow furrowed in concentration. The boy next to her balances the skeleton of a kite like it's a rocket prototype.

The girl looks vaguely familiar, though I can't place her at the moment. Before I can choose between acknowledging them or retreating, she squints up at me.

"Hey, Mister! You're Ms. Fia's friend, aren't you?"

I blink, caught off guard. Then it clicks. She's Daysha, from the youth center—the one Thandi congratulated on her scholarship. The boy with her is new to me, though.

Daysha straightens, giving me a very scientific appraisal. "You are," she says, nodding as if she's solved the problem before I can answer. "I remember. You played in the pick-up game, right? You were making googly eyes at Ms. Elowen." She giggles.

Well, damn. Not exactly the legacy I was aiming for. But she's not wrong. And apparently, even the kids noticed.

The boy—Ricky—scowls. "Hey. Nobody's allowed to make googly eyes at Ms. Thandi."

"Says who?" Daysha shoots back.

I want to know, too, because I'll be doing a lot more than making googly eyes at Thandi.

"Says me." Ricky folds his arms like a tiny enforcer. "She's family now. Googly eyes are forbidden."

I bite back a laugh. *Family*, huh? That's new. But I'm not about to argue with a kid ready to duel me over it. What Ricky doesn't know won't hurt him.

Ricky is still glaring at me when I drop to a crouch in the grass beside them. "So," I ask, nodding at the neon paper and crooked frame, "what's the plan here? You aiming for orbit or just to clear the jungle gym?"

Daysha grins, tape hanging off her wrist. "We're optimizing lift."

"Yeah," Ricky chimes in. "But the wing angle keeps collapsing."

I lean closer, ignoring the sweat sticking my shirt to my back. The frame's just a little too tight at the corners. I pinch the spar, twist, and nudge it into place. "There. Just need to adjust the tension."

They both test it, eyes going wide when the paper snaps taut.

"It's perfect!" Daysha squeals. Before I know what's happening, they're already yanking me up, sprinting for the open field.

I stumble after them, dragged into the chase, the kite string bobbing in Ricky's hands as it leaps skyward. Daysha's laugh carries over the grass, sharp and wild. Ricky whoops beside her.

And me? I'm thinking two things at once: first, thank God I didn't skip cardio, because these kids are Energizer bunnies. Second, what the hell have I gotten myself into?

The answer streaks in neon paper across the sky: abundant joy all over their faces that's worth every step.

Eventually, the wind falters, the kite floats back to earth, and we jog back across the field, breathless.

Ricky's still grinning when he says, "Hey, you never told us your name, Mister. Can we call you Google?"

Daysha bursts into another fit of giggles, nearly doubling over.

I shoot them both dirty looks, even though the corner of my mouth threatens betrayal. "Absolutely not."

I straighten and offer both hands for high-fives. "I'm Ronan. Put 'er there."

They slap my palms with enough force to sting, and we're still catching our breath when Ricky's lip quirks. "You're not so bad. Though you're still not allowed to give googly eyes to Ms. Thandi."

I cross my heart, expression solemn. "I hereby swear that henceforth, there shall be no more googly eyes in the presence of Ms. Thandi."

Daysha narrows her eyes. "What do you think, Ricky? Do you believe him?"

Ricky snorts, unimpressed. "Nope."

I can't help it. I laugh, the sound escaping me before I can stop it. For these two, I don't mind being the punchline.

"Hey, Mr. Ronan," Daysha pipes up, eyes bright. "Why don't you come to the youth center and build more kites with us? We've got harder ones we want to try."

I open my mouth to say no—that I'm busy, that I've got more formulas to map. But they're both looking up at me with such hope in their expressions that none of my excuses seems to matter.

I sigh. *Fuck it.* It's a good cause. And if Fia and Thandi can spend half their lives at that center, I might as well join the club, too.

Besides, I can't help the smile tugging at my mouth. There'll be more opportunities to make those forbidden googly eyes at Thandi.

"Okay," I say, raking a hand through my hair. "When are we doing this?"

"Every Wednesday at six," Ricky says firmly.

Daysha shoots him a look. "And Thursdays at... um... five."

Ricky's brows lift, catching on fast. "Saturdays too!"

I stare at them and shake my head. Am I seriously being scammed by two ten-year-olds?

"Deal," I say, smiling at the two rascals. "We'll start next Wednesday." I offer, since my Saturday is already spoken for.

"Deal!" They fist-bump like they've just closed a million-dollar contract, grins splitting their faces.

I'm about to turn and head back to my notes when a thought strikes me. I glance over my shoulder. "Hey, do you two come here often?"

They're already bending over a stack of UNO cards, bickering about who shuffled last, when Daysha glances up. "Yeah, but we always go home before dark."

I nod, filing that away. "Does an ice cream truck ever go by?"

"Yeah!" Daysha gushes. "They have bubblegum, strawberry shortcake, orange creamsicle—oh, and the Ninja Turtle one with the gumball eyes."

Ricky shrugs, more measured. "It's here on Wednesdays and Fridays. Today's Friday." His lip quirks. "I don't like it, though. I'm lactose *tolermant*."

Daysha bursts out laughing at the word, but Ricky just shrugs again, dead serious. "If you want a cone, though, it'll be by in like five minutes."

And as if the universe is listening, music starts tinkling in the distance. The ice cream truck rolls into view, tinny notes trailing from it like the Pied Piper of Hamlin.

Kids from every corner of the park are already scrambling to their feet, sprinting across the grass in hot pursuit. I hang back for a second, watching them go. I can't help but think of Thandi—of the terror she must have felt once, hearing the same cheerful tune under very different circumstances.

I say my goodbyes to Daysha and Ricky and drift toward the truck, but I keep off to the side, letting the kids swarm ahead. They jostle each other in line, voices sharp with excitement, while the vendor, a cheerful woman in a sun visor, calls out flavors like she's auctioning happiness.

The melee of scents assaults me at once: Syrupy snow cones bleeding red and blue into paper cups. Nutty cones dipped in chocolate, the shells already softening in the heat. Sticky-sweet icicles, pure sugar on a stick. And of course, creamy vanilla in a halo of warm waffle cone.

I write it all down, take it all in to be recreated later. The kids' faces glow as they clutch their choices, laughter spilling into the humid air. For them, this is childhood's sweetest reward. But not Thandi. I think back to that day in the lab, her body small and vulnerable in my arms. What must it be like to have something so ordinary, so sweet, forever marked by pain? The weight of her suffering tears at me, and I know somehow that I have to help fix this.

Mom always pushed me to find my purpose, and the more time I spend with Thandi, the more I realize all of it may be tied to her.

Even beyond the science, now that I've held her, tasted her, I don't want to ever let go.

A mosquito buzzes around my face and dive-bombs at me, biting my forearm. I slap it, putting an end to the mini Nosferatu, but not before a bump swells red and bright on my arm.

I'm cursing under my breath when someone says:

"Don't scratch that."

The voice is thin but firm, and my hand freezes midair.

I glance down at a tiny old lady. She can't be more than five feet tall, silver hair knotted into a bun, yellow floral dress fluttering in the breeze. Her blue eyes, creased at the corners, are sharp as glass.

"You'll scar," she adds, wagging a finger. From the purse at her elbow, she produces a bottle of calamine lotion, the label faded with age.

It's so quaint, so absurdly on brand, that I almost chuckle. Hell, when was the last time I saw calamine lotion?

Before I can protest, she tips some onto a cotton pad and dabs it across the welt.

"There. Better than scratching yourself raw."

I manage a quiet thanks, though I feel faintly ridiculous—towering over her while she fusses over me like I'm a boy who's scraped his knee.

She pats my arm. "Always better to treat a wound properly," she declares, then she moves off, leaving me with a pale pink smear on my arm.

Well, that was unexpected.

The chalky scent clings to my skin, oddly comforting. I lift my arm, sniff once, shake my head, and laugh.

Then, for the hell of it, I catalogue that too.

I'm back at RT Laboratories, but distracted as hell. Thandi will be here any minute.

I check my watch. Ten minutes to go. But damn, this woman is the worst at texting. No traffic update, no sweet nothing to tide me over.

Meanwhile, it's taken all my willpower not to bombard her all day.

Okay, so maybe she *has* been in touch. My phone's full of her messages—sweet, quiet, and thoughtful in that Thandi way. All since Fia's party, and at least two today.

But that was five hours ago, damn it.

I huff and straighten the already spotless lab for the third time.

By the time I'm done, my phone buzzes. She's here. I hustle to the lobby to let her in.

"Hey," she grins, a little shy.

She's got a backpack slung over her shoulder and is dressed down in a zip-up hoodie, shorts, and a t-shirt that reads *Never Trust an Atom. They Make Up Everything*. That's my Thandi—nerdy, sharp, gorgeous.

"Hey, yourself," I purr, pulling her into my arms and sweeping her off her feet. "You made it."

I kiss her softly, then bury my nose in her neck. "Mm. You smell good, too."

"Thank you." She tilts her head, amused. "You going to put me down, or…?"

I waggle my eyebrows. "Or?"

She bursts into laughter. "You're an idiot, you know that?"

"A very charming idiot," I correct, finally setting her down. I offer my hand, and satisfaction floods me when she slips hers into it without hesitation. "Come on. Let me show you the place."

I lead her down the hall, and she's already wide-eyed, taking it all in. "This is all yours?"

I nod, pride constricting my chest. "Yeah. Though I haven't been actively involved until recently." I pause. "I took a break when Mom got sick. We did some of our best work together here," I say quietly.

She squeezes my hand. "That's really special. I understand why it could take some time to return."

I glance at her, caught off guard by how easily she gets it. Most people would have given me some polite line, but to her, it's obvious.

I smile. "I'm ready now, though. It just feels right."

Thandi's eyes meet mine, and for a moment, the world narrows to her. I want to hold her, kiss her—make love to her. But I force myself forward. She deserves the tour I promised.

"How was your meeting with Dani?" I ask. I'd suggested we meet earlier, but Immerscent had claimed her day.

Thandi's face lights up. "Really good. I think we're on track to present the Sugar Hill concept to the board soon."

I laugh, the moniker catching me off guard. "Sugar Hill concept? I like that."

She grins. "It has a certain ring to it."

We stop at the first glass-walled lab, where Elsa, our newest research fellow, is zipping up her backpack. She spots us and waves, "Hey, Mr. Thorne, I'm heading out. Don't stay too late!"

"I won't," I call as she sprints to the car waiting out front for her.

I turn back to Thandi, gesturing around the room. "This is our immunotherapy division. Most of our revenue comes from monoclonal antibody contracts. Glamorous, I know."

"Hey, I make my living from smells," Thandi's tone is wry. "No judgment here from me."

See? I told you she's perfect.

I smile and lead her deeper inside, pointing out workstations for prestigious researchers and detailing our latest releases, when she stops dead in her tracks.

"What?" I ask, skidding to a halt beside her.

"That's a Biacore, isn't it?" she breathes, pointing at the SPR system still idling in standby.

Forget perfect. I might be in love.

I don't care that I'm grinning like a maniac. Usually, I temper my enthusiasm and keep it simple for investors. But with Thandi? I let the geek in me loose.

"Yeah. Watching binding curves resolve in real time never gets old."

It's stupid, but it feels good not to hold it back, not to dumb anything down.

Thandi's answering smile is pure delight, and suddenly I can't wait to show her everything else.

We head to the drug delivery lab, followed by the diagnostics division. I may be doing the tour, but Thandi has me seeing everything with fresh eyes. I'm practically swooning from her company and her pointed questions. I never realized how much of myself I've kept muted until I hear her voice ring through these halls.

Her observations pull me closer. Instead of scents, I'm cataloguing each of her reactions—precious infinity stones from a night that's already reconstructed my entire universe. I glance over, tucking away all of them:

Thandi, leaning over the chip platform, eyes shining, asking: "Are you using staggered herringbone mixers?"

And her low whistle at the lab-on-a-chip biosensor we hope will revolutionize treatment for Alzheimer's and Parkinson's.

We end in the regenerative medicine division, where incubators are humming, and the glow of bioreactors paints the room in soft gold.

"This is one of our newer divisions, but one of the most special," I say, a little tentative. "They grew a skin graft scaffold last year that saved a burn patient. I think Mom would be really proud of that."

I'm a little hoarse saying it out loud. It's the first time I've let myself acknowledge it.

"Oh, Ronan, that's amazing. This is huge!" Thandi exclaims, and I allow myself to bask in it.

I've given this tour before, but always with my mask on, always detached, never letting on how deeply personal all of this is to me. But tonight, with Thandi at my side, I'm finally sharing, not just selling.

"Thanks for letting me show you all of this," I say, once we've looped through the core wings, Thandi matching me step for step.

"Of course. This has been wonderful."

"My pleasure," I murmur, kissing Thandi's temple. And it has been. I haven't held back. I've let the young man who practically lived here with Mom shine through.

But there's still one more stop.

"There's something else I'd like to show you."

"Oh?" Thandi's brows lift as we turn off the main passage into a new wing that still smells of drywall and cement.

At the end of the hall, plastic sheeting hangs across a doorway, taped in crisscross patterns.

The new wing.

I haven't brought anyone here since construction started.

I pause, my fingers brushing the seam. My heart hammers. This isn't just lab space. It's *her* space. Mom's place—my tribute and her legacy, wrapped in one.

I glance at Thandi. She's waiting, curious, her hand still in mine, even though I know my palms must be sweaty by now.

"Ready?" I ask.

When she nods, I tear the seam open and lead her inside.

Threshold
Ronan

We step through the plastic sheeting, and my heart is thumping like crazy. My palms are definitely sweaty. None of it is sexy, but I won't let Thandi's hand go for anything. Not even to soothe my own nervousness.

"Well, this is it," I say, and fuck if my voice doesn't croak like I swallowed gravel.

Jesus Christ, Ronan, get it together.

I rake a hand through my hair, and the whole thing comes tumbling down. The tie bounces to the floor, skittering into the dust.

Great.

"Sorry," I mutter, bending to snatch it up, cursing under my breath. So much for making a good impression.

"Hey." Thandi's soft hand lands on my shoulder. "It's okay. Take your time."

I look up, and she's staring at me with the most tender expression. There's far too much understanding in her big brown eyes.

I jerk to my feet with a nod, clearing my throat. "Yeah, okay. Let's try this again." I pull my hair back, but now she's looking at me with the strangest expression.

"What?" I ask. "What is it?"

Her eyes widen. "What? Nothing."

"Can't be nothing if you're staring at me like that. Is there something in my teeth? Spit it out, Pink—I can take it."

"It's not that." She bites her bottom lip, her gaze darting at me from under her lashes.

Damn it, it's kind of sexy. Now I'm a basket of nerves *and* turned on.

Worse, Thandi's *still* staring at me. I take her hand again, hair tie and attempts at looking presentable forgotten.

"Come on, baby, talk to me," I coax, and she makes a soft sound.

"It's nothing. It's just your hair…." She's biting her lip again and … is she fidgeting?

Wait. My nervousness ebbs.

Oh. That's the issue.

"What about my hair?" I lean in now with a grin.

Thandi gestures helplessly. "Nothing. I've just never seen it like this. It's … nice."

"Nice?" I scoff. I run my fingers through it and shake it out for dramatic effect.

It's not the first time a woman has commented on my hair. Objectively, I know it's striking, both in color and length, but I've never had much vanity about it. Its purpose has always been practical:

Besides my eyes, it's the one thing that marks me most distinctively as my mother's son.

But seeing Thandi's reaction? Yeah, I can't help taking advantage.

"Admit it. You like me in thirst-trap mode." I hook my thumb in the back of my t-shirt and waggle my eyebrows. "Want me to take off my shirt?"

"What? No! Of course not," Thandi protests, but the way her eyes jump from my head to my chest suggests that she *very much* wants me to take off my shirt.

I file that little nugget away for later.

"You sure?" I tug at my collar, deliberately hiking up the fabric to flash a slice of abs. What? I never said I wasn't vain about *everything*.

"I thought you were giving me a tour." Thandi folds her arms and glares. Well, tries to. Hard to shoot daggers while sneaking peeks at my stomach.

"Fine. Let's go." I take her hand again, still smiling. The nerves are gone, burned off like morning fog. And of course, it's because of her.

We walk deeper into the new wing, and I wonder what it looks like through Thandi's eyes—the bare drywall, rolled-up carpet, and the remnants of old cubicles. Probably nothing more than chaos, but I can already see the skeleton of possibility behind the detritus.

"Where are we?" Thandi asks. "Is RT Laboratories expanding?"

"Yes," I swallow. "This will be the Rosalind Thorne Institute of Neuroscience, with a specific focus on olfaction."

It's still hard for me to say it; still hard for me to accept the fact that she's gone.

Thandi's eyes widen. "Oh, Ronan. What an amazing tribute."

I nod. "Mom was a scientist like you." I smile. "She was even obsessed with scent, though she was primarily interested in emotional regulation."

Thandi loops her arm through mine. "She sounds like a woman after my own heart."

That gets me. Not only because Thandi is right, but I just know Mom would have loved her too.

"She was a survivor," I say, leading Thandi to the space where the first lab will be.

It's still pretty bare bones, but at least the ductwork is in. Someone's labeled the segments in marker: *volatile capture/odor isolation*, and I know Thandi will appreciate the fiber-optic cabling that will feed into the high-resolution neural imaging rigs. We walk past a row of unfinished workstations where a portable fume hood sits in its crate. Chalked notes sprawl across the subfloor in thick white lines, marking where equipment will go.

We circle back to the doorway, where I let my eyes travel over it—the scaffolding of a future Mom will never see, though it should have been hers.

"She fought pancreatic cancer for almost a decade." My voice breaks. "It's been a year since she let go."

Thandi doesn't rush to fill the silence. Instead, she's almost reverent in her stillness as she stares across the room. Finally, she turns back to me. "I'm sorry for your loss, Ronan. But looking at this, I think your mom would be very proud of the legacy you're building."

"I hope so," I murmur. I never cared to live up to James' expectations, but when it comes to Mom, there's no room for error.

I take a deep breath, trying to shake off the melancholy that's descended on us like a shroud. "Anyway, I've thought about dedicating something to her for a while, but when she left me her estate—and her research—it was a done deal."

Thandi's look is thoughtful. "I'd love to learn more about her work one day."

That scuttles some of the clouds away. Because it's not just a line. I can hear the genuine curiosity in her voice.

I'm so glad I brought her here.

"I'll send you some of her bibliography. Maybe RT Laboratories and Immerscent can dream up something together."

"Promise?" Thandi props her hands on her hips, eyes narrowing in mock challenge.

The look is so much like Daysha testing my commitment to kite-making that I can't help but laugh.

"Promise," I say, leaning in to kiss her again.

"Okay, don't get too excited—" Thandi starts, and I immediately spin in my chair to face her.

"Well, you know if you say that, I'm going to get worked up."

She rolls her eyes even as she reaches into her backpack. "I brought a sample of the Sugar Hill prototype."

"Baby…" I'm over there in a heartbeat, peering over her shoulder. Her ass looks great in those shorts, so I give it a little squeeze too.

"Ronan," she gasps. "Focus!"

I caress her delectable curves before pulling away. "Okay. Fine, I'm behaving now. Show me."

Thandi pulls out her tablet and a small vial along with it. "Now bear in mind this is only a rough attempt, so temper your expectations, but I'm feeling good about this direction."

It's the first time I've gotten to be so close to her genius. Of course, I've seen the numbers, even analyzed some of her formulas as part of my initial assessment, but that's all theoretical. This puts me up close and personal with her craft in a way that feels special.

I uncork the vial and my eyes flutter shut at the first whiff. I have to give myself a minute.

I've analyzed and recreated thousands of scents, but there's a delicacy to Thandi's work that is stunning. I love the science, but half of Shezmu has always been instinct—art. Thandi's method is different but no less beautiful. There's no rough improvisation here. This formula is elegant, achingly precise.

But that's not what grabs me by the gut.

What I smell is like a single violin note vibrating in the air—clear and sharp. Her Sugar Hill shorthand is perfect, because I'm suddenly on a rollercoaster, hurled backward and forward at once. Back to that first night at Tino's, when she ordered me a gin and tonic. The herbaceousness and citrus notes are all here, but the vial's real power is in its resonance. In possibility. That's the forward thrust.

I have to turn away as my eyes smart with tears. Because what Thandi has captured isn't a drink, but a moment of recognition—the instant she shattered my mask and asked me to step into the man beneath.

I'm once again back at that tiny table, surrounded by the evidence of her authenticity—and shocked at being so clearly seen. Beside it is the fragile spark of hope, the wistfulness of wondering what it would be like not just to reveal that man, but to *be* him.

Ever since I met Thandi, I've tried to understand why Tino's was such a turning point. Sure, it was the first thaw in the tension between us, but smelling the prototype, I've finally figured it out.

For months, I was grieving, directionless. Stumbling from one pleasure to the next so I could forget. Pushing everyone away with my brashness and disaffection.

I hated that Ronan.

I'm still not sure he's completely left.

Yet, even irritated, that night, Thandi saw a better man in me than I thought I was.

She's just like Mom in that way. Seeing the best in me, buried under the worst.

And now I have no choice but to make both of them proud.

"Pink," I breathe, and it spills out like a prayer. "You've done it."

I sweep her into my arms.

"This is fucking brilliant."

Special Delivery
Thandi

I warned him it was just a rough sample, but Ronan doesn't seem to care. He's bent over the vial, inhaling, eyes half-shut in concentration. When he exhales, he murmurs something under his breath as his pen scratches across his tablet.

I'm still tweaking, fussing with ratios and not entirely convinced the balance is right, but watching him makes me hopeful. With Ronan, there's no pretense. And right now, he's totally absorbed, scrawling down possibilities like the future itself is whispering to him.

I don't even know what he's recording, and maybe I don't need to. What matters is the way he makes me feel as I work beside him. Like we're in this together. A team.

I'm still reeling from the attraction between us, but this is even more unexpected. It's trust, acceptance. Something I never imagined. Not that others haven't tried, or I haven't either. But there's always been a barrier, a wall that I couldn't overcome.

I'm not an easy woman to love.

Not with my secrets.

Yet, something's different with Ronan. The walls are less like stone and more like hedges—a garden with the gates flung wide. And now, we're in a rhythm I longed for and didn't know I needed.

Ronan comes up for air, dragging a hand down his jaw. He sniffs my vial again, then pivots to his workbench. I watch as he measures compounds. There's a boyish spark in his focus, a guileless passion that is disarming.

I can't help that I'm falling for him even more.

A minute later, he's back at my side, holding out a fresh sample.

"Okay," he says. "What do you think of adding this?"

I take it from him, turning it in my hand. At first, I think he's remixed the proportions, but when I bring it to my nose, I realize I'm wrong.

He hasn't modified the notes. The foundation is intact. What he's added is something else—an accelerant. A catalyst that makes the top notes flare, then vanish, leaving the heart to unfurl and linger, even as the base notes threaten to intrude.

It's like trying to catch a firefly in the split second before it blinks away.

The effect startles me. Instead of being tantalized by the earlier bright citrus, I'm chasing the warmth beneath. The fragrance itself seems to murmur: *Stay. Don't skim the surface. Come closer. Keep going.*

I look up, heart in my throat. "You didn't change it, and yet, it's better."

Ronan rubs the back of his neck, almost self-conscious. "I didn't need to change it. I just wanted to make sure the heart didn't get lost."

I lower the vial. Somehow, I manage to choke out, "Thank you."

Before I can stop myself, I fling my arms around Ronan. He makes a startled sound, then folds me in his embrace like I've always belonged there. His scent, his warmth, his strength—they're everything I didn't know I was searching for.

I tilt my face up, and he kisses me, softly first, then deeper. When he pulls back, the curve of his mouth is wicked.

"So why didn't you tell me this is what I had to do to make you throw yourself at me?"

"Stop!" I laugh against his chest, still clinging to him.

I told him earlier we'd be ready to preview the concept with the board soon, but now I'm certain. There are refinements to make, of course—tweaks I want to share with Sammie and the rest of the team. Already, my mind is darting ahead, wondering if the patient protocols for this one need to be different.

I steal a glance at Ronan, a wave of tenderness rising in me. He's clicking away at his laptop, but somehow he feels my stare. His gaze meets mine, sultry and knowing, and my breath catches.

"Thandi." Ronan closes the space between us.

He takes my hand and presses a kiss to the center of my palm. His lips linger, teasing the soft skin. He turns his head, tongue stealing out to trace a burning path from my lifeline to my wrist.

I gasp, heat flooding my body. Ronan kisses me again, and that heat ignites into flame.

He calls my name. There's a promise there as he bends closer, our breaths mingling. His arm slides around my waist, and my grip tightens on his shirt. When I cry out, he cups the back of my head in that tender way I'm coming to expect.

"Ronan…" I whimper.

And then his phone buzzes.

Ronan freezes, chest rising and falling as he catches his breath. "Shit," he mumbles. "Sorry, baby, I'm expecting a call. I need to take this."

I swallow, nodding. Disappointed, but a little relieved. Probably not the best idea to ravish Ronan on a laboratory floor, anyway.

"Yeah, okay, I'll be out in two minutes," Ronan answers the phone. He glances at me, looking for all the world like a kid caught with his hand in the cookie jar. His grin is sheepish, even though his eyes are still hot, still fixed on my mouth.

We're not finished.

Not by a long shot.

Still, I can't help being a little suspicious. I narrow my eyes. "What are you up to? I hope you're not planning anything devious."

Ronan's smile only grows more wicked. "Hold that thought."

He disappears down the hall. A moment later, I hear muffled voices, then the growl of a motorcycle pulling away. When he returns, he's holding a large pizza box.

My jaw drops. "No!" I grab his arm, practically bouncing when I see the familiar Tino's logo stamped across the lid.

"How much did you have to pay Tino to convince him to deliver?" I demand. "He's even militant about takeout unless it's leftovers."

"Nothing. I just told him his favorite person was working late." Ronan grins, utterly smug. "And that I'm your boyfriend now."

My mouth falls open.

"What?" I punch him in the arm, mostly to hide the flush rising in my cheeks.

Ronan shrugs, but there's uncertainty in his eyes. "I am, aren't I?"

I stare at him.

I think about how many times he's saved me, the way he held me at Fia's, the affection and pleasure he's given so freely. And tonight—what he's revealed about his past, even as he's nudged me toward my future.

And just like that, it's settled.

"Yes," I say, stepping closer and wrapping an arm around him, not caring that the pizza box is wedged awkwardly between us. "Yes, you're my boyfriend, Ronan."

I expect some witty Thorne-esque quip, but he just kisses the top of my head and begins plating the pizza, a tiny smile on his lips.

And for some reason, that tiny gesture hits me harder than any lavish declaration ever could. Already, my defenses are in shambles.

Steadying my breath, I follow him as he sets the pizza box down on the lab bench, then finds a roll of paper towels and some soda cans in the staff kitchen. We end up with disposable plates and cups like two interns pulling an all-nighter.

When he flips the lid open, I actually gasp. On one side of the pizza is pepperoni; on the other is Tino's famous mushroom with white sauce.

"Okay, now this is just crazy. Do I need to call? Is Tino sick? Did you put something in the water?"

Ronan blinks at me, all wide-eyed innocence. "What? Why?"

"It's half-and-half," I say, jabbing my finger at the perfect line down the middle of the pizza. "Tino doesn't do half-and-half."

"Sure he does," Ronan says smoothly, sliding a paper plate toward me.

I narrow my eyes. "He must have been abducted by aliens. Wait—are you an alien?"

"Or," Ronan drawls, "maybe he just loves you enough to make an exception."

"Highly unlikely!" I scoff, rolling my eyes as I stuff a pepperoni slice in my mouth.

Ronan watches me chew, a crooked smile tugging at his lips. "I don't know. You'd be surprised at how many of us would give you the world, Thandi."

I almost choke on my pizza and have to force it down with a drink. How can he say things like that so easily? The soda bubbles sting my throat, and I can't tell if I'm lightheaded from the sugar, the grease, or Ronan.

"Why would I need the world?" I mutter, not quite able to meet his eyes.

Ronan reaches over and tilts my chin up. "You'll never know until you ask."

"Says who?" I tease, though my voice is trembling. It's easier to do that than focus on the weight of his words.

Ronan's thumb brushes over my mouth, lingering on my bottom lip. "Didn't you ask at the party? Didn't I give you what you needed?"

"That's—" Breath abandons my lungs. My lips are tingling where he touched them, and I'm on fire, melting from his words and the memory of what we shared.

"That's what?" Ronan demands, eyeing me over his slice of white mushroom.

"You know what," I shoot back, barely able to grip my next slice thanks to the tremor in my hands. "You're not playing fair."

"Fair?" Ronan throws his head back and laughs. Laughs! The man is incorrigible. He pats his thigh. "Come here, baby."

I eye him, but do as he asks. I move over, perching gingerly on his lap. "What do you want?" I pout, laying my head on his shoulder.

"Just this," he murmurs, weaving soft kisses from my temple to my cheek. I shiver when he nuzzles my neck.

"Ronan," I plead, as memories of Fia's bedroom come rushing forward.

"I know. I've got you." Lacing his fingers with mine, Ronan kisses the tender spot beneath my jaw. His mouth slides up, hot against my ear. "I can't wait to make love to you, Thandi."

God. His words jolt through me. My heart stutters, misfires, and picks up a new rhythm. I want to say something, but all I can do is release a helpless moan.

I don't think. I just drag his mouth down to mine.

Ronan tastes like pizza and root beer and something deliciously forbidden. His stubble scrapes my chin; his hand burns at my waist. My fingers tangle in his hair, and then I'm clutching at his shoulders. I hold on for dear life because if I let go, I'm afraid I'll lose myself.

Ronan groans, steadying me, even as he nips my lip and his tongue slides against mine. He reaches beneath my hoodie to find my breast. Those knowing fingers circle and press my nipple, and I slump against him, dazed. Desperate cries escape me. All I know is I want more.

By the time we pull apart, I'm aching, and the thick ridge of Ronan's erection juts against my hip.

We're both panting. I can hear his heart galloping against my ear, and pride swells in me.

I'm not the only one undone.

"I can't wait to make love with you, too," I whisper.

Ronan shudders, and the sound he makes is low and tortured. His jaw ticks, and his forearms are taut with strain. A gust of air bursts past his lips.

"Fuck. You'll be the death of me." He still manages a roguish smile. "You're lucky, I refuse to let our first time together be in a lab."

I dip forward and steal a quick kiss. "Well, you started it."

"So this is my punishment?" Amber eyes dance with amusement.

"Mm hmm."

"I'll take it."

Smiling, Ronan presses his forehead against mine. "Let's finish this pizza so you can tell me about your parents' dinner. Now that we're official, I don't want to embarrass myself."

Casserole
Ronan

Dinner with Thandi's family is kind of a big deal.

I even brought a dish. Well, that was Fia's idea.

I'd planned on bringing an excellent Château Margaux, but she called that lazy. Said I needed to put in real effort. So instead of a bottle of Bordeaux, I ended up in her kitchen, roasting zucchini, peppers, and eggplant until the place smelled like Tuscany. Fia ran the whole operation like basic training. Apparently, blistered edges are mandatory.

Now I'm balancing a casserole dish of vegetarian baked ziti under one arm—Winston strikes me as more of a quinoa-and-kale guy than steak and potatoes—and a bottle of Rosalind's Trace in the other. It seemed fitting, since Iris knew my mother.

The vibe I'm going for is safe—comforting. Something that says, *Don't worry, he's domesticated.* Only time will tell if I've nailed it. If baked pasta and a sweet vintage can't buy goodwill, I'm out of ideas.

Thandi keeps reassuring me her parents are harmless, but I'm still nervous. Iris is as sharp as they come, and no father is blasé about his only daughter.

As charming as Winston was at the fundraiser, something tells me I'm going to get grilled harder than Fia's veggies tonight.

Taking a deep breath, I raise my hand and ring the bell.

"Coming!" A muffled voice sounds from within, followed by thundering footsteps.

The door swings open to reveal a breathless Daysha and Ricky. "Mr. Google!" they shout in unison.

"That's it—" I say, pretending to walk away. "I'm going home."

"No! We're kidding!" Ricky giggles while Daysha grabs the hem of my shirt. They both begin dragging me inside, and I feel like a clown with a juggling act, trying to keep a hold on my presents.

"Easy, guys—" I stumble over the threshold and teeter into the hall as the kids keep tugging me forward. I have no idea how they're doing it. This kind of berserker's strength has to come from sugar.

"Ricky? Daysha? Who's at the door?" Iris' dulcet tones filter down the hallway. She hurries over when she sees me being mobbed by two pint-sized scientists.

"Oh gosh, Ronan! I'm so sorry." Iris shoots a stern look at Ricky and Daysha. "Come on, kids, you know better than this. Let Mr. Ronan go. Why don't you two go help set the table?"

"Yes, ma'am," they mumble, contrite, and shuffle down the hall.

"I hope you don't mind a little extra company," Iris says with a laugh as she watches them go. "Weekend science camp was cancelled, so Daysha's having dinner with us until her mom gets off work."

"Nah, they're great kids," I say with a grin. "The more, the merrier."

I shift the casserole dish into her hands before I drop it. "Thanks again for having me. These are for you."

Iris' eyes widen. "How thoughtful! You didn't have to do this." She hugs the dish closer to her chest. "And the casserole smells wonderful."

"The wine is from Mom's vineyard," I blurt, then instantly feel like an idiot. Real smooth, Ronan.

"I know." A hint of pink touches Iris' almond-cream complexion. "Honestly, I hoped you'd bring some. We're huge fans of Rosalind's Trace over here. I won't admit how many bottles we go through in a season."

"She's not wrong," Winston ambles in, wearing a "Sous Chef" apron. He plucks the bottle of Rosalind's Trace from me. "That wine has rescued me from the doghouse more times than I can count."

"Oh?" I ask, instantly relaxing.

Winston winks. "Best peace offering."

"Okay, rule number one: someone has to stay in the kitchen." Thandi barrels around the corner, spatula in hand. She's wearing the same apron as Winston, except hers reads "Head Chef" across the front.

"Dad, you know I'm working on that roux. And you need to check on your salmon. Mom, those blanched vegetables are looking good. I—"

She skids to a stop when she spots me, eyes wide, fingers tightening on the spatula.

"Ronan ... you're already here."

"Hey, baby," I say softly.

"Hey," Thandi breathes, and for a second the world narrows to just the two of us.

She's all soft and pretty in a yellow spaghetti-strap romper scattered with tiny white flowers. Even under the apron, it shows off her legs, and of course, she smells incredible. Today it's something warm and coconutty, with a hint of lychee and strawberry underneath.

She looks like a snack and smells like dessert.

I lean in and kiss her cheek. "Thanks for doing this. I'm really looking forward to this evening."

"Me too," Thandi whispers, just a little breathless. I like that I can affect her like this; that she wants to be with me, too.

"Ronan brought us a dish," Winston says behind me.

"And some wine," Iris adds.

And just like that, reality rushes back in. Thandi and I shift apart.

"You didn't have to do that, Ronan. You're our guest."

"I wanted to," I insist, my gaze locking with hers.

"Thank you," she murmurs, still looking adorably flustered. But then a determined look crosses her face. Turning on her heel, she glances over her shoulder.

"Come on, everyone, let's get you fed."

"Ricky, honey, pass the spring rolls."

"Daysha, last helping of mac and cheese, okay? You've got to eat your vegetables."

"Peanut, this jambalaya is amazing."

"Ricky, betcha can't stuff *two* sausage rolls in your mouth at once!"

"Winston, you know you're supposed to be watching your pressure. Put that salt shaker down."

"Damn it, Iris. It was just a sprinkle."

My head swivels back and forth as the conversation ricochets across the table. Winston argues for his right to a little more seasoning. Thandi piles another spoonful of mashed potatoes on my plate without asking; Ricky and Daysha squabble over who's the faster swimmer.

I'm dazed, heady on the chaos, the warmth, the laughter. Leaning back in my chair, I take it all in with wonder.

This is what a real home feels like. I know most families aren't like the one I grew up in, but I'm still fl oored by the care and acceptance the Elowens give each other, and everyone around them.

I think of how fragile my father's ego was, even with everything we had. Hard to process how a family like this, who's endured so much grief, still opens their hearts so freely.

I clear my throat, reaching for lighter ground. "So, how's the kite-fl ying going?" I ask Ricky and Daysha, who are practically vibrating in their chairs at the promise of peach cobbler.

"So good!" Ricky grins. "We made a new one yesterday."

"Kites?" Thandi asks, smiling at me, and it's enough to leave me distracted. I almost forget what we're talking about.

"Yeah," I say, shaking myself. "I was scoping out Anchor Park for some labs and found these two engineers conquering the skies."

"Mr. Ronan helped us fix it when it wouldn't fly," Daysha says, in a tone that suggests maybe I've earned a sliver of her respect.

"Wait, you were at Anchor Park alone?" Iris says sharply, and even I freeze. It's the first time I've ever seen a crack in her calm demeanor.

Silence settles over the table.

"Ricky, Daysha, answer me!" Iris' hands tremble. No—her whole body is shaking, her eyes white with fear.

The kids flinch and clam up. Ricky's shoulders curl forward until his head nearly touches the table.

Before I can blink, Winston is at Iris' side. He wraps his arm around her. "It's okay, my love. They're here; they're safe."

Across the table, Thandi looks ashen. She half rises, ready to go to Iris, until she sees Ricky's wounded posture. Her eyes flutter shut, and when she opens them again, I see the moment she decides to set her pain aside, to shoulder the weight herself.

The joy, the warmth of before, is shattered. My stomach churns at the knowledge that my question broke it.

That's why James says I ruin everything I touch.

My throat aches. I want to fix it, to say something, but all I can do is watch as Thandi kneels by Ricky and hugs him tightly.

"Come on, Ricky, hold your head up. Mama's not mad at you. She's just worried. Why were you and Daysha at the park?"

But Ricky won't speak. His tiny fists are clenched, tears streaming down his cheeks.

God. My chest contracts. What have I done?

Suddenly, I'm back at another table, much larger and colder than this one. I'm late, after staying outside too long. So late that I don't have time to change for dinner. So I sit, with a grass-stained shirt and bruised knees, braced for rebuke and the thunder of a fist against my back.

My father's voice is sharp and derisive. His glare of disapproval pierces me from across the table.

"Look at you, always a goddamn mess. You'll never amount to anything at this rate."

His chair scrapes against the hardwood. His footsteps are heavy as they approach my chair.

I bite my lip hard. I know better than to lift my head.

He raises his hand.

I close my eyes.

And tense—

"Don't be mad at Ricky, Mrs. Elowen."

I gasp as Daysha's voice pulls me back from the edge.

"It was my idea to leave science clinic and go to the park," she says. "We just wanted to test the kite. We didn't mean anything bad."

Ricky manages to raise his head from Thandi's chest. His voice wavers. "Please don't send me back to the group home. I promise we won't do it again, Mrs. Elowen."

Now Daysha is crying too.

I'm gutted. I push my own chair back. I should leave—the fly in the ointment that's contaminated everything. This evening has been so beautiful, and I don't think I can bear to see the inevitable.

Because I know what comes next: *Pain, humiliation, the growing kernel of rage.*

I'm standing, about to apologize, when the Elowens do something unexpected.

Iris closes her eyes and breathes through her panic. Then she darts to our side of the table. Winston is right behind her. Together with Thandi, they form a tight circle around Ricky and Daysha, enveloping them both.

Iris takes Ricky's hand and kisses his forehead. "I'm sorry for raising my voice at you, Ricky. I didn't mean to scare you. I just love you and want you to be safe. And sometimes safety means we can't do the things we like—not in the same way."

Winston looks from Ricky to Daysha. "We talked about stranger danger, right?" The kids nod. "The park isn't always safe for kids, so if you want to practice on your kites, one of us has to be with you, okay?"

They nod again, and Winston shakes his head. "Nope, I need to hear you say it."

"Yes, sir," Ricky mumbles.

"Yes, Mr. Elowen," Daysha echoes.

I clear my throat, the words rough. "I'm happy to pitch in. They already got me to promise in blood that we'd get together three days a week."

"A blood oath?" Thandi makes a show of looking fearfully between the two kids. "You guys are ruthless." She leans in conspiratorially. "Tell me how you did it."

"They were merciless." I clutch my wrist. "Just took off my bandages this morning."

At that, both Ricky and Daysha give teary giggles.

In that moment, the look Thandi and I share steals my breath: tenderness, gratitude—and beneath it, something that scares me.

A sense of belonging.

A place where I'm welcome beyond a mother's unconditional love.

"Baby—" I begin to whisper, when Winston's sharp voice cuts across the room.

"There's one very serious thing that hasn't been addressed." He turns to Ricky.

"Son, I heard you mention the group home." Thandi releases Ricky and lets her father pull him close. "You're an Elowen now, and we don't throw away family. Even if we argue, even if we get upset. Understand?"

Wide-eyed, Ricky nods.

"You can't get rid of us now, Rickster," Thandi growls, going in for a tickle, and the ugliness pops like a bubble. Everyone is smiling and laughing again, though Thandi and Iris are still wiping at tears as they fold everyone into another group hug.

"Son, what the hell are you doing?"

"Huh?" I look around and realize Winston's talking to me.

"What is it?" I ask, alarmed.

"Why are you hanging about like a spare tire? Come on in here."

I splutter, not sure if that's an insult or an invitation.

"Well?" Iris raises an elegant brow.

And just like that, I'm folded into their circle of trust, too.

Collage
Ronan

Ricky is already asleep when we peek in; brow furrowed, caught in a dream he can't shake. Thandi brushes a kiss against the crease and smooths his hair back with her palm. He exhales, his face softening into peaceful rest.

"Thanks for being so good to the kids," Thandi whispers as she eases the door shut behind her. Daysha's tucked into the guest room down the hall. After the long, emotional night, Iris let her stay.

The energy and chaos of earlier have quieted into something richer, almost sacred.

It's nearly ten, and even Iris and Winston have said their yawning goodnights. Thandi and I stand on the landing, the glow from downstairs catching the rosy tints in her hair and the caramel depths in her eyes.

She takes my breath away.

"Tonight was a lot, huh?" I say, pulling her close. Already, it feels so natural that I can't imagine not having her warmth against me.

"Mm-hmm."

For a moment, Thandi softens, leaning entirely into my strength. I tighten my arms around her, letting her know that I'll always be her anchor when she needs it.

Eventually, she pulls away and grabs my hand. "Come, let me show you around. We got so busy with dinner and the kids, I never gave you the tour."

I lace my fingers with hers. "Lead the way."

The Elowens' home is a cozy two-story craftsman with a tasteful addition that takes nothing away from the home's warmth or history. The stairs creak as Thandi guides me downstairs, her hand never slipping from mine.

To the right of the hall is a study framed by thick white columns and built-in shelves stacked with books. This is unmistakably Iris' space. Research notes rest beside a laptop, a wall calendar is pinned up with color-coded tabs, and a pile of bills tells me Thandi's mom does much more than science here. She manages the family itself.

One wall features a collage of photographs, mostly of Iris and Winston throughout the years. An oversized frame dominates the center. In it, Thandi's parents are barefoot on the beach, the tide curling at their ankles. Their faces are joyful as they stand beneath a wedding bower threaded with palm fronds, ginger lilies, and birds of paradise. Beside them, Thandi grins, showering them with rose petals from a basket.

"That was their twentieth anniversary in Montego Bay," she says, running her fingers over the frame. "They renewed their vows that summer."

I nod, studying the picture longer than I mean to. I'm caught by how Iris leans into Winston, her hand curled against his chest—almost exactly like Thandi leaned into me outside Ricky's bedroom. The resemblance stirs something startling within me. I realize that I'm already hoping that what I feel with Thandi endures just as fiercely as what Iris and Winston share.

I kiss Thandi's fingers, still conjoined with mine, and the look she gives me is so sweet, I have to capture her lips until she melts into me again.

I take in the rows of books, the worn desk, the framed photos crowding the walls. Everything feels well-loved and lived in. Nothing is frivolous or pretentious here.

"Did your parents ever think about moving?" I ask quietly. "With your success... I imagine you could set them up anywhere."

Thandi shakes her head, her lips curving, not quite into a smile. "We waited for years, hoping that Tess would just... show up at our door one day. We thought if we left, she'd never find her way back. So we stayed."

I can hear the ache in her voice. And after witnessing the Elowens' capacity for love tonight, I have a new understanding of how much Tess' absence must have devastated them.

Thandi stares out of the window, where a breeze is shaking the trees.

"With time, we'd done so much to honor her; it didn't make sense to leave. Even when I offered my folks a bigger place, it didn't feel right to them."

Her gaze returns to mine. "I get it. I feel it too."

Her words linger between us, tinged with love and a loss few can imagine.

"Come on," she murmurs, and we continue down the hall.

The living room is a wide, warm space, anchored by overstuffed couches and built-ins similar to the ones in the study. But it's the gallery of frames along the mantle that steals my attention.

Two girls, sweet mirror images, smile at me from an array of vignettes. I can tell them apart, not just because they're wearing different-colored dresses. Thandi, more serious, is instantly recognizable—and she is holding a LEGO masterpiece in at least one photo. Tess, meanwhile, radiates mischievous energy, playacting with dolls or leaping above jump rope. And yet, despite their differences, the twins are arm-in-arm in almost every photo, grinning like they're sharing secrets.

I'm gutted. Until now, Tess has existed in the abstract, in conversation—in the weight behind Thandi's eyes. But here, she is vivid and undeniable.

The ache in my chest grows the further we move along the visual sequence: grinning vacation pictures with a youthful Iris and Winston, shared violin recitals, sports meets with medals…

Then, abruptly, the symmetry ends.

Only Thandi is on the stage, clutching a bouquet. Thandi alone breaks the tape at the finish line of a race. Next, she is in cap and gown, solitary and brilliant, her valedictorian sash catching the light. By the time we get to an image of Thandi, Iris, and Winston moving boxes into a Howard dorm room, the pattern is clear. Laughter that was doubled has been halved—every new milestone is now a testament to achievement as much as absence.

Thandi follows my gaze. "I miss her so much," she whispers, lips trembling. "She was my best friend."

I reach for her, pressing a kiss to the top of her head. "I'm so sorry, baby. Both of you deserved so much better."

Tears rush down Thandi's cheeks. When I sink into the recliner and tug her onto my lap, she curls into me with a sound of distress. I kiss her face, her hands, her trembling lips as I rock her back and forth, soothing her pain—letting her know that I can shoulder it too.

Grief settles around us, heavy with the weight of potential lost— of lives that could have been lived.

Neither of us speaks.

Some things don't need words.

Loss is its own language.

I don't know how long we stay like that, the darkness deepening outside. I stroke Thandi's back and think about my samples from Anchor Park. I need to get working. I can't afford to wait; not when Thandi's pain is still so fresh.

As if sensing my thoughts, she stirs against me. "Want to head to the kitchen? I should probably pack some lunches for the kids; save mom a little work in the morning."

"Of course. I can help."

The kitchen is bright even now, white cabinets gleaming in the glow of the pendants. A bowl of tomatoes rests on the counter, and the ghost of Thandi's jambalaya lingers in the air. She reaches for a cutting board and begins arranging utensils for prep.

"Okay." I roll up my sleeves. "Where do you need me?"

"Can you grab the bento boxes from the dishwasher? I'll get the leftovers from the fridge."

I open the dishwasher and grab the boxes, handing them to Thandi. She places them side-by-side on the counter, neat compartments ready to be filled.

"Want me to uncover everything?" I ask, nodding at the bowls of leftovers.

"Would you?"

"Of course, baby." I peel back the covers and grab some serving spoons and a spatula, which I pass to Thandi.

She slices thick squares of my baked ziti, nestling one into the corner of Ricky's bento box, then adds grilled chicken to the next. A spoonful of Iris' *arroz con gandules* and the last of the peach cobbler follow, each tucked into their respective compartments.

Turning back to the cutting board, Thandi begins throwing together some sandwiches, layering ham and cheese between slices of bread. She cuts them into neat triangles before slipping them into sandwich bags for recess.

We work side by side, the quiet from the living room lingering between us. Thandi packs Ricky's box; I mirror her with Daysha's. It feels oddly ceremonial: two children, two lunches, twin gestures of care.

"Almost done," Thandi says, wiping her hands on a dish towel. "Can you grab the lunch bags from the cabinet above the fridge? You're tall enough to reach them."

"Sure thing." I stretch, pulling down two canvas bags while Thandi rummages in the fridge. She grabs a pair of juice boxes, then nudges the door shut with a graceful hip bump that leaves me distracted.

The juice boxes are bright impossible flavors—Gobsmacked Grape and Outrageous Orange—and my mind flits back to Ricky and Daysha in the park, racing over the grass, the neon kite bobbing above them.

I lean against the counter. "Can I ask you something?"

Thandi glances up. "Sure."

"When I ran into the kids at the park, Ricky said you were family," I say carefully. "And I couldn't help noticing your dad referred to him as an Elowen tonight."

Thandi smiles, slipping the Ziplock into place before passing me Daysha's lunch bag.

"That's because he is. We're still in the process, but my parents have been conditionally approved to adopt him. It isn't official yet. There's paperwork, court dates, home visits … but he belongs with us."

Thandi slips Ricky's bento into his bag, smoothing the zipper shut. Her hand lingers on the lunch bag, thumb brushing over the canvas.

"Ricky's spent all his life in the foster system. He's been through so much. More than any kid should have to. And my parents…" Her smile deepens. "They've opened their hearts to him completely."

I slide Daysha's juice box into her bag and press the Velcro flap closed, the sound loud in the hush of the kitchen. Now Ricky's pride at the park and his terror at being sent away this evening make sense.

"That's amazing," I say. "He seems like such a sweet kid."

"He is." Thandi comes to stand beside me, her shoulder brushing my arm. "It's only been a couple of weeks, but it's crazy how much better he's already doing."

"Better?" I slip my arm around her shoulder, and she hugs my torso.

"Mm-hmm." Thandi leans into me. "His last foster placement was bad. Neglect, and…" She shakes her head. "They'd even taken him off his ADHD meds. By the time I found out, he was really struggling."

For a moment, I can't breathe past the rage coursing through me. What kind of family takes their responsibility to a vulnerable kid and perverts it?

"Took him off his meds? What the fuck for?" I growl.

"Honestly, I can't figure out if the Glens were trying to save a buck, or if Astor's outreach has just been that aggressive." Thandi's voice is rising now, her chest heaving against mine. "They had him on those ridiculous PlayMist EDU inhalers that are not safe, not tested, and shouldn't be near any kid!" Her hands squeeze at my sides, agitation pouring through her grip.

Every nerve in my body freezes.

"Astor?" I gasp.

I've felt this dread before. Once, in Fia's town, a decade ago. Gut-wrenching bile rises in my throat, along with the certainty that my father's depravity is destroying lives again.

Thandi's sigh is bone-deep. "Yeah. They're Immerscent's biggest competitor. In the last year, Astor's released a slew of commercial scent products. I don't think scent therapy should be unregulated, but at least they were marketing to adults. Now—" her lips thin into a grim line. "They're focused exclusively on kids."

"*Kids?*" Horror snowballs as memory resurfaces. "Even when I worked with Mom, we had evidence of how catastrophic that could be for developing brains."

"Not according to Astor," Thandi mutters with a bitter twist to her lips. "They're leaning hard in the opposite direction. Now they're preying on parents and cash-strapped school districts, peddling Play-Mist as a medical intervention."

Thandi's shoulders sag. "We helped Ricky, but there are so many other kids being harmed. I don't know how we get to all of them."

"Yeah," I croak, choking on the panic clawing at my throat. Thandi's sweet warmth may be next to me, but suddenly I feel cold, so cold.

I'm an idiot.

My method strips context by design. I blindfold myself first, convinced distance makes me unbiased. People pay me obscene sums for that blindness. Yet now I'm struck by the arrogance of it— the privilege in being able to ignore the context.

While I sat in my office, ignoring competitor environments in the name of objectivity, James was busy building this. Not just chasing Immerscent. Hurting kids like Ricky.

Now, once again, he's threatening the people I care about most—

And everything Thandi and I have been building.

I stare down at her, and her face lifts to mine, her smile soft and radiant. She's my sun now. The first thought when I wake up, and the last before sleep. I clutch her tighter, terrified. Her kind heart, her brilliance, her fierce passion... they're too precious to lose.

But the truth pounds in my temples:

Will she still want me? Will she still look at me like this when she finds out I'm an Astor?

Sleepless
Ronan

The ceiling glares at me, blank and cold. My eyes burn, but sleep won't come.

Moonlight pierces the blinds, catching on the picture frame on my dresser. Mom stares back from our last photo together, the corners of her eyes crinkled with so much love—even through her pain.

I wish she were here now.

I wish I could hear her voice, bright, clear, and full of conviction. I wish she could tell me how to protect Ricky and the other kids hurt by Astor.

And how not to lose the woman I'm falling in love with.

I curse, hurling the covers aside. The wood floor chills my feet as I cross to the window. The city unfurls beneath me in miles of twinkling lights. My reflection wavers against the glass, a ghost over Kenleigh.

Thandi's words echo in my mind. Ricky's sharp eyes, his quick smile—held hostage by a company that carries my bloodline. For years, I've avoided my father; hidden behind the safety of distance. But distance won't stop James from pumping poisons into young bodies.

That's when I hear her voice reaching across the space of a decade to ask the same thing of me now, as she did then:

"I'm not asking you to fix anything. Just go see it for yourself."

Except this time, I do have to fix it.

I'm no longer young, foolish, or powerless. If there's a way to stop Astor, I'll find it.

I throw on a T-shirt and grab my keys, the stairs creaking under my weight as I jog downstairs. The garage lights flood the concrete in sterile white. Two shapes wait side by side: the Maybach gleaming with finesse, and the Lexus' muscular menace.

I already know which one I'm taking. Tonight, I need armor to match the battle raging in me.

Sliding into the Lexus, I grip the wheel and let the silence wrap around me. I don't know where I'm going, yet, only that the road feels like the answer. The only place to begin this reckoning.

I gun the engine, roaring into the quiet streets.

The farther I drive from Kenleigh, the more the world hums with life. A delivery truck rumbles through an intersection; a pair of laughing college kids stumble out of a diner. A plane takes off, a single pinpoint of light in the distance. I consider speeding through all of this modernity and pushing into the wooded byways—letting the open road swallow me until dawn.

But that's when I see the billboard—three stories high, burning like a beacon against the night.

A man and a woman embrace, half-reclined against each other. His mouth hovers above hers, their eyes locked in adoration. A curlicue of pink-violet smoke coils between them.

WhiffRush **is For Lovers** is slashed across the bottom.

The image is obscene in its perfection—harm dressed up as romance; poison cloaked as desire. I tighten my grip on the wheel, and before I can think, I'm signaling, switching lanes, taking the exit into downtown Chesden.

A mega gas stop sprawls before me, row after row of pumps gleaming beneath the vast overhang. This is no grungy movie gas station, but a glittering complex. The convenience store is slick— one of those places that sells everything from groceries to imported cigars. The front windows throb with neon decals. *WhiffRush Sold Here,* pulses in purple, next to *Fresh Coffee* and *Ice Cold Beer.*

I ease the Lexus into a parking spot and turn off the engine. For a minute, I just sit there, breathing deeply, trying to organize my thoughts. Then I step outside.

A gaunt figure stirs near the ice maker. The woman's smoke-roughened voice rasps out.

"Spare a dollar, sir?"

My hand goes automatically to my wallet. But before I can tug it free, she adds with a wheeze of laughter, "Thanks, man. Ain't nothing crazy. Just looking for a little WhiffRush hit."

I freeze.

The sign flickers above her, the purple glow bleeding across her hollowed face.

"Sorry," I mumble. Shaking my head, I slip my wallet back into my pocket, the weight suddenly as heavy as a stone.

"Fuckin' loser!" she hurls at my back as I step through the convenience mart's automatic doors.

She's not wrong. Not with everything Astor's done.

Hunching my shoulders, I hustle inside. Behind the counter, a dark-haired young man in a muscle tee looks up from his phone.

"Hey, man. Let me know if you need anything," he calls.

"Thanks," I murmur, already heading down the aisle.

I haven't paid attention to James' products before, but tonight I'm going to learn them all.

WhiffRush takes up half a rack between gum, condoms, and flavored lube. The packaging continues the theme from the billboard—edgy fonts over silhouettes of entwined bodies. I see that this product, at least, is intended for adults. I grab some packs from a box labeled *"Now, in Exotic Flavors."*

Unfortunately, Astor's integrity ends there.

I find *PlayMist* nestled beside asthma rescue inhalers and sinus sprays. This is the product that hurt Ricky—or at least a variation of it. My fingers tighten around one of the pastel plastic pumps. I want to dash them all to the floor, crush them under my heel. Because while I will never absolve the Glens, it's not hard to see how the placement next to real medical devices could lure an unsuspecting parent.

Nothing turns my stomach, though, like the bright cartons of *Sniffz* tucked next to fruit snacks and pudding cups, their wide-eyed cartoon mascots beaming with joy. Suddenly, a memory from the pickup game at the youth center rushes back to me. A gaggle of rowdy kids, jostling out of the doors after the match:

"Let's hit the gas station and get some Sniffz!"

"I'm getting the cherry one—and the one that smells like fire!"

"I'm getting, like, five vials. I'm this close to finishing my PlayPack."

At the time, I'd smiled listening to them, thinking it was all harmless fun. If only I'd realized the net James had already cast over them.

I snatch a handful of each flavor, my arms filling fast. The door tinkles; other late-night stragglers flit in and out, grabbing gum or asking for change. Nothing could be more ordinary. Yet, I feel like I'm standing in a minefield, knee-deep in Astor's rot.

The clerk flashes a smile as I approach the counter.

"If you're a fan of these," he says, tapping the WhiffRush packs as he scans them, "we'll have the new flavors in next week. Heard they're supposed to be wild."

He moves to the Sniffz, beeping them across the scanner. "You got kids?"

"No, these are for kids I mentor," I lie, hoping he'll stop asking questions.

"Sweet." He shoves the last box onto the pile. "Need a bag?"

"Yes," I say quietly. "A bag."

He pulls one free, shaking it open. I reach for it, and his eyes widen as they drop to my watch.

"Damn, is that a Patek? Yo, a Nautilus 5711 is insane." His grin stretches. "Hey, maybe you should check out the premium line. Quality stuff."

He slides a matte-black card across the counter with a chuckle. "Beyond my price range, but figured you might appreciate it."

I flip the card over, surprised to see how close the location is to my neighborhood. "Thanks, I'll check it out tomorrow."

"No problem. Just so you know, that spot's open twenty-four hours. You look like you could use some help getting the devil off your shoulder."

My jaw tightens as the words lodge deep. What if the devil is your father?

I slip the card into my pocket and head for the door. The woman at the entrance hasn't moved, but someone else has patronized her in my absence. She's slumped sideways against the brick wall, a crumpled takeout container near her hip. Her fingers are slack around a neon-green inhaler.

I stare, the bag swinging like an accusation at my side.

I've seen enough.

If James was disappointed in me before, when I'm done with him, he's going to regret I was ever born.

The storefront gleams in muted black glass, the only signage a heavy gothic A above the door. Even at two in the morning, there's a valet post, and a pair of men in fitted polos rush forward as I pull up.

"Welcome, sir. This way, please." They gesture at the black carpet leading to the entrance, where a couple is presenting ID.

When I step forward, the bouncer gives me a sharp nod and speaks into his earpiece. "Incoming. One for the VIP lounge."

"Do you need my ID?"

He laughs, glancing over my shoulder at the Lexus and down at my wrist. "No, man, you're good."

Inside, music throbs in a low, sensual beat, and the air is perfumed with something engineered to soothe. Chrome shelving lines the walls, illuminating inhalers in black rhodium, platinum, and chrome. Cartridges glitter like jewels in the near-dark, their labels embossed with names like *Obsidian Rush* and *PlayMist Prime — Midnight Edition.*

A hostess who could be Amber's sister greets me with a glass of sparkling wine and a sway of her hips. She drags an appreciative look over my body. "Welcome to Prime. A curator will be with you shortly. Cristal, while you wait?"

I raise an eyebrow but take the glass. The flute is chilled to perfection, bubbles rising in a golden stream.

As if on cue, someone materializes at my elbow. This woman is sharply dressed in a slate gray suit, glasses glinting on her ebony face. Her four-inch heels are silent on the soundproofed floor.

"Good evening, sir. I am Solé, your curator. Whom do I have the pleasure of serving?"

"You can call me Ansel," I say, shaking her hand.

"Excellent, Ansel. Please allow me to show you to your scent suite."

We pass a counter where uniformed staff in black guide customers through "tasting rituals," misting testers into the air. The group inhales with reverence, heads tilting back, eyes half-shut.

"What are those?" I ask, pointing to a row of black pods with velvet curtains.

Solé smiles, perfect teeth flashing. "These are our care pods. VIPs like you will receive a more personalized experience, but we guarantee transformational care for all. With just a few key pieces of information, guests can receive a free assessment tailored to their needs. Shall I show you?"

I nod, and she ushers me into one of the cocoons. The pod is as simple as it is luxurious: a plush leather chair and a sleek console set into the wall. I sink into the seat, ensconced in seductive comfort.

Solé gestures to the Bose headphones, and I slip them on, the buzz of the lounge vanishing instantly. Her fingers fly across the console, and the voice that fills my ears is smooth, almost tender:

"Good evening, Ansel. I'm Alaia, your wellness assistant."

Solé leans against the pod with feline grace. "You may speak to her or type your responses. You may also go straight to the questionnaire."

A glowing panel slides into view. I swipe at random, and questions spill across the screen:

Please enter your height and weight.

Do you ever experience shortness of breath?

Rate your sleep quality.

Have you noticed mood swings, focus issues, or changes in appetite lately?

Of course, my answers are nonsense, intended only to test the technology. Still, by the time I am halfway through, I'm chilled to the bone.

This is Immerscent's philosophy. These are Thandi's meticulous client care protocols hollowed out, her rigor replaced with digital mimicry.

The violation is appalling, not just because of the risk of harm or the blatant data harvesting, but because James' playbook hasn't changed. What he wants, he takes without respect for rules or ethics. Especially when the innovator is a woman.

He did it to Mom when he stole her company. Now Thandi is in his sights.

My heart pounds, the blood throbbing in my temples at the theft—the desecration. Cursing, I yank off the headphones.

"Is everything alright, Ansel?" The faintest furrow mars Solé's brow.

"I've seen enough," I bark, jerking to my feet. I can barely think for the storm of rage and disgust roiling in me.

"Of course. I understand if the pods do not meet your standards. That is why we've prepared a scent suite," Solé intones, entirely misreading my agitation. Her feet move rapidly across the floor.

The scent suite is a luxurious microcosm of the entire lounge. A hostess circles with another round of drinks, while another offers charcuterie and caviar. I have my own "tasting" counter, behind which is a heavily tatted and pierced man in a Matrix-style outfit, whom Solé introduces as my "mixologist." Here, I can select any of the existing flavors, or the mixologist can craft one for me.

As soon as Solé leaves, a slim man wearing a lab coat approaches. His mild-mannered face and clinical outfit are a stark contrast to the moody excess around me.

"Ansel, I'm Keith Harrington, chief scientist here at Prime. How might I assist you this evening? Perhaps a custom blend? Or are you in the market for a gift?"

I'm about to wave him off when I pause.

"Actually—" I lean against the counter. My gaze sweeps over the rainbow of vials. "Tell me about the science behind Prime."

Imposter
Ronan

Mom always said there are no coincidences.

Tonight, I'm inclined to believe her, and it has nothing to do with mysteries of fate or spirituality.

Because what I'm hunting isn't chance. It is intention honed to a dagger point.

A sickly-sweet haze burns through the air as I crush and liquefy the three samples on my bench: a garish packet of Sniffz, a slick box of WhiffRush, and the PlayMist Platinum from Prime.

My conversation with Harrington was ... illuminating to say the least.

You'd think, after all the suffering James has inflicted, nothing could surprise me. Not after Mom, after Fia, Ricky, and what I saw at Prime.

Still, I frowned when Harrington mentioned G protein–coupled receptors and signal cascades. I froze when he referenced research on allosteric modulation. Dread loomed at his excitement over shared receptor families.

Each innovation he named is familiar.

They were all a focus of Mom's during her career.

A coincidence? I wonder. Or something else?

Surely, even James wouldn't stoop that low?

I notch the flame higher, stripping away the mid-weight compounds until the haze sours, then thins, and only an oily residue clings to each beaker.

I'm already gloved, pipettes clicking in my hands as I fill one glass slide after the other.

I stain the WhiffRush dregs first, slip the solution under the microscope, and bring the lens into focus. The glow isn't random. It blooms into a lattice, its sharp planes locking into a grid I know too well.

My pulse spikes. My hands shake as I dip the pipette back into the WhiffRush remnants, draw, and test again. The same lattice, spectral and stubborn, glares back at me.

I inhale, trying to steady myself as I reach for Sniffz. I draw and stain, and the fluorescent pattern flashes into place within seconds. My stomach churns. I test again with a fresh sample, a second slide, a second stain.

Still no change.

Next is PlayMist Prime. I grit my teeth as I splash drops hastily over the slide, praying for a deviation. The grid flares bright as ever. I dip, repeat, test again and again. Nothing shifts. The glow holds fast. Indelible, distinctive, utterly damning.

The bench screeches across the floor as I jerk to my feet. Anger and pain claw at my throat. Suspecting is one thing. Knowing nearly drives me insane.

Every sample, every single product, contains the same foundation, the same blueprint.

Not a note, or a fragrance, but a bespoke allosteric modulator, brilliant and unfinished.

RT3.

Mom's last formula.

I curse, my voice echoing through the empty lab. I'm railing at yet another deception, another bone-deep betrayal: Mom's science pilfered to fuel Astor's twisted empire.

James' infernal smirk blooms in my mind. He thinks he's untouchable? I'll find him and drag his sorry ass to the depths of hell and back.

I'm reaching for my keys, fists already clenched, pushing past the lab into the hallway. But just as I'm hurtling past my office, the thin glow of construction lights behind the new wing's cellophane entrance stops me cold.

And it's Mom's voice again, calling from the reaches of memory, that reminds me what matters:

To my beloved son, Ronan Thorne, I bequeath all intellectual property rights associated with Thorne Therapeutics, including patents and proprietary formulations developed under the company's name.

I go utterly still. So still I can hear the rush of blood in my veins, every note of the wind whistling outside.

These aren't just Mom's formulas anymore. *They're mine.*

What does James always say?

That I don't understand power—how to find it, how to seize it, how to wield it.

I unclench my fists and stare at my hands. They're strong hands, uncannily similar to the ones James never hesitated to rain down on me until I was large enough to be a threat of my own.

No. I won't become him, and I won't use his methods. Because that kind of man didn't hold Mom through the end. That kind of man doesn't get to cherish a woman like Thandi.

I'm not James, and I won't succumb to his poison. Not for Mom, not for Thandi, but for myself. I've seen enough pain and bitterness. It's time to build something better.

Besides, I don't need to become James. Not when Mom has handed me the most incisive weapon of all.

Now there are only two questions: how to tell Thandi, and when I should use it.

Grilled Cheese
Thandi

"This is just a start, but the next phase could be synthetic receptors or engineering pathway bias," I finish updating Trent on the Sugar Hill concept. "But as is, we'll be ready for the IPO next week."

"So Thorne was worth it after all." Trent leans back in his chair with a grin.

I'm working from home today, so Trent and I are having our Monday meeting in my condo's private garden. The little bistro table between us is littered with paperwork. I have a ton to finish for the IPO launch, but at least here, away from the office chaos, I can focus.

I can't help the flush of pleasure warming my cheeks at the mention of Ronan. I turn toward Junie, who's gurgling as she digs a hole in the sandbox with a tiny red shovel. Her star-shaped sunglasses catch the sunlight.

"Yeah," I say softly.

Worth it doesn't even begin to describe what's blossoming between me and Ronan. A month ago, I thought Trent was crazy. Today, I'm floored by everything Ronan has brought into my life.

I think back to dinner with my parents, how natural it felt to have him there. It was special. Perfect. Because with Ronan, I don't have to be. Or maybe it's that with him, I don't have to keep *doing*.

My heart clenches as I remember how he held me in the living room. More than anything, with Ronan, I don't have to be alone. His shoulders are strong enough to bear the weight of my secrets.

I've never had permission to rest—not with Tess as my unresolved question. I'm still searching, still rushing forward, but the journey is a little less daunting now. Maybe it's Ronan's confidence, his protectiveness, or our surprising partnership, but I'm … happier when I'm with him. And it feels different, deeper than anything I've ever known.

I guess Dani was right after all.

"Good," Trent says, bringing me back to the present. "No wonder Fowler was excited. He said Thorne previewed the concept with him at your dad's fundraiser. Sounds like he's ready to lock it in."

"I didn't realize you knew Fowler," I say, bending to hand Junie her sippy cup.

"Yeah, our families go way back. He and my father were country club buddies. I even got a couple of steers from his ranch."

"He seems like a good guy."

"He is. Anyway, let's map out the next steps with the board. Clara and Marisol will get it, but you know how ornery Niko can be. Let's—" Trent pauses as his phone buzzes. "Wait, sorry, I have to take this."

"Of course."

Trent flashes me a grateful look. Scooping Junie up, he props her on his hip as he wanders out of earshot.

While he's gone, I check my messages. My smile blooms as soon as I spot Ronan's text:

Ronan: Can I tempt you with lunch? I could swing by your office.
Me: WFH today, but yes. About to take a break now, if that works for you?
Ronan: Perfect. I'm in the area, so I'm 15 mins away. See you soon, baby.

Baby. My breath catches. My stomach stitches itself into tiny knots at the endearment. It's not just the word; it's the fact that I can hear Ronan's deep voice, his exact emphasis, as if he were breathing it against my ear. Of course, that flings me right onto the path of perdition, straight into the memory of his kisses in Fia's bedroom.

The memory of his fingers caressing my neck.

I shiver.

Down, girl. It's just a lunch date, I remind myself, pressing my phone to my chest. It doesn't slow my racing heart, but skimming the rest of my texts helps distract me.

There's a text from Dani reminding me to review the IPO launch marketing plan; a delivery confirmation for the bath bombs I ordered; and a long, confusing message from Dad about a venue. He's clearly typing on the go, and the text is garbled enough that I make a note to return to it when I'm less preoccupied.

Trent is still deep in his conversation, Junie cooing along beside him. He's nodding, a smile softening his features. Whoever he's talking to, at least it looks like good news. I start thumbing through Dani's marketing plan, and before I know it, the concierge is making her way across the grass, one hand shading her eyes from the sun.

"Ms. Elowen?"

"Yes?"

"A Mr. Thorne is here to see you. Shall I send him over?"

"Please." I smooth my hand over my leggings and the oversized button-up I'm wearing. Do I look frumpy? I didn't give my outfit a second thought with Trent. Now I'm wondering if I should have changed.

Too late—the concierge disappears, and Ronan steps through the glass doors and onto the grass. Of course, he's in full business mode today, in a sharply tailored suit that makes his hair look as burnished as a penny. He's carrying a brown takeout bag in one hand and a cardboard tray with two lemonades in the other. He stops short when he sees Trent and Junie in the distance.

"I'm sorry, baby. I didn't realize you had company."

I wave him closer. "Trent is hardly company. Besides, we were finishing up anyway."

"You're sure?"

"Positive."

"I hope you brought your appetite," Ronan says, setting the bag on the table. Whatever's inside smells heavenly, like milky, cheesy goodness.

"I'm starving," I say, looping my arms around his waist.

He tugs me forward by the lapels of my shirt. "Just for food?" he murmurs, with a wicked grin.

"You offering something else?" I ask breathlessly.

"Mm hmm. Let's call it dessert." Ronan nuzzles my neck. "This is a cute look, by the way. I don't think I've ever seen you this casual."

"Are you calling me high maintenance, Thorne?" I narrow my eyes at him. My attempt at sternness is ruined when my voice wobbles, thanks to the butterfly kisses he's trailing along my skin. I whimper as his teeth graze my throat.

"Ronan," I gasp.

"I missed you," he whispers against me.

"We just saw each other yesterday." I'm trembling in his arms, need tingling through me.

"Exactly. An eternity," Ronan purrs, pulling me tight against him.

I think I just might melt when my stomach beats me to the punch. It growls ferociously.

Ronan chuckles, then steps back. "Okay, let's get some food in you."

"Sorry." I manage a sheepish look. "I had an early start and didn't grab breakfast."

"It's a good thing I'm here, then." Placing a soft kiss against my temple, he begins unpacking the food.

"What is it?" I ask, leaning on tiptoe to peer into the bag. "It smells so good.

"The ultimate Monday comfort food—grilled cheese and tomato soup."

My eyes widen. "Don't tell me you went to Grate Expectations? That food truck always has a line down the block. I could kiss you right now!"

Smirking, Ronan leans forward and taps his cheek. "Put 'er there, then."

"Silly." I lean in and kiss him. It's only noon, yet his jaw is already stippled with shadow. The rasp of stubble sensitizes my lips, leaving them tender, faintly bruised. The memory of that same roughness against my inner thighs sparks heat low in my belly, and a sound slips out before I can stop it. My hand drifts to my mouth.

"What?" Ronan's eyes blaze over my face. We're close enough that I can see the sudden expansion of his pupils.

Heat rushes to my core. God, I need to get control of this. I can't keep melting into a needy puddle the minute Ronan is near.

"Nothing," I say hoarsely. I meet his eyes as I brush my thumb over his cheek. "I thought this was supposed to be a five o'clock shadow. It's midday."

Ronan turns his face and licks over my palm. His eyes are whiskey-dark, his tongue hot and soft against my fingers. "I shaved this morning, but it grows quickly. You like it?"

I nod, my breath catching as he dips lower, sipping at my pulse.

"I'll remember that," he murmurs—half promise, half threat. A hot ache throbs deep inside me, and the rest of the world falls away until there's only Ronan. He shoots me a knowing look, then eases back. He passes me a sandwich and a container of tomato soup before taking his own seat.

"Eat. And I expect to see an empty plate, given your lack of breakfast."

I roll my eyes, but warmth blooms in my chest. I dip the cheesy, crusty edge of my sandwich into the soup. "Thank you for doing this."

"Any time." Ronan smiles, but after a minute, his expression falters. His gaze drifts toward Trent. "Thandi, I need to tell you something important. Do you have a moment after Trent leaves?"

"Of course. Is everything alright?"

"Honestly, I'm not sure." His tone is grim. His hands close around the edge of the table, knuckles stark against the metal. I've seen him worried, even frustrated, but never like this. Unease coils through me. What could shake him this way?

I place my hand over one of his. "Whatever it is, we'll work through it together, okay?"

Ronan nods. "I—"

"Oh, thank goodness, you're here! Peanut, I need you." Dad bursts in, his locs a lion's mane around his head. He's so harried that he must have lost his hair tie somewhere.

I'm sorry, I mouth to Ronan, who only shakes his head.

"Dad, what's going on?"

"Ronan, son, good to see you," Dad gasps, skidding to a stop in front of us. He leans forward, propping one hand on his hip.

"Winston, why don't you sit?" Ronan rises, offering his chair. Dad collapses into it with a grateful huff. "Thanks, son."

I frown, taking in his heaving chest and the perspiration dotting his brow. "Have you been running? What's the emergency?"

"We lost the venue for the Blue Moon celebration."

"The what?" I press my lemonade into his hands.

"The Blue Moon celebration this weekend," Dad says, drawing long and deep on the lemonade. "Mark had lined up the lake house on the Susquehanna, but it fell through at the last minute. The owner's got a family emergency. And now we're stuck without a venue for the club's most mystical moment of the year!"

"I'm sorry, Dad," I sigh, finally piecing together his garbled text. Every year, Dad and his friends hold a 'healing retreat' timed with major moments in the lunar cycle. Apparently, this year is extra special thanks to a rare Blue Moon.

"Remember, during the pandemic, you let us use Immerscent's rooftop for our singing bowl harmonization? Any chance that's an option again?" His eyes gleam with desperate hope.

"I'm sorry, Dad, one of our suppliers booked the space for a business event. It's free next weekend, though."

Dad drops his head into his hands, shoulders slumping. "The Blue Moon will be gone by then. We'll miss it."

He looks so dejected, I can't help pulling him into a hug. "Come on. Don't give up. We'll think of something. I'll call Fia. Maybe one of the venues we considered for the fundraiser is available. It's short notice, but—"

"What about the vineyard?" Ronan asks.

My head snaps up. "What vineyard?"

"Thorne Run. It's right on the estate, and there's plenty of space. We host events there all the time, precisely because of the views. I'm not sure exactly what you need, but I can't think of a better spot to see the moon."

"You mean it?" Dad pops up in his seat.

Ronan shrugs. "It's not a big deal. I'm happy to arrange a tour for you and your friends. There's also plenty of room in the main house if you need to spend the night."

I stare at him, my heart pounding at his generosity. I can't believe he'd go out of his way for my family like this.

"Ronan…" I breathe.

He raises a hand to the back of his neck. "You're both making far too much of this. I'd be happy to have you."

"Son, you're a lifesaver." Dad shoots me a look. "I knew this one was a keeper."

"Dad!" Heat floods my cheeks, but he's already buzzing with excitement, his imagination catching fire.

"We'll take it—but only if you two join us."

"Dad … that's the day before the IPO launch. I'm slammed, and I'm not sure Ronan needs to be dragged into this."

Dad folds his arms. "Let the man speak for himself. And a healing celebration before your IPO launch is auspicious—some might even say lucky. Are you sure you want to miss it?"

I sigh and toss Ronan a look that says, *You talk some sense into him.* But he surprises me by nodding.

"Sure. If it's important to you, I'll come. What time is the celebration? If it's in the evening, it could work even with your IPO schedule. What do you say, baby?"

It's hard to say no after everything he's done for me. And now this....

"Fine," I relent. "I'll come."

"Excellent!" Dad claps his hands together. "Ronan, son, would you like to be initiated into the singing circle?"

I groan. You can never say Winston Elowen isn't an optimist. Ronan is just starting to sputter and back away when Trent returns from his call.

"Good news, Thandi—whoa. This is quite the gathering."

"Ronan brought me lunch," I explain. "And Dad dropped by with a last-minute wrinkle in an event he's planning."

Trent nods, clapping Ronan on the back and greeting my father. "Well, I'm afraid I'm adding another wrinkle of my own. Thandi, how do you feel about flying to Austin this evening?"

"This evening, as in tonight?"

"Yeah. That was Fowler on the line. He wants to host something for Immerscent at the country club's speaker's night tomorrow. He suggested you could be the guest of honor—use the moment to bring in some additional investors for the IPO. He's even managed to convince Yanovich of that new perovskite solar firm to come, and you know how rarely he's seen in public."

My head spins at both the magnitude and the suddenness of it, but I can't deny the opportunity. No, this is bigger. Once-in-a-lifetime. Not just because of Yanovich, but because women like me don't get invited into these hyper-exclusive, tradition-steeped spaces. It's going to be a rough week, but I'd be a fool to turn it down.

I meet Ronan's eyes, and his expression is almost panicked. I'd agreed we'd talk about whatever was weighing on him, but now there's no time. I need to get ready for the trip.

I ignore Trent's startled look as I rush over to Ronan and fling my arms around him. "I'm so sorry, but I have to do this. We'll talk as soon as I'm back, I promise."

"Of course, baby. Go show these old farts what you're made of. I'll be here, waiting."

Trent stares from me to Ronan. "So it's settled then?"

"It's settled," I say.

I hug Ronan and Dad, then grab my things and follow Trent and Junie out. Trent's already pinging Dani and calling my assistant as we hustle across the lawn. I should be grateful, but I'm too distracted.

Too worried about Ronan—and the shadows in his eyes.

Volley
Ronan

"She's going to hate me."

"She's not going to hate you."

It's Thursday evening, and I'm so wound with anxiety that I haven't slept more than a couple of hours since Thandi left for Austin. Tonight, Fia's with me in my gym, helping me burn off the excess energy.

"I'm the son of the man who endangered her foster brother— and who's trying to steal her protocols. She's going to hate me."

"Ronan." Fia catches the medicine ball against her chest with a grunt, sweat streaking down her temple. She holds it for a second before hurling it back at me. "Thandi is not that kind of woman. She may be shocked and confused, but she's not going to hate you. Besides, you're nothing like your father—and you're not responsible for what James has done."

The ball slams into my palms. I feel its weight reverberate through my shoulders as much as her words.

"You really believe that?"

"I do." Fia catches the ball as I toss it back to her. "Do you need to tell her? Yes. Will it be a big deal? Absolutely. But you've also spent the last decade deliberately crafting a legacy of your own. Let her in. Show her who you are and what you believe in."

I grunt and shift to the battle ropes, seizing the thick coils and snapping them against the mat in alternating waves. Sweat flies with every strike, the thud of the ropes echoing in my chest.

Across from me, Fia rolls her shoulders and wheels over to the rowing erg. She straps in and then pulls in a precise rhythm.

"So you're saying I shouldn't call her and bare my soul?"

Fia rolls her eyes. "Only if you want to throw her off her game during one of the biggest moments of her life, then sure."

"Do you always have to be so logical?"

"To a fault." She grins.

I drag the edge of my shirt across my forehead. "What about this weekend at the Blue Moon celebration?"

"Won't that be a bit awkward, surrounded by her family and friends? And probably not very fair to her. She'll be out of sorts and forced to play it cool, so Winston's moment isn't overshadowed."

I let the ropes fall with a frustrated thud. "When, then?"

Fia stays quiet through two reps, then looks at me. "I love that you want to face this head-on, but you need to create a space that's quiet, intimate—where she can feel emotionally safe. Remember, this timeline is one you're creating. Rushing could backfire. Let her come home, enjoy the celebration together, and tell her once the IPO is launched on Tuesday. She has too much on her plate right now to process anything else."

I sigh. "Okay."

Fia eyes me. "Besides, it's not like you don't have other things to figure out."

"Things like what?" I ask, picking the ropes back up.

"Like what you're going to do now that you have the power to take down Astor. I don't see how it survives an intellectual property suit. RT3 is too distinctive not to be traceable to Rosalind." She shakes her head. "I gotta say, that's some *cojones grandes* on James' part. When do you think he did it?"

My whole body tenses at the thought. "I'd imagine it must have been soon after Mom was diagnosed—right after her company went public."

Fia's eyes widen. "You mean as part of James' takeover of the board?"

"Yes and no." I set the ropes down and move to the water station, refilling my bottle. "I talked to Frederick last night to better understand what happened—what Mom knew."

"And?"

"And it turns out the betrayal ran deeper than the board. Not only was James colluding with the chair to buy up a controlling share of Mom's stock, but he also bought out her lead scientist. She always suspected he'd stolen her work, and since Astor swallowed Thorne Therapeutics, the non-compete clause never came into play."

I tighten my grip on the bottle. "Besides, she was sick by then, and once James had the board strip her of the CEO title, there wasn't much she could do."

"That bastard." Fia shakes her head.

I think of all that Mom lost, and Frederick's words keep ringing in my head: "*She was adamant, Ronan. Said you were the only one she trusted to safeguard her work. That you'd understand when the time came.*"

I have to act, and it must be not only decisive but strategic. It won't pay to underestimate James.

"I've already spoken to Aamir. He's preparing the paperwork for the suit. But I need more time to dig into Astor's operations. I may hold the trump card, but everything about this has to be planned. James won't make it easy, and I'll need maximum leverage."

"Agreed."

Fia pulls away from the rowing machine and wheels up to me.

"Now tell me. How can I help?"

Top Notes

Priority
Thandi

The first thing I do when I land is call Ronan. I swear the phone only rings once before he picks up.

"Thandi. You're back?"

"Yeah," I breathe, cradling my phone to my ear. The last few days in Austin were a blur. What started as an evening fireside chat turned into a morning meeting with Fowler and Yanovich, which spun into introductions to half their circle. Before I knew it, I was clearing my schedule and spending the rest of the week in Trent's city.

Now, 120 hours later, I'm exhausted but proud of what I've accomplished—Fowler promised not to sell a single share for six months, Yanovich came in with a seventy-five-million-dollar indication of interest, and there were so many other commitments of support that I'm still reeling.

I've been in full business mode, with barely a chance for anything beyond a few texts to Ronan. Now that I'm back, though, it's crazy how much I've missed him.

"Monday feels like a lifetime ago. I wish you could have come with me. How are you?" I ask, nudging the door to my condo open and dragging my carry-on behind me. Of course, I haven't forgotten what he was so desperate to tell me before I left.

"I wish I could've come with you too, baby. And I'm good—minus your abandoning me mid–grilled cheese. It's been a busy week. Tell me about Austin," he says against a backdrop of clinking cutlery. Somewhere in the distance, a microwave hums, then beeps.

My curiosity gets the better of me. "What are you doing over there? Are you cooking?"

"Only if microwaved s'mores count as meal prep."

"Ronan," I laugh, "don't tell me you have a sweet tooth."

"Mm-hmm. You didn't know?"

"Nope." I sink onto the couch and kick off my pumps.

"I'm surprised."

"How would I know that? Although you really liked those funnel cakes at Sugar Hill Park…" I muse, rubbing my instep.

"Those were fine, but I much preferred what I had at Fia's party instead."

"What you had—" I start to ask, then his meaning registers. I gasp, suddenly too warm despite the condo's blasting AC.

Ronan's laugh is dark, silky. "You disagree? I thought you were very sweet."

"That's…" My voice comes out strangled. "Thank you."

I can barely think past the blood pounding in my veins, the memory of Ronan's touch, his sinful kisses on my skin, the intensity of the pleasure he gave me. I clutch the phone tighter.

"Still here?" His voice is rough, gravelly—proof I'm not the only one affected.

"I'm here. Just a little breathless," I confess.

"Good. Then maybe tonight we can continue where we left off."

The question hangs between us, but my body and my heart already know the answer. There's no doubt. I want him completely—in every way. "I'd like that," I whisper.

Ronan groans, the sound fanning my flames even higher. His breathing is heavy, silence thick on the line before he finally says:

"I can't wait. Now, seriously, tell me about your trip."

I sigh, leaning into the cushions. I tell him about Fowler's lock-up, Yanovich's surprising commitment, and the other potential investors, plus the deal that came together at a private rodeo show.

"That's quite the whirlwind, but none of it surprises me. I knew you'd hit it out of the park," he says—and I believe him. I can hear the pride in his voice through the line.

I just wish he were here so I could see it in person.

"Thanks. I'm still stunned by how quickly it all happened, but it was worth it." I pause. "But enough about me. Ronan, you were worried when I left. I know there was something you wanted to talk about. I'm sorry we didn't get to it."

"It's fine," he says, surprising me. "Your jetting off turned out to be a good thing."

"How so?"

"Gave me a moment to step back, gain some perspective. It can wait. Let's show up for your dad and get past your IPO launch. Sound good?"

I frown, recalling the anxiety etched across his face before I left. On Monday, whatever he'd been agonizing over didn't feel like something that could wait. Now he's saying the opposite. I only hope he's not putting on a brave face because the IPO is so close.

"Are you sure? I ask, my voice uncertain. "If it's important—"

"It can wait, baby. Trust me."

"Alright…"

"Besides, this evening is much more important. I don't want anything getting in the way of holding you in my arms again."

Some of the tension leaves my shoulders, and I can't help smiling.

"So that's your only priority, sir? Getting me into your bed? What about the moon? Spiritual fellowship? Communing with nature?"

"You'll always be my number one priority, Thandi."

My lips part, the breath knocked out of me for the second time this evening. "Ronan…"

Ronan makes a soft, inscrutable sound. "I'll see you this evening?"

Of course, there's only one answer, after his searing declaration—now that I know, for Ronan, I come first above all else. It's heavy and freeing all at once. And dangerously close to something much deeper we're both circling, but not ready to say yet.

For now, I nod and imagine his arms around me.

"Yes," I murmur. "I can't wait."

The condo is quiet except for the shuffle of papers and the low hum of the espresso machine. Dani and I have colonized the window seat, our legs folded up between cushions and files, IPO binders spread across the ledge like a battlefield. She's in soft gray sweats, glasses slipping low on her nose as she marks up another draft of the press release. A cup of matcha sits cooling at her elbow, long forgotten.

I lean back against the glass, the city skyline at my shoulder, and skim through the interview prep she's outlined—CNN, Bloomberg, even a late-night slot that makes me groan out loud. Dani just smirks, unflappable as ever.

"Don't worry, we'll control the message," she says, tapping her pen against the page. "You were already going in strong with the Sugar Hill concept, but Fowler's six-month lock-up, Yanovich's seventy-five million indication, and the book already being oversubscribed—that's the bang we were hoping for. Analysts will eat this up. It tells the market Immerscent isn't just stable, it's irresistible."

Her tone softens as she sets her pen down. "I mean it, Thandi. I'm proud of you. Watching you close these deals, watching you step into this moment… It's everything I knew you were capable of."

My throat tightens. "You've been with me every step of the way, D. This was a team effort. Three years ago, you took a chance on me when all I had was my research and a dream. I couldn't even pay you!"

Dani grins. "Ogilvy was boring anyway. This was the better bet. And let's be clear, I'm very happy with my salary now. But if you're offering a bonus, I won't complain." She winks. "Evelyn's been hinting about the Seychelles."

"I think we'll all need a vacation after this." I laugh. It's my turn to wink. "And I'll see what I can do about the Seychelles, because happy wife—"

"Happy life," Dani finishes with a grin. "Okay, let's go over the press release one last time, and then I'll get out of your hair." She fixes me with a pointed look. "Also, you better not be planning to work all evening. I need you fresh tomorrow—I mean it, Thandi."

"Calm down. I couldn't work tonight even if I wanted to. Tonight's one of Dad's lunar celebrations."

"Oh?"

"Yeah, it's a big deal. Apparently, tonight is a blue moon."

Dani's eyebrows lift. "Whew. Good omen? That's pretty powerful on the eve of an IPO launch."

I lean over, peering into her eyes like I'm checking for fever. "Are you okay? Who are you and what have you done with Dani?"

"What?" She crosses her arms.

"Aren't you the same woman who told me astrology is for fools? Who cackled when Pluto got demoted for that very reason?"

"This isn't astrology. The moon's gravitational force has been scientifically proven to have real-world effects. Just look at the tides. Besides…" A rare tinge of pink creeps into Dani's cheeks. "Evelyn's been teaching me a few things."

"Okay, forget what I said earlier. We are absolutely getting this woman to the Seychelles. She's out here working actual miracles."

I flop back against the window seat, giggling as Dani balls up a piece of paper and tosses it at me.

"That's my cue to leave," she pretends to huff, gathering her things. She pauses mid-motion, laptop half-slipped into its sleeve.

"Oh, I forgot to mention, something popped up in alerts this morning. Looks like Amber bought the rights to that journalist's photos from your dad's fundraiser. A normal person would be ashamed of what happened, but her publicist is spinning it into fodder for her reality show." Dani shakes her head. "Go figure."

I groan. The last thing I need is to relive Amber's sabotage attempts, especially not with online drama that could spook investors. "How bad is it? Will it hurt us tomorrow?"

"No," Dani says slowly, slinging her bag over her shoulder. "It might actually be helpful."

"Helpful? How?"

"Let's just say the coverage of you is very sympathetic. And there's some chatter about Ronan, thanks to video footage a guest uploaded. Last hashtags I saw were about chivalry not being dead."

I press a hand to my temples. "There's *video*? It was a private event."

Dani shrugs. "Comes with the territory these days, I'm afraid. I'll keep monitoring, but I'm not worried. Most of the attention's on Ronan anyway. It's next to impossible to find anything about him, and that only fuels the fascination."

I sigh.

Dani turns as I walk her to the door. "Disconnect this evening, Thandi. Enjoy yourself—and rest. You've earned it, and you won't get another chance next week."

Easier said than done. Still, I nod.

"Thanks, Dani."

We hug, and she promises to check in first thing in the morning.

Once she's gone, I lean against the closed door, breathing deeply, trying to shift gears, now, to something much more lighthearted. After all the travel, part of me wishes I could stay in, curled up with a glass of wine—and Ronan. But Dad would be disappointed if I bailed at the last minute.

Time to rally.

I head to the bedroom and start tossing an overnight bag together.

This will be fun, at least.

Blue Moon

Ronan

Thandi arrives first, as I suspected. Like me, she must want a little time alone before the rest of the party arrives. My heart is in my throat, and I'm out the front door before her sleek BMW i7 rolls to a stop.

Mr. Hensley is descending the stairs, a valet in his wake, but I sprint ahead before they can reach her. "I've got it, Mr. Hensley," I call.

I jog down the last few steps, open Thandi's door, and offer her my hand. She slips out gracefully, passing her keys to the young valet without looking away from me. My hands are shaking just at the sight of her.

"Hey," I breathe.

"Hi." She smiles and wraps her arms around me. And damn if it doesn't feel like home. I lift her off the ground, holding her close, inhaling her familiar scent. She makes a startled sound, but she doesn't pull away—and that means everything. All the tension and nervous energy drains out of me, leaving only the tenderest emotions behind.

"It's good to see you," I murmur.

"You too," she whispers, and when she tilts her sweet face up to mine, I can't resist capturing her lips.

I savor her, teasing at the seam of her mouth with my tongue, and she opens for me without hesitation. The breathy sound she makes kindles the embers of my desire, igniting them to a flame. I tighten my arms around her, crushing her breasts to my chest, and she whimpers.

"Ah… pardon, Mr. Thorne." Behind me, Mr. Hensley clears his throat.

I groan, stealing one last kiss before pulling away. "Yes?" I try not to sound irritated.

"Where would you like me to take Ms. Elowen's bag?" He's already pulled Thandi's duffel over his shoulder.

Of course, Hensley is the picture of professionalism, but he's not fooling me. His eyes are dancing; he's far too pleased with himself. I know what he's thinking: Thandi is the first woman I've brought to Whitlow since I moved out in my 20s. By the time he and Mrs. Jackson compare notes, I'll never hear the end of it.

"Baby, I've prepared your own suite, or you can share mine. Any preference?"

"Yours is fine." She brushes my shoulder. "Now, put me down."

I set her on her feet, but I know I'm grinning like an idiot at her choice. I stare at her, taking in her beauty. Her linen dress and leather sandals are the picture of late summer ease. She looks exhausted but happy.

Fia was right. Waiting to talk about James makes sense. I can't throw another challenge at her right now. Not with so much on her shoulders.

"What?" she demands, smoothing her hand over her dress.

"Nothing. Just admiring the view." Smiling, I extend my hand. "Come, let me show you around."

The guests start arriving at the vineyard around six, just as the sun is low enough to cast shadows across the vines.

I don't even have to guess which car is Winston's.

It's hard to miss the VW Microbus with *Celestine* emblazoned on the side and a hand-painted yin-yang stenciled on the back hatch. Its mint-green paint catches the light, solar decals glinting as it rolls to a stop.

The hum of the electric engine fades to the creak of the sliding door as Winston steps out in worn leather sandals. His salt-and-pepper locs are pulled into a loose queue over one shoulder, and he's wearing linen drawstring pants and a batik shirt in crimson and indigo. Several strands of beads adorn his neck and wrists. He tilts his head back as though greeting the heavens, breathing deeply, before opening the passenger door with a flourish.

Iris emerges in a flowing cream caftan and scarf, her hair pinned into a low bun. She's balancing a mason jar pitcher of something labeled "hibiscus-ginger tonic" in one hand and a novel in the other.

Thandi and I hurry over. I take the pitcher from Iris while Thandi folds both arms around her parents.

Iris squeezes my hand. "Ronan, what a beautiful place. Thank you for having us."

I smile. "I'm just happy I could help."

We've entered the wooded border skirting the vineyard rows, where we'll set up camp. The air is cooler here, and light dapples through the leaves. Winston whistles low as he surveys the clearing.

"This energy?" he says, voice reverent. "It's a blessing. You can *feel* it."

"*Can* we feel it? Or is that just the breeze?" Thandi teases, rubbing her hands together.

I take them in mine and warm them between my own. She's right; it is unseasonably crisp for early September. The DMV is notorious for its false fall high jinks, though. Next week we'll probably be in shorts again, but for now the chill lingers.

Thandi shoots me a grateful look as I massage warmth back into her fingers. She's wearing one of my sweatshirts over her dress, and it dwarfs her frame. The sleeves are scrunched up to her elbows, and the hem drapes almost to her knees. I can't help but bite back a smile at how adorable she looks. I need to find more excuses to put her in my clothes.

"I'm just saying, Peanut," Winston declares, throwing his arms wide and turning in a circle. "This land is ready for healing. You feel that hum? That's alignment."

Thandi only laughs. "If you're happy, then I'm happy, Dad. That's all that matters."

Just like at dinner, I'm struck by the affection between them, so genuine, so easy, it almost hurts. Mom was my world, but even then, there was scant physical affection in our house. And James— he always favored the stick over the carrot. I can't imagine having the kind of closeness Thandi shares with her parents.

As I try not to stare at the Elowens, I think about the weight of legacy. A man like me, who was nurtured in dysfunction, probably shouldn't even think about becoming a father. But if I ever had the honor, I'd do things differently.

Unbidden, my eyes slide to Thandi. She's always beautiful, but today she's glowing. It's only been a few weeks, yet the realization sears through me: I want more with her. Much more than business.

Winston's already offloading the van, humming to himself as he wrestles with a crate. Thandi peers inside, incredulous.

"Dad, what's all this stuff? Just how many boxes are in here?"

"Enough to get the job done," he answers with a wink.

Iris adds in a dry voice, "He insisted we bring the rosewood incense and the *mbira* to add to the atmosphere."

"You're going to play?" Thandi asks, reaching for the wedge-shaped wooden instrument with its gleaming metal tongues.

"Absolutely. Mark and I have something special planned for peak moonrise."

I have no idea what they're talking about, but before I can ask, Winston approaches and sweeps me into a hug. He smells of sandalwood and citrus balm, and for a moment, it's as if he knows the thoughts I was battling earlier. I stiffen. I'm stunned—starved—uncertain what to do with this fatherly affection.

When he pulls back, he's beaming. "Son, I can't tell you how much your hosting us means. Here—" He presses a carved mahogany box wrapped in recycled sari cloth into my hands. "A token of our appreciation."

"You didn't have to do that, Winston," I protest, easing the lid open. Inside, crystals catch the light, next to several neatly wrapped bundles and hand-labeled tincture bottles. Bemused, I examine one. "I'm afraid you'll have to explain what's in here."

"Blue Moon circles are potent. A perfect time for renewal, transformation, and forging bonds," he says with great ceremony. "This is just a little something for you and Thandi, to magnify connection, open your heart chakras, and keep the energy flowing."

Thandi's eyes widen. "Wait, what?"

Winston nods, plucking out a bottle labeled *Moonfire Elixir: For Vital Magnetism*. "Shatavari, rose, cordyceps, damiana. Increases blood flow—"

"Dad, no. We are *absolutely* not talking about libido enhancers right now." Thandi snatches the bottle before he can finish. Behind her, Iris chuckles.

"What?" Winston looks genuinely baffled. "It's just adaptogens. Good for the root chakra."

"He made the labels himself," Iris offers.

"I did," Winston confirms proudly. "And there's more.

He pushes aside the tincture bottles to reveal two jewel-toned sarongs, a pouch of smooth crystals—rose quartz, carnelian, amethyst, and moonstone—plus a neat packet of dried petals for bath infusions. There's even a sweet, herbaceous massage oil that makes the entire box smell like a moonlit greenhouse after rain.

I raise a brow. "This is... extremely thorough."

"Check the QR code." Winston notches his chin proudly. "It opens a playlist."

"Oh my god. How is this happening?" Thandi moans, mortified.

I laugh and draw her close, delighting in the way she buries her face against my side.

"All right." Iris steps forward, gently closing the box. "That's enough moon medicine for tonight. Winston, at least let them get through dinner first."

"What did I say?" Winston splutters as Iris steers him back toward the van. The box remains in my hands, fragrant and heavy with significance.

"Well, that was unexpected. It's the thought that counts?" I murmur, kissing the top of Thandi's head once her parents are out of earshot. "It *is* very thoughtful, though."

I'm still struggling not to laugh, but I can't resist lifting the lid again, staring at the entire experience Winston has curated.

Thandi sighs, shooting me a sheepish look. "Welcome to my childhood," she says wryly. But her fingers linger for a second on the sari cloth.

And later, when no one's watching, I scan the QR code anyway.

Ledgers
Ronan

Of course, Thandi is the type of woman who ends her relationships in healthy, well-adjusted ways. She's still friends with her ex. So much so that Micah is now Winston's apprentice. I try to imagine showing that level of composure after losing Thandi.

I can't.

I narrow my eyes and rearrange the blankets Iris asked me to unpack for the fiftieth time while I surreptitiously observe the other man.

He's probably six feet tall, with tanned skin and sandy blonde hair that falls to his shoulders in waves that manage to look both perfect and uncombed. He's probably one of those people who doesn't shampoo and instead swears by apple cider vinegar and unicorn tears. There's a thick silver band on his thumb, a turquoise one on his pinky, and a few tattoos in a foreign script on his forearms. One of them is curved into a crescent moon.

Naturally.

Micah says something, and Thandi smiles, sweet dimples flashing. He smiles back, but something flickers across his expression for a heartbeat—too fleeting for anyone not watching closely to notice. But I see it. I know that look.

He's not over her.

For a moment, I feel an unexpected pang of sympathy. I don't blame him. I've only known Thandi for a few weeks, and already I can't imagine what it would take to get over a woman like her.

Still, it's hard to see them together.

I'm not jealous.

Not exactly. Logically, I know their relationship is in the past.

It's just that, even as far as Thandi and I have come, it irks me that Micah seems more embedded in her life than I am.

Paradoxically, hope glimmers as I take in the other man's aesthetic. He's got the whole artistic, vaguely androgynous, "I manifest tantric energies" vibe. There's nothing granola about me; I've also got at least seventy pounds of muscle and several inches on him. (Vanity, sure, but I'll take my wins where I can get them.) Yet, despite our differences, I see that Thandi has a type: tall, unconventional, and definitely rougher around the edges than she is.

Whatever I feel about Micah, it is reassuring to know that I'm not a complete aberration. Look, we all want to be special, but I'm a data man. Outliers are fleeting. Trends have staying power.

The thought cools my nerves and calms my baser instincts. So I leave the blankets behind when Thandi calls me over to meet Micah. I smile, shake his hand, and try not to think about the fact that he's held Thandi in ways I haven't. I keep smiling, even as every cell in me wants to whisk her away.

"Hey man, good to meet you." Micah nods.

"Likewise." I might actually preen when Thandi loops an arm around me. Even better, the gesture is guileless and unconscious—an instinctive gravitation toward me. I tug her closer, savoring her warmth against my side. What was I worried about again?

"Winston told me you own the vineyard. I'm sorry for your loss. Rosalind was an amazing woman."

I swallow hard. Mom's name is still a live wire, zinging straight through my chest. "You knew her?"

Micah nods. "Rosalind made a point to source from local artists. Since my specialty is ceramics, she approached me about designing and supplying the custom corks in the gift shop. We've been working together for the last three years."

Grief presses in on me, and with it, guilt. I feel like a cad for my earlier uncharitable thoughts. The crazy part is I've seen the corks. I even remember Mom showing me a shipment. Micah is talented.

I clap him on the shoulder. "I didn't know. Thanks for supporting us. Your work is beautiful."

"Thanks." Micah hesitates, then glances at Thandi before looking back at me. "Say, man. Could I grab you for a second? There's—"

"Okay, gather around, folks. Your gifts are here!"

Winston bursts out from behind the van, arms full, cradling a wicker basket piled with small linen bundles.

Thandi slaps a hand to her forehead. "Here we go again."

"What?" I turn to look at Winston.

Whatever Micah was about to say evaporates as he chuckles. "He's doing the thing."

"What thing?"

"The gift bundles," Thandi says. "He's been making personalized ones since I was a kid. It's like WebMD, but with herbs."

God help us all.

Sure enough, Winston moves from guest to guest, radiating purpose and delight, his basket swinging from one arm like an apothecary Santa Claus.

"For your knees, Nancy—ashwagandha with turmeric and a topical rub. Do not microwave it," he warns, handing over a drawstring sachet like it contains state secrets.

"Steve! Your acid reflux? Slippery elm and papaya enzymes, just like I promised."

"Oh, and Micah—something for that hairline you keep complaining about. Rosemary and castor oil. Organic."

Micah lifts it like a trophy. "Respect."

I glance over at Thandi, and her face is a mix of affection and exasperation. My laugh slips out before I know it. Besides, I feel a little better knowing that while our box may have been the most extravagant, Winston does this to everyone.

Well, he's not the only one who can spread a little cheer. Once everyone tucks away their gifts, I call them over. The best part? Thandi still doesn't release me, even in front of this extended group of family and friends.

"Good evening, everyone. I'm Ronan Thorne. Welcome to Thorne Run Vineyard. We're delighted to host you for your celebration. First, a round of applause for Winston, for bringing us all together."

"Woo!" Micah whistles, and hoots and cheers erupt from the group, now swelled to about fifteen guests.

Hilariously, once Winston becomes the center of attention, he's quick to wave us off and rub a sheepish hand to the back of his head.

"As a token of my appreciation," I continue, "everyone here will receive a free bottle of Rosalind's Trace, and we have vouchers for fifty percent off in the gift store."

Another cheer rises as, on cue, two vineyard staff emerge with tickets. I checked the forecast, and there's still plenty of time before sunset. A little shopping won't impact the festivities.

While the group lines up for their vouchers, Thandi goes to Iris to offer her mother her free bottle and tickets. She knows how much Iris loves the rosé.

Instead of joining the queue, I find the man of the hour frowning at the ceremonial circle he's been arranging with Iris' blankets.

"Problem?" I ask.

"Hey, son. Thanks for treating the group. Gives me a bit more time to figure out this setup." Winston props his hands on his hips.

"What's wrong?"

"The ground's soft," Winston says, his gaze fixed on a patch near the fire pit. "Normally we'd spread blankets in a circle, but with last night's rain…" He shakes his head. "No sense leaving folks with wet backsides. And it's crisp out here tonight. Comfortable if you're moving, less so if you're sitting still."

I follow his line of sight, nodding. He's right.

"I've got some old wine crates in the cellar," I say. "Sturdy enough to use as benches. Not fancy, but they'll keep everyone dry."

Winston grins. "Now, that's a fine idea. Let's haul a few up and see how they do."

We fall into step together, heading to the main building, where the cellar awaits. The air smells of rain-drizzled earth and wood-smoke from the fire pit.

"I know I said it before, but I really appreciate this," Winston says. He glances at me, mouth tugging into a half-smile. "I know scientists like you find this kind of thing hard to believe in. But like I told Iris and Thandi—it's doing no harm, right?"

I shrug. "I used to be more rigid about this stuff. But when Mom got sick…we tried everything. Acupuncture, Reiki, massage, herbal therapies—you name it." I glance down at the path, remembering all those waiting rooms. "I went with her to every appointment and learned a little along the way. Not enough to explain the how, but I saw the difference it made. She was more comfortable. That was all I cared about."

Winston doesn't answer right away. I've come to think of him as a whirlwind of creative energy—colorful stories, offbeat jokes, a kind of joyous unpredictability that fills a room. But here, in the hush between us, is something more poignant. His eyes are sharp and assessing. And his comfort in the stillness reveals more than any words could.

After a while, he says, "I began my spiritual practice because the hardest thing for us to confront is change. It's good when a man isn't afraid to let go of beliefs that no longer serve him."

The words are heavier than I expect, striking close to truths I'm surprised Winston can discern. It feels like I've spent a decade letting go—shedding the Astor name, my inheritance, and any preconceptions that James will ever be the kind of father Winston is.

The sun sinks lower as we walk, the sky streaked in orange and pink. Crickets begin their chorus, and somewhere a cardinal trills.

The main building rises ahead, and we step through the front doors into the tasting room, which is bustling with the members of our little moon party, buying gifts and sampling vintages.

Downstairs in the cellar, the air is cooler and rich with the scent of oak. Rows of barrels line one wall, and in the corner, crates are stacked almost chest high. A few are filled with empty bottles waiting to be cleaned and reused.

I lead Winston over, bracing against one of the stacks. "The empties are behind these. We'll have to shift a few out of the way. How many do you need?"

Winston rubs his chin, considering. "Akila and Jinhee can't make it anymore, but that still leaves us with sixteen, I think."

I grunt as I shift one of the crates heavy with bottles. "Not a problem. We've got enough."

"Amazing." Winston steadies the edge of the stack while I slide another full crate out of the way.

I nudge another crate aside, Winston spotting me again, the two of us working in a quiet rhythm. We've pulled aside nine of the sixteen needed when Winston releases the crate he's holding and turns to me.

"My Thandi," he says quietly. "She's golden. Both of my girls are—" He pauses, a flicker of grief crossing his face. "Were."

He shakes his head once, like he's brushing the shadows away. "But Thandi…she's always been a fighter. You know why I call her Peanut?"

My hands still on the crates. "Why?"

"She was a tiny thing as a baby—underweight. When they told us we were having twins, it was touch-and-go at first."

Winston stares out of the window into the fading light. I'm quiet as I wait for him to continue.

"There was a problem. Thandi and Tess were sharing the same placenta, and Thandi was at a disadvantage. The doctor called her the donor twin—smaller, weaker, at risk of not making it." Winston sighs, his eyes soft with memory. "But somehow, they both pulled through. And Thandi—she came out yelling her little lungs off."

Winston laughs, the sound rich and warm in the space between us. "You know what's funny?"

I swallow, my pulse picking up. This is it—the talk I half-expected at the family dinner that never came. My throat feels tight. I hear the weight behind his tone and ask almost reverently, "What is?"

He smiles. "She's still that way. Still fighting for her place. Always giving more of herself than she probably should."

Winston's gaze pierces mine. "She needs a soft place to fall, son. Someone who won't take advantage of her kindness. And more important than that—someone who'll love her enough to show her she deserves kindness, too."

There's a pressure in my chest, heavier than any crate in the room.

"I'd never take advantage of Thandi's kindness," I say, my voice rough with all the emotions I can't yet name. But I am sure of one thing: "All I want is to be the man she can count on," I tell Winston. "I'd give her the world if I could."

Winston studies me, arms folded. Then, slowly, he nods.

"Good." He reaches for an empty crate, brushing it clean before lifting it off the stack. "It's not my way to interfere, and Thandi is her own woman. But as a father, I see things…"

I set the last crate down, brushing my hands off on my pants. "And?"

"And you're moving fast. That's not a bad thing. Nature—and love—have their own rhythms. I just wanted to make sure I wasn't mistaken in my assessment of you."

"Does that mean I've passed the test?"

Winston chuckles. "For now," he winks.

I grin. "Well, now that's settled, I'll go grab a cart. Sixteen of these is a lot to carry, even for two men."

Winston claps me on the shoulder. "Good thinking. Let's make this easy on our backs."

I head back to the first floor and almost crash into Micah at the top of the stairs. He's holding a box of his ceramic wine stoppers, and they rattle dangerously before he cradles them to his chest.

"Whoa," I say, stepping back. "Sorry, man, didn't see you coming."

"No worries." He lifts the box to inspect it. "No corks harmed in the process," he laughs.

"I'm relieved."

Micah glances over his shoulder as though making sure he's out of earshot. "I hate to do this, Ronan, but I need to ask about payment."

"Payment?" My brows lift as I lead Micah to the privacy of the back office.

"Yes, we submitted our invoice to Mr. Astor three months ago. I don't mind carrying some costs, but we're still a small business. I won't make next month's payroll if this continues."

The mention of my father alone is alarming, not to mention the disgraceful situation Micah has been put in.

"You worked with James on invoicing?" I ask, my mood darkening. I knew my father had commandeered the vineyard for his own use, but I don't understand why he was involved in its finances. Even with Mom sick, those details should have been handled by the vineyard staff.

"Yeah. Things were fine until about nine months ago when Suzie, the manager, left. Then we dealt exclusively with Mr. Astor." Micah shifts the box in his hands. "Unfortunately, it hasn't been great. This is the second time we've missed a payment."

"First, let me apologize for this unacceptable situation. James is no longer involved with Thorne Run. If you need anything, you can reach out to me directly," I say, striding to the desk and logging into the computer.

It only takes a few clicks to pull up Micah's invoice. He's being charitable—if not downright modest. The $9,200 payment is more than 120 days late, and it turns out it covers far more than corks.

There's a contract for an entire collection of cheese boards, coasters, even tasting cups—all delivered, and not a cent paid. My jaw clenches. He trusted us, and James left him hanging.

"Micah, let me assure you this is not the way Thorne Run does business." I yank open the desk drawer, pulling out my checkbook. It takes less than a minute to write the amount owed, tear the slip free, and press it into his hand.

Micah's shoulders sag with relief, and for the first time, I see the exhaustion carved into his features—the weight of stress he's been hiding.

"Thank you. We're doing well, but we've only become profitable in the last couple of years. A lot of that is thanks to my new creative partner, Nia. I can't afford to let her go."

He hesitates, then admits quietly, "My only other option would have been to refinance my home."

I'm appalled that Thorne Run has pushed this artist to the brink. And it makes no sense. I reviewed the estate paperwork with Aamir after the will reading, including the vineyard's topline revenue. Thorne Run is comfortably profitable. There's no reason it should be cash poor.

"I should probably head back." Micah smiles. "Thanks again."

"No problem," I murmur, but my mind is racing. Every instinct is screaming that something is very wrong here.

I don't have much time to contemplate it, though, as Winston pops his head into the door. "Son? Everything all right? We'll need to head back with that cart soon, if we want to set up before dark."

Shit. I completely forgot about poor Winston and his moonrise mission.

"Of course," I say, hurrying over to reassure him.

I head to the storeroom to grab the cart, but my mind is still on Micah's desperation and the sick suspicion that there's far more to the late payments than just James's negligence.

Joy
Ronan

Joy erases everything.

It's hard to fixate on James in the glow of the fire with Thandi leaning against me and the mbira vibrating through the clearing.

Winston is joined at the center of the circle by Mark, a husky accountant with thick silver hair, and Nancy, a slender dark-haired woman with a haunting voice.

Winston plucks the mbira in his lap, liquid notes shimmering. Mark answers with a drumbeat, deep enough to resonate in my chest. And Nancy, grinning, shakes the hosho as she begins to hum—a low, almost otherworldly sound that threads through the music like smoke.

Above us, the blue moon blazes. Not distant and cold as its name implies, but a heavy, luminous orange, so close we can almost touch it.

And still, none of it is as beautiful as the woman in my arms.

Everyone finds their perches—crates, camp chairs, even a flat log someone dragged over. I'm glad to see them comfortable. As for me, a little damp is no problem. The vineyard crew laid a sheet of tarp under one of Winston's blankets earlier, so I stretch out on the ground.

Thandi joins me, curling into my side, a tiny comma of affection. When I wrap my arms around her, I realize she's shivering.

"You're cold?" I ask, dismayed.

"A little," she admits. "We've been out here for a while."

She's right, of course. The musical performance is the capstone to an evening of food, blessings, and incantations. I've never experienced anything like it. It's also been a lengthy program. At almost 10 o'clock, the temperature has dropped with the hour. No wonder Thandi's teeth are chattering.

"Come here," I say, pulling her into my lap. "Better?"

She nods, a pleased hum escaping her as she burrows close. I let out a yelp when her ice-cold fingers slip under my shirt.

"Jesus, your hands are cold. Am I just a giant heater to you, now?" I tease.

"Sorry." She has the decency to flush. "I'm freezing, and you're *so warm*."

"Hmm." I press a kiss to her forehead. "You can use me any time, baby."

"Why do I feel like there's a double entendre in there?"

"Because there is?" I grin.

"Behave," Thandi growls, poking her fingers into my side.

"Mm… yeah, that's it. Just a little lower…" I fake a moan, and she can't help laughing.

"You're incorrigible. How a brilliant man can also be such a fool is beyond me."

"I'm only a fool for you, Thandi," I say, cupping her face in my hands.

"Oh, Ronan…" Her lips part on a shaky breath.

The last thing I see before capturing her mouth is the firelight dancing in her eyes. And then I am lost. We both are, as her lips seek mine—warm, yielding, and everything I've ever wanted. When I pull away, she's trembling again. But this time, it isn't from the chill.

"Should we go up?" she whispers, and I'm swept away in anticipation. In a yearning so fierce it steals my breath.

"You're sure?" I ask, my voice unsteady.

She nods, and I watch as a delicate shudder seizes her.

It's enough. I lift her in my arms and make my way to the edge of the circle.

By now, Winston has invited everyone into the center to dance. Limbs wave, and hips sway, and between the laughing and the twirling, they're all too preoccupied to notice our exit.

My heart is pounding, and I kiss Thandi again. Her tongue caresses mine, and it's like being enveloped in sweet fire. She tastes like s'mores and a hint of grape. I can tell she had the Merlot instead of Rosalind's Trace. Knowing she, too, prefers the earthier wine fans my flames higher. I hold her poised, crushing her lips against mine. Her fingers tangle in my shirt, and when I nip her bottom lip, she moans.

"I want you so much," I groan.

"Me too." She clings to me like a vine, making delicious sounds— needy little cries that have me rock hard in seconds.

I never noticed how large Whitlow was until now. It takes an eternity to stride to the main house, cross the foyer, and climb the stairs to my suite. I take the steps two at a time, and as soon as we pass the threshold, Thandi yanks her sweatshirt over her head. One-handed, I undo her dress, shoving the bodice down her shoulders. Pearl buttons pop, pinging to the floor, and she gasps.

"Sorry, I'll replace that," I mutter as I carry her to the bed.

Thandi buries her face in my neck, shoulders shaking with quiet laughter.

"What?" I growl.

"Why are you always ripping my clothes to shreds? First, my zipper. Now this?"

"Those were accidents. This isn't, though—" I slide my hand under her dress and rub over the damp crotch of her panties. Gently, I tug the fabric aside and caress her where she's opening to me. She arches like she's been struck by lightning as my fingers smooth over silken heat and delicious wetness. She's already drenched.

"Ronan," Thandi whimpers, her thighs squeezing around my hand.

"You're so wet, baby. Why didn't you tell me?" I ask, placing the tenderest kisses along her collarbone.

I keep stroking between her legs, bathing in her desire. She's so soft here, and sliding my middle finger through her heat is like a little taste of heaven. When I press my thumb to her clit, a hoarse cry bursts from her lips.

"You like that?" I nudge her legs further apart, dragging her panties off so I can touch her freely.

"Yes, Ronan, I—"

"What?" I rub her clit in a sinful rhythm.

"Oh god!" Her body jerks and her words fragment, tapering into a moan. She shakes her head, unable to catch her breath.

"I guess that means I should continue," I smile against her skin. She's so responsive, so sexy. She makes me feel like the most powerful man in the world.

I'm the one gasping, though, when I ease my finger inside her. She's small and sleek, and now I'm doubting whether this powerful man can hold it together when it's time to fuck. And the way Thandi writhes and mewls my name doesn't help my control. But she's mine to cherish, and I'll take all night if I have to.

I groan and begin a gentle thrusting. She won't be able to take me without some stretching, so I add another finger beside the first. Thandi arches, her hands fisting in the sheets. Her eyes are scrunched tight, and I press a kiss to each of her closed lids.

"Look at me, baby."

Her lashes tremble, fanning across her cheeks, but slowly she opens those big brown eyes.

"That's my girl. Is this okay?" I thrust into her again, pressing on her clit at the apex of the caress.

"Yes," she whines. "Don't stop, please."

Her hips rock against my palm. I pick up the pace, thrusting hard and deep. She cries out with each movement, and watching her pleasure overtake her is the most beautiful thing I've ever seen.

I keep stroking her, and feel her orgasm building in the pulsing of her inner walls. I chase it, curling my fingers forward, calling her ecstasy forth in a liquid rush.

She comes with a broken cry, her entire body shuddering, her release wetting her thighs. I can't help running my fingers through it. Is there anything sexier than the proof of her pleasure?

By now, her dress is tangled about her hips, exposing her to me. She's bare except for a silken arrow of hair over her mound. I caress her curves and kiss that sweet landing strip.

"Have I told you how lovely you are?"

"Oh, god, Ronan. How can you be so…" Thandi makes a helpless gesture.

"So?"

"Intense." She gasps, flopping back onto the bed.

I kiss her fiercely. "Is that a problem?"

"No." She smiles, brushing my cheek. "Not a problem at all. Thank you for that."

"Don't thank me." I roll on top of her. "I'm not done with you yet."

Thandi chuckles. "Am I allowed to shower at least?"

"Why do we need showers?" I demand, unbuttoning each of the tiny buttons down the front of her dress. Well, what's left of them, anyway.

"We don't, but I'd like to. I feel like I've been sitting around in the grass all day." Thandi's lips quirk up. "Besides, after that orgasm, the water will help me stay awake. I've waited too long to be with you to end up passing out before the main event."

I suppose that's fair, and knowing she wants this just as much as I do makes everything better. I tug her dress off until her lacy bra is the only thing that separates us. For a moment, I lean back and just admire her smooth brown skin, the lush swells of her breasts above the cups of her bra, her slender waist, and her rounded hips. Heck, even her small feet with their pink toe polish are sexy to me.

"Fine." I brush my lips over hers. "You take the main suite, and I'll use the guest bath down the hall."

"Mm." She pulls me down for another kiss before sitting up. Of course, I enjoy the view of her glorious ass as she pads over to her bag. I'm about to say everything she needs is in the bathroom when she pulls out a tube of face wash and a mystery bottle with a dropper. I keep my mouth shut. I know better than to get between a woman and her skincare.

For some reason, though, the dropper reminds me of the oils in Winston's kit. My brows shoot upward as an idea dawns. "Baby, should we use the stuff in your dad's box? Just so you know, my massages are legendary."

Thandi glances over her shoulder with a laugh. "Well, if they're legendary, I can't turn one down, can I?"

"You can't." I saunter over and palm her ass, my hand sliding forward to cup her softness. Her pussy is still wet, and she collapses against me as soon as my fingers touch slippery, sensitive skin. She's trembling.

I'm tempted to lift her onto the dresser and take her right there, but I promised her a shower, and I'm a man of my word. I release her with a kiss to her temple.

"Come," I say, grabbing the wooden box from the dresser. "Tell me what's in here before you go."

Thandi nods, taking a shaky breath. She pulls out the oils, explaining their supposed benefits. A diligent Winston has left a guide to the crystals, so I read that and put them aside. My fingers brush over the sarongs.

"What are we supposed to do with these?"

Thandi flushes. "Well, we can lay them on the bed for the massage, or we can wear them."

"Wear them?" I frown.

"Mm-hmm. They're supposed to match."

"Show me," I say.

Thandi shakes her head, smiling as she loosens the fabric. The sarong is a sweep of jewel tones that catch the light as she folds it lengthwise.

"Are you going to undress?" she asks.

"Baby, you don't need a sarong as an excuse to get me naked," I tease, waggling my eyebrows. I tug my T-shirt over my head and catch the way her eyes trace the planes of my chest, then follow my hands as they go to the waistband of my pants.

"Hush." She bites her lip. "This was your idea, remember?"

"Mm-hmm." I hook my fingers in the waistband and shuck my sweats and boxers off in one motion.

Thandi's eyes go wide, and she makes a strangled sound.

"What?" I stalk closer. "We're even now."

"Yes... that's..." She clears her throat, clutching the sarong tighter. She stares. Satisfaction surges through me.

"Like what you see, baby?" I shake my hair loose, strands falling over my shoulders. She gasps softly, and the wicked part of me wants to keep pushing her.

"Don't worry—" I brush a kiss across her cheek. "I'll take my time. We'll fit together perfectly. Do you trust me?"

She nods, swallowing.

"Good."

"Stand still," she whispers. Her hands tremble as she loops the cloth low around my hips. Her fingers graze my skin while she knots the ends at my side.

I spread my arms. "Have your way with me."

Thandi laughs, tucking the edge into place. "There."

"That's it?" I glance down. "Feels like it'll fall off with a breeze."

Her lips curve. "It won't. But if it did—isn't that the point?" She tugs the knot again, and I'm acutely aware of her hands at my waist.

She lifts the second sarong, equally vivid in indigo. "I could tie it like yours, or like this." She crosses the fabric over her chest and knots it behind her neck, halter-style. The drape skims her hips and falls to her knees.

"See? Matching." She spreads her hands, mimicking me.

My gaze travels from the knot at her collarbone to the curve of her hips to the length of her legs. "Baby, I don't stand a chance next to you."

"Flatterer." She shakes her head. "Think you've got the hang of it?"

"I don't know… maybe I should untie it, let you be the judge."

"Nice try." Thandi rises on tiptoe to kiss me. "Practice while I shower. I'll evaluate when I'm back."

I tug her close, capturing her lips before she can escape. "Fine. But I expect a hands-on assessment."

"You have my word," she murmurs against my mouth. Then she slips away, hips swaying as she heads to the bathroom.

I groan, watching her go, then grab my things and head for the shower down the hall. Not even ice water could put out this fire—or get Thandi out of my head.

Crystals
Ronan

I finish showering first, but that's okay. I use the time to prepare for Thandi instead of just waiting around like a schmuck. Condoms are by the bed, and I lay out the massage oils, choosing the one that smells the most like her—roses and sandalwood. I set the stones in warm water to take the chill off, imagining how they'll feel against her skin. While they heat up, I even read about the crystals.

Turns out amethyst is for calm, which I could use a dose of, given how fast my heart is beating.

Moonstone is for intuition. I smile, turning the pale oval over in my hands. I think of how far Thandi and I have come. It's always felt like some invisible force was leading me here, guiding me to her. Even in the beginning, when it made no sense, I knew I wanted to be by her side.

Now, I want so much more.

Maybe that's why Winston placed carnelian here, too. Heat, I've got covered. But courage? I need help with that to finally open up tonight. To say the things I've been holding back.

And lastly, there's rose quartz for tenderness.

For love.

I stare at the words for too long, their weight heavy in my chest. I'm standing at the edge of a precipice, ready to leap.

But is Thandi?

The bathroom door opens, and there she is, as if summoned by my thoughts. Light spills around her in a soft halo, and breath abandons my lungs.

She's wearing nothing but the indigo cloth, the sarong riding low on her hips, exposing rows of glittering chains draped over her taut stomach. Each is studded with semi-precious stones, and every time she moves, they catch the light. Her breasts are proud—her nipples the sweetest shade of cocoa. Under my gaze, they darken and pebble, begging for my attention. She's so gorgeous, I can't believe she's mine to cherish.

"It's fucking insane how stunning you are," I gasp, closing the distance between us. Thandi grips my forearms as I slip my arm under her hips and lift her so we're face to face.

"Ronan..." she breathes, her voice soft, helpless. I can feel her heart hammering against mine.

"I'm going to make you feel so good," I vow, placing her on the bed.

"You always make me feel good," she whispers, and my heart soars.

I want to shout from the rooftops—tell the world that she's mine. I nuzzle her neck, and her pulse jumps under my lips. Maybe that means her heart is soaring, too.

"Ready for your massage?" I ask.

"Yes. Word on the street is they're legendary." Thandi settles against the pillows with a smile.

"They are. And tonight, you're getting the blue moon special," I say with a grin. "You'll be asking for my autograph after this."

"Okay, now let's not get too carried away."

"You don't believe me?"

"I'll make my decision once I feel the results."

"Prepare to be amazed." I waggle my eyebrows.

Thandi laughs. "Alright, maestro, consider me prepped, then."

"Perfect." I set the massage oil on the bed beside her, my fingers brushing the jewels at her waist. "What are these, by the way? They're stunning."

"They're waist beads. I had them custom-made a long time ago. Call it a relic of my hippie upbringing." Thandi ducks her head. "I don't wear them often, though. Just on special occasions."

"Baby…" Warmth fills my chest. Knowing that she wanted this enough to adorn herself for me only makes me want to hold her even more. I tilt her chin up with my finger.

"Tonight means the world to me, Thandi. More than you'll ever know."

Thandi's large brown eyes meet mine. "Me too," she whispers.

Something in her gaze speaks to the yearning inside me. Something that makes me think I might not be alone on the precipice. I want to believe that we're both suspended on the edge of something as vast and luminous as the blue moon against the window. Something that will eclipse us if we let it.

My hand trembles as I cup her face. My thumb brushes her cheek, and she leans into me like a flower. When my lips find hers, it's the sweetest thing in the world. I kiss her, gasping at the electric pulse between us—the gravitational force drawing us toward something irreversible. I linger, teasing her lips one last time before pulling back.

"Ready?" I ask.

Thandi nods.

"Then turn over, baby."

She rolls onto her stomach, presenting me with her back. Her smooth brown skin and feminine curves are a feast for the senses. The sarong rests just beneath the twin dimples at the base of her spine, emphasizing her rounded hips and perfect ass. Unable to resist, I brush my hand down her back. Her waist is so slender that my splayed hand completely spans it. She's so petite that I feel like a brute by contrast—the beast to her beauty.

I stare for a moment before drizzling the warm oil down her spine. When Thandi gasps, the sound goes straight to my dick. It's hard not to imagine how we'll fit together when she's all but naked before me, with only the thin indigo cotton separating us.

The oil trickles in a ribbon over her skin before I spread it with my palms, smoothing it across her back in long strokes. Her muscles loosen beneath my hands, and the smallest sigh escapes her. I reach for the first stone, testing its heat against my wrist before touching it to her skin.

"Not too warm?" I ask.

"Uh-uh," she mumbles. "It's perfect."

I place the moonstone just below her shoulder blades, smiling at how shaky her voice already is.

And here she was doubting my prowess.

The groove of her spine beckons me. I sweep my hands in an outward arc, and Thandi's breath rushes out in a soft puff. She shifts on the mattress.

I grab the rose quartz, resting it in the middle of her back. Covering the stone, I smooth the oil in circles, coaxing Thandi's muscles to yield. She presses her cheek into the pillow, her frame softening beneath me. Clearly, she needs this.

"Still okay?" I ask, and she makes a muffled, dreamy sound, encouraging me to continue.

I keep smoothing my palms across her back, then pause, frowning, when I find a knot. I rub once, then circle back, pressing in with my thumb.

Thandi moans and immediately slackens under my touch.

Got it. I can't help feeling a little smug. What? I'm not just a pretty face. Years of rowing and workouts have been my therapy. I know a tight rhomboid when I feel one.

I shift lower, tracing Thandi's sides. Another knot waits there, deep in the muscle. I apply careful pressure, kneading until it relaxes. Thandi sighs, and I can almost feel the exhaustion leaving her body.

She's carried so much this week; it's no wonder she's wound tight. The least I can do is help her let go.

I drizzle more oil over her skin, and my hands drift to the small of her back. Placing first the carnelian and then the amethyst, I work in slow, grounding strokes. She groans, going boneless beneath me. But I'm anything but loose as I shift her sarong low enough to access the upper part of her hips. I want her so badly, my hands are shaking.

So much for those magic hands I bragged about earlier.

Thandi's breathing is deep and soft—relaxation and arousal threaded together. Her skin gleams in the lamplight, and her fingers twitch against the sheets. I swallow hard, pulse racing at the sight, the sound—the intoxicating scent of her. When I slide my hand down to her hip, her heat sears me to my core.

"On your back, sweetheart."

Thandi pauses, a fine tremor rippling through her frame. Then she rolls over.

She's flushed, lips parted—breath coming in ragged pants. Her nipples are hard, and from the way she shifts on the bed, I know how much she wants me.

Desire flares bright and hot. My dick jumps, eager to give her everything she needs and more.

"Jesus, Thandi, do you have any idea what you do to me?"

"Ronan…" She makes a needy sound.

"Mm … I've got you, baby." My hands hover over her breasts, and she jerks as drops of warm oil slither over her nipples.

"Is it too hot? Am I hurting you?" There's no way for me to hide the huskiness in my voice.

"No, it's okay," she shivers. "It feels good."

"Good."

I love seeing her like this, overcome by her pleasure. I cup her breasts, savoring their soft weight. They need to be handled delicately, just like the rest of her. Because, of course, she is a treasure.

My treasure. I spread the oil, massaging in hot circles, brushing over the hungry peaks of her breasts with each pass.

Soon she's trembling, mewling softly as I pluck her nipples. I caress her left breast, then draw the tip into my mouth. Thandi's body surges upward, a shout bursting from her lips.

"That's it," I murmur, dragging my teeth across the stiff peak. "Just feel."

"Ronan, *please*," she cries, tangling her fingers in my hair.

I know what she wants, but I'm not ready to give it to her yet. I want to savor this moment a little longer.

Splaying my hand between her shoulder blades, I hold her poised as I sip at her, tugging on the velvet peak until her nipple is swollen and rigid on my tongue. I worry it between my teeth, then nurse at her until she writhes and moans. She shudders when I move to her other breast to lavish it with the same treatment. By the time I lift my head, she's moaning and shaking in my arms.

Fuck it. I need more. Growling, I yank her hands over her head, caging both wrists in my fist. She's arched up in offering to me as I push her sarong aside, dipping between her legs. A groan escapes me at the proof of her desire. She's drenched for me all over again.

"You're so sensitive. So perfect. It makes me want to do wicked things to you," I confess, kissing her temple, her trembling eyelids. And then I'm bending to her breasts again, licking and suckling. I flick over her nipple, pressing the bud to the roof of my mouth with my tongue.

Thandi's eyes are wide—*wild*—as she gasps my name.

But I'm not done with her.

"The only thing I want more," I confess against the swell of her breast. "Is to taste you."

I slide down her body, and she gives a desperate cry as I spread her wide. Every part of her is beautiful, but here, she's a fucking masterpiece. I hold her open with my thumbs, loving the way her arousal spills over my fingers. I revel in her wetness, caressing her satiny petals.

And her scent— *God*. My eyes roll into the back of my head.

"I could bottle this." My smile is wicked against her thigh. "Maybe I should create it in the lab."

"Don't you dare," Thandi hisses, managing to sound mortified and excited at once. She props herself up on her elbows to glare at me.

"No?" I laugh. "I'd call it Heaven and inhale it when you're not around."

"Ronan, I swear to god, if you—ah!"

"Mm." Whatever insult Thandi was about to hurl evaporates as I lap at her entrance.

Instead, she moans like a woman in torment as I taste her. I've always loved eating pussy, but she makes me want more. I want to explore every inch of her. I want to catalogue every reaction, every moan, every sigh.

So I do.

Thandi whimpers, her head lolling on the pillow. She's lost in her pleasure, eyes glazed, her hips rocking in a sensual rhythm.

"Baby, you taste so good." I groan, dragging a finger through her slit. "Look at how pretty your pussy is. How wet you are for me."

Thandi struggles to focus, and her dazed expression ignites all my baser instincts. She's sexy, adorable—and I feel like the big bad wolf before a lamb. Devious. Ravenous.

I devour her, swiping my tongue along her labia, then nursing her clit. Her arousal drenches my face, and her wet, salty perfume tantalizes my senses. Moaning, I thrust my tongue inside, tasting her deeply.

Thandi thrashes against the mattress. Her eyes are screwed shut, and her fists are clenched in the sheets. She spreads her legs, giving me greater access, exposing her dripping pussy to my hungry gaze.

I can see all the way up her body—the curving lines of her hips, her stomach tensing as she fights for control. The tight buds of her nipples point upward, and I almost lose it when she starts teasing them with the flat of her hand. It's the most erotic thing I've seen, and I'm so hard it hurts. I usually pride myself on control, but with Thandi like this, I'm not sure how much longer I can last.

I move closer, sucking her clit, while I dip my fingers into the well of her desire. I slide two fingers in, pumping into her heat.

Thandi cries out, her back arching off the mattress. Her fingers grip my wrist. "More," she gasps. "Harder, please."

She doesn't have to say another word. I increase my pace, feeling the gentle contraction of her muscles, driving her toward ecstasy.

Her voice is an anguished whimper as she teeters on the edge. She's almost frantic, her nails digging into my wrist, scoring my skin as she grinds against my hand. The coil of tension inside her winds tighter, and then she explodes in a tremulous rush.

"Beautiful," I breathe.

The moment she comes, I crawl up her body and nudge her hand aside, taking her nipple into my mouth with a rough suction. I almost come right then and there as she lets out a high, plaintive wail.

I can't wait any longer. I slip on the condom and position myself between her legs. She's almost delirious, still shaking with the aftershocks of her pleasure. Her thighs fall apart, and she moans, welcoming me.

God, I want her so badly I could shoot right then and there. But I won't. I refuse to fuck this up. Taking a deep breath, I ease forward, nudging her entrance. She immediately bears down, trying to lure me in. Her sweet little pussy contracts around the head of my dick, and the sensation grabs me by the balls.

Jesus Fucking Christ.

"Fuck!" I'm forced to stop. I'm panting, my arms on either side of her, trembling as I fight for control. I suck in a breath and pause, letting her feel the heat emanating from my body. Then, slowly and deliberately, I push forward.

She's deliciously wet, impossibly tight. Her body fits me like a satin glove. Our cries meld together as I begin to move, stroking shallowly at first. Thandi whimpers, and I hold still, letting her adjust to me.

"Are you okay?" I whisper. "Is this too much?"

Her only answer is to wrap her legs around my hips, pulling me closer. I moan as I slide all the way to the hilt. I start pumping, then bend forward, crushing my lips against hers. Thandi answers with equal hunger, moving beneath me. Our tongues tangle in a frenzied dance. She's more beautiful than I could have ever imagined. Hotter than my most fevered dreams.

This is what I was afraid of from the moment I saw her. That she would burn me alive with a passion so honest, so true, I would never recover from it. And now that I've tasted her fire, I know I'll never be the same.

I touch her clit, and she begins trembling, rocking against my hand. My hips surge forward, pumping faster. She makes a keening sound as she nears her peak, her body fluttering in my arms like a hummingbird.

"It's okay, baby, let it happen," I coax, stroking her pussy. "Come for me."

Thandi's eyes go wide as the first wave of pleasure breaks over her. She screams my name as she tumbles over the edge. Her cry triggers my own avalanche, and I come hard. I let out a roar as I pour into her, pounding her into the mattress.

Thandi moans and clamps down on my dick, each pulse of her quivering pussy squeezing every drop from me. I throw my head back as her name breaks on my lips. I'm not a man anymore, just a mindless shaft, a humble piece of clay in her hands, ready to be shaped to her will.

"God, Thandi." Cradling her face, I kiss her. And as always, she welcomes me without hesitation. Her mouth is soft and full, her tongue lazy against mine. She's sweet. So sweet.

I stop moving as she holds me in her body. Her eyes are locked with mine with such tenderness that it shatters every cell in me. At that moment, I know without a doubt that she's wrecked me from the inside out. Every nerve, every breath, every heartbeat. I'm falling in love with her, and I don't know how to stop it. It doesn't matter anyway because I don't want to. I'm too far gone, too addicted to her light.

"I love you." The words spill from me before I realize it. Thandi's eyes widen, and for an instant, everything freezes. I can't think, can't breathe, too afraid to even blink as she holds my heart in her hands.

Then she smiles.

"I love you too, Ronan."

God. No one told me joy could feel like this. Like my heart clawing out of my chest. So pure, so full it hurts.

I sweep Thandi off the bed and take her against the wall, her sweet little pussy gripping me with every stroke. When she's crying and clawing at me again, I lower her to the floor, crouching over her on all fours.

Some might say this position isn't romantic, but I disagree. This way, I can surround her, shield her from anything that would hurt her. Cherish her like I plan to do for the rest of my life.

I kindle her fire again, rubbing her clit and stroking her pussy so she can take me like this. And when I slide in at last, we're both in deeper than we've ever been before.

Thandi whines, straining against me. She doesn't have to say it. It's perfect, but I know it's not complete for her. Not yet.

"I got you, baby," I murmur.

My hands slide up her throat. The delicate column bobs as she swallows. Inside, where she's caressing me, I feel her gentle contraction, and the rush of wetness that tells me she knows what's coming next—and how eager she is for this peak.

I caress her neck, coaxing her to lift her head. The graceful line of her throat is exposed, but for now, I don't linger. Instead, I caress

her face … her arched back … the sweet curves of her breasts ….
her straining nipples.

Then, only then do I trail my hand up to her throat once more.

"Breathe," I say, fingering the veins on either side of her neck.

Thandi gasps.

I press harder.

Giving her what she needs. Hearing her cry of ecstasy.

Letting her world go deliriously, gloriously dark.

Pancakes
Ronan

Morning dawns in a gentle haze, sunlight teasing at my eyelids. I blink awake, feeling more rested and content than I have in months. I smile as the night's memories rush back to me.

Thandi was beautiful. Perfect. Her passion is a gift I can't wait to savor again.

Now she's a warm bundle sprawled across my chest, her breath feathering against my skin. I rub slow circles over her back, drinking in the peacefulness of her expression. For a long moment, I just hold her, wondering how the hell I got so lucky.

I brush my thumb over her cheek and press a kiss to the crown of her head. The ghost of the rose and sandalwood massage oil lingers on her skin, soft and sweet.

My mind drifts to Fia's party, to dinner with her parents, to the circle under the moon—and now, this moment. And I can't shake the feeling we're at the start of something beautiful.

I don't know how long I lie there with Thandi in my arms, her breathing in my ears as the light inches above the horizon.

I could stay like this forever. But today is a big day for her—the IPO launch, months of work coming to fruition—and I want to make sure she starts it strong. Careful not to wake her, I ease away from the bed and pull on a pair of drawstring pajama pants.

The first thing I do is open her duffel and ring housekeeping, asking them to press her business suit. She deserves to face the day looking every bit as formidable as I know she is.

I pad downstairs, humming under my breath. The house is quiet, with a stillness that only comes in these early hours. Before long, the staff will be here, bustling about, preparing Whitlow for another day. I set the coffee to percolate, breathing in the first rich curl of steam, while I rummage through the pantry.

IPO launches call for strawberry pancakes. And maybe some eggs too, for ballast.

It's not much, but it feels like the only contribution I can make to Thandi this morning: feed her, steady her, and make sure she knows she's not alone. That feels especially important after my conversation with Winston in the cellar.

I'm pulling scallions and bell peppers from the fridge when Mrs. Jackson wanders in, already sharply dressed for the day.

"Well, this is a rare sight." She smiles as she sets a kettle to boil for tea.

Heat crawls up my neck. After all these years, she can still make me feel like a teenager sneaking into the house past curfew.

I clear my throat. "Yeah. Woke up ravenous. You want anything?"

"Oh, no, my waistline is well past its pancake era. Tea is quite sufficient." Her eyes glint with a rare hint of mischief. "Besides, I wouldn't want to take anything away from Ms. Elowen."

I point the spatula at her. "You've been talking to Hensley, haven't you?"

Mrs. Jackson hides a sly grin. "I have many sources of intelligence."

I fold my arms, giving her a look. "So it *was* Hensley."

Mrs. Jackson sips her tea, eyes sparkling. "We are *all* delighted to meet Ms. Elowen. A welcome change if I say so myself."

I raise a brow. "First of all, was that a dig at my previous dates? Also—'all?' Is the whole house tracking my relationship?"

She only shrugs. "We're just happy for you, Ronan. There's a lightness to this place since you've come back—almost like the mistress is still here."

Mrs. Jackson's eyes become uncharacteristically misty before she steels herself again. "In any case, we care for you. We're here to support you and this new relationship. And we'll continue to hope that one day you'll make Whitlow your permanent home."

Her words hit me in the chest: the mention of my mother, the blessing on Thandi and me, the hope that I might one day root myself here. I'm touched. Overcome. And I have no idea what to say.

So I do what I've always done—I hide the burn in my eyes by turning back to the stove, fussing with the omelet, and rescuing the pancakes before they get too crisp.

She walks up beside me and pats my shoulder. "We're proud of you."

I swallow. "Thanks."

Mrs. Jackson nods, satisfied. She downs the rest of her tea and is halfway to the door when I remember something else.

"Mrs. J," I call softly. "Can I ask you something?

She pauses. "Yes?"

"Micah, the ceramicist who makes the gift shop's accessories, told me yesterday he hadn't been paid in over four months. Even more surprising, he said James was the one handling the invoice. Do you know why that might be?"

"Not directly, no," Mrs. Jackson says carefully. "But I understand certain… irregularities were behind the manager, Suzie Chalmers' decision to leave."

"Irregularities?" I echo, studying her face. As always, she is a master of tact—and as always, what she leaves unsaid speaks as loudly as her words."

"I know nothing of the vineyard itself, but I can say the past year has been unusual. If not for certain reserves of mine, we may have been in a much more precarious situation. I leave it to you to unearth the context." She inclines her head. "Enjoy your pancakes."

I watch her walk away, posture ramrod straight, heels echoing against the marble floor. My mind is still churning with her words. I'm on the verge of chasing after her when the doorbell rings.

I glance at my watch. It's barely 7 a.m. Too early for deliveries. Too early for anyone sane to visit.

Who the hell shows up at this hour?

I stride to the foyer, irritation prickling at the interruption— first my preparations for Thandi, now my chance at clarity with Mrs. Jackson.

I pull open the heavy oak door—

And freeze as the last person I expect is on the other side.

James stands on the threshold, face mottled with rage, a magazine crumpled in his fist.

"You ingrate!" he snarls.

And before I know it, he lunges, his fist aiming straight for my face.

Confrontation
Ronan

I may be big, but I'm not dumb—or slow.

James should know that. He paid enough to make sure I was quick on my feet.

Rowing, rugby, boxing, tennis, Taekwondo—even a brief flirtation with water polo.

So when he barrels toward me, my reflexes are instinctive. I duck his fist and drive my shoulder into his solar plexus.

He sprawls onto the pavers, the stupid paper he was holding fluttering at my feet. I scoop it up as the old dinosaur struggles to rise, daring to look shocked that I knocked him on his ass.

Time isn't as kind as it used to be. He still can't stand. I loom over him, nudging him with my foot. "Try that again, and you'll need a stretcher."

James purples with rage. "Do you take joy in embarrassing me, boy?"

I don't know if he's referring to me knocking him down or something else. What I do know is that I have no time for his bullshit. And at seven in the morning? You have got to be fucking kidding me.

"What the fuck are you doing here?" I growl.

"That!" James jabs a finger at the paper. He lurches to his feet.

Exasperated, I glance down at what I'm holding. At first, I think it's some business document, but no, it's The Daily Graph. A goddamn tabloid. The fact that James is not only reading it but working himself into a frenzy over it is so absurd I almost laugh.

"What's the matter? Can't figure out the Sudoku again?" I toss over my shoulder, turning away in disgust. I'm pissed he'd pull this shit. And even more pissed he'd pull it after my night with Thandi.

"It wasn't enough for you and your mother to conspire against me. Now you're fucking the competition?" he snarls.

I spin and am on him before he can blink. It happens so fast, he gasps as I crush his collar in my fist. I yank him close until our faces are inches apart.

"Say one more word about Thandi, and I will end you right here." My voice is deadly soft—frigid.

James' eyes widen. This close, I can see the red rimming his irises and the sallow tint of age in his complexion. I stare him down, years of pent-up rage radiating from my body. He's cast a shadow over my life for too long, his disapproval and cruelty leaving scars I still can't erase.

I hate pointless violence, but there's a part of me that is spoiling for this. A part of me that dares him to cross the line. He thinks I betrayed him? I can show him that in one brutal way, I can still be his son.

"Master Thorne, is everything alright?" Hensley appears in the doorway with two of the estate's security staff behind him.

His words stop me in my tracks. Not because I've lost control, but because he never calls me that. I'm Ronan—Mr. Thorne in public, and when he's feeling charitable to the whelp he raised. The choice is deliberate, a message to James about who is in charge now. The armed guards underline the point in brutal ink.

I release James, shoving him backward. "Get the fuck out of here. If you set foot on this property again, I'll have you arrested for trespassing."

Disbelief, ever-persistent anger, and something much less common cross James' features—defeat. Twice now, he's lost to me. First at the will reading and now this. Our gazes meet. I see the recognition in his eyes and grudging respect. A young Ronan would have reveled in it. Instead, my contempt grows for the man who still considers humiliation and domination as the only pathways there.

James smooths the wrinkles in his lapel. He's about to say something when Thandi's sweet voice drifts through the door.

"Ronan? Are you okay?"

Fuck. This isn't how I want Thandi to find out about James. Not right now. Not after what we shared.

"Hensley," I say sharply.

He nods. "I'll see to Ms. Elowen." He closes the door behind him, leaving the security guards to stand sentinel.

James' mouth curves. "You haven't told her, have you?"

"You have no idea what you're talking about," I say coldly. "Now, leave."

He rolls his shoulders, straightening his jacket. "I'll see you around, *son.*"

My heart hammers as I watch him go. His car disappears down the drive, and only then do I look at the tabloid. Now that I can focus, I see it clearly: a photo from Fia's party. The split-second after Amber shoved Thandi is frozen in print. In the image, I'm standing behind Thandi as she falls into my arms. Beneath it is a silly column rife with speculation.

I've spent years and a fortune scrubbing my digital footprint. The reporter can barely piece together who I am now, let alone my connection to James.

I frown, staring at the piece. In all the ways I've defied my father, this seems the most trivial. I didn't even know Astor was Immerscent's rival until recently. So why is James this furious? This desperate?

Unless…

I think back to his bloodshot eyes, his sallow color, Mrs. Jackson's and Micah's words echoing in my head.

Something else is going on here.

I head back to the house, crumpling the article in my fist. I need to get to the bottom of this.

But first, I need to make sure Thandi's okay.

Love and Fear
Thandi

This isn't how I expected to start my morning.

Alone after a night of ecstasy with Ronan, and our declarations of love.

Is it silly that I wanted to snuggle with him? Make love again before the insanity of the IPO launch?

But his side of the bed is empty, the sheets cool. I brush my hand across the hollow he left, and anxiety churns in my gut. Ronan wouldn't toy with me. Wouldn't fake what I saw in his eyes when he held me close.

Would he?

My hands tremble as I feel for my discarded sarong and knot it around me, covering my nakedness. When I turn, I notice my suit, freshly pressed, hanging from the hook on the door. A single red rose is tucked into the jacket pocket.

My tension eases.

Smiling, I pluck the rose from the jacket, burying my nose in its velvet petals.

He hasn't forgotten. This wasn't just some cruel game. The proof is right here.

The bile in my stomach ebbs. I set the rose on the dresser, then shower and dress, eager to find the man I love.

Downstairs, the house is hushed, the stillness magnifying Whitlow's grandeur, steeped in an almost eerie sense of history. My heels sound too loud on the marble as I cross the foyer, and I pause, suddenly uncertain which way to go. There's no sign of the staff—or Ronan—and the last thing I want is to get lost in this mansion's maze of rooms.

I'm about to choose a cavernous hall to the left when a commotion near the entrance drifts towards me. Two voices are raised in anger, and even muffled, I instantly recognize one as Ronan's.

I frown. I've seen Ronan in a hundred mercurial moods—mischief, wry humor, unpredictable brilliance. Rage has never been one of them.

What could make him this furious, this early?

The coil in my stomach tightens as I stride to the front door. It's slightly ajar, and through the crack I glimpse black uniforms. *Is that security?* Is Ronan in danger? *What on earth is happening?*

"Ronan?" I call, my voice sharp with worry. "Are you okay?"

I edge closer, only to be stopped by Mr. Hensley, who steps briskly into the hall and shuts the door behind him. "Good morning, Ms. Elowen. Did you have a restful evening?"

"Good morning, Mr. Hensley. I slept well, thank you." I try to peer around his shoulders, now blocking my view. "I heard shouting. Is everything all right? Where's Ronan?"

Hensley gives a clipped nod. "Mr. Thorne is dealing with an unannounced guest, but he has the situation well in hand. He asked me to convey that he'll be with you shortly."

"Are you sure? I saw security out there."

"Nothing but a precaution." He beams—pleasant, immovable. Whatever is happening, there will be no negotiating with him.

"I'd feel a lot better if I could talk to Ronan," I say slowly.

"And you will. Mr. Thorne assures me that he will be with you in a few minutes." Hensley clasps his hands behind his back.

"But—"

"Mr. Thorne has prepared you a special breakfast." Hensley smiles down at me. "Shall I show you?"

I hesitate, suspicion pricking at me. Something is happening beyond that door, and I know I'm being kept out. But the reminder of Ronan's thoughtfulness—the rose upstairs, and now this—tugs at me.

I sigh. "Okay."

"Right this way, please."

Hensley leads me down a corridor into the kitchen, and my heart skips a beat at the feast on the island: A fluffy omelet is cooling on one plate, toast stacked neatly beside it. Next to them is a stack of strawberry pancakes and a cloud of whipped cream in a porcelain dish. A small vase of wildflowers, hastily gathered, brightens the center.

It isn't perfect. One place setting is only half-finished—fork askew, and napkin missing. But it's obvious which plate is mine. A folded note rests beneath it, my name scrawled in Ronan's handwriting. I slip the note from beneath the plate and unfold it, my heart already fluttering.

My love,

You made me the happiest man in the world last night. This morning, it's my turn to sustain you. Here's a little nourishment to carry you into your big day. I know you're going to knock it out of the park.

—Ronan

By the time I reach the end, my throat is tight. Warmth blooms in my chest, chasing away every trace of the unease I felt earlier. This is Ronan—the man who doesn't just say the words but finds ways to show them. He loves me. Even though I'm a bit broken. Even if I'm not perfect.

I'm terrified by how much I already need him, how much I crave his tenderness. Not just words whispered in the dark, but gestures like this—simple, deliberate acts of care that steady me. That remind me that even the broken can find happiness.

I press the note to my lips, the paper cool against my skin, before setting it gently beside the vase of wildflowers. Relief softens my shoulders. Our love is real. And it's strong enough to carry me through whatever today brings.

Smiling, I perch on one of the stools at the island and cut into the omelet. The first bite is rich with herbs. *Ronan never told me he was such a good cook!*

I pour myself a cup of coffee, inhaling the fragrant steam. I'm reaching for the stack of strawberry pancakes, fork poised, when footsteps sound in the hall. Ronan steps into the kitchen, an apology already on his lips.

"Thandi, I'm so sorry, baby. I didn't mean to leave you alone like this." He comes up behind me, wrapping me in his arms.

I immediately lean into him. "It's okay. I was a little worried, but when I saw this—" I shrug, smiling. "Thank you for breakfast. It's wonderful."

Placing his hands on either side of the leather stool, Ronan spins me around to face him. Only then do I register what he's wearing—or rather, what he isn't. He's shirtless, powerful shoulders and sculpted abs on display. His sweatpants ride low on his hips, drawing my eyes downward. I swallow, suddenly feeling too warm in my jacket.

"What?" he asks softly.

"You're…very distracting in this," I whisper, brushing my hand over his shoulder.

"Yeah?" Ronan grins.

"Yeah." I cup his face between my palms and kiss him. When our lips touch, it's languid, full of need.

"Mm." Ronan pulls back with a purr. "Good morning to you, too."

I sigh, softening against him. "What happened out there? Mr. Hensley said there was an uninvited guest?"

Ronan stiffens, his brow darkening. "Yes. He's gone now, though."

I wait, hoping he'll say more. When he doesn't, the fork trembles in my hand. I'm out of sorts. The rose, the note, this breakfast—they all say the right things. But his tension, his secrecy, after we promised to give ourselves completely to each other, is jarring. I keep turning over the pieces, and it's an equation I can't balance.

I lift my hand, tracing the furrow in his brow.

I hate to ask. I'm scared to shatter the fragile dream we started building last night, but I need to know.

"Ronan…" I stare into his eyes, desperately searching for the meaning behind all of this. "Is everything okay? Are *we* okay?"

His eyes widen. "Thandi," he says roughly, crushing me to him. "You've done nothing wrong. Everything I said last night—I meant it. I love you. I need you. I want to be with you for as long as you'll have me."

"Then why are you hiding from me?" My voice breaks, barely a whisper. My eyes burn with the tears I'm fighting to hold back. "Why won't you tell me what's wrong?"

"Thandi," Ronan calls me, but I can't lift my head.

Something inside me buckles, collapsing in on itself. I thought I could silence it—the accusing voice that won't let me rest. It hisses that dreaming of love without justice for Tess is betrayal. That this discord, this fracture, is only what I deserve.

"Baby, please, talk to me." Ronan's voice breaks. He kisses me in frantic succession—my forehead, my cheeks, the curve of my neck. His stubble rasps against my skin, his arms caging me, as if he can hold me together by sheer force of will. But I'm frozen, locked in sorrow and shame.

"Thandi!" Ronan gathers me in his arms and curls me to his chest.

Reluctantly, I lift my eyes to his. I try to speak, but only a broken sound emerges.

"Listen to me. Please." Ronan cups my chin. "The man who showed up just now—it was my father."

"Your father?" I echo.

"Yes." His voice is grim. "This is what I wanted to tell you before you left for Austin. I love you. I knew I was falling for you, and my father—he's not a good man."

"But what does that have to do with you?"

Ronan shakes his head. "I... I've been ashamed. Scared it would change how you see me."

I grip his hand. "Ronan, I'd never judge you for your father's sins. You have to know that."

"*Don't*—" His voice is tortured. "You can't say that until you know everything."

My lips part. I'm about to brush his protest aside when I see the tension in his muscles, the wildness in his eyes. He's afraid. Just as afraid as I am.

It guts me. The Ronan I love is bold. Being with him makes *me* braver. Seeing him like this means whatever his father has done must be egregious. As I study his clenched features, I wonder if I'm ready for the answers I'm seeking.

"Why didn't we talk about it when I arrived?" I ask.

Ronan sighs. "Yesterday was your dad's celebration. Today is one of the most important days of your life. I wasn't going to ruin that with my family drama." He raises his hand before I can speak. "And before you say anything, no, I wasn't going to keep it from you forever. I thought tomorrow, after the IPO launch, was best. Then we could talk without distractions."

"What about now?" I say gently.

He sets me back on the stool with a bitter laugh. "Because the truth is, I'm not ready. I wish I were a better man, a braver man—but I'm not ready."

He turns away, shoulders hunching as he shoves his hands into his pockets. "You're the best thing that's ever happened to me, Thandi, and the thought of losing you is tearing me apart. I hate to admit it, but I'm scared."

When he turns back to me, his eyes are bloodshot, haunted. "I practiced this. I had a script. It makes me feel like a loser, but I didn't plan to say it like this. I thought I had more time. I can't do it on the fly." His voice breaks. "Give me one more night," he pleads hoarsely. "Please, Thandi."

One more night. As if time alone could protect us from the monster hiding between us.

But he has laid himself bare, exposing his deepest fears to me. And isn't that what love is?

I slip away from the island and wrap my arms around his waist. "How about a compromise?"

"What's that?" Ronan asks, hope and dread warring in his eyes.

"We don't have to discuss it now. But it won't help to put this off either. Can we talk tonight?"

He gives a curt nod, though every line of his body stays rigid.

I place my hand on his arm. "You love me, right?"

"With everything I have," he croaks.

"Then whatever this is—we'll get through it together."

Something in him softens at that, enough to ease both our fears.

I lay my head on his chest, listening to the strong, sure beat of his heart. "We can get through anything, as long as we don't give up on each other," I say.

And, God help me, I hope I'm right.

Launch Day
Thandi

My heart is heavy as I pull out of the driveway. I never thought I'd see Ronan so full of doubt. Even when I roll down the glass and he leans in for a kiss through the driver's side window, his gaze is shadowed with worry. Last night's euphoria feels strangely distant, like a dream already slipping away.

I wave, and he waves back. He doesn't go inside as I drive off. Instead, he watches me go, his powerful form shrinking in the rear-view mirror until it's just a blur.

We'll be okay, I tell myself. *We have to be. What we have is too special.*

Gripping the steering wheel, I draw in deep breaths. I need to get it together. I'm no use to Dani if I can't focus.

But my mind keeps circling back to Ronan and his terror. I feel a surge of guilt. Of course, I knew about Rosalind and how much her memory lives beside him every day. But he's never spoken of his father. I assumed they were estranged, not fractured by a secret so dark its scars haven't healed.

I should have seen it, but I was too consumed by my own pain to notice.

I'll do better. If Ronan is brave enough to reveal his fears, then it's my turn to help him heal.

By the time I pull into my parking spot at Immerscent, I'm still disoriented, but determined. I've never given up at the first sign of a challenge, and I'm not about to now.

Dani's waiting for me as soon as I enter the doors just off the parking deck. "CNN is confirmed for 3 PM, and Bloomberg wants an interview at five. It'll be tight, but I think we can make it. Briefer is in your inbox, but I've got a copy here."

I nod, thumbing through the document she hands me, but the words all run together on the page. I'm still trying to get my head in the game.

Dani casts a sharp look over me. "You okay? You seem out of it."

I sigh. Of course, nothing slips past her. "No, but I'll push through."

"What happened? I thought you were supposed to be relaxing after Austin?" We step into the elevator, and I hit the button for the lobby.

"I was. I *did*…"

"But?"

"Ronan and I sort of had our first fight this morning."

Dani clucks her tongue. "Oh geez, I'm so sorry, Thandi."

I roll up the briefer diploma style, my hands clenching around it. "Thanks. We're talking this evening. Hopefully it'll be fine."

Dani glances at me. Gently, she takes the paper from my fingers. "Evelyn and I also had rocky patches in the beginning. We still do. It's bound to happen when two people are so different. But what always saves us is our trust in each other—and the fact that we're both all in no matter what."

Dani smiles, tilting her head. "I don't know what happened, but that man has been falling in love with you since the pick-up game. Hell, we might have even won if he hadn't been so busy chasing you." She squeezes my arm. "I don't think he's going to give up without a fight."

I swallow past the lump rising in my throat. "I'm not giving up either."

"Good. Then whatever this is, you'll get through it."

I draw a breath, squaring my shoulders as the elevator doors glide open. The weight of the morning lingers, but it's not crushing me anymore. I smooth a hand over my jacket, fingertips brushing the outline of the rose tucked into my pocket.

I couldn't leave it behind.

Not when it's a reminder of Ronan. Of everything worth fighting for.

I'm smiling by the time we step into the lobby. I've found my center again.

Around us, the air thrums with anticipation. Staff are either rushing about or glued to the two massive screens near the front desk. One flashes Immerscent's ticker, the other is tuned to CNBC, where talking heads speculate about our debut. A countdown clock ticks away in the corner of the broadcast feed, marking the minutes until the market opens.

The hum of activity falters when Dani and I enter. Heads lift. Then, as if on cue, a cheer rises from the staff, applause echoing through the lobby. Analysts, assistants, engineers—their faces alight with pride and excitement.

Heat blooms in my chest, buoying me. I lift a hand in thanks, smiling. "Thank you. Truly. But save your energy—we've got a big day ahead."

The clapping softens into laughter, and with it the anxiety I've been feeling all morning.

"Thanks for the pep talk," I tell Dani, squeezing her hand. "Let's do this."

She grins. "Any time. I'll confirm Bloomberg and line up Trent for *Fortune* and *Forbes*. They'll want the board chair's perspective on governance and how we scaled responsibly. That way you can stay front and center on vision and product."

"Perfect. I—"

I never get to finish.

My parents burst through the lobby doors, their faces ashen. Ricky is sobbing between them, cheeks wet, chest heaving raggedly.

Scattered applause still echoes in the atrium, but it's as if the sound belongs to another world. My vision tunnels. Dani's hand is still warm in mine, but I barely feel it.

Mom's eyes lock on mine, wide and unblinking. Dad's lips press into a grim line. Ricky stumbles forward between them, his small body shaking.

I rush to meet him, dropping to my knees and folding him into my chest. His sobs rattle against me as I cradle the back of his head. My gaze jerks up to my parents.

"What happened? What's wrong?"

"It's Daysha," Ricky wails. His little fists clutch my jacket as he tries to speak through hiccupping breaths. "She's missing."

Search Party
Thandi

I'm falling apart.

Breaking.

Not this. Not again.

Lights strobe against the darkness, a mad flicker of red and blue across the looming shadows of the trees. News helicopters whir overhead.

Anchor Park is a hive. The entire youth center is out here. When one of us is in trouble, we answer the call to fight. We don't abandon our own.

And we're not alone. People of every age fan out across the grounds: Immerscent staff, volunteers from other communities, teenagers still in their school hoodies, parents clutching flashlights in trembling hands.

In the main clearing, searchers sweep in slow, methodical rows. Here, deep in the woods, the search is more desperate—people calling for Daysha, their voices muffled by the dense underbrush. I try to shout her name again, but my voice cracks, hoarse from hours of use and my tears.

Police dogs dart through the brambles, handlers urging them forward, their leashes taut. Radios crackle with clipped updates. The cold from the Blue Moon Festival still clings to the air, seeping through my jeans and into my bones. I tighten the hood on my sweatshirt, breath fogging in front of me as I push deeper into the shadows.

The IPO launched without me, interviews postponed, Trent taking the ones that couldn't be moved. I can't think about business right now. Not with another piece of my heart missing. First Tess, now Daysha. When will it end?

"Thandi."

Ronan wraps his arm around me, and I let him pull me close. His chest is warm against my side, his breath against my hair. He's here. He came the moment the news broke, offering his strength and comfort. Suddenly, our argument this morning feels insignificant. Pointless. How can I care about his past when he is so unfailingly, so lovingly *present*?

"What?" I whisper.

Ronan sighs. "It's getting late, baby. We should head back to the park."

"I can't go back. Not yet." My voice trembles.

"I know you don't want to, but it's too dark to make more progress. Besides, you're exhausted. You've done as much as you can here."

"But—"

"He's right." A commanding voice slices through the cold air. A flashlight beam swings between the trees as Detective Simone McNamara approaches, branches crunching beneath her boots.

"My team will stay out here a bit longer, but I'm asking all civilians to go home for the night. We're not giving up on Daysha—" She cuts through my protest. "But we need to be our best for her, and we can't do that in these conditions." McNamara's tone softens. "Besides, I need to ask you some questions, Ms. Elowen."

I don't like it, but I have no choice. I nod and let the detective lead us back to the right side of the park, where the police have set up a makeshift command center. My parents are already here, standing in a little cluster as they speak with one of the officers. Poor little Ricky is sullen beside them, nursing a cup of cocoa. They turn when they see me, and as one, we rush to each other.

I feel Dad's arms around me, and I bury my face in his chest. He smells like he always does of soap, aftershave, and the faintest hint of plaster. It's almost exactly like that day twenty years ago, except this time I feel the tremor in his body, and the defeated slump of Mom's shoulders. I realize with sudden clarity that they've borne too much—that I must be the foundation now.

I curl my arm around Ricky and huddle in Mom and Dad the best I can with my free hand. For a long time, we don't speak, sorrow rushing beneath us like a river. Most people will never experience the storm we've weathered all these years. We're still sifting through the wreckage of Tess' kidnapping. And yet, by God, somehow lightning has struck us again.

For a moment, the thought almost unravels me. I'm battered, a house on shifting sands.

And then Ronan is there, behind me, his shoulders broad enough, his arms wide enough to close the space that mine can't reach. I lean against him, tears clouding my vision.

"Pardon me…" Detective McNamara clears her throat.

I step away, hastily wiping at my eyes. "Yes."

"I hate to interrupt, but it's good you're all here. I need to go over the details of the incident one last time."

"Sure," I say, and McNamara nods.

"This way, please."

Floodlights cast a hard white light over the command post—a tangle of tents and folding tables. The ground is hard underfoot, scattered with the detritus of defeat: half-empty water bottles, discarded gloves, and empty snack wrappers. A junior officer with a black trash bag and a litter picker in hand moves through the scene, slowly restoring order to the chaos.

A portable generator coughs somewhere near the line of cruisers, and the faint static of police radios drifts through the air. The crowd of volunteers has thinned to clusters of tired silhouettes returning equipment, their voices low and raw from shouting into the cold.

Detective McNamara herds us toward the main tent, where a few officers hunch over glowing screens. My parents look pale in the floodlight, and Ricky's cocoa cup trembles in his hands.

"Is there somewhere they can sit?" I ask. My voice comes out steadier than I feel.

McNamara nods, signaling to a young female officer with dark skin and a neat bun. She pulls two folding chairs from the back of a cruiser. I help Mom and Dad into them, then press Ricky's shoulder until he sits too. For a moment, I just stand there, breath fogging in the light. Then I turn back to McNamara.

"Alright. What do you need to know?"

McNamara sits across from my mom, steepling her fingers beneath her chin. Her trench coat pools around her boots, the hem dragging in the dust. "Let's start from the beginning. Just tell me what you remember, in your own words."

Mom's lips tremble before she presses them together. When I reach out and rub her shoulder, she shoots me a grateful look.

"Sundays are our nights with Daysha," she says slowly. "Not every single week, you understand, but most weekends. Her mom's an ER nurse, and it's a huge help not to have to hire a sitter. The cost, you know?"

She stares at her hands. "Daysha stays over, we do science home-work together, and we take her to school with Ricky in the morning." Her eyes lift. "Aliyah's a fine woman. A good mom, doing the best she can. Daysha's father passed away three years ago."

McNamara nods, pulling a slim tablet from her coat, the screen's glow catching the lines around her mouth. "But last Sunday was different."

It isn't a question.

"We were all at the Blue Moon Festival, so Aliyah paid her nephew Stephan to stay with Daysha overnight and take her to school in the morning."

"The Blue Moon Festival?" McNamara asks, her stylus pausing midair.

Dad's throat works. I can't bear to see this wonderful, kind man blame himself for any of this. I go to him and wrap my arms around his shoulders, whispering that he has nothing to be ashamed of. He closes his eyes and nods once, jaw tight, but he still can't speak.

So I tell McNamara about the Blue Moon festival, what it is, and the joy it represents.

"Got it." She glances up from her tablet, her tone gentling. "Sounds like a beautiful event. Good on you, Mr. Elowen, for making it happen."

She makes a few more notes, then looks back up. "Where was Ricky if you were all at the vineyard?"

"My sister lives with my mother in Bethesda," Mom says. "Ricky spent the night with them. Winston and I picked him up this morning."

"So how did you know something was wrong?"

"Ricky and Daysha have been working on building kites for their physics class," Mom explains. "The project was due today, so they wanted to meet early to practice their presentation. I told Stephan we'd swing by Aliyah's place, but he said we could meet at Shimmy's."

"The diner?" McNamara asks.

"Yes." Dad finds his voice. "Stephan said Daysha wanted pancakes. It's across from the park."

At this, Ricky starts sniffling again, and I go over to him, pulling him into my lap, letting him bury his face in my neck as his tears fall.

"The strawberry ones are her favorite," he hiccups. "She always says they're good luck."

I hold him tighter, staring past the tent flap to where the floodlights burn against the night, and wonder how a world so bright can feel so dark.

Ronan stands beside me, a silent sentinel. His fingers gently stroke my neck, reminding me of his presence. I am so grateful that he's here.

"And what happened next?" McNamara asks softly, her gaze shifting between my father and Ricky.

"They walked through the park," Mom whispers, staring into the distance. "*I don't know why they walked through the park.*"

My heart splinters into a thousand pieces. Ricky, Mom, Dad—how can we survive this? Daysha has to be okay. Because I don't know how we live through this again.

"We waited at the diner," Dad says hoarsely. "But Stephan never showed up. When we went looking for him, we found him at the park. He seemed confused—frantic. Said Daysha went to the bathroom, and he couldn't find her."

"How old is Stephan?"

"Nineteen. He's a sophomore at UDC."

While Dad speaks, the young officer who brought the chairs bends to whisper something in McNamara's ear. A flicker crosses the detective's face, confirmation enough: Stephan must still be in custody.

McNamara grunts. "I've spoken with folks in the neighborhood tonight. Everyone's stunned. They say the park's always been safe, even for kids." She sets her stylus down, brown eyes sharp and searching. "Sounds like you all disagree."

Mom flinches as if struck. The light drains from her face; she's slipping under, swallowed by the dark well of memory.

"Can they go?" I manage, sharper than I intend. "My family's been through enough. I'll answer the rest of your questions."

Ronan shifts beside me. "Baby, are you sure about this?" His voice is low, his brow furrowed with concern.

"I'm sure," I say, not looking at him. "They need rest. I can handle this."

He hesitates, then nods, but I can still feel the weight of his gaze, as if he's ready to catch me if I fall.

McNamara studies me for a long moment. The tent is so quiet I can hear the whisper of her coat as she shifts in her chair. Then she jerks her head. "Of course," she says. "Officer Hayes will see them to their car."

Mom blinks, as if surfacing from deep water. Dad steadies her arm while Ricky clings to his empty cocoa cup, the paper dented from his fingers. I don't move until they're gone, their shadows swallowed by the glare of the floodlights beyond the tent.

McNamara returns to me. She folds her arms. "I have a lot of questions for you, Ms. Elowen."

Red
Thandi

"This isn't the first kidnapping at Anchor Park."

McNamara frowns. "What?"

"My twin sister Tess disappeared here twenty years ago."

For a heartbeat, even the generator outside seems to pause. Then McNamara straightens, the line of her shoulders rigid.

"Hayes—see if you can pull that case file. Twenty years back."

"Yes, ma'am." The young officer pivots toward her laptop, fingers flying over the keys.

I frown as the screen's glow flickers against the tent wall. Ronan drags an empty chair closer and takes my hand, his thumb brushing across my knuckles.

"Isn't that why you wanted to talk to me?" I ask.

"No…" McNamara mutters, tension rippling through her voice. "We found something at the scene. They told me you were an expert."

Rising, the detective moves to the white folding table and pulls two small baggies from a banker's box. The harsh light glints off the plastic as she sets them down.

Each holds a WhiffRush inhaler.

Beside me, Ronan gasps. I don't blame him. My own breath catches like I've been struck.

McNamara's lips tighten. She hesitates, her gaze flicking to Ronan. "You and Mr. Thorne are…?"

"We're together," I say firmly. "He's family. He stays."

"Thandi…" Ronan breathes my name. He lifts our joined hands and presses a kiss against my knuckles.

I smile, caressing his face. We're both a bit crazy—two lost souls finding our way back to wholeness. But he's mine, and now, more than ever, I refuse to lose another person precious to me. I'm not letting him go.

McNamara watches us in silence, something unreadable in her expression before she schools her features.

"Very well." Her tone is clipped. "Your father said the boy, Stephan, seemed confused—disoriented. The interviewing officer noted the same." She lifts a baggie, the bright red inhaler gleaming inside. "Could this have anything to do with it?"

"Well," I say slowly, "it depends on how much he's used, but yes."

"What do you mean?"

"My specialty is scent-based technology. My company, Immerscent, stimulates memory through targeted olfactory–limbic pathways." I sigh. "Despite what people think, memory is malleable. Without proper controls—without rigorous clinical protocols—the hippocampus can become overstimulated. That can trigger distortions in recall, even full-blown confabulations. False memories."

McNamara raises an eyebrow. "And?"

"And that's just the effects that we know of. This is still an emerging field, Detective. We *don't* fully understand how scent technology affects the brain. That's why Immerscent refuses to work with children." I point to the red inhaler. "WhiffRush is made by Astor Pharmaceuticals. Unfortunately, they have no such qualms, despite the science being unsettled."

"So you're saying they're marketing to teens?"

I incline my head. "Adults, too—but we're their biggest competitor. They haven't captured our market share, so they've shifted their focus to young adults. Even kids." My voice hardens. "I wish I could say this was their only product on the market."

"Fucking corporations," McNamara hisses, then quirks her lip. "No offense."

I shrug. "None taken."

"Look, I need you to break this down for me, Ms. Elowen, so I can get this straight. I was never a science whiz." McNamara flashes a quick grin. "*Wuthering Heights* was more my speed."

When my brows fly up, she laughs and gives an elegant shrug.

"So you're telling me this kid, Stephan, got high on this crap—" She waggles the plastic-wrapped inhaler. "—and hallucinated what happened?"

"Maybe. It's possible that his WhiffRush use affected his memory of what happened to Daysha—especially if he uses it daily. We've seen it in some clients seeking rehabilitation for what we'd normally classify as addiction." I release a frustrated breath. "The problem is I don't know exactly how Astor's products work. I haven't studied them."

"I have," Ronan says quietly.

I stare at him in shock.

"My late mother was also a developer of scent-tech," he continues, squeezing my hand even as his eyes plead for understanding. "She had the opportunity to study Astor's products. As her research assistant, I helped."

I'm speechless. My heart is racing. Even though Ronan is right beside me, it feels like this morning all over again—like he's drifting away from me. The specter of our argument looms in the back of my mind. What else don't I know about him?

McNamara is as silent as I am, waiting for Ronan to drop the next bombshell.

His gaze never strays from mine. "Unlike Thandi's work, Astor's is… messier. There are no clinical controls. And the technology itself isn't refined. It affects memory, yes—but more than that, it alters mood regulation and impulse control. That's really the root of the addiction Thandi described."

"I see a lot of addicts in this line of work. Erratic behavior, mood swings… and yes, memory issues." McNamara exhales, rubbing a hand over her face. "I'm guessing Daysha's mom didn't know any of this—or she never would've asked Stephan to watch her daughter. The question now is, what do I *do* with this?"

I don't look away from Ronan. I breathe deeply, reminding myself of our vows this morning, of Dani's words about being all in. *I have to trust him.* I have no choice. Finally, I find my voice again.

"Well," I murmur, "I can't say how badly affected Stephan is without seeing his scans. But unless you have a real reason to believe he's complicit in this, you might as well let him go."

I swallow hard, as I think of the fight ahead—of another case that could vanish into fractured memory. My hands shake as I turn to McNamara.

"If he's been using WhiffRush, the only thing you have on your hands right now, Detective, is one very unreliable witness."

"Shit." McNamara folds her arms. "The chief's going to be pissed. The kid's our only lead. He's—"

"I found those case files, Detective."

Hayes rushes over, laptop in hand, eager and a little breathless. She can't be more than twenty-one—barely older than Stephan himself.

McNamara straightens, taking the laptop from Hayes. "Show me."

I watch, almost in slow motion, as she scrolls through the file. The silence stretches, heavy and endless, as she absorbs each detail. I can't quite look at Ronan, but I don't want to untangle my fingers from his either. He holds tight to me, and I feel his fear for Daysha—for *us*—in the grip of his hand, a desperate mirror of my own.

The scratch of McNamara's stylus against her tablet sounds too loud in the quiet tent. Suddenly, she makes a sharp sound and pivots toward me.

"You were there," she breathes.

"Yes." My eyes burn under the harsh lights. "I can't remember, though. Not everything. Not enough for it to have mattered."

To my surprise, she sets the tablet down and rests a hand on my shoulder.

"I'm sorry for your loss. And for what you've been through." McNamara's voice softens. "I've seen too many of these..." She shakes her head. "You're a very lucky woman, Ms. Elowen."

"Thank you," I manage, beating back the guilt, the pain of forgetting. But there's something in her words that leaves me gripped with terror.

"Does that mean you don't think we'll find Daysha?" I gasp.

"No," McNamara says quickly. "Of course not. We've lost some time, but the window hasn't closed yet. We're not giving up on Daysha, Ms. Elowen. I'm not. I swear my badge on it."

I can't speak. It's hard not to say the quiet part out loud—about the number of little Black girls who go missing, the level of effort poured into their cases, and the system that too often looks away. Did the cops do everything they could to find Tess?

Maybe.

Probably.

I study McNamara's silhouette: strong, elegant, her close-cropped natural hair touched with silver at the temples.

Twenty years ago, there wasn't a detective who looked like Simone McNamara at the MCPD on Tess' case. Maybe that will be the difference.

I press my face into my hands. I don't know. What I *do* know is that back then, far too soon, they simply stopped looking.

Ronan pulls me into his arms. Whatever lies between us doesn't matter. I don't resist.

"Is that all, Detective?" he asks. "Do you need anything else?"

McNamara sighs, the fight leaving her shoulders for a moment. She rubs the bridge of her nose before lowering her hand.

"Not right now," she says. "I want to review the files from the old case more closely. It's a long shot, but maybe there's a connection." Her gaze drifts toward the laptop, the screen's blue light cutting across her face. "At this point, we can't afford to leave any stone unturned."

Ronan nods, helping me to my feet. "Come on, baby. Let's go home."

"Wait—" I place my hand on his arm, stopping him.

"There are two," I say to McNamara. "Why are there two?"

"What?" McNamara pauses, halfway through gathering her things.

"There are two inhalers," I press. "Where did the other one come from?"

McNamara stutters, "We found it in the park. I—"

"I found it near the bathrooms, along with a child's bracelet," Hayes interrupts.

The soft-spoken rookie steps forward. "Since Stephan said Daysha disappeared when she went to the restroom, I thought it was important to catalogue."

"Near the bathrooms?" Ronan blurts even as I practically shout, "A bracelet? Where?"

We stare at each other, start again, our words tumbling together.

"What—"

When—"

McNamara raises her hand. "Let Hayes speak."

"I was with Brooks when he answered the call from your parents," Hayes says quickly, glancing toward McNamara. "He's my training officer. The red inhaler was in Stephan's pocket. But when I showed him the green one, he didn't recognize it."

McNamara's expression sharpens. "Go on."

"I thought it was strange, but he was pretty torn up, so I didn't press." Hayes shrugs. "Besides, like you said, those inhalers are sold everywhere. It could be anyone's."

My pulse hammers so hard it hurts. I can't seem to draw a full breath. For a second, all I can hear is the whir of the laptop and the rush of blood in my ears.

"Can I see the bracelet?" I croak.

Hayes blinks, glancing toward McNamara for permission. "It's been bagged," she says quietly. "Do you want her to look, Detective?"

McNamara hesitates, studying me. Then she nods. "Show her."

The bag crinkles as Hayes passes it to me. Inside is a small, colorful bracelet strung with plastic beads. White cube letters spell out *L-O-V-E*, threaded between yellow charms and hearts.

Daysha's favorite color.

I start to tremble. My fingers skim frantically over the plastic, turning the bag again and again.

Then my world stops.

I shouldn't touch it, but I can't help it. The harder I stare, the more the world narrows to one impossible bead: **Ds.**

The memory is so vivid it leaves me gasping.

Daysha had wanted to learn the entire periodic table with me. She laughed when we reached Darmstadtium, insisting it must stand for *Daysha's symbol.* This spring, I found the charm in a specialty science shop and tucked it alongside the chemistry set I got her for her birthday.

I trace the outline of that single bead through the bag.

Ds: Darmstadtium. Rare, exuberant, *impossible to capture.*

A sound explodes from me before I can stop it, a half-sob, a wretched moan of torment. My knees buckle.

Ronan catches me before I hit the ground. "What..." his voice breaks. He clutches me tighter, shaking his head. "Is there anything we can do?"

McNamara's face looks deeply lined, weary when she finally meets our eyes. I'm surprised I can even see her through the blur of my tears.

"Look," she says quietly. "I wish I had easy answers, but I won't lie to you. This isn't a simple case." She knots the belt of her trench coat. "My problem isn't resources—" She shares a look with Hayes. "It's keeping this case a priority."

McNamara sighs. "You're both high-profile people. The biggest thing you can do for me right now is buy me time. Show the world that *you're interested,* so they stay interested too."

Her words strike like a bolt to the heart. I stiffen in Ronan's arms.

I'm not a religious woman, but I can't help thinking there's a reason Daysha was taken on the day that marks the culmination of my life's devotion to Tess. If there's one thing I have in abundance right now, it's attention.

I blink rapidly, raising my eyes to the ceiling. "I'm listening. I got you, sis," I whisper.

"Thandi?" Ronan's voice wavers.

"Put me down." I'm already shifting, struggling to get to my feet.

He makes a questioning sound, but releases me.

"We need to find Dani," I say. "I'm going to hold a press conference."

Impact
Ronan

Show me a woman braver and more beautiful than Thandi.

I'll wait.

I watch as she approaches the podium with Dani in tow, the fiercest determination on her face. Cameras flash, tiny supernovas scattered across the sea of faces in Immerscent's packed conference room. The reporters call her name, a hundred questions crashing over one another in a rising tide. Beyond the floor-to-ceiling windows, Chesden gleams in the dark, the city stretching toward the horizon.

I held Thandi in that tent and finally understood why she is so remarkable—how she survived Tess' kidnapping to become one of the most brilliant and powerful women in the world.

I've studied reaction pathways all my life, but I've never seen anything like the alchemy of how she transmuted her pain into action. Not for her sake, but someone else's.

It only makes me more ashamed of my cowardice.

Because, unlike Thandi, all *I feel* is fear.

Fear that we won't beat the racing clock to save Daysha.

Fear for the white lie I told McNamara about how I learned about Astor's products.

It wasn't a complete untruth. I assisted Mom in her analysis, but we didn't know back then that Dad would steal her company and research to build the empire at the root of this horror. And of course, my deepest understanding of James' harm is far more recent, thanks to my visit to Prime.

Now, alongside my fear for Daysha's survival is fear for my own. For Thandi and me. I'm terrified that I wasn't man enough to confess the truth about James this morning, and now it's a ticking time bomb between us.

Anxiety roils in my stomach. *We just have to get through this press conference,* I remind myself. *Then we'll be fine.*

Dani kicks off the briefing, dragging me from my thoughts. Thandi steps to the podium, looking both tired and resolute. Behind her, Daysha's smiling face fills the screens—a ten-year-old in a yellow hoodie, dimples deep, eyes bright with mischief.

"Good evening. I'm Thandi Elowen, president and CEO of Immerscent. I'm speaking to you tonight not about my company's public offering, but about a beautiful girl who went missing today in Anchor Park—Daysha Howard."

Murmurs ripple through the crowd. A few reporters leave, but most freeze in place, recalibrating. Shock gives way to action. Fingers fly across laptops. Phones glow as others text furiously, no doubt alerting their editors that Thandi is about to break the most unexpected news in Immerscent's history.

"You might ask why I've chosen to focus on Daysha instead of Immerscent's future on such an important night," she continues with a tight smile. "The answer is simple. Immerscent would never have existed if someone hadn't invested in me when I was a geeky kid obsessed with science."

Her voice wavers. "But Daysha is so much more than that. She's brilliant, sweet, and kind—and she deserves a chance to grow up. Not just because she could be our next great inventor, but because her life matters. Help me find her. Every second that passes is one second too long without her home."

What began as a buzz swells to a roar. Cameras flash, reporters shout, jostling for attention. Thandi raises a hand, and—miraculously—the noise dims.

"I want to thank the MCPD and Detective McNamara for their tireless work on this case. And to support their efforts, I'm personally offering a reward of $150,000 for any credible information leading to Daysha's safe return," Thandi finishes.

Dani strides forward, then, sweeping the crowd with a critical gaze. "We'll now open for questions," she says briskly, her voice amplified through her lapel mic.

Hands shoot up.

"Ms. Elowen!"

"Ms. Elowen, over here!"

"Ms. Elowen, Jessamyn Mutu with *the New York Times*." A slim, dark-skinned woman with a regal afro projects over the din, her tone clipped and commanding. "The initial reports suggest that either the child's babysitter or the kidnapper was intoxicated on WhiffRush. Can you comment on that? Would you say Astor Pharmaceuticals is complicit in this incident?"

Of course, I hold my breath at the mention of Astor.

Not out of any anxiety for James—fuck him and his cruelty. Let them drag him through the mud. He's earned it. What sends my heart racing is something far more urgent. I know my father. Once Thandi speaks, she'll go from distant threat to immediate enemy.

I have to be ready to protect her.

Thandi sighs. "I'm not privy to all the details of the case. That's a question for the MCPD. Who can say if these products played a role in Daysha's kidnapping?" Her gaze is sharp. "It is a reminder, however, of how nascent the science is and why Immerscent has always prioritized rigorous client protocols and clinical consultation over commercial use."

"Okay, but help us play this out—a thought experiment, if you will." A grizzled man with a hastily-knotted tie interrupts. "Matt

Hastings, *The Christian Science Monitor.* Doesn't research suggest that products like WhiffRush can impair executive functioning, potentially creating an even more volatile situation for this child?"

"Based purely on the science, yes," Thandi says slowly. "But I am not an expert in Astor's products. It would be best to reach out to them for clarification."

"But—"

"Next question, please," Thandi slices through his protest.

She powers through the next volley of questions, fielding everything from her connection to Daysha to whether the kidnapping will affect Immerscent's stock value.

"I hope it rises," Thandi says evenly, "when investors see that the brand they're committing to isn't just innovative, but human."

A chastened silence follows, broken by a ripple of applause from the Immerscent staff clustered at the back of the room. Thandi is about to call on a freelancer when a woman's voice cuts through the blur.

"Ms. Elowen—Karen Whitfield, *The Baltimore Sun.* Twenty years ago, a girl was also kidnapped in Anchor Park, but the case was never solved. My sources tell me that girl was your sister, Theresa Elowen. Do you think her kidnapper is back?"

The room freezes.

Then detonates.

Reporters surge forward, shouting over each other.

I watch in slow motion as the words hit Thandi like blows. She freezes, her gasp audible even over the cacophony.

Relentless, Whitfield projects over the noise. "You are the only living witness to that incident, Ms. Elowen, but reports say you couldn't remember what happened. How does it feel knowing the kidnapper may still be out there?"

The crowd spirals into frenzy.

I don't even register the decision to move. One second I'm at the edge of the room; the next, I'm shoving through the crush of reporters, taking the steps two at a time.

Dani is moving too, striding from the opposite side of the stage, but I reach Thandi first.

She's gripping the podium, white-knuckled, eyes wide and unfocused, her breath coming in shallow bursts. I grab her and pull her close, my arm tight around her waist.

"What the fuck is wrong with you?" I snarl at the reporter, the words tearing out of me before I can stop them.

The room erupts, the chaos doubling instead of stopping.

"Ms. Elowen, is it true?"

"Ms. Elowen, can you still not remember the kidnapper?"

"Are you a key witness in this investigation?"

"Ms. Elowen, is that why you founded Immerscent?"

The questions fall like a rain of bullets, each one more brutal and merciless than the last.

Dani strides toward us, shoulders squared. She steps in front of us at the podium. "That's enough," she says sharply. "Ms. Elowen has to leave for another engagement. I'll take your questions."

I breathe a sigh of relief—until Thandi, my sweet virago, surprises me yet again. She straightens and reaches past Dani to reclaim the mic.

"Thank you, Karen, for the question." Her voice is calm, clear steel.

The room goes silent.

"Yes, it's true. My sister's kidnapping is the reason I founded Immerscent. I still don't remember what happened, and it eats at me every single day. That's why finding Daysha matters. I couldn't get justice for Tess..." She takes a breath. "But I won't stand by and let it happen to another innocent child."

The tension in the room pops like a balloon bursting. Because really, what else can be said in the face of such truth?

The rabble dissipates into a hum. Reporters glance at each other as if realizing they've witnessed something far bigger than a headline. Even Karen Whitfield lowers her recorder, lips pressed together before she tucks it away.

Dani nods in satisfaction, her expression reflecting the same fierce pride swelling in my chest.

"Thank you." She raises her hand before the reporters can interrupt again. "That's it for our press conference today."

As we cross the stage, I can't help glancing at Thandi's profile—the lift of her chin, the curve of her cheekbones, the quiet fire that never seems to dim. *God, I love this woman.*

But I'm no fool. Reporters don't stay docile for long, not when blood is in the water. Every instinct screams to get her out before they remember what they're here for.

We're halfway to the exit when I spot Greg Owens, my father's longtime PR lead, lingering at the back of the room.

Except he's wearing a press badge for some random independent outlet, not an Astor tag.

I frown. What the fuck is he doing here?

Is that why James has been spiraling—monitoring tabloids himself? He's lost his communications lead?

Owens leans toward the reporter beside him—a dark-haired, middle-aged man with a *Washington Post* badge—and whispers something I'm too far away to catch.

I try to track it, but my focus is on Thandi, on getting her out of this room in one piece.

"Ms. Elowen! Just one more question!" the Post reporter blurts.

"Sorry, that's all for today, folks," Dani snaps, steering us toward the door.

My hand is on Thandi's elbow. Now that she's moved mountains, I can feel what it's cost her—in the tremor of her fingers, the falter of her step that only I'm close enough to notice.

"Come on, baby," I murmur, wrapping my arm around her shoulder, steadying her as the crowd keeps roaring, cameras flashing.

I'll never be as heroic as she is. But I can take her home, care for her—and finally erase the secrets between us. I can endure the pain of her disappointment because I see now that a lie will rip her away from me forever.

And I won't survive it.

I'm not an alchemist like her.

She told me she wouldn't judge me for my father's sins, and I have to believe her. After her courage today, there's no other path forward.

I just didn't realize I'm already too late.

The funny part is that it happens in slow motion—the karmic impact that destroys my world.

We keep walking. I'm bracing, tucking Thandi closer to me as I prepare to push through the sea of paparazzi outside.

"Ms. Elowen! Please! One last question before you go." The plea comes from the back of the room again.

Dani makes an irritated sound, while Thandi frowns and slows. She whispers to Dani, who shakes her head—terse, emphatic. But when Thandi whispers again, she relents. Sighing, she nods, granting permission.

Smiling tiredly at me, Thandi squeezes my hand. She slips from my fingers as she pivots back to the podium.

"Yes," her voice rings out, soft but clear. "I'll take one last question."

The reporter stands, victorious. "Ms. Elowen—Josh Christopher, *The Washington Post*. You've shared your gut-wrenching past and your reservations about Astor's approach—" A slow, deliberate smirk curls Christopher's mouth.

"But can you really claim to be different when you're romantically involved with Ronan Thorne, James Astor's son?"

The room goes still.

Thandi jerks as if she's been struck.
Slowly, helplessly, she turns towards me.
Our eyes lock.
And that's the moment my universe goes dark.

Shame

Thandi

The biggest thing Tess taught me is to fake it until you make it. She was good at that.

The first time we jumped off the pier at Grandma Moses' house, she was more scared than I was. It was a warm spring day, just before she was kidnapped. I was the better swimmer. Besides, she hated getting her hair wet.

My fear wasn't of the water itself, but knowing Daddy had warned us not to go in without him or Mom nearby.

But the moment you told Tess she couldn't do something, she latched onto it—especially if she didn't want it in the first place. As soon as Daddy said no, she decided we had to jump in.

So we stood at the edge of the dock, peering into the blue-gray water. It wasn't deep—maybe six or seven feet—but it felt endless to me. The surface was calm enough to mirror the trees, and the wooden planks under our feet were warm from the sun. Tess wore a pink swimsuit covered in yellow stars. Mine was white with blue stripes.

I glanced over and saw her fists clenched, her bottom lip caught between her teeth. For a second, I thought, *Maybe she'll back away this time.*

"We should go back," I said.

She was quiet for a long moment, breath shallow, toes curling over the edge. Then she grinned. "I'll be a mermaid; you'll be

Aquagirl. We're gonna jump in to save Shani and Miss Becky from an evil octopus!"

Shani and Miss Becky were our favorite American Girl Dolls. They were in the cabin, not the water, but I got what Tess was putting down. I stared at her, half shocked that she made *me* the superhero. That never happened.

"Octopuses can't live in fresh water," I pointed out, squinting at her.

By then, the old Tess was back, vibrating with energy, her trepidation evaporating like dew in the sun. She stuck out her tongue, grabbed my hand, and shouted, "On three!"

I wanted to argue, to stall, but she was already counting. "One... two..."

The air smelled of sunscreen and something metallic from the old ladder. Birds warbled from the trees behind us.

"Three!"

Her small hand squeezed mine, and then there was no more wood beneath our feet, just the dizzy drop and the rush of cold as we hit the water.

For a moment, we were both under, sunlight breaking apart in shards above us. My ears filled with that humming silence you only hear underwater. When I surfaced, gasping, Tess was already kicking away from me, her laughter ringing out across the cove.

"See? Easy," she shouted, hair plastered to her forehead.

But even then, I remember thinking how far the pier suddenly looked—how wide the distance between us had become.

Ever since that day, I go back to it—to the memory of her hand in mine as we leaped together—whenever I'm facing something terrifying. When I'm at the precipice, staring into the unknown.

That memory is what kept me moving forward tonight. It's what allowed me to stand here and answer all these stupid fucking questions when all I want to do is search for Daysha. To scream at fate for doing this to us again.

That, and Ronan.

Knowing he's just at the edge of the room, catching his encouraging smile every time I glance over, buoys me up. So I grip the podium and smile instead of drowning in my despair. I love him so much, and I don't know how I could survive this without him.

Not after twenty years of treading water.

Not when I'm now even farther from the pier.

I'm tired. My eyes burn from staring at Dani's talking points and the endlessly flashing cameras. But Daysha's bright, smiling photo across the room keeps me grounded, reminding me why I'm here.

I glance at my phone. We're almost done. Dani and I agreed on thirty minutes. I'll take a couple more questions, and then we can get out of here.

By reflex, I look across the room, searching for that familiar shock of auburn hair.

The amazing thing about having a man built like a bruiser is that it's impossible to lose him. Ronan's leaning against the wall, arms crossed, towering above the reporter beside him. He winks at me and tips his chin up—encouraging and sexy all at once.

Nodding back, I square my shoulders. I lean into the mic, ready to get this over with and curl into his arms again.

The freelancer to my left raises her hand. I'm about to give her the floor when another voice rings out:

"Ms. Elowen—Karen Whitfield, *The Baltimore Sun*. Twenty years ago, a girl was also kidnapped in Anchor Park, but the case was never solved. My sources tell me that girl was your sister, Theresa Elowen. Do you think her kidnapper is back?"

I gasp. It's like hitting cold water again, but this time, I'm not in my grandmother's sheltered cove. Tess' hand isn't in mine. I'm spinning, churning, caught in a riptide. No swimming lessons, no talking points could prepare me for this: free-falling, naked, my deepest secret—my deepest shame—suddenly laid bare.

I can't speak; I can't think. I don't know how to find the surface.

And then—oxygen.

Ronan is at my side, holding me up, shielding me. When? How? I don't know, and I don't care. All I can feel is relief—his warmth, his solidity, the deep, all-consuming surge of his love.

He's barking something at the reporter, but everything sounds garbled, like there's water in my ears. I cling to his warmth and his strength. His arm tightens around me, and my heart expands.

I can breathe again.

Because he's here with me, I'm not naked anymore. I can do this. I can pretend to be a superhero one more time, because Daysha's in the arms of a monster, and I can't stop hunting until she's free.

Closing my eyes, I inhale deeply, then take the mic once more. I push through the pain and the panic and tell the room my truth. And just like that day with Tess, as soon as I leap, I'm freer. It's easier than it seems, just like she said.

The room goes so quiet it feels unreal. The reporter, Whitmore, nods, tucking her recorder away with grudging respect. I haven't rescued Daysha yet, but I'll live to fight another day.

I glance toward Ronan and Dani, and they're both watching me with such pride it makes the whole ordeal worth it.

And just like that, we're at time. Dani's ending the press conference, and Ronan's already guiding me off the stage. He curls his arm around my shoulders, tucking me close so that he's between me and the crowd. His powerful body blocks the room from view, and my world narrows to just us. Just like we were last night.

"Come on, baby," he murmurs, and for once, I don't try to be strong or witty. I just lean into him.

But then something strange happens.

A *Washington Post* reporter calls from the back of the crowd, demanding a question. There's something in his tone I can't place, something more than journalistic persistence. I can't name it, but I feel it, like a current shifting under still water.

At first, we ignore him. Dani leans close, reminding me that even with Daysha's crisis, I can't postpone tomorrow's IPO interviews. We'll have an early start, and I need to rest.

She's right. I relent.

We stride toward the exit, and I brace myself for the wall of paparazzi waiting beyond the doors—the flashing cameras, the crush of bodies, the next barrage of questions. Even this, I remind myself, is visibility. The world loves a spectacle, especially when it's tinged with a Black woman's pain. I'll give it to them if it keeps the search light focused on Daysha.

My fingers brush the door handle when the *Post* reporter calls out again. I'm exhausted; Dani's already irritated. But if he's this persistent, maybe it's important. And honestly, I'll take any question from the biggest paper in the DMV if it means more eyes on Daysha's case.

And so we stop. I pivot back to the stage.

The reporter grins as I return to the podium, but even though he's smiling, it isn't pleasant. The sense of wrongness prickles at the back of my neck. I'm frowning, realizing too late that this is probably an ambush, a smear to distract from the case or tarnish the IPO.

Damn it, I should have listened to Dani.

But what James Christopher shouts isn't about Daysha or Immerscent.

It's something far worse.

"Can you really claim to be different," he sneers, "when you're romantically involved with Ronan Thorne—James Astor's son?"

I hear the words. I understand each one.

But together, they don't make sense.

Ronan? James Astor's son? Impossible.

Ronan's last name is *Thorne*. He's nothing like that maniac.

No one that gentle, that deliberate, could be.

I think of his grief over his mother, the wing he built in her memory, the quiet devotion he turned into purpose.

How could *he* be connected to a man who poisons children?

I'm about to scoff at the absurdity. I tap the mic, eager to put Christopher in his place when something rushes back to me:

"Thandi, I need to tell you something important. Do you have a moment after Trent leaves?"

"The man who showed up just now—it was my father."

I knew I was falling for you, and my father—he's not a good man."

My hands tremble on the podium, as a horrible feeling churns in my gut. I remember the look of panic on Ronan's face when we were interrupted by Dad that afternoon with Trent. I think of the empty bed after our night of passion and his secrecy this morning.

I swallow, gasping for breath. I'm sinking again.

So I do what's become instinct in these last two months: I turn to him. To the one constant, the one who's been my anchor, my lifeline.

Our eyes meet.

And the tether snaps.

Because I see the fear in his gaze—the same fear I saw this morning at breakfast.

I'm unmoored, tossed out to sea again, but this time it isn't panic. It's agony. After Daysha's kidnapping, after being stripped bare in front of the world, this is too much to bear. My heart feels like it's consuming itself.

It can't be true. It *can't*. The man I love can't I love can't share blood with the one who hurt Ricky.

He wouldn't stand beside me at the podium, wouldn't eat at my parents' table, wouldn't help tuck Ricky into bed—and keep that secret.

There's no way Ronan could be the son of the man who's spent years trying to destroy Immerscent, whose products have harmed the people I love and mocked everything I've built.

Could he?

Ronan makes a broken sound and lurches toward me. I'm used to him being powerful, but now his fists are clenched, his shoulders hunched. He looks so, so frightened. *So small.*

"Baby," he chokes out.

And then I know.

I know it in the marrow of my bones—in the hollow, haunted space Tess left behind—that it's true.

I'm running before I can think. Off the stage, away from him, shoving past Dani. She calls my name; her fingers graze my arm, but I tear free. I don't even know where I'm going. I just know I have to *get out.*

The door looms ahead, a blur of light and movement. Paparazzi. Cameras. Too many eyes. I skid to a stop, pivot, and bolt for the elevator instead. That's right. My car. I can go to the parking deck. Anywhere but here.

I mash the button, praying the doors will open fast.

Behind me, the conference room is a roar of chaos. Dani will handle it. She always does.

But that's not what scares me most.

It's the sound that follows— the soft rhythm of footsteps closing in behind me.

I don't need to turn around to know it's Ronan. Even with my heart breaking, our souls are still connected. I'm shaking, pressing the button desperately. I can't see him; I can't touch him. I won't survive it if I do.

I stare at the digital display, counting down the floors as the elevator descends. Four ... three ... two...

Come on, come on, I plead. *Almost there.*

The elevator dings, and I hear the shift in Ronan's footsteps— the staccato beat as he breaks into a run.

"Thandi, wait!" His voice is raw, torn. "Please, baby, don't go. I can explain."

He's so close I can feel his heat. So close I can smell his familiar, comforting scent.

I can't. I can't do this. My world is shattering.

He catches my elbow just as the doors open.

"Don't!" I gasp, wrenching free. "Don't come any closer. Let me go."

I don't know if I mean now, tomorrow, or forever.

Ronan jerks back, blanching. His face twists in an agony that mirrors my own. He watches me as the doors slide shut, his image blurring through my tears.

I touch my cheeks, and there's water, salt water everywhere. I can't stop the rain, can't stop the deluge.

Because I'm drowning again.

I collapse onto the floor and sob until I can't draw another breath.

I lie there, unable to believe my beautiful dream is over. I squeeze my eyes shut, holding onto the image of Ronan's smile, his soft kisses, the way his body fit perfectly with mine. Holding onto the precious partnership we built in just a few weeks.

I thought we had a lifetime.

Turns out it was all a mirage.

I don't open my eyes until the elevator doors part onto the parking deck.

Coming Soon

BY DEVIN EM

Coming February 14, 2026
Vanilla After You

Brokenhearted and reeling after Ronan's betrayal, Thandi Elowen is forced to confront the fallout—both to her heart and to the company she's fought to build. As old wounds resurface and new threats emerge, the carefully balanced life she's created begins to fracture.

For Ronan Thorne, regret is no longer enough. Desperate to prove that he's worthy of Thandi's love and trust, he's willing to risk everything to make things right. But as danger closes in from all sides, Ronan may have to confront the possibility that love, once tested, doesn't always wait—and that the woman he loves may already be slipping out of reach.

A powerful conclusion filled with romance, suspense, and hard-won healing, *Vanilla After You* delivers the second half of Thandi and Ronan's unforgettable love story—and their guaranteed happily ever after.